AF489610

The Dreams We Chase

also by h.k. green

The Road and The Rodeo Series

The Pieces We've Lost

The Chances We Take

The Hearts We've Broken

The Dreams We Chase

Standalones

Playing With My Heart Strings

Short Stories and Novellas

Paper Rings

The Dreams We Chase

H.K. GREEN

Copyright © 2026 by H.K. Green.

All rights reserved.

No part of this book may be reproduced in any form or by any electronic or mechanical means, including information storage, without written permission from the author, except for the use of brief quotations in a book review.

No generative A.I. was used in the writing of this book. No part of this novel may be used in any way to train, improve, or aid the use or advancement of A.I. in any way without express permission of the author.

This is a work of fiction. Names, characters, places and incidents are either products of the author's imagination or used fictitiously. Any resemblance to actual persons, living or dead, business establishments, events or locales is entirely coincidental.

Editing by Andrea Halland, Editing by Andrea

Cover Design and Formatting by H.K. Green

Paperback ISBN: 979-8-9909156-7-1

For the ones who take our hands and walk with us through the shadows, reminding us that even in the darkest times, we never have to fight alone.

"There's a day when you realize that you're not just a survivor, you're a warrior. You're tougher than anything life throws your way."

BROOKE DAVIS, *ONE TREE HILL*

playlist

i miss you, i'm sorry | Gracie Abrams	2:47
Family Line | Conan Gray	3:36
We Hug Now | Sydney Rose	4:08
Growing Pains | Ethel Cain	5:28
GRAVE | Avery Anna	3:11
Sparks | Coldplay	3:47
Senses | MICO	2:39
Staying | Lizzy McAlpine	2:31
THE LONELIEST | Måneskin	4:07
My Heart is Buried in Venice | Ricky Montgomery	3:04
Gilded Lily | Cults	3:32
Way down We Go | KALEO	3:33
Let Down | Radiohead	4:59
Indigo (feat. Avery Anna) | Sam Barber	4:46
The Fall | Cody Johnson	3:17
Carry You Home | Alex Warren	2:46

Thank you for picking up *The Dreams We Chase*. This is book four in The Road and The Rodeo series and can be read as a standalone. However, for the best reading experience, I recommend starting with *The Pieces We've Lost* and *The Chances We Take*, followed by *The Hearts We've Broken*.

Additionally, please note that The Road and The Rodeo is a five-book interconnected series that progresses in a chronological timeline. While the main couple gets their HEA/HFN at the end of this book, there may be side stories and plot points that are not immediately resolved and will run through the series.

The Road and The Rodeo is a cowboy romance series, but it's also a sports romance series, so just like the previous books, rodeo plays a major role in the plot. Team roping and barrel racing are the main focus of several chapters, but other events are discussed.

In rodeo, the animals are extremely well cared for, and that is reflected in my story. Rodeo is not meant to be an act of animal cruelty, and thus no animals are injured during the events of this story (although it can happen).

If you've read my prior books, you know that most of the stories I've released are fairly lighthearted. However, while *The Dreams We Chase* focuses on the romantic relationship between the main characters, the story also explores more serious and dark topics that may be triggering for some readers including domestic violence and child abuse.

I worked with local law enforcement officers, various sensitivity readers, and domestic violence survivors during the drafting and editing processes to ensure that the characters and events in this book are handled with care and depicted with as much authenticity and integrity as possible.

If you feel trigger warnings are spoilers, or do not need them, please skip the next section. Please take care of yourself and do what is best for your heart and mental health.

The epilogue of this book does include a pregnancy announcement from a supporting character.

If you, or someone you know, is experiencing or has experienced domestic violence, help is available. The National Domestic Violence Hotline is available 24/7 by calling 1-800-799-7233 or by texting the word BEGIN to 88788.

You are not alone.

This book is intended for adult readers and contains mature themes, including explicit, on-page sexual content and explicit language. If needed, please refer to the back of the book for closed-door modifications.

Additional on-page contents include:

- Abandonment
- Abuse from a parent (physical, emotional)
- Alcohol consumption
- Anxiety and anxiety attacks
- Blood and gore depiction
- C-PTSD stemming from traumatic childhood events
- Domestic violence/partner or family member assault
- Flashbacks/nightmares
- Gun violence resulting in death
- Kidnapping
- Physical violence
- Pregnancy announcement from a supporting character (Epilogue)
- Rodeo events (barrel racing, team roping); no animals are injured
- Stalking and harassment
- Underage drinking

rodeo 101 + law enforcement acronyms

Alleyway: In barrel racing, the entrance to the arena where the horse and their rider begin their timed run.

Barrier: In a timed event, the line stretched across the front of the box that the contestant and their horse cannot cross until the steer or calf has a head start.

BOLO: Be on the lookout

Box: In a timed event, the box is the area where the horse and rider back into before they make a roping or steer wrestling run.

Breaking the Barrier: Failure to give the animal enough of a head start before a roping or steer wrestling event, resulting in a ten-second penalty.

Chute: A specialized, narrow corridor designed to hold a calf or steer and release it for a roping run.

Circuit: Geographical regions in which PRCA contestants compete. Each athlete designates a home circuit based on their home address or preference. There are twelve circuits in total.

Cinch: The leather or fabric band that secures the saddle to the horse.

Cloverleaf Pattern: The most common pattern in barrel racing both for amateurs and professionals consisting of only three barrels set up in a very specific, precisely measured way that is standard to every professional competition. Two barrels are set up directly across from each other horizontally and then one single barrel is set up above the bottom two but directly in the middle.

CNFR: College National Finals Rodeo

Dallying: The act of wrapping the rope around the saddle horn for the header to secure his catch.

Header: In team roping, the cowboy who ropes first and aims for the horns.

Heeler: In team roping, the cowboy who follows the header and aims for the hind legs.

Honda: The knot through which a rope passes through on its way to becoming a loop. Also referred to as the hondo.

Legal Catch: Three ways to acceptably catch a steer in competition: around both horns, half-head, or around the neck.

MHSRA: Montana High School Rodeo Association

NHSFR: National High School Finals Rodeo

NFR: National Finals Rodeo. The premier rodeo event by the PRCA, which showcases the talents of the PRCA's top-fifteen money winners in each event as they compete for the world title.

Nodding: A signal that a cowboy gives when he is ready for the gate or chute to be opened.

No Time: The failure to make a qualified run in timed events due to a rule infraction, which includes an illegal catch or no catch.

PFMA: Partner or Family Member Assault

PRCA: Professional Rodeo Cowboys Association. The oldest and largest professional rodeo-sanctioning body in the world.

SAR: Search and Rescue

Standings: In professional rodeo, a cowboy's success is measured in earnings. There are several sets of standings where cowboys can keep track of where they rank.

WPRA: Women's Professional Rodeo Association; one of the largest rodeo sanctioning bodies in the world, exclusively open to women.

WRCA: Working Ranch Cowboys Association. A professional association that produces the World Championship Ranch Rodeo, an event that showcases the skills of the working ranch cowboy.

series recap

From *The Pieces We've Lost*—**Ellison** and **Colter** have been happily married for a year and are living on the family ranch in Silver Creek. Colter is still team roping with Reid and managing the Carson family ranch, and Ellison works as a vet tech in Miles City. She also teaches kids in the community how to ride horses and travels to rodeos with Colter and the guys often.

From *The Chances We Take*—**Isabelle** (Ellison's best friend) and **Reid** are in a long-distance relationship but are very much in love. Reid lives in Silver Creek and still competes with Colter at rodeos, and Isa lives in Houston and works with bookstores managing their social media marketing. They visit each other in Montana and Texas as often as they can.

From *The Hearts We've Broken*—**Juniper** just moved to Minnesota to work in a cancer research lab. **Mikey** recently moved onto a small plot of land on the Carson ranch and is still a bull rider. They are in a long-distance relationship, though they were fake dating for three months prior to breaking up temporarily then getting back together in an official relationship.

Jake and **Hayden** are both single and competing in rodeo. Jake is a tie-down roper, and Hayden is a team roper. They both live in Silver Creek and travel with their buddies—Colter, Reid, and Mikey—to rodeos.

SIERRA

Sometimes the real monsters weren't the ones hiding in the shadows under your bed or in your closet. Sometimes the real monsters were the ones who were supposed to protect you from them in the first place.

A steady drumming in my temple matched the pace of my racing heart as I took in my surroundings. The world around me was devoid of color, everything in shades of gray.

Glass shards crunched under my body as I hauled myself to my feet, muscles shaking on the verge of giving out. An acrid, coppery scent filled my nostrils, and warm liquid dripped down my cheeks.

Tears?

I pressed my fingers to the skin under my eye, wincing at the sting of pain that came with it before my hand retreated back down under my gaze.

No.

Blood, like melted honey, clung to my fingertips.

The remnants of liquor bottles covered the hardwood floor, and I debated reaching down to grab one of the jagged pieces. It would be so easy, too easy, to get it over with. End all of this—all the fear, all the pain and suffering—for good.

After taking a deep breath, I carefully stepped over the dark figure lying on the floor, heading to the kitchen counter. My heart hammered against my ribs as my vision tunneled on the phone, the whole reason I'd gotten up from a heap on the floor in the first place.

My fingers moved on their own, pressing buttons as though it were muscle memory, even though my limbs trembled as I raised the phone to my ear.

A few heavy moments passed, hanging still in the silence of the dark, sleepy street of my neighborhood.

They say monsters aren't born. They're made.

A feminine voice crackled in my ear. "911, what's the address of your emergency?"

But who gets to decide what makes a monster?

sierra

Montana was populated by men with small penises. At least that's what I could only assume when an ugly, lifted Chevy Silverado cut me off for the third time today. I banged my fist against the steering wheel, hoping the blaring of my horn would get the message across that they were a major fucking asshole.

I wasn't even driving slow—I was going ten over the speed limit. And I couldn't just slam on my brakes. I had a damn horse trailer for God's sake.

In hindsight, I should've seen this coming. Driving in Goldfinch *sucked*. There were way too many people on the roads and only one route I could really take to get anywhere.

As if the universe sensed my frustration, another idiot in a compensator truck changed lanes, swerving in front of me without using their blinker.

Laying on the horn, I mentally cursed the TV shows that made Montana so popular.

Stupid college boys, with their stupid ugly-ass lifted pickups, who don't use their stupid-ass blinkers.

How hard was it to flick a simple switch and use your turn signal? Then again, college boys—and men, really—were lazy and didn't do anything extra, even if their lives depended on it.

My stress levels weren't up only because of the horrible drivers, though. My anxiety spiked every time I came within a five-mile vicinity of this town.

Deep breaths, Sierra.

I slowly inhaled, counting to four. After holding my breath for four beats, I exhaled, releasing the air for another four.

All I had to do was make it to the fairgrounds in one piece, run the pattern, and then I could get the hell out of here.

My dog, Pancho, stuck his head out the window, tongue lolling in the breeze and tail wagging a mile a minute. His furry butt wiggled as he nipped at the air then spun in circles in the passenger seat before sticking his head out the window again.

At least someone was enjoying themselves.

I sighed as I took in the familiar surroundings. Pale-blue mountains stretched toward the sky in one direction, dark tree silhouettes dotting the hills and ridges. In the other direction, the land stretched on for miles, bordering the Sapphire Gulch Creek that ran through the valley the town was nestled in.

Goldfinch hadn't changed much since the last time I'd been here—five years ago. The population had grown, a phenomenon most college towns experienced, but for the most part the businesses and neighborhoods looked the same. Some houses appeared to have had better days, the paint on their siding now weathered and cracked, but most seemed to have gone through modern updates.

I knew every inch of this town, every side street and backroad, yet I could never muster up the courage to drive past my old house.

The house that was never a home.

I wondered if anyone lived there now or if it was vacant, haunted by the ghosts of my childhood.

I knew exactly which street it was on. Physically, I could probably still drive there blindfolded, but, mentally, I couldn't do it.

The truth was, I never wanted to stay in Montana. The winding dirt roads and sprawling landscapes held too many memories—ones I yearned to remember and ones I wished I could erase from my mind.

My goal was always to get out and never come back. And a few times I did get out, but something always brought me back. Whether it was a rodeo, a court date, or something else stupid. This place, as beautiful as it was, had a death grip on me I couldn't shake.

I stopped at a red light, and my knuckles paled as my hands gripped the steering wheel tighter.

"Stop it! Don't touch her!"

Glass shattered somewhere to my right, and my body recoiled as I sucked in a breath, heart thumping as my chest tightened like an iron suit of armor. My eyes darted toward the floorboards, frantically searching around for the shards. Warm liquid dripped down my palms, and I lifted my hands off the steering wheel, turning them over. My hands shook, but there was nothing there. There never was.

Pancho tilted his head at me and whined, the sound breaking me out of my panic.

It's not real. It's not real. It's not real.

The blast of a car horn pulled me out of my daze, and

I looked up, noticing the light I'd been stopped at had turned green. The car behind me changed lanes, speeding by as the driver flipped me off.

I pressed my foot down on the gas pedal, and the engine rumbled as I slowly started to inch along again.

My heart still raced in my chest, but I had to pull myself together.

It was one day.

A few hours.

I inhaled through my nose and exhaled a couple of long breaths through my mouth until I gathered my composure again. Pancho licked my arm in an attempt at comfort, and a wobbly sigh fell from my lips.

"What do you make of all this, Pancho?" I asked, even though I knew he wouldn't answer.

He lifted a paw in the air, which was good enough for me.

I huffed out a laugh, shaking my head. "All right, bud. Let's do the damn thing."

I pulled into the parking lot of the rodeo grounds about five minutes later. The rodeo didn't start for a few more hours, but I needed to let my horse, Lucky, get settled and rest for a while before warming him up for competition.

I hopped out of the pickup, fully intending to leave Pancho in the cab with the window rolled down. He had too much energy to be running around, and he was a bit of a pain in my ass. That dog found trouble wherever he went. My life would be a bit easier today with him in the truck. But he clearly had a different idea when he leapt over the center console to jump out of the vehicle and take off running.

Goddammit.

"Pancho! Come back here, asshole!" I yelled as I ran after him.

He'd run up to a random group of strangers and started jumping up on one of them. The damn dog was rubbing his back against the poor man's leg, front limbs splayed out as he sat up on his hindquarters.

The man reached down to pet him, his straw cowboy hat blocking his face. His friends just laughed, arms crossed in amusement. They looked vaguely familiar, but I couldn't place who they were from afar. The rodeo world was close-knit, though, so I wouldn't have been surprised if I'd seen them before on a big screen at a competition.

When I finally caught up to my devil dog, I leaned down to grab his collar so I could pull him away. "I'm so sorry about my dog, he's—" I started to apologize, catching my breath. But as I stood up, I came face-to-face with a familiar pair of ocean-blue eyes.

Ones I remembered all too well.

How could I ever forget eyes like his?

Five years could do a lot for a person. His jaw was more defined, having lost the pesky baby fat in his face, and he could actually grow facial hair now, although it was still a bit patchy and looked as though he kept it short— clean and well-trimmed. His hair was slightly darker than it was when we were kids, now more of a sandy brown or a dark, dirty blond. Lean muscle rippled in his arms, a tell-tale sign he was no longer a boy—no longer the boy I'd fallen in love with at sixteen, despite knowing I could never have him, would never subject him to the pain I'd endured as a child.

My first love.

My first loss.

Decades could have passed. An infinite amount of time apart wouldn't have mattered.

I'd have recognized him anywhere.

"Hi, Skip." The corner of his lip twitched, and amusement shone in his gaze, but I didn't miss the crack—ever so subtle—in his voice when he said my childhood nickname.

Hayden.

hayden

S-sorry." Sierra's face flushed, and her mouth gaped as though she wanted to say something else but couldn't. Instead, she blinked a few times before picking up her fluffball and running off.

My vision was glued to her as she left, and I only lost sight of her when she disappeared behind a row of pickup trucks and trailers.

"Who was that?" Colter asked once Sierra was out of earshot.

"That"—I paused, sucking in a breath—"was Sierra Bayley."

I'd seen her in passing over the years—on arena jumbo screens and social media posts—but nothing could compare to seeing her face-to-face. Not much about her had changed, despite the amount of time that had passed since she'd last spoken to me. Her hair was dark now, nearly jet black instead of her natural blonde. Even though she ran away from me today, I knew she still carried herself with the same take-no-shit attitude and sass she'd developed in high school. Her TV interviews said as much.

Sierra wasn't always like that—confident, intimidating, *radiant*—but I knew she didn't let anyone see what was underneath her tough exterior.

Only me. Once upon a time.

Blonde hair cascaded over my thigh as we lay on the old, ratty couch in Keenan's basement. Sierra's head lay in my lap, and her bare feet rested on the arm of the couch. My fingers gently brushed through the tangles in her hair as music thumped around us. No one at this party—if you could even call it that—seemed to be paying any attention to us, all of them too busy dancing and getting drunk off the cheap liquor Keenan stole from his parents.

"Do you ever worry about the future?" she whispered, looking up at me with her emerald-green eyes.

All the time, *I thought. "Sometimes. What are you worried about?"*

She fell silent for a moment. "Do you think we'll still be best friends in the future? Still be…us?"

Without hesitation, I said, "Yeah. Yeah, I do."

I think we'll be together in every lifetime. Every universe.

I didn't think there could ever be another version of me without Sierra Bayley.

I didn't want there to be.

Once bright irises muddled in an instant, her gaze cloudy and exuding sadness. "I hope so."

Mikey's laughter brought me out of my temporary daze before his jaw dropped with realization. "Wait, was that girl your ex? The one you were talking about when we were in Cheyenne?" When I didn't confirm nor deny, he slapped his knee. "Hot damn! I didn't know you had it in you, Hayden. She's a smokeshow, that's for sure."

"Whoa there, Michael. Juniper might castrate you if you're not careful." Jake chuckled.

"Hey, I never touched her, man," Mikey protested, crossing his arms defensively. "No one ever said anything about looking. Besides, I'm sure June would agree."

I shot him a sharp glare. If looks could kill, he would already be six feet under. "Well, I'm saying something about looking."

Four heads snapped toward me with widening eyes and raised brows, but I held my chin high, standing my ground. Even if Mikey's comments were only meant as jokes toward me, I didn't want them bringing her into it.

Sure, I was quiet and kept to myself most of the time, but Sierra wasn't just any girl.

No, she was special. She was the type of girl people wanted to go to bat for and defend in rooms and conversations she wasn't in.

I'd defend her to the grave.

"I was kidding, Haydie." Mikey raised his hands in resignation. "But I hear ya."

"Let's just go," I grumbled. I didn't want to stand here and talk about Sierra. Talking about her would only lead to questions—questions I wasn't sure I knew the answers to anymore.

And the answers I did know weren't mine to share.

"Man, it's great to be back in our hometown, isn't it?" My roping partner, Keenan Chase, patted me on the shoulder after he'd tracked me down.

Keenan was my closest friend growing up. Our parents were best friends—our dads worked together at the Gulch County Sheriff's Office before his dad medically retired—

so we'd practically known each other since the womb. We both grew up in Goldfinch, then competed in high school rodeo together before ultimately going separate ways for college.

Keenan had gone to school in Wyoming, and I'd stayed to compete on the SGU rodeo team. When we graduated from college, we kind of fell out of touch—Keenan moved to Nebraska, and I moved to Silver Creek—but happened to reconnect last year before the NFR. After a day of playing catch-up, we decided to enter up together for the following year. It'd be just like old times, except we were much better than we were as teenagers.

"Mm-hmm," I grunted in response.

"Come on, Hazey. What's with the sad face?" Keenan poked me in the ribs.

I side-eyed him, eyes narrowing as I scrunched my nose. "That's just my face."

"Nah, you're not normally this…broody. Does it have anything to do with a certain someone whose nickname rhymes with tippy?" He seemed to take the hint with the glare I gave him, because he threw his hands in the air in surrender. "Hey, I was just curious. Have you—"

"We ran into each other earlier. Her dog jumped on me." I chuckled. "She ran off pretty quickly after, though, so no. And this was the first time I've seen her in…"

Five years, my brain screamed in my ear, filling in the blanks I didn't want to say aloud. *You haven't seen her in five years.*

I coughed. "It's been a long time."

"Damn, I'm sorry, dude. I know you two were close. I, uh"—Keenan scratched his head—"I don't know exactly what happened after we graduated, but I'm here if you want to talk about it."

"Thanks," I mumbled, knowing it probably wouldn't be something I talked about. With anyone. "I'm going to warm up Peanut Butter."

Keenan laughed, his eyes squinting to slits as his shoulders shook. "Man, I can't believe your dad let you name that horse Peanut Butter."

I shrugged. "I was fourteen." The name may have been a tad ridiculous, but it was special to me. It meant something.

I started running Peanut two years ago for competition. I ran her in practice arenas a lot when I was in college and just starting my professional career. She was young, although competition came naturally to her—a good thing, because two years ago, the horse I ran all throughout my childhood and college suddenly passed. Team roping required not only a reliable human partner, but also a reliable horse, and Peanut was consistent. Plus, it seemed special to compete with the horse who grew up with me… and Sierra.

"Hey, girl." I patted Peanut's neck, and she chuffed in greeting.

I tacked my horse, careful to double-check all of the equipment to make sure everything was tight and secure, then warmed her up, taking a couple laps around one of the smaller pens behind the main rodeo arena.

When I was on the back of a horse, the world around me seemed to pause. Equine therapy was a thing for a reason. The animals were great for emotional regulation because they mirrored a person's emotions. A horse could sense your anxiety or stress, so it was important to keep your emotions in check. Throughout the years, riding became my comfort, my stress relief. It also didn't hurt that some of my best memories involved horses and Sierra.

"It's a beautiful day for a rodeo. We've got some talented cowboys and cowgirls competing today. Let's kick off the fun with bareback riding!" The rodeo announcer welcomed the crowd after the National Anthem played and a prayer wishing safety on all the participants was said.

I hadn't seen Sierra since our run-in earlier this morning. I was sure we'd both been warming up our horses and preparing for competition, but it still didn't stop me from looking for her.

"You must be real down bad for that girl, Haydie." Jake laughed.

I crossed my arms, feigning disinterest. "What do you mean?"

He shrugged, leaning against one of the arena panels. "You keep looking around. I'm guessing for her. Unless there's another girl here you're trying to find?"

Mikey came sauntering up then, adding in his two cents. "Which, if you were, no one would be judging, least of all me. But then I'd have to repeat my earlier statement because I would have never expected that coming from you."

"I'm not—" I started to protest, but Keenan threw his arm around me.

"And denial is a river in Egypt, my friend."

I rolled my eyes, shaking him off. "Shut up."

"Leave him alone, you guys." Colter shoved Jake away, the latter making a dramatic show of it, pretending to trip over his feet. "Unless you want me to remind you of the past six months, Mikey?" He raised his brows at the bull rider then turned to Jake. "I don't think I even have to say anything about you."

Jake's mouth pressed into a hard line, like he knew exactly what Colter was alluding to. "Believe me, Colt, I would if I didn't have morals."

"Wait, you have those?" Reid teased, covering his mouth with his palm.

Jake shot back a flashy smile. "Hard to believe, ain't it?"

"Don't you have to compete?" I muttered.

Jake had grown up competing in both steer wrestling and tie-down roping, but more recently he was only competing in tie-down.

"Ah, yeah, I suppose so. See you on the other side." He gave us a mock salute then took off in the other direction.

"Up next in the team roping, we've got a duo who grew up right here in the Gulch! Give them a big home welcome, folks. Hayden Watkins and Keenan Chase!"

I led my horse into the roping box on the left side of the chute. Keenan adjusted his cowboy hat on the other side, looking to me for the signal. Peanut was ready to run, and I backed her up as far as I could. Once I'd readied myself and checked that Keenan was also ready, I nodded and the steer was released from the chute.

Peanut took off, her hooves pounding against the dirt. I swung my rope over my head, keeping my eye on the honda and my target. When the time was right, I threw my rope, the loop falling perfectly over the steer's horns. Jerking out the slack, I dallied as Peanut ran past the steer in a curve, turning the animal so Keenan could follow up on roping the legs.

Once he'd caught the hind legs, the time stopped. Keenan let the rope go slack, and my horse followed the steer as it ran, my rope still attached to its horns, guiding it to the end.

"How about a five-point-nine!" the announcer called out.

"Hell yeah!" Keenan pumped his fist in the air.

Once the steer was out of the arena, Keenan and I rode next to each other down the side of the arena to get out before the next team started their run.

I nodded, dipping my chin slightly in acknowledgment, and he laughed.

"Always the stoic one, Hazey."

hayden

MAY, SENIOR YEAR

Let's goooo, Hazey! It's graduation day!" Keenan ran past me, slapping me on the back, as we headed toward the school entrance from the parking lot. "Bro, I never thought this day would come. Thank fuck, or my senioritis probably would've taken me out."

I chuckled at him. "You've had a case of senioritis since the first day of sophomore year."

"You're damn right I have. It's been a long four years, and now I'm ready to spread my wings and fly. Caw caw!" He flapped his arms and made squawking noises as he zigzagged through the cars.

I rolled my eyes and pulled my phone out of my pocket to send a text to Sierra.

I'll see you in there, Skip

"Hurry up!" Keenan yelled at me over his shoulder.

I picked up my pace, taking the front steps two at a time to make it to the doors before Keenan could close them in my face for being too slow.

The atrium was already crowded with our classmates and family members who had gotten to the graduation ceremony early. Congratulations and chatter about college plans echoed through the halls.

My eyes scanned the sea of people in the lobby outside the gymnasium. No sign of Sierra yet. It wasn't like her to be late for anything, much less something as important as graduating high school.

"Yo, Chase! What's good, buddy?" One of Keenan's friends, Jack, pulled him into a bro hug.

"Not much, just ready to get this shit over and done with." Keenan's mouth curved into a flashy smile, the type that had all the girls in our class falling at his feet.

"A-freaking-men, dude. I can't wait to get out of this town for good." Jack threw his arm over Keenan's shoulder as they climbed up the short set of stairs leading to one of the common areas.

I checked my phone, noticing Sierra hadn't read my message yet. Thinking maybe she just didn't get the notification, I shot off another text to her.

> Are you going to be here soon?

After scanning the gymnasium for Sierra—maybe she'd gone inside early—I realized I still needed to grab my cap and gown.

"Hey, Hayden!" A few of my classmates called out their greetings as I passed them in the halls.

I waved at a couple of them and gave the others a brief hello or a head nod.

Today would likely be the last day I saw a lot of them. Most of my friends planned to go to school out of state—

or at least out of Goldfinch. I, on the other hand, was perfectly okay with going to school at Sapphire Gulch.

I'd tried to get Sierra to apply for SGU with me. If I was able to get a rodeo scholarship, there was no way she wouldn't also get one. But she'd brushed me off or changed the subject every time I'd asked, a sad glint in her eyes.

I knew she had a complicated relationship with her family. If I was being honest, "complicated" was an understatement. Her dad was a piece of shit, and everyone in town knew it. Spencer Bayley had been arrested more than a couple of times in the four years I'd known Sierra. I probably knew far more than she intended. Even though she tried her hardest to keep secrets, I could read her like a book.

Something was bothering Sierra. I knew it because she'd been avoiding me all week, and a bad feeling settled in my chest.

"Skip! Wait up!" I called her name down the hallway, but she didn't stop like she normally would, keeping her head down as she continued walking through the waves of students trying to get to class.

Slamming my locker shut, I jogged after her, eventually catching up. She was no match for my five-foot-eleven stature.

"Sierra, hey." I lightly touched her elbow, but she flinched back like my hand was a hot iron that just branded her skin.

Recognition, then something like shame, flickered in her expression. "Oh, hey, Hayden." She wouldn't maintain eye contact with me, her emerald eyes always averting toward the ground or the ceiling.

"Is everything okay?" I asked, trying not to sound overly concerned.

Her walls immediately went up like a shield, and her mouth set into a hard line. "Why wouldn't everything be okay?"

I tried not to let it hurt me, but Sierra and I didn't keep secrets, and knowing she was holding things back from me stung. Especially since I was confident I already knew what she was keeping from me. "I just feel like you've been avoiding me. You know you can talk to me if you need anything, right?"

Her gaze flicked up and down and back up. "Yeah, whatever. I've been busy, okay? You don't need to keep tabs on me."

I knew she didn't mean it. This was her defense mechanism. She pushed people away so she didn't have to be vulnerable. I'd known her for over two years now—spent almost all of my weekends with her—so I knew when she was trying to deflect.

It was hard to stand by, though, especially after knowing what had happened last week. My dad didn't want to tell me, but I would have found out eventually.

Everyone would.

The slam of a locker forced me out of my thoughts, and I remembered where I was.

Cap and gown. Right.

It was like I was in a trance, moving through a dream sequence where everything was distorted and blurry. All I could think about was Sierra as I moved through the motions to get my cap from my locker and shrug on my graduation gown.

It wasn't until Keenan grabbed my hand to pull me down the hallway that I snapped out of it.

"Hazey! Come onnnn!" he whined.

As he dragged me toward the gymnasium, I checked my phone again. It was almost time for the ceremony to start, and I still hadn't gotten a response from Sierra.

"Party tonight, girls. You coming?" Keenan winked at a couple girls as we passed them in the hall, and they all nodded excitedly.

I rolled my eyes at him and shook my hand free from his grasp.

"You hear from Skippy yet?"

I shook my head. "No, not yet. Have you seen her?"

It was hard to recognize anyone in the sea of navy-blue graduation caps and gowns, but Sierra wouldn't have come to graduation just to ignore me.

"Nope. I'm sure she'll show up. Don't worry. Relax a little, dude." Keenan grasped my shoulders, massaging the tension out of them.

"Yeah, you're right, she's probably just late."

"Welcome to the graduation of the Goldfinch High School class of…" The school superintendent stood in front of a podium at the end of the gymnasium. Graduates sat in alphabetical order facing the podium, and everyone else in attendance sat in the bleachers. I was near the back, and I couldn't really tell who was in front of me, but Sierra should have been in the first few rows.

I strained my eyes to see if it was even possible to tell she was here from the back of her head. Or maybe her graduation cap? Most of the girls in my class talked about decorating their caps with flowers and glitter. Sierra was never that type of girl, but maybe she put horses or something on it.

Then I remembered; all the seats were labeled with our names in case someone ended up being late. It was drilled into our heads that we needed to be early, and I was sure people were too scared to show up late, if not for the embarrassment of walking in late, then for the subtle threats our class advisor gave us.

I held my breath as I mentally went through all of the last names of kids in our class as my eyes wandered over each row.

My heart dropped when I found her seat still empty.

Holding my phone between my knees, I sent off another string of texts.

> Where are you?

> I'm getting worried Skip

"Friends, family, faculty, and staff, we are here today to recognize an incredible milestone for these young men and women."

A few speeches dragged on, but the only thing on my mind was Sierra and her empty seat.

"It is my honor to present to you the graduates of Goldfinch High School."

The first couple rows stood up and moved in a line just like we had practiced.

"Lydia Rebecca Abbott."

"Elizabeth Grace Arnold."

"William Rye Bailey."

"Sierra Madeline Bayley."

She's not here.

An awkward silence filled the gym for a split second before the commencement continued like nothing had happened. Some kids were bound to not show up; it was expected.

"Keenan Matthew Chase."

Like the showboat he was, Keenan hit some kind of wild pose after he'd received his diploma, and the gymnasium burst into laughter. He may have been an idiot, but he was a lovable one, that was for sure.

"Hayden Andrew Watkins."

The crowd clapped, and my friends whistled as I walked across the stage to get my diploma. Cameras flashed as I plastered on the most convincing smile I could while trying to ignore the pit in my stomach telling me something had gone horribly wrong.

Is everything okay?

Text me back

Sierra, please

sierra

The name of this next cowgirl might be familiar to some of you folks. Today, she's blazing back onto her old stomping grounds like a wildfire! Let's see if this cowgirl's still got it!"

Lucky shook his head as we waited at the end of the alleyway to start our run. I turned him around in slow circles to keep him calm.

Anticipation bubbled in my chest as the crowd roared around us, but I kept my breathing steady. Lucky fed off my energy. If I was anxious and ready to run, he would be, too, but if I was cool, calm, and collected, he'd lock in exactly how I needed him to.

"Running today on Ace's Lucky Charm, we've got Sierra Bayley!"

I set my hands on the reins as the announcer called out our names, adrenaline pulsing through my veins. "Steady," I murmured.

Leaning slightly forward into a ready position, I guided Lucky until he was lined up with the last barrel straight ahead at the end of the arena. My calves squeezed Lucky's flank to let him know to go, and he took off in a run down the alleyway as I pointed us slightly toward the right barrel. This allowed us to approach it at an angle, creating a pocket to turn around the barrel without knocking it over and adding five seconds to our final time.

Dust flew into the air as we raced toward the barrel. My ears pulsed with the noise of the crowd surrounding us as well as the steady rhythm of hooves pounding into the dirt.

As we reached the barrel, Lucky slowed ever so slightly. I pulled the reins in my right hand toward my hip, using my other hand for balance and my outside leg to apply pressure and control his turn. Once we were around the barrel, we cut through hazy clouds as I pushed him toward the next one on the other side of the arena, repeating the turn before finally racing toward the final barrel to finish the cloverleaf pattern.

After rounding the final barrel, Lucky knew exactly what he needed to do.

"Go, go, go!" I gave him a couple soft kicks to get him moving into a sprint down the final stretch of the arena, the wind ripping through my hair, blowing it behind me.

"How about fifteen-point-three-six seconds for Sierra!" the rodeo announcer called out. "That'll put her at the top of the leaderboard!"

"Atta boy, Lucky." I smiled, patting his neck as we exited the arena.

After dismounting my horse, I started to lead him toward one of the holding pens to wait until the end of the rodeo. It wouldn't be too long now.

A few other barrel racers who competed against me in high school were circled up, and whispers rose into the air when I passed by.

"I'm surprised she decided to show her face back here again."

"Bold move, that's for sure. I can't believe she's still competing. I'd be too embarrassed to leave my house."

"She's so aggressive. I'd keep a close eye on my horse and gear. You know the saying, 'The apple doesn't fall far from the tree.'"

A muscle in my jaw ticked, but I took a deep breath and ignored them, biting back the remarks I wanted to make.

"I heard her mom ditched town and just disappeared."

"I mean, can you blame her? I would too if my husband…"

Shut up. Shut up. Shut up!

Those girls knew *nothing* about what my mother and I had been through. They only knew what the newspaper articles said.

I blinked away any memories that threatened to pop up in my brain.

You're a good person, Sierra. You did what you had to do to keep everyone safe.

Instead of letting their petty comments get to me, I dusted myself off like the cowgirl I was and headed back to the arena to watch the rest of the barrel racing and the bull riding.

By the time the smell hit my nostrils, it was too late.

"There's a trailer on fire!" a panic-laced voice cried from the direction of the parking lot.

"Someone get help!"

Black plumes of smoke billowed into the air from the area I parked my trailer and pickup, and I sprinted toward the parking lot. Lucky was still in one of the holding corrals, and it was a good thing because *my* trailer was the one currently going up in flames.

Pancho.

"Move!" I pushed people aside as I ran toward the fire. "Pancho!" My voice cracked as I screamed for him.

I'd left him in the small living quarters of the trailer after he'd run off toward Hayden because it was air conditioned and I didn't trust him not to jump out of the pickup again. He was only two, and despite being trained, I swore the dog had half a brain cell. His puppy tendencies took over when he got excited. Besides, it was too hot to just leave the windows down, and I wasn't going to leave the vehicle running for hours on end.

Why didn't I just keep him with me? Or better yet, board him at a kennel for the day.

A firm hand grasped my arm. "Wait!

"Wait a second, you little shit. You're not fucking going anywhere." Pain shot through my limbs as the grip on my arm tightened enough to leave bruises. I'd have to wear a long sleeve to school again or my teachers would ask questions.

I flinched, my eyes squeezing for a moment. Although the reaction was subtle enough no one else would pick up on it—especially with all the commotion relating to the fire —I still mentally kicked myself.

You're safe. It's not real.

I tried to shrug off the man, but his grip tightened, preventing me from moving toward the burning trailer.

"It's not safe to go over there!"

I whirled around on him, trying to rip my arm from his hold. "Let go of me! That's *my* trailer, and my dog is in there!" Agony clawed at my chest as I fought against the man restraining me. I choked out a sob. "Let go!"

Pancho and Lucky were all I had.

I couldn't lose him.

"It's okay, sweetheart, someone got him," he reassured me, pulling me toward safety. "Look." He pointed toward another man in a cowboy hat holding Pancho in his arms. Pancho wiggled against the man's chest as he tried to lick his face, tail wagging rapidly.

I huffed out a sigh of relief knowing the little devil dog was safe.

I walked over to the man holding my dog. "Thank you for getting him out safely."

He gave me a confused look. "What do you mean? Your dog wasn't in the trailer. He was running around barking, and it got my attention. Your dog led me over here, but the trailer was already on fire."

Already on fire? How did Pancho get out then?

There was no way for my dog to open the door to the trailer, and I'd sworn I locked it anyway. Even in a small town like Goldfinch, I didn't trust anyone enough to keep my trailer unlocked.

My brows furrowed. "Huh. Well, thank you for looking after him."

The man nodded. "No worries. Sorry about the trailer." Once he'd handed Pancho over to me, he walked away with his shoulders slightly slumped.

Sirens wailed as the Goldfinch fire and police departments peeled into the parking lot. Luckily for other people—unluckily for me—my trailer was the only one that had been engulfed in flames, and all the other vehicles and trailers were able to be moved before any damage was done.

By the time the firefighters extinguished the blaze, the only thing left was a sad, broken skeleton of metal. The horse trailer—my only home at the moment and means of transportation for Lucky and our gear—was completely and utterly unsalvageable.

The rodeo had long concluded when a firefighter walked over to me. I stood from my crouched position, picking up Pancho so he wouldn't take off.

"Excuse me, miss, are you the owner of this trailer?"

I nodded.

"I'm a lieutenant with the Goldfinch Fire Department. We've cleared the area, so it's safe to gather any belongings that may have survived the fire as well as any personal items left in the pickup truck."

I pulled my lip between my teeth. Both of us knew it was unlikely anything was left.

"Kearns! You're going to want to see this," one of the other firefighters called out.

"Actually, hold tight." The lieutenant dipped his chin at me before heading back to the trailer.

I observed their conversation from afar, unable to hear exactly what they were talking about. One of the firefighters disappeared into the rubble, reemerging with something in his hand. The lieutenant crossed his arms as they continued discussing.

Footsteps crunched in the gravel to my right, and I turned my head to see who it was.

Hayden. Again.

"Hi." His voice somehow calmed the thoughts bouncing around in my brain.

"Hey."

"What happened?" He gestured to the pile of rubble that used to be my horse trailer.

I snorted. "Great question. I guess that's what all the firefighters are trying to figure out." I let my shoulders drop. "Sorry, it's just…"

"Miss." The lieutenant from earlier, Kearns, came back. "We found this in the back of the trailer. In a pile of hay…er, well, what used to be hay."

My eyes narrowed. "What am I supposed to be looking at exactly?"

"It's the butt of a cigarette," Hayden muttered.

"This is likely what started the fire," the firefighter explained.

"It's not mine. I-I don't smoke." After realizing how ridiculous that sounded, I blinked, shaking my head. Of course it wasn't mine. I was competing in the rodeo the whole time. They never insinuated it was mine either. "Sorry, I'm just processing all of this."

"Of course." The firefighter nodded. "Do you have any idea where it could have come from? Anyone you know who would have been smoking around the trailer?"

"N-no. I don't know anyone else here. I travel alone."

Hayden's face fell for a brief moment, and a wave of guilt washed over me, but it wasn't exactly a lie. I was practically a stranger to Hayden at this stage of our lives.

"It's likely that whoever had the cigarette threw it through the window of the trailer. Probably just negligence, but we have to rule out all the other options, so we'll need to hold on to the pickup as evidence."

Hayden's brows shot up. "What, you mean like foul play?"

Kearns shrugged. "Maybe. Or like I said, it was probably just an accident."

"Apparently the door to the living quarters got opened," I mumbled. "Pancho, er, my dog was inside the trailer, but by the time anyone got over here, the trailer was already on fire and my dog was outside. There's no way for him to open the door himself, so I don't know…"

Both of the men gave me strange looks, and my eyes flicked to the ground.

"Maybe I just left it unlocked."

"That's certainly interesting." Kearns tapped his lips, as though deep in thought. "Well, for the moment, don't worry too much about it. For all we know, it was someone being careless."

I nodded slowly. "Right."

After I exchanged my information with the fire lieutenant, he left me with Hayden.

I opened my mouth to say something, but my phone interrupted, pinging with a text message.

UNKNOWN NUMBER

Shame about the fire. What a lucky dog.

Who is this?

UNKNOWN NUMBER

I'd quit while you're ahead.

Who knows what could happen.

I reread the text a few times, my heart rate increasing with each pass.

"You okay, Skip?" Concern painted Hayden's features. "You look like you've seen a ghost."

I swallowed the lump in my throat. "Y-yeah. I'm fine. I'm gonna go." I pointed my thumb over my shoulder.

The problem was, I didn't have anywhere to go.

"Where are you going to go?"

Of course he'd call my bluff.

I shrugged as I forced out a laugh. "I don't know. I'll figure it out." Spinning on my heel, I started to walk back to the arena. Surely there'd be someone who could board my horse and drop me off at a hotel or something.

"Skip," Hayden called out the stupid childhood nickname, but I ignored him and kept walking. "Sierra, wait."

When I didn't stop like he wanted, he started to follow me.

"Come with us."

That was enough for me to stop abruptly in my tracks, causing him to bump into my back with an, "Oof."

"What?" I needed to make sure I heard him correctly.

"Come on the road with us. We have plenty of space and—"

I cut him off, holding up a hand. "I don't think that's—"

"Come on, Skip, let me finish a sentence for once." He chuckled before I could finish my own interruption.

"It's okay, Hayden, I don't want to overstep."

"You wouldn't be. Where are you going to go instead?"

"I'll stay in a hotel or something until I can get my pickup again, then…" Truth was, I didn't know what the fuck I was going to do. A fire investigation could take anywhere from a few days to a few weeks. I couldn't just stop competing, but even if I wanted to go on the road, I didn't have a way to transport Lucky. Unfortunately, horse trailers cost a pretty penny, too. Not to mention all the gear I'd lost in the fire.

"Don't lie to me, Skip." His voice softened. "We don't do that, remember?"

"Okay, fine. I don't have a plan right now, but, like I said, I'll figure it out. I don't want to be an inconvenience."

"You're the farthest thing from an inconvenience to me."

"I don't know how long it'll be, and I'd just be in the way." I started sputtering out any excuse I could think of.

Because I didn't want to step on anyone's toes. Definitely not because I was scared.

"Stay with me. Please."

"Don't go." His eyes glistened from the emotions welling up in them. "Stay with me. Please. Even if it's just for tonight."

How could I not do anything—everything—he asked of me?

I huffed out a breath, knowing he wasn't going to give up so easily. "Fine. But as soon as I get a new trailer and my pickup back, I'm leaving."

His brows furrowed, but he still laughed like he already knew he wasn't going to let that happen. "All right, Skip. Come on. Let's get out of here."

hayden

AUGUST, FRESHMAN YEAR

In a town like Goldfinch, the first day of freshman year was just like any other first day of school, especially when grades seven and eight attended in the same building.

Although the school was decently sized in terms of small towns (the population of Goldfinch was around thirty thousand, but the university made up a significant percentage with nearly ten thousand students), you knew *everyone*. At least, you knew everyone in your graduating class. Goldfinch only had one middle-slash-high school—with a student body population of around a thousand students—and one elementary school, so I grew up alongside all of the kids in my class.

Being the new kid at a school where everyone played in diapers together was like the equivalent of supergluing a neon sign to yourself, so it didn't come as a shock when all eyes were glued to the unfamiliar blonde who stepped on the bus that first day.

She kept her head down, little tendrils of her hair falling

into her face to nearly cover it, but every time she passed by a row of seats, her head would tilt up slightly. She wore long sleeves despite it being the middle of August, and they were pulled down to her knuckles, her thumbs hooked in the cuffs.

Her steps were slow and cautious. Like if she made a wrong move, something would go terribly wrong.

Keenan nudged me with his elbow, breaking my attention away from the new girl. "Are you listening to me, Hayden?"

"Huh?" My eyes flicked back toward the aisle.

She was only a few rows in front of our seats in the middle of the bus; we weren't quite cool enough to be at the very back of the bus like the sophomores.

"Sorry, what were you saying?"

"I was asking if you saw the new video game that GearWorx came out with. It looks sick, dude." He waved his arms around wildly as he started describing what the game was about. Something about monster mutations, super soldiers, and a post-apocalyptic world.

I had completely tuned him out when the girl reached our row, going as far as to turn my head the opposite direction of Keenan to look at her.

Sad, emerald-colored eyes locked onto mine.

"Hey." I raised a hand in a wave.

She flinched—the tiniest little movement; if I'd blinked, I would have missed it—those eyes darting to my open hand, but she quickly recovered, mumbling a timid, "Hi," as her face flushed bright pink.

Before I could say anything else, she brushed past me, finding a seat a few rows back.

When I looked at her over my shoulder, I caught her looking at me, though.

"Hayden!" Keenan whined, grabbing my sleeve. "You're not listening to me."

"Sorry, sorry. Start over. I'm listening now, I promise."

But I wasn't, not really. Because my mind was glued to the new girl with the sad eyes sitting just a few rows behind us.

By some stroke of fate, the new girl was placed in the same homeroom class as me and Keenan.

Most of the desks were already taken by the time she walked in, everyone choosing to sit in the little groups they'd formed since elementary school. My eyes tracked her as she found a spot near the back corner of the room —the opposite corner from where I sat.

The classroom buzzed with conversation about summer break and what everyone did.

"Dude, my parents took me to Deadwood this summer, and it was *so cool*," Keenan blabbed to his other friends, Jack and Andrew, as he tapped his pencil against the wood top of his desk.

Tap. Tap. Tap.

I gently grabbed the end of the pencil near the eraser, stopping him from hitting it against the desk.

"Whoops, sorry, Hayden," he apologized, but five minutes later he was tapping the pencil again.

"What did you do over the summer, Hayden?" Andrew asked.

I shrugged. "Not a whole lot, honestly. Dad was working a lot this summer, so we—"

"We got to ride in the cop car with them that one

time!" Keenan cut me off. "We didn't get to catch any bad guys, but they let us turn on the lights and the sirens."

I chuckled, adding to his outburst. "We did. That was really cool."

"All right, settle down, class." Our teacher, Mrs. Gibbs, clapped her hands at the front of the classroom to get everyone's attention.

The chatter dwindled to just a few hushed whispers.

"We've got a new student joining us today!" Mrs. Gibbs exclaimed, gesturing toward the new girl, whose face was now bright red. "Why don't you stand up and introduce yourself? Don't be shy, honey."

All of my classmates—myself included—turned around in our seats, which I'm sure didn't help ease her nerves. I didn't like getting called on in class for normal things like answering a math question, much less having to introduce myself to people I didn't know.

The girl looked like she would have rather swallowed a mug full of nails as she reluctantly stood. Her eyes bounced around the room before they finally landed on me and stayed there. I offered her a small smile, and it seemed as though her shoulders relaxed.

"Um…" Her voice was soft but sweet, if not a bit timid. "I'm Sierra." She swallowed, her fingers fiddling with the right-hand cuff of her long sleeve, rubbing back and forth, back and forth like a bow on the strings of a violin. "Sierra Bayley."

Bayley. Bayley. Bayley.

I swore I'd heard that name from somewhere, but I couldn't place it.

"Where did you move here from, Sierra?" Mrs. Gibbs prompted her to continue, even though Sierra had already started to sit.

She cleared her throat, straightening her posture again. "Ponderosa Valley. Can I sit now, please?" As she waited for a response, she pulled her lip between her teeth, shrinking her body like she wanted to disappear.

"Of course. Everyone, make Sierra feel welcome here."

A chorus of, "Yes, Mrs. Gibbs," rose from the classroom. Everyone else had faced forward in their seats again, but I was still looking over my shoulder at Sierra.

She must have noticed I was staring, because her lips twitched up in a tiny smile. And for the first time today, her eyes didn't look as sad.

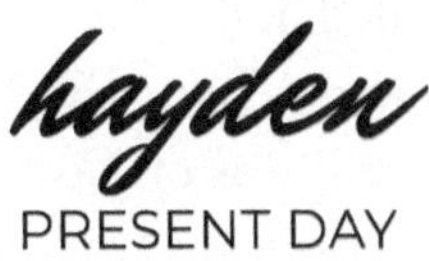

CHAPTER SIX

T his one's yours." I gestured to the guest bedroom across the hall from mine, then to the door at the end of the hall between the bedrooms. "The bathroom is there."

Pancho happily trotted into the guest room, pouncing on the bed to curl into a ball on the fluffy, lilac-colored comforter. The corners of my lips lifted at the sight of him making himself at home.

Sierra shifted awkwardly on her feet, her gaze glued to the floor. "I—you didn't have to..." Her voice trailed off. "Thank you, Hayden."

I leaned against the doorframe as she carried in what few belongings she'd been able to salvage from the fire. "Let me know if you need anything, okay, Skip?"

Her eyes flicked up to mine, and she gave me a small nod. "I will."

After Sierra agreed to come back to Silver Creek with me, we untacked her horse and got him loaded in my trailer. I'd told the guys that I would be a little longer so they could hit the road without me. Thankfully, they hadn't argued or asked questions, but I knew I'd have to formally introduce her soon.

We got Lucky settled in the pasture with Peanut as soon as we made it home. The only equipment that was salvageable from the fire was on his back at the time, so it didn't take long to clear space for it in the barn.

Luckily I had everything else Sierra might possibly need, so she'd at least be covered until she figured out what she was going to do.

I didn't want to think about her leaving again, so once she closed the door behind her, I walked out to the living room, gazing out the window into the pasture.

Her horse seemed to be content, which offered some sense of relief. I only hoped Sierra would be as happy to be staying with us as Lucky and Pancho were.

Down the hall, a door closed, followed shortly by the shower turning on.

I figured Sierra would want some time to adjust and settle in, and I wasn't too keen on just waiting for her out in the kitchen like a weirdo, so I scribbled *Going to the grocery store* on a sticky note. I put it on the counter in case Sierra got out of the bathroom and wondered where I was, then hopped into my pickup to drive into town.

The blend of harmonica and guitar filled the cab as "Save My Soul" by Noah Rinker started to play when I turned the key in the ignition.

I wasn't necessarily low on groceries, but Sierra had lost basically everything in the fire, so I wanted to make sure she had everything she needed. After grabbing a cart at the front of the store, I walked down each aisle, meticulously searching for her favorite things—at least the things I knew were her favorite when we were in high school.

I probably looked ridiculous to other shoppers, grabbing items seemingly with no rhyme or reason—or consideration for health, for that matter.

Looking down at the array of items in the cart, I decided I should probably grab some ingredients to make an actual meal. I turned the cart around, heading back to the produce aisle to grab carrots, celery, and an onion.

After about twenty minutes of searching, I was satisfied with the food items I'd gathered. I headed over to the health and beauty aisle to grab a few essentials before checking out.

"Hayden?" a familiar voice called out behind me.

Spinning around, I came face-to-face with one of the bartenders at Rudy's. "Oh, hey, Liv."

Liv was a few years younger than me and Sierra, but we'd always gotten along fine. I was sure she'd had a bit of a crush on me when she first started working at Rudy's, but nothing ever came of it. In fact, she started dating one of her coworkers recently.

She looked at my cart and then chuckled. "Interesting choices you've got there. Shopping for someone special?"

"W-what makes you say that?" I stumbled over my words.

She grabbed the box of tampons in my cart and held it up, raising her brows.

"Oh. Uh…right, well…" I cleared my throat, snatching the box out of her hands. "I have a…uh…an old friend is staying with me for a while. I thought I'd do her a favor and stock up the bathroom."

"That's considerate of you." She patted me on the back as she passed by. "You're a good guy, Hayden. I hope I get to meet this girl."

I shook my head, suppressing a laugh. "I'm sure you will."

She raised her hand in a wave as she disappeared around the corner, leaving me to grab the shampoo, conditioner, and soap she'd always liked—the fancy kind that smelled like lavender. I picked up a few more things, then checked out.

When I walked through the front door of the house, Sierra was waiting on the couch.

She narrowed her eyes at the bundle of grocery bags in my arms. "What did you get at the store?"

I set the grocery bags on the counter, keeping the one with toiletries in my hand. "Go ahead, take a look. I'll be right back."

I hurried down the hall to the bathroom, unpacking the soap and personal items, putting them in plain sight so she'd be able to see them easily.

"Hayden?" Sierra's voice had a hint of surprise to it.

I couldn't hide the grin on my face when I came back out to the kitchen to find her with one hand on her hip and a bag of peanut butter cups in the other.

"What is all this?" She held up the bag of candy and gestured to the other things I'd bought with her in mind.

"Those are your favorites," I pointed out as nonchalantly as I could, which admittedly wasn't very well.

Her eyebrows furrowed. "They are. But how…"

I stepped closer to her. "You think I don't remember every single thing about you? You are…*were* my best friend in the entire world, Skip. Forgetting someone like you isn't that easy."

It was nearly impossible, actually. Sierra, and everything about her, left a permanent imprint on my heart. Knowing her—*loving her*—had altered my brain chemistry.

"I'm sorry," she murmured.

I rested my elbow on the counter, leaning into it so I was eye level with her. "Sorry for what?"

"For…everything. For leaving."

I reached out, my thumb brushing the hair out of her face, across the faded pink scar on her cheek below her left eye. I remembered the first time I noticed the scar—two years after we'd graduated high school, two years after she'd left for the first time—and my stomach felt like it was tying itself up in knots.

I half expected her to flinch back like she sometimes did, but her eyes just flicked to my retreating hand. "You did what you had to do to survive, Sierra. I don't hold any of it against you. I never have. Never will."

I may not have known the full story of why she left our senior year of high school, or even why she left five years ago for the second time, but I knew what she'd gone through when we were kids. That, to me, was enough.

She exhaled a heavy breath, tucking her hair behind her ear and straightening her posture. "I'd like to start over, though, if that's possible. Be…friends again."

Friends was the last thing I wanted to be with Sierra—I didn't think it was possible for us to be just friends—but if that's what it would take to get her back, then it was a start.

"Friends sounds great, Skip."

CHAPTER SEVEN

sierra

Classic country music played from the speakers overhead in Rudy's—one of Miles City's local bars—as Hayden and I walked through the double doors. The scent of stale beer, aged wood, and a plethora of sweaty bodies greeted us. The bar seemed pretty packed for a Thursday night, but it was summer vacation, and college classes would be starting up again in a few weeks.

"Come on, they're probably all in the back playing pool." Hayden reached for my hand but pulled away when our fingers nearly touched.

My heart screamed at me to take his hand, to make up for all of the time we'd lost, but the darkest part of my brain reminded me that it was my fault and he deserved better. Maybe we'd be together if I hadn't left so many times.

I cleared my throat, choosing to stuff my hands in my pockets. "Lead the way."

College-aged kids crowded the dance floor, couples flinging each other around in a swing dance.

"Hayden, you made it!" One of the cowboys—a tall

man with medium-brown hair and warm, honey-colored eyes—who gathered around the pool table slapped Hayden on the back, pulling him toward the game.

"Thank God you did." Another—a blond with short, cropped hair—handed him a pool stick. "For a second I was worried I was going to have to play with Mikey."

"Hey, you idiots, don't be rude. Who's this with you, Hayden?" A woman with dark hair and piercing blue eyes, who appeared to be around the same age as us, pushed off from her position against the wall to approach me. "I'm Ellison Carson."

She extended her hand to shake, and I took it.

"Sierra…" I cleared my throat. "Bayley."

"How do you know Hayden?" she asked.

The shortest of the men—with a thick mustache and tattoo sleeves covering his arms—cut in with a stupid grin on his face. "Wait, wait, wait. Haydie, isn't this your—"

"Sierra's an old friend," Hayden answered before he could finish his sentence.

I had to admit, it stung a little. I didn't know why; I was the one who suggested we be *friends* again in the first place, but "friends," and especially *old* friends, didn't feel like the proper way to describe who Hayden was to me. Who we were to each other.

"She's staying with me for a while. Her trailer caught fire at the rodeo in Goldfinch."

"Oh, that was yours?" Ellison's eyes widened.

I crossed my arms over my chest, suddenly feeling a bit self-conscious. "Yeah…"

"Well, shit, I'm so sorry. If you need anything, let us know, okay? I'm sure Hayden's got you all taken care of, but any friend of Hayden's is a friend of ours. Anyway, sorry, I got a little sidetracked there." She grabbed the arm belonging to a man who had on a navy-blue pullover and a straw cowboy hat. "This is Colter, my husband."

"It's nice to meet you, Sierra." He took off his hat to shake my hand.

The cowboy who originally greeted Hayden introduced himself next. "I'm Reid Lawson."

Hayden introduced the final two. "The short one's Mikey Tucker, and the blond one is Jake Flynn."

"It's nice to meet you all." I offered a pathetic attempt at a smile. I recognized Colter, Reid, and Mikey's names. They were big-name athletes in the rodeo world, although Mikey had more of a reputation with women than for winning buckles up until recently.

"You're doing pretty well for yourself in the barrel racing this year, aren't you?" Colter asked.

My cheeks flushed, and I ran my fingers through my hair. "Yeah, I'm currently sitting fourteenth in the world standings. It would be my first NFR if I made it."

The NFR, the pinnacle of rodeo events, had always been my dream. I never went to college, so I didn't get to experience a CNFR, and I wasn't quite good enough in high school to make it to the NHSFR, despite how much Hayden hyped me up.

"The NFR has always been her dream," Hayden whispered, so quiet I didn't think anyone else heard him besides me.

"That's impressive. You were at the Houston Rodeo earlier this year, weren't you? I think I remember hearing your name," Colter continued, either not hearing or ignoring Hayden's statement.

I nodded. "I was."

"Well, are you any good at playing pool? We can do teams of three?" Reid suggested, handing me a pool stick.

Shrugging, I laughed. "Sure, why not? But what about you?" I pointed to Mikey.

"They don't want me to play pool because of *one time*," he grumbled, but there was a glint of humor in his eyes.

"First of all, it was more than one time. Secondly, how many times do we need to tell you this? Let's see, there was that time a couple of years ago, and then…" Reid teased, pretending to count on his fingers.

Mikey groaned. "All right, all right, I get it! I'm going to get a drink."

"Okay, now that that's settled, let's make this fair," Jake piped up. "Colter, Reid, and Ellison, one of you has to split up. Ellison, why don't you play on my team?"

"What? Why?" Colter protested.

Jake rolled his eyes. "Have you *seen* your wife play pool? She's better than all of us."

Colter shrugged. "Well, I can't exactly argue with that, but why do *you* get her on your team?"

I watched their exchange, unable to help the small grin pulling at my lips.

"We're always on a team together. Let's mix it up." Ellison playfully nudged Colter. "How about me, Jake, and Sierra on a team? Then you, Reid, and Hayden?" She turned toward me. "Unless you want to play with Hayden."

"Me?" I pointed at myself with my thumb before shaking my head. "I'm fine with whatever."

"Losers buy the next round?" Jake looked around the group for approval.

"You're on." Reid nodded. He turned his head toward me after racking the balls. "Do the honors?"

Lining up a shot, I squinted one eye and hit the cue ball, aiming for the ball at the top of the triangle. The shot had just enough force for the balls in the second row to ricochet toward the pockets in the middle of the table. A solid-colored ball rolled directly into the pocket on the left side, and Ellison pumped her fist next to me.

"Atta girl!"

My next hit wasn't so lucky, setting up Hayden for an easy shot.

The game went back and forth for a while. After Colter missed a shot, I stepped up to the table. Our last ball was right next to the eight-ball, making for a risky shot.

I popped my knuckles before bending down and hinging my hips back so I was eye level with the table. At the last second, though, my eyes flicked to Hayden, who was staring at me with an intensity I'd only seen once in my life.

Blue eyes deep as the ocean peered into mine as Hayden's fists grasped the sheets next to me, his body hovering over mine, warmth radiating off his skin.

A sigh fell from his lips just as…

My wrist slipped right as the pool stick made contact with the ball, and, instead of hitting the final solid ball, the cue ball bounced off the eight ball, gently knocking it into the pocket.

"Shit, sorry guys," I muttered to my team as Colter, Reid, and Hayden celebrated.

Mikey chuckled, raising his beer bottle to me. "Join the club, Sierra."

"How about those drinks, ladies and gents?" Jake threw his arms around Colter and Reid as they walked toward the bar. "Sierra's paying!"

"I can pay if you want me to," Hayden's voice rumbled in my ear, slow and low.

I jumped as my eyes darted toward him. He was close

enough that I could feel the warmth from his body. "It's fine, I've got it. Fair's fair, right?"

"Hi, guys!" The bartender, a blonde girl with a round face and green eyes, smiled when we stepped up to the bar.

"How's it going, Livvy?" Mikey leaned against the bar.

"Great! We've been busy. All of the themed nights that June, Nico, and I came up with have been a hit! I'm a little nervous about how busy it'll get when classes start up again, though." Her attention shifted to Hayden, then to me, then back to Hayden. "Hayden?" She drew out the word with a sly grin. "Who's this?"

"I'm Sierra. Hayden's an…old friend." I mimicked the wording he used to introduce me, even though my teeth ground together as I said it.

"Aw, is she the one you were buying tampons for at the grocery store?"

Hayden's face flushed bright red as he stammered an incoherent string of words, and the rest of the guys burst into laughter.

My brows shot up. "Wait, you did what?"

Hayden wrung his hands together. "I just thought you might need some things. It's not a big deal. Come on, guys, just order your drinks."

"Can you get us five shots of Pendleton, a tequila soda, and whatever Sierra wants, please, Liv?" Colter, still chuckling, was the one to give the order.

"I'll just do a vodka soda," I said, still thinking about Hayden buying me personal products at the grocery store. If it were anyone else, it would be weird, but Hayden had always tried to take care of me and make sure I was comfortable. It was nice to know that even five years later, he hadn't changed.

After we'd gotten our drinks, the guys went back to the

pool table, but Ellison and I found a high-top and some stools.

"So, you grew up in Goldfinch?" Ellison asked. "Hayden mentioned you two went to high school together."

I hesitated for a moment. "No, I actually grew up in Ponderosa Valley but moved to Goldfinch right before starting high school." Barely anyone knew why my family moved from Ponderosa Valley to Goldfinch. There wasn't exactly a proper way to say the reason you moved was because your dad was arrested for assault and wanted to avoid contact with the cops who knew his face.

"Ah, okay. That's when you met Hayden, then." It was more of a statement than a question, but I nodded anyway.

"Yeah. We did high school rodeo together and everything. He and his family helped me a lot. They let me ride their horses for practice and competition until I was able to get my own."

"I'm not surprised about that. He's very kind." She took a sip of her drink. "Has he always been such a man of few words? I've only ever known him to be quiet. He's opened up the last couple years, but when I first met him, I think he said maybe five words to me." A small laugh bubbled out of her.

To any normal person, it would have been funny, too, but something in my heart dropped. "No. He hasn't always been that way."

sierra

Sierra! Get the fuck down here, or you're going to miss the bus! I have better things to do than drive your sorry ass to school!" The masculine voice boomed through the house, rattling the picture frames hanging on my wall.

My eyes flew open, and I scrambled to reach for my phone, knocking it off the nightstand in the process. It fell face up, and the screen illuminated, displaying the time.

No, no, no.

My alarm hadn't gone off, and the bus would be here in five minutes. Practically leaping out of bed, I threw on a pair of jeans and a long-sleeved shirt, not bothering to brush my hair or pull it back into a braid. That would take too long.

I grabbed my backpack, making sure my homework was in there—forgetting that and having to call home would be like setting off a ticking time bomb—then ran some toothpaste over my teeth and tongue.

"Sierra!" the voice, angrier, called out again.

"Coming!" I forced my voice to be strong and unwavering. I couldn't show how anxious I was.

Darting down the stairs, I brushed past the figure at the base of them, silently praying that I could make it out of the door quickly and quietly.

I pulled my bottom lip between my teeth, biting until the metallic tang of blood filled my mouth. My eyes squeezed as I waited, but the impact never came. Letting out a sigh of relief, I made it out the front door with my backpack hanging off one shoulder and my shoelaces still untied.

Leaves crunched under my feet as I jogged down to the bus stop. It was late September, and the weather could be unpredictable, but at least this morning there was a chill to the air. Long sleeves weren't as out of place as they were in July or August.

"Good morning, Miss Bayley," the bus driver, a kind old man named Mr. Hughes, greeted me.

"Morning, Mr. Hughes," I huffed, a bit out of breath.

I'd been attending high school in Goldfinch for a little over a month now, but people still stared at me like I was a wild animal at the zoo. To be fair, I wasn't going out of my way to make friends, but that didn't mean I wanted to be a spectacle.

I'd at least developed a routine: Get on the bus, say hello to Mr. Hughes, avoid everyone's gaze, and sit near the back of the bus until the blond-haired boy I met the first week of classes—Hayden—inevitably tried (and usually succeeded) to talk to me.

I'd never admit it to anyone, but despite my cool demeanor and general distaste for people, I actually enjoyed talking to him. Something about Hayden was... calming. When I was around him, it was like driving under a bridge in a rainstorm. Even if it was only temporary, his presence made me feel less on edge.

I slumped down in my seat next to another quiet girl named Clare, swinging my backpack around so it rested on my lap. We didn't talk much on our bus rides, but she always saved a spot for me. I liked to think we had some kind of mutual understanding.

Keenan and Hayden were already in their seats two rows in front of me—the two rambunctious boys were among the first people to get on the bus since they lived outside of town. Keenan always sat by the window, and Hayden sat in the aisle.

"Hey, Sierra." Hayden flashed me a toothy grin, never once taking his eyes off me.

My lips had a mind of their own, curling up into a smile as my cheeks flushed. "Hi, Hayden."

Keenan pulled on Hayden's arm, and he reluctantly shifted his attention off me. But after a little while, Hayden turned back to me, ignoring Keenan and whatever elaborate story of the day he was trying to tell. "Do you want to come over to my house after school?" When I didn't respond, he added quickly, "We have horses."

I suppressed a giggle, because what a way to convince a girl. "Oh yeah?"

He blushed, and as he raked his fingers through his shaggy blond hair, a few strands fell over his forehead. "Yeah, one of our mares just had a filly. So, do you wanna?"

I pulled my bottom lip between my teeth as I weighed my options. I could go to Hayden's house and potentially get in trouble, or I could go home and potentially get in trouble. I thought the answer was pretty obvious.

"Let me ask my mom if it's okay."

He flashed me a bright smile then looked at me expectantly.

"Oh, now?" I asked when a few moments of him staring at me passed.

He nodded again, a tint of pink spreading into his cheeks.

"Okay." Pulling out my phone, I typed out a message to my mom.

> Can I go to a friend's house after school?

MOM

> Sure, just make sure you're back home in time for dinner.

My heart lurched in my chest, but another text came through.

MOM

> Who is it?

I resisted the urge to roll my eyes like a petulant child.

> Just a friend I met at school

> They have horses!

MOM

> Okay... let me know if you need me to pick you up.

Three dots appeared and disappeared, but after a while, nothing else came through.

Butterflies fluttered in my stomach as I triumphantly announced, "She said I could go."

"Awesome! You're going to love the horses and all the animals we have!" Hayden tugged on Keenan's sleeve. "Keenan, did you hear? Sierra's coming to hang out after school!"

Keenan groaned before his head popped up over the seat. "Aw, you're so lucky, Sierra. My parents won't let me go to Hayden's during the week because they say I won't get my homework done if I do."

"I mean, they're kinda right, though." Hayden laughed. "You get distracted pretty easily."

When the final bell rang at school, Hayden was already waiting by my locker.

"You ready?" he asked as I grabbed my things.

"Yep," I replied, awkwardly shifting on my feet. "But aren't we just riding the bus?"

Hayden shrugged. "My dad's picking us up."

A million thoughts surged through my mind, but the only thing that came out of my mouth was, "Oh."

"Don't worry, he's cool." Hayden's phone buzzed, and he quickly glanced at his messages. "Come on, he's out front."

"All right." After double-checking that I had everything, I followed Hayden outside.

A sheriff's deputy vehicle was parked in front of the school, and I froze.

What are the cops doing here? Did something happen again?

"Hi, Dad!" Hayden called out as a man who could be his older, taller twin stepped out of the vehicle in a GCSO uniform.

Dad? His dad's a sheriff's deputy?

"This is my friend, Sierra." Hayden waved me over, and I realized I was still frozen in place at the top of the steps.

Reluctantly, I descended the stairs, crossing my arms over my chest when I reached the bottom. "H-hi."

"It's nice to meet you, Sierra. I'm Roy." He offered his hand, but my body instinctively shrunk back. His eyes widened a bit, but I snapped out of it to shake his hand, hoping he didn't read into it too much.

"Thanks for having me over." I didn't have very many friends growing up. The few I did have never came over to my house, so more often than not, I didn't get invited to theirs.

"Of course. I'm glad my son is making friends. Right, bud?" Mr. Watkins ruffled Hayden's hair, and he protested, smoothing the strands back out with his hands.

Once we got into the vehicle, Hayden and his dad immediately engaged in conversation, a small mercy for me. Most parents wanted to ask their kid's friends questions, and that was overwhelming for me. It was one of the reasons why I didn't go out of my way to make a lot of friends.

"Do you have homework?"

Hayden shook his head. "No, I got most of my work done during class."

Mr. Watkins's eyebrows raised in the rearview mirror. "Most?"

"Okay, I have like two things I need to do, but I'll get it done, I swear." Hayden rolled his eyes, but his dad didn't even react. "Can we go see the horses?"

His dad chuckled. "Does Sierra want to see the horses?"

"Of *course* she wants to see the horses, Dad!" Hayden insisted. "I led with that, obviously."

"Sierra?" His dad made eye contact with me through the rearview mirror.

"Yeah, that sounds fun. I like horses. I used to ride sometimes."

"Well, there you have it." Mr. Watkins chuckled at the same time Hayden's head popped around the seat to look at me.

"No way, really? You ride? You should do high school rodeo with me!"

"Oh, I don't know." I looked down at my feet. "My parents probably wouldn't let me. I don't even have a horse."

"That's okay! Plenty of kids don't have their own horses. You could use one of ours, and you could practice here, and—"

"Hayden." Mr. Watkins laughed. "Let the girl breathe."

"Sorry, it's just that Keenan is my only close friend who does rodeo. The rest of the girls who do rodeo from GHS are kinda mean, and the other guys are more interested in the girls than rodeo."

I held back a snicker at his comment.

Mr. Watkins chuckled awkwardly, scratching his head. "All right, well…"

I didn't think Hayden's dad really knew what to say, which prompted Hayden to continue. "You'll think about it, right, Sierra?"

I pursed my lips and nodded.

The remainder of the drive was fairly quiet, and about five minutes later we turned off the main highway onto a long gravel road with a headgate sign spelling out *Watkins*. Off in the distance stood a farmhouse with a barn and fenced-in arena. Cattle lowed in the distance, and when we pulled up to the house, a Corgi ran up to the passenger side.

Hayden hopped out of the pickup truck, looking like he intended to head immediately to the stables, but his dad stopped him. "Go say hello to your mother first! She's probably got snacks for you two."

"Okay…" He drew out the word. "Come on, Sierra!"

Hayden took off, leaving me standing next to the pickup branded with the GCSO logo and *Sheriff* on the side.

"Thanks for the ride, Mr. Watkins," I mumbled awkwardly.

"You're very welcome, Sierra. Hayden's a good kid, you know. Any friend of his is welcome at our place any time."

You probably wouldn't be saying that if you knew who my family was.

I offered a terse nod then speed-walked to catch up to Hayden.

The scent of freshly baked cookies hit my nostrils the second I opened the front door. I wasn't sure what I was expecting his house to look like, but the homey atmosphere, warm lighting, and family photos lining the wall in the entryway felt right.

I slid off my shoes, placing them neatly by the front door, and padded forward into the open-concept kitchen and living room.

"You must be Sierra!" a woman, who I assumed was Hayden's mother, exclaimed.

"That's me." I gave her a small smile.

Hayden sat at the kitchen island, so I joined him, sliding onto a stool next to his.

"Do you like peanut butter cookies? I just pulled a batch out of the oven." His mom held a tray out toward me. White sugar dusted the tops of the fork-indented cookies.

"Peanut butter is my favorite." I took one off the tray and took a bite, groaning as the flavor burst across my tongue. "Mmm, these are *so good*."

My cheeks heated as Hayden and his mom both laughed, but after I realized they weren't making fun of me, I joined in with them.

"I can't remember the last time I had a cookie that good. Thank you, Mrs. Watkins."

She offered me a wide grin, the corners of her eyes creasing. "Oh, please call me Mae."

"Mom, I was telling Sierra that she should join the high school rodeo association with me and Keenan," Hayden mumbled through a mouthful of his peanut butter cookie.

"Don't talk with your mouth full, Hayden," Mae scolded.

He swallowed. "Sorry. But what do you think? She should join the team, right?"

"Well, I don't know. Does she—"

"She has riding experience, Mom. She doesn't have a horse, but I told her we have plenty and—"

"Whoa, whoa, whoa, son. Slow your roll there." Mr. Watkins walked into the kitchen. "Hello, wife." He planted a kiss on Mae's lips.

"I think I'd be interested in rodeo…maybe," I whispered.

Hayden's head snapped toward me. "I *told* you guys!"

Mr. and Mrs. Watkins shook their heads, looking at their son with what seemed to be a mix of pride and amusement.

"We're going to go see the horses," Hayden declared, reaching for my hand as he hopped down from the stool.

The sudden movement startled me, and I pulled my hand away, smacking the underside of the counter in the process.

Hayden didn't seem to notice, but embarrassment still flooded over me.

"S-sorry," I apologized for no reason. "Um, can I have another cookie?"

"Of course, dear. Take as many as you'd like."

I tried to ignore the concern in Mae's voice as I grabbed two cookies with a muttered, "Thanks," and took off after Hayden, who was already at the front door.

We walked side by side toward the stable and pasture, neither of us saying a word.

When we got to the fence, he started pointing out the horses and telling me their names.

"This one's Bullseye." He gestured to a big bay gelding and then a smaller mare. "And this one is Buttercup. The baby is in the stables right now, but we can go see her in a minute." He must have caught me staring at Bullseye, because he asked, "Do you want to pet him?"

I nodded, approaching the horse slowly from the side, the back of my hand stretched out so he could sniff. Bullseye nuzzled his nose into my hand, and I rubbed it along his muzzle.

"He likes you."

"I like him, too," I murmured.

We spent some more time with the older horses while Hayden told me all about their histories and which one he was going to be riding for rodeos. Then he gestured for me to follow him into the barn.

"This one's the mom. Her name's Bagel." He pointed

to a beautiful roan. "The baby doesn't have a nickname yet."

The foal, who had a beautiful chestnut-colored coat, tried to stand, but her knees wobbled a little, pulling a giggle from my throat.

"She's the color of peanut butter." The thought slipped out, but Hayden just looked at me and nodded.

"Yeah, she is. I like that. Peanut Butter."

"Hayden!" a voice called out from the main house a couple of hours later

"Oh, shoot, you need to get home, don't you?" he asked.

We'd lost track of time playing with the horses, barn cats, and the Corgi, whose name I learned was Reggie.

I pulled out my phone, looking at the time. "Yeah. My mom told me I needed to be back by dinnertime."

"My dad can give you a ride home. So your mom doesn't have to come all the way out here."

"Oh…okay." No one had ever dropped me off at my house or even come near my place. I wasn't necessarily ashamed of where I lived, but I also didn't really want Hayden and his family to know—not after seeing the way they interacted with each other today. Like a normal, happy family.

Things had also been okay between my parents since we moved here, and I didn't want to ruin that by having to introduce them to Hayden's dad. I wanted to continue being friends with Hayden, and I wasn't sure if his parents would let him hang out with me if they knew about the stuff that sometimes happened at my house.

"Come on!" Hayden took off toward the house, making me jog to catch up with him. "Dad! Sierra needs to get home! Can we give her a ride?"

A few minutes later, Mr. Watkins emerged from the house. "Sure thing. Did you two have fun?"

Both Hayden and I nodded.

"We should name the foal Peanut Butter, Dad," Hayden declared.

"Peanut Butter, eh?" Mr. Watkins glanced between the two of us, a knowing look on his face. "I like it."

Twenty minutes later, we made it back into town. I gave Mr. Watkins the general directions of my neighborhood but didn't give him the exact address.

"You can drop me off up here. Thanks!" I unbuckled my seatbelt, even though we were still a few blocks away from my house.

"This is where you live?" Hayden's dad asked as he pulled over to the curb, a suspicious tone to his voice.

"Yep!" My lie came out a little bit too enthusiastically.

"We'll wait out here until you get inside."

My heart started racing. "No, no, that's okay. I can manage. T-thank you for the ride. I'll see you tomorrow, Hayden."

I got out of the car and slowly started to walk up to the house that wasn't mine, looking over my shoulder to see if they were still there. Sure enough, they were. I turned around to give as convincing a wave as possible, and the vehicle slowly pulled forward.

Once they were out of sight, I sprinted the three blocks back to my house.

hayden

Ⅰt's a beautiful day here in Billings, Montana. We're looking at clear, blue skies and sunny weather all day long. Next up, we've got 'Big Iron' by Marty Robbins." The local radio station blared in the cab of my pickup truck as Sierra and I drove toward Billings for a three-day rodeo.

"So…" Sierra fidgeted in her seat, picking at the skin around her fingernails.

"So?" I repeated, taking my eyes off the road for a second to look at her.

She forced out a laugh, the sound sharp and harsh. "I don't know, honestly. I'm not sure what to do or say right now. Being back here, with you, it's…" Her voice trailed off, but a multitude of questions fired off in my brain.

Why did you just leave?

Was it me? Did I do something wrong?

Where have you been all these years?

Why didn't you reach out? Why didn't you tell me you were okay?

Instead of saying any of those things, I threw out a

random word that seemed fitting enough for the occasion. "Weird?"

She nodded. "Weird." Shaking her head, she huffed out another laugh, although there was no humor in it. "I guess. How have things been?"

My grip tightened on the steering wheel.

How was I supposed to answer that? What was the correct way to explain that she was my entire world? That my entire being seemed to rotate on an axis around her, and when she left without saying a single word, a part of me fractured, shattering into a million tiny pieces on the floor.

When I didn't answer right away, her face contorted into something of discomfort. "Sorry, that was also… weird. I'm not good at this, Hayden." Taking a deep breath, she continued. "I really do want to start over. I also know I owe you some explanations, but I'm just not ready for that yet. Is that okay?"

Without thinking, I reached over, taking her hand in mine and squeezing.

One. Two. Three.

A silent message. A promise.

"I'll be here when you're ready. I'll always be here, Skip."

Even if it tore me up from the inside out, I'd always be there for her.

"Remember that time we broke into the football field our junior year?" I changed the subject in an attempt to lighten the mood. "I thought for sure Keenan was going to get us caught."

It worked, and Sierra's shoulders shook with laughter. "Yeah, I do. Those were the days, weren't they? We were fucking delinquents."

"We?" I laughed. "If I recall correctly, it was you who said we should hop the fence."

She shrugged with the same devilish grin from back then. "Technically, it was Keenan's fault. He's the one who got us there in the first place."

"Hello?" I answered my phone on the third ring, the caller ID displaying Keenan's name.

"Wanna go on an adventure?" His voice was low and hushed, although there was a hint of anticipation.

I rubbed my eyes. "It's like two in the morning, dude."

Something rustled in the background of the phone call. "Exactly. It'll be fun."

"What do you have in mind?"

"Well, I'm kinda already here, and I need your help so I don't get caught."

An involuntary groan rose from my throat. "Where are you?"

"SGU..." His voice trailed off. "The football stadium."

"Keenan," I hissed. "If you get caught, you're going to get banned for life. GCSO doesn't have jurisdiction on campus, so our dads can't do anything!" Not that our dads would do anything to begin with. If we played stupid games, we won stupid prizes.

"I know. That's why I need your help getting out of here. Bring Sierra, too. Hurry."

"You owe me." Grumbling, I rolled out of bed and pulled on some clothes. My dad was on night shift, so he was gone, and my mom was a heavy sleeper.

I dialed Sierra's phone number, praying she'd pick up.

Come on, Skip, *I thought.*

She picked up on the fourth ring, her voice groggy and laden with sleep. "Hello?"

"Hey. Did I wake you?"

"Um, yes?" she said, like it was the obvious answer.

"You're gonna think this is so dumb, but I need your help, Skip. Well, Keenan needs your help."

She groaned, a similar reaction to mine. "What did that idiot do now?"

"He broke into the football stadium at SGU, and he needs our help getting out of there."

"Oh my God." She let out a dramatic sigh, exasperation in her voice. "Is he trying to get banned?"

I chuckled. "I know."

"All right. Come pick me up. You have thirty minutes before I go back to sleep and you two are on your own."

Thirty minutes later on the dot, I pulled onto Sierra's street. She climbed out of her window and dropped to the ground with an oomph *before running over to my pickup.*

Her breathing was heavy as she climbed in the passenger side. "Let's make this fast. If my parents figure out I'm not asleep, I'm in deep shit."

A few silent minutes passed as we drove through town.

Sierra finally scoffed. "What the fuck was he doing breaking into the football stadium anyway?"

I shook my head, shrugging. "Beats me. It's Keenan. When has he ever been logical?"

She snorted. "Fair enough. He'd better hope none of us get caught. Especially you, Mr. SGU Rodeo Team Scout."

"I'm not the only one they're looking at, and you know that."

Sierra fell silent, and I knew right away the conversation was over. I'd been trying to convince her to come to SGU with me after graduating for a while now, but the answer was always no. I didn't understand why she was so against the idea. Yeah, we wouldn't be getting out of Goldfinch, but at least we'd be together.

Keenan was nowhere in sight as we pulled into the stadium parking lot. I parked next to his truck, and Sierra and I both hopped out, heading toward the fence.

"Should we jump it?" Sierra looked at the fence then back at me, a devilish smirk on her face.

"What? Why?" I'd always been the rule follower of the three of us.

"I mean, we're already here, so why not?"

I sighed, never able to say no to her. "Fine. Five minutes. Then we're getting the hell out of here."

Sierra climbed the fence with ease, hopping down onto the other side. I followed closely behind, and we stepped out onto the turf. The stadium lights overhead were off, but it wasn't difficult to spot Keenan's figure on the fifty-yard line. He was lying on his back, looking up at the sky.

We ran over to him, and he perked up, looking ready to run away.

Once he realized it was us, he pressed a hand to his chest. "God, you guys scared me! I thought you were campus police."

"I thought you needed help getting out of here. Your truck is parked outside."

He shrugged. "It got you guys here, didn't it?"

"So you lied," Sierra deadpanned.

"Come on, Skippy. Live a little." He patted the ground next to him.

She plopped down, lying on her back with her knees bent. I lay down next to her, sandwiching her between me and Keenan.

"Don't you guys want to get out of here one day?" she asked.

I turned my head toward hers, noticing how her green eyes stared off into space above us.

She continued. "There's a whole world, a whole universe out there, and we're stuck here in the middle of buttfuck nowhere."

I hadn't really considered the world outside of Goldfinch. I hadn't considered the world outside of Montana, because Sierra was here, and she was my world. I knew I'd always said I wanted to go to SGU, but if she asked, I'd follow Sierra to the ends of the Earth.

"I'd like to get out. See the world a little, then maybe come back," Keenan admitted.

"Hayes?" She looked at me.

"Yeah. Maybe." If it meant being with her, there wasn't anything I wouldn't do.

As though she decided then and there, she announced to us, "I'm going to be a champion barrel racer one day. Travel all around the world to compete. Houston, Pendleton, Cheyenne, and Las Vegas. I'm going to do all of it. We all will. I'm sure of it."

The clank of chains cut through the silence hanging around us, and we perked up.

"Shit, we gotta go, guys." Keenan shot up to his feet, grabbing Sierra's hand to pull her up.

I sprang up as well, running after them, and just in time.

We entered the tunnel under the bleachers where the concessions were and turned the corner just as a flashlight beamed behind us.

"Who's there?" a booming voice called out.

"Run!" Keenan whisper-shouted at us.

I was sure whatever security was here could hear our feet as they pounded against the ground. My lungs burned as we made it to the gate, the padlock undone—presumably by the security guard.

Keenan's shaky, out-of-breath laughs filled the air. "That was close."

"We are never doing that again," I scolded him.

"Come on, you have to admit that was kinda fun."

"I think being asleep would be more fun, but yeah, it was kinda cool to be on the field," Sierra admitted quietly.

"I need to get Sierra home." I pointed at Keenan. "You get home safe. Text me when you're at your house. Don't get pulled over."

He gave me a mock salute. "Got it, Chief."

I shook my head, thinking of the memory.

"When did you start running Peanut Butter?" Sierra asked in a soft voice.

The claws of grief gripped my chest, but I swallowed down the lump in my throat. "Full time? Two years ago. But after graduating from SGU, I started practicing with her more because Bullseye was getting older. He passed a couple of years ago. Peanut's young, but she's good at what she does."

"Damn. I'm sorry about Bullseye. He was a good one." Sierra pursed her lips.

"When did you get your horse?" I asked.

"About four years ago, I think. I'm sure you know, but I didn't enter into the WPRA until recently. When I left, I traveled around for a bit, competing in smaller-scale rodeos." She huffed out a laugh. "Guess I couldn't quite get rid of the itch."

"You've always been a natural competitor." I teasingly nudged her with my elbow. "Racing's in your blood, Skip."

Her eyes flicked to me, an ocean of emotions swirling in them. "That was always our dream, wasn't it? To make it to the NFR together."

I nodded.

I didn't know if it was still her dream, if her plans still included me. But, even if I had to watch from the sidelines, watching Sierra succeed was always going to be part of mine.

hayden

When we arrived at the rodeo grounds, Colter, Reid, Mikey, and Jake were already there. Keenan texted, letting me know he was about twenty minutes out.

The group of us would be camping out at the rodeo grounds for the weekend. Jake normally bunked with me in my trailer, but with Sierra coming with us, he tagged along with Colter and Reid. Ellison stayed home this time, even though she was normally on the road with us a lot.

"All right, who wants a beer?" Jake pulled out a set of lawn chairs, setting them up next to Colter's pickup.

Colter raised his hand, and Jake tossed him a can before giving Mikey one, too.

"Reid? Hayden?" He held up a beer in each hand.

"Ah, why the hell not? Just one, though." Reid put his hands up so he was ready to catch the beer.

I shook my head. "I'm good, thanks."

"Does your lady want one? Maybe the dog wants a drink, too." Jake tipped his head toward Sierra and Pancho.

She appeared to be looking for something in the cab of

the pickup. Pancho was gnawing on a chew toy at her feet, behaving for once.

"She's not my lady, and you can ask her yourself when she gets over here."

Jake shrugged, cracking his can before plopping into a lawn chair. "So, are we allowed to ask questions about her yet?"

"Ooh, I have some questions!" Mikey raised his hand and started waving it around.

"Fine." I rolled my eyes. "You each get *one* question."

Reid scrubbed his face, scrunching his nose. "I don't think I want to participate in this."

"Wait, does that mean I can steal his question and have two?" Jake asked, leaning forward in his seat.

I shook my head. "No."

Mikey groaned. "You're no fun, Haydie."

"I don't have to answer any of your questions, so you should just be happy I'm letting you ask."

Jake spread his legs as he leaned back into his chair. "Fair enough. Okay, what's the story between you two?"

Loaded question.

Blowing a raspberry, I leaned against Colter's truck. "We met in high school. She moved to Goldfinch at the beginning of our freshman year, and we became really close. It was her, me, and Keenan pretty much all through high school. I convinced her to join high school rodeo. She rode one of our horses, so she was always at my house practicing. Then I went to college, she left, and we just fell out of touch, I guess." I was leaving out *a lot*, but Jake should have been more specific with his question if he wanted all the details.

Mikey tapped his fingers against his lips. "So, did you guys date or what?"

I shook my head.

"But I thought she was your ex?" he asked.

Making a buzzer noise, I put my hands in an X gesture. "You already asked your question."

His eyes lit up. "Oh, so you didn't date, but you did—"

The jingle of Pancho's bell cut him off.

"What are you guys talking about?" Sierra's eyes narrowed as she approached us. "Pancho, down."

"Nothing important." I shot a glare at Mikey and Jake, a silent warning for them to behave.

"Okay then…"

"Want a beer, Sierra?" Jake piped up.

She shook her head. "No, I'm all right. I was going to put Pancho in the trailer, then I'm probably going to take Lucky around a few laps to loosen up before the rodeo starts."

I pushed off the pickup. "Good idea. I'll come with you."

Colter and Reid agreed in unison. They got up from their chairs, and we all went our separate ways, leaving Mikey and Jake alone.

"This next pair of cowboys comes from our home state of Montana. Put your hands together for Hayden Watkins and Keenan Chase!" The rodeo announcer called out our names as the rhythm of drums from a country rock song played over the speakers.

Keenan and I backed our horses into the roping boxes as the arena erupted into a chorus of cheers. Peanut shook her head as we settled into a ready position at the back corner of the box.

I looked over to Keenan, and he dipped his chin, letting me know he was set, his rope at the ready. Taking a deep breath, I nodded, and the steer was released from the chute between us.

I gently squeezed my calves against Peanut's side, signaling for her to burst out of the box and follow behind the steer. I swung my rope over my head, waiting for the perfect window to throw the rope over the steer's horns.

Team roping required precision—if you threw your rope even a hundredth of a second too soon or too late, you could miss.

The loop floated in the air, finally dropping over the steer's head. I pulled the rope tight, dallying it around my saddle horn. Peanut pulled ahead of the steer along the arena fence, and she took a turn toward the inside of the arena to turn the animal's trajectory, giving Keenan access to the hind legs.

I watched as he swung his rope a few times over his head and then released the loop, catching the hind legs of the steer.

"Five-point-nine seconds!" the rodeo announcer hollered, and cheers erupted from the crowd.

When I looked past the arena fence, the world seemed to still as I made eye contact with emerald-green eyes. Sierra clapped and then placed her fingers in her mouth, letting out a loud whistle for us.

After letting Peanut cool down, I took all her equipment off and put her in one of the temporary stalls for the rest of the rodeo.

Barrel racing would be starting soon, so I went to check on Sierra.

She should have been warming up Lucky by now, but I couldn't see her anywhere.

I spotted her at the stables, pacing back and forth so much I was sure she'd wear a trail into the dirt. Jogging over to her, I called out, "What's wrong? What happened?"

She was never like this before a competition. Sierra was always calm and locked in. Something had to have happened. She looked like she was on the verge of frustrated tears, hands on her hips as she continued walking in circles.

"Sierra. Tell me what happened." I placed my hands on her shoulders to stop her.

Her eyes flicked up to me, then she took a deep breath. "I left for a second to grab something, and I came back to this." She lifted one of the straps on her saddle. At first, I didn't think anything was wrong, but then I noticed the frays. Someone had cut the strap, just enough that if used while riding, it would have snapped.

"You can use mine." The offer was immediate, instinctive.

"But—"

I cut her off. "You can use mine, because racing with this one is too much of a risk, and you've come too far to get injured. But we also need to report this."

Sierra nodded, like she knew arguing with me would be pointless.

"Wait here, and I'll grab my saddle."

I did my best to keep my cool as I marched away from the stables toward the parking lot, but I was sure smoke was billowing from my ears.

"Yo, Hayden, wait up! What's wrong, man?" Keenan asked, trying to keep up as I walked with long strides to the horse trailer.

"Someone tampered with Sierra's saddle. It's a good thing she actually inspects her equipment now, because if she'd ridden Lucky with that saddle, either one of them could have gotten seriously hurt."

When we were younger, Sierra would get in such a rush to race that she would sometimes skip steps, not taking the time to check everything. It took her saddle slipping down the side of her horse to finally make her realize that it was okay—necessary even—to take the time to double-check, hell, even triple-check her equipment before a race.

"Seriously?" Keenan matched my urgent pace. "Who would do that?"

"I have no idea, but after I get her my saddle, we're going to report it."

Keenan vocalized what I was concerned about. "Are they going to be able to do anything?"

"They'd better fucking try. Whoever it was committed a crime, and she could have gotten seriously hurt. And so soon after her trailer burned down in Goldfinch?"

He hummed in agreement. "Yeah, that's odd. Could it just be a coincidence, though? Or a jealous competitor? She is one of the best in the world right now."

"I mean, we haven't heard anything back about the trailer. They found a cigarette butt as the cause of the fire, and that could easily have been negligence. But a tampered saddle? I find it hard to believe that's accidental. That leather's tough. And jealousy is no excuse for destruction of property," I pointed out.

"Yeah, no, you're right," he agreed. "You think someone is targeting her, though." It came out as more of a statement than a question.

I didn't want to think about that.

"I'm just looking out for her. I won't let anything happen to her."

We'd reached the trailer by now, and I lifted my spare saddle off the rack in the back, inspecting it for anything out of the ordinary before heaving it over my shoulder to carry back to Sierra.

"You didn't do anything with the saddle, right?" I asked her when we got back.

She shook her head. "No. Haven't touched it."

"Good. We need to report this to the rodeo association and the police."

Her face blanched. "Are you sure? I mean, it could have just been—"

"An accident?" I cut her off, shaking my head. "No. You know just as well as me, Skip. This was intentional. A cut like that doesn't just happen. It's day one of three. Better to play it safe than regret it later."

"Okay." Her shoulders drooped, but she didn't argue.

I knew Sierra didn't like to get the police involved in her life, considering what she'd gone through as a kid, but reporting the saddle was important. Her dad may have been in prison, but that didn't mean someone wasn't after her.

I set the saddle down, hooking a finger under her chin and tilting her face up toward mine. "Focus on racing, and I'll take care of it, yeah?"

She rolled her lips between her teeth and nodded. After I confirmed she was okay, I made Keenan stay with her while I went to report the incident to the stock contractor. Unfortunately, since neither I nor Sierra were around when it happened, nothing might come out of it, but I still needed to try. We at least had the evidence that the saddle was cut, so that was a start.

I would also be making a police report, because there was no way I was going to gamble with Sierra's safety. Maybe there were fingerprints on it that could trace back to whoever did this.

By the time I got back from talking to the stock contractor, rodeo secretary, and police officers stationed at the rodeo, the barrel racing had started.

"Running next on Ace's Lucky Charm, we've got one tough cowgirl out of Goldfinch, Montana. Let her hear you, folks! We've got Sierra Bayley!" the rodeo announcer called out as Sierra and Lucky exploded out of the alleyway, racing down the arena toward the first barrel.

Dust rose in the air, surrounding the pair in a cloud as she maneuvered around the first barrel. They cut through the dust like a knife, heading toward the next barrel as fast as a flash of light. Her hair billowed behind her underneath her cowboy hat, and her face was set in determination. They were a lethal pair, all muscle and athleticism.

Her turns were tight but skilled enough not to knock over the barrels. After rounding the second barrel, the pair made their way to the third and final barrel.

"Let's help her home! Come on, Sierra!" the announcer cried over the loudspeaker.

Lucky's muscles rippled as he sprinted the homestretch, Sierra urging him on with gentle kicks and control on the reins.

When they crossed the time barrier, the announcer called out, "Fifteen-point-six-seven! That time will move her up to the top of the leaderboard!"

Sierra leaned forward in her saddle, patting Lucky's neck with a brilliant smile on her face as they exited the arena.

sierra

We filed a police report in Billings for the tampered saddle, but we hadn't received any news by the end of the rodeo weekend. There were no witnesses, so there were no leads. The only fingerprints that were found on the saddle were mine and Hayden's, so that was a bust, too.

There was no time to dwell on it, though. The county fair and rodeo in Miles City was this weekend, so the only thing on my mind was another barrel race. This one was at least local, so we didn't have to do a lot of driving. Looking forward, though, we had a lot of miles ahead of us. In a couple weeks, we'd be traveling all the way to Oregon for the Pendleton Roundup, then we'd turn around and drive to North Dakota. That would end our long stretch of competitions until mid-October, when we'd go back to Billings for the last big rodeo of the season.

My first order of business was fixing the saddle. It was returned to me by the time we left Billings, so at least I didn't have to shell out money for a replacement. Not to mention the time it would take to break in a new one.

Unfortunately, I still didn't have my pickup back, but Hayden had offered to either drive me into town or let me use his.

I, selfishly, opted for driving myself. I left Pancho at the house with Hayden, figuring he could keep himself entertained. He'd taken well to Hayden in the short time we'd been staying with him.

The roads were quiet, which was surprising at this time of day. I would have thought more people would be out and about given it was mid-afternoon on a weekday, but Silver Creek and Miles City weren't large in population by any means. I appreciated that, though. I preferred a slower pace of life to the hustle and bustle of a larger city or even just a larger town like Goldfinch.

In the five years that I'd been away, I spent a lot of time in small towns—for rodeos and just exploring, seeing the world like I'd always promised myself I'd do.

My favorite was a sleepy little town nestled in the mountains of Colorado. While it had the classic small town charm, the people weren't nosy like the typical stereotype. They were friendly, of course, but they respected the privacy of their residents. If juicy gossip was what you were looking for, Cedar Bluffs was the wrong place to be, which was perfect for me. It wasn't like my name was huge —I was by no means a celebrity-level rodeo athlete like Colter Carson, Reid Lawson, or Mikey Tucker—but if anyone were to look me up, the articles associated with my last name weren't the most sparkling. What happened had nothing to do with me, but family reputations tended to follow a person around.

After the…incident…I left Goldfinch for a while. I had to come back to testify a few times, but after the case was over, I never wanted to set foot back in Montana again. I did once, and that was the nail in the coffin for me. After that, I changed my phone number and truly started over, setting my sights on being anywhere but my home state. At least until I entered into the WRCA and my schedule brought me back.

I hadn't spoken to my mother in six years. She made her choices, and I made mine, but our lives weren't connected anymore. I hoped she was able to find peace, but I couldn't look her in the eyes after what she allowed to happen, even after I begged and cried. Because by the time she finally decided to take a stand, it was too late, and our lives were forever changed.

I turned onto the main road in Miles City, pulling myself out of my well of thoughts. If I treaded through them too much, I was sure to drown, and I needed to keep my head above water.

The bells on the front door of the saddle shop chimed as I walked in. The smell of leather and oils hit my nostrils, and a girl with dark hair popped her head around the register to greet me.

"Hi! Is there anything I can help you with today?"

I stepped up to the counter. "I'm looking to get a saddle repaired. It's in my vehicle, but I can go grab it. How long would something like that take?"

"Hmm…" She typed a few things on the computer. "We can have it done for you in a couple days. Does that work?"

"That'll be great. Thank you."

I brought the saddle inside, exchanging it with the girl working. She gave me a quote on what the repair would cost then collected my phone number and email address for invoicing and updates.

"Thank you so much, Sierra. We'll keep you updated."

"I appreciate it. Thank you. Have a good one."

She waved as I headed toward the front door. Before I could stop myself, the bells jingled, and I ran into a solid chest.

"S-sorry." I took a step back, throwing out a quick apology to whoever I'd run into.

"Oh, hey, Sierra."

Reid Lawson.

"Hi. What are you up to today?" I put my hands in my back pockets.

Reid ran a hand through his hair before clearing his throat. "Had to come pick up a saddle. You leave Hayden at home?" he joked, and it immediately lightened the mood.

"Yeah." I laughed. "I'm not really doing anything exciting, and I left Pancho with him. Some days I think the dog likes him more than he likes me."

"Hayden tends to have that effect."

You have no idea.

A moment of quiet passed between us before Reid said, "I don't know if it's something you'd be interested in, but I have a practice arena if you want to use it. We all have days where we just hang out and get some runs in. We can get some barrels to set up, no problem."

I raised my brows. "Yeah, that'd be great. Thanks, Reid."

"It's nothing." He waved me off. "Any friend of Hayden's is a friend of ours."

"I appreciate that. Well…" I started to head out the door, but Reid started speaking again.

"You know, Hayden doesn't talk very much—even less about his personal life and girls—but I'd always had a feeling there was someone special to him. We were on the rodeo team together in Goldfinch, and even when we reconnected after college he never…anyway, I'm glad he has you. And if you need anything at all, just let one of us know. We're all family around here."

I wasn't sure what to say; I was so caught off guard. Instead of fighting to find words, I just nodded in acknowledgment. Then I rushed out the door, shaking my head, trying to wrap my brain around what that all meant.

Instead of heading back to Hayden's right away, I drove around town, running some quick errands and familiarizing myself with the town. I hadn't had much of an opportunity to map out Miles City yet, something I always made an effort to do in an unfamiliar place. It made me feel more comfortable when I knew where I was going and had an exit strategy.

After looping around town a few times, I went to the farm and ranch supply store to pick up some feed for the horses and dog food for Pancho as well as the convenience store to get more hair dye—my roots were starting to show, which, unfortunately as a natural blonde, made me look bald—then headed back to the house, driving a little slower than normal to decompress.

"Hey, how was your day?" Hayden asked over the music filtering in from the kitchen speaker as I walked through the front door.

I placed my boots on the mat and headed through the living area into the kitchen. Hayden was busy making dinner, flitting from the counter to the stove and then back. "It was…good?"

"Good to hear. Did you get your saddle fixed?"

I nodded as I leaned my elbows on the bar top side of the counter he was working at, looking at him through the kitchen passthrough. "What are you making?"

I knew what it was from the smell filling the kitchen alone, but I wanted to hear it from him.

He reached into the cabinet above the counter, pulling out various spices and seasonings. "Chicken and dumplings. Wanna help?"

"Yeah. What do you want me to do?"

He smirked, the corners of his mouth crinkling. "Is that even a question?"

I rolled my eyes, heading around the half wall to wash my hands. "Just thought I'd ask. Didn't know if you wanted to change it up."

"Old habits die hard, Skip."

He'd already started to cook the chicken, but the vegetables still needed to be cut and the soup hadn't been started yet. Hayden was always better at making the dumplings, so it made sense that he'd start there. Part of me thought he was waiting for me, knowing that I'd want to help, just like old times in the Watkins family house with Mae.

I started chopping carrots, and the two of us fell into a comfortable silence as we worked. Soon the only noise in the house came from the sound of vegetables snapping and George Jones's serenading voice playing through the speakers.

I began cutting an onion as the butter in the pot started to melt, and Hayden started humming behind me. Taking a sneaky peek at him, I watched as he swayed his hips to the music and had to pull my bottom lip between my teeth to suppress a laugh.

As though he could sense me watching him, he glanced over his shoulder, his lips curling up into a grin.

"I didn't know you were such a good dancer," I teased.

He laughed, the sound bubbling over. "Bullshit. I've always been a great dancer."

My cheeks heated. "I suppose you're right."

Setting down whatever he was working on, he walked over to me, carefully taking the knife out of my hand and setting it on the cutting board.

"Come on. Dance with me." He placed one of my hands on his shoulder as he set his on my waist, then laced our fingers together with his other hand.

The song had changed to Chris Stapleton's cover of "Tennessee Whiskey," and Hayden's hand on my waist tapped to the beat as he spun us around the kitchen. For a moment, it was like we were kids again, without a care or worry in the world. We were still best friends, and neither one of us had left. Neither one of us had broken the other's heart—*I* hadn't broken his heart yet.

I didn't know how he could forgive me. I wouldn't have forgiven myself if I were him. And as much as I wanted him back—wanted to try again—I couldn't.

"Hayden," I whispered.

"Hmm?"

"Friends…friends don't do this kind of thing."

His eyes gleamed, like he was hurting on the inside but trying to put on a brave face. "We've never been just friends, though, have we?"

Before I could answer, the smell of burning butter hit my nostrils.

"Oh, shit!" I pulled away from Hayden, breaking us apart, to run over to the stove.

Laughing, we both looked at the damage in the pot.

"What a waste of butter," I sighed.

Hayden shrugged. "It was worth it to dance with you one more time."

I rolled my lips between my teeth, awkwardly shifting on my feet. "I'm gonna start over on this. You should get the dumplings finished."

Falling back into silence—this time with tension in the air—we finished cooking the meal.

Maybe I shouldn't have been so stubborn. Maybe I should have held my tongue. This wasn't what Mae had taught us, cooking silently instead of in a kitchen filled with laughter and love pouring out.

But I couldn't change the past, a fact that haunted me every day.

We each plated our own food, sitting across from each other at the dining table.

"Thank you for helping." Hayden smiled, although it was a bit sad.

I poked my fork around my plate. "Of course."

He nodded, digging in, so I followed suit. Even with a single bite, the flavors bursting on my tongue were able to bring the childhood memories flooding back.

hayden

I think at this rate, you'll be able to join the team by next year! You're picking up everything so fast." Alyssa, one of the older girls in the high school rodeo association and a cousin of mine, was talking to Sierra in the arena at my family's place.

A radiant smile flashed across Sierra's face, though she still seemed a bit shy. "Thanks."

"Keep working at it. If you ever want to practice with someone there to give you tips, you have my phone number now." Alyssa spun on her heel to head to her pickup, giving Sierra a quick wave.

"She's really good," she whispered as she passed by me.

"I know," I whispered back.

Sierra was still standing in the arena with her hands in her pockets, staring at the horse my parents let her ride.

"What are you thinking about?"

She turned her head toward me. "Nothing." Her eyes betrayed her, though, deep, green pools of sadness.

"You sure? You can tell me, you know."

Sierra sighed, the whoosh of the air leaving her lungs

piercing through the silence between us. "My grandparents had horses. That's where I learned how to ride. I miss them."

"Are they…" I hesitated asking whether her grandparents were still alive or not.

"Dead? No. They're still alive. The horses, too, if that's what you meant."

"Oh." I rolled my lips between my teeth. "Why don't you go see them?"

"Because I can't," she snapped, and my eyes widened at her tone. "Sorry. I just can't go see them, okay?"

"Okay. Do you want to go inside? My mom's cooking dinner. You can stay if you want to."

She pulled out her phone to look at the time. "I can stay for a little while, but then I have to get back home. My mom can come pick me up, though; it's fine."

I nodded. Sierra had been really resistant to accepting rides after that first time she came over to the house last fall, despite offers from both me and my parents.

My dad had pulled me aside after we'd gotten home from dropping Sierra off.

"Do you know where your friend lives?" he asked. "She just moved to town, right?"

I shook my head. "Yeah, she just moved here, but she hasn't mentioned where she lives. She rides the bus and gets on at the stop on Sparrow Lane, though. Why?"

"That house we dropped her off at last night? I don't think she lives there."

"Oh, huh. Yeah, I guess not."

I'd asked her about it the next day at school, and she ignored the question. After that, she didn't let my parents drive her home anymore.

We headed into the house, and I kicked off my boots by the door.

"Mom, we're coming inside for a little bit! Sierra's going to hang out!" I called out, even though I was sure she was just in the kitchen.

I popped around the corner, and, sure enough, she was getting dinner ready.

"Smells good, Mom."

"Thank you, honey. Do you two have homework you need to get done? Sierra, dear, are you staying for dinner?"

Sierra shifted back and forth on her feet. "I'm not sure."

"You're more than welcome to, dear." She flitted from one end of the kitchen to the other, chopping up vegetables and checking whatever she had on the stove.

"What are you making, Mom?" I asked, trying to peek over her shoulder.

"Chicken and dumplings."

On my way back to Sierra, I stole a carrot from the counter. "Ooh, my favorite. Mom makes the *best* chicken and dumplings, so you should definitely stay for dinner."

Sierra shrugged. "I guess I can ask my mom and see."

"Awesome! Hey, aren't you warm? You've got a sweatshirt on still." I tugged on the part of her sweatshirt sleeve covering her elbow, and the cuff hiked up a little ways, revealing dark splotches on her forearm. "Sierra…"

She pulled away, angrily tugging her sleeve back down.

My mom was still preoccupied with dinner, so I lowered my voice, pulling her aside into the hallway. "What happened?"

"Nothing." Her response was flat, devoid of emotion.

"Sierra."

Her nostrils flared. "Nothing happened, Hayden, okay? Just leave it alone."

"If you're in trouble, my dad—"

She put up a hand to stop me, annoyance flaring in her eyes. "Fine. I tripped down the stairs and bumped my arm, okay? Happy?"

No, I wasn't happy. Not at all. But if continuing to push the subject was going to push her away, then I'd let it rest for now. I'd be keeping a closer eye on her, though. My dad always told me to look out for my friends—to help people whenever I could—and that's what I was going to do.

"Hayden, honey, could you help me with something?" Mom called from the kitchen.

"Coming!" I gave Sierra one last look. "You can turn on the TV or do whatever you want. I'll be over there in a second."

She nodded, the tension from our confrontation still radiating between us in waves.

"Can you make the dumplings for me?" Mom had all of the ingredients laid out on the counter. We used to do this when I was younger. She taught me how to make all of the dishes she made and said that one day I'd be grateful to know how to make something other than instant ramen or microwave macaroni and cheese.

"Maybe Sierra wants to help, too," I suggested.

Mom nodded. "Go on and ask her. She can help with the soup."

Sierra was sitting on the couch with her knees tucked up to her chest. The TV wasn't playing, so she was just sitting in silence, staring into space.

I approached her slowly, taking care not to startle her.

"Hey, do you want to help with dinner? My mom said you could help her with the soup."

She nodded, slowly getting up from the couch. "Yeah, I'll help."

We washed our hands at the kitchen sink together, taking turns rinsing them under the faucet.

"Do you want to roll up your sleeves, dear?" Mom asked Sierra.

I didn't need to be looking at her to know she froze.

"Oh, n-no, I'm okay. They won't be in the way."

"Okay, if you're sure. You'll want to melt this butter in the pot, then you can add the vegetables and let them cook for about five minutes." Mom gave her some instructions, and Sierra jumped on it.

We worked in comfortable silence as the meal started to come together.

The dumplings were always my task for the meal and had been since I was a kid. I'd perfected it by now at age fifteen—not that it was a particularly difficult task to begin with, but compared to my classmates, I was ten steps ahead when it came to cooking.

Before long, the rich aroma of chicken broth and vegetables had enveloped the kitchen. Mom had taken the drop dumplings I'd made and put them in the soup that she and Sierra had put together. Now, all that was left to do was wait until they were done cooking.

"How are you liking school, Sierra?" Mom asked while she cut up some fruit.

Sierra and I had migrated to the stools by the kitchen island, and both of us sipped on cans of soda.

"I like it." She took a small drink. "It's different from my old school, but everyone is nice. I like my classes, too."

"Oh, I'm so glad!" Mom smiled. "I'm sure Hayden has

already told you this, but if you ever need anything, we are only a phone call away."

Sierra's cheeks flushed pink, and she tugged her sleeves down even more. "Thank you. I-I appreciate that."

If Mom noticed, she didn't say anything. "All right, kids, dinner is ready. Why don't you dish up first, Sierra? Go ahead, help yourself."

She hopped down from the stool, shyly walking over to the stove. Mom handed her a bowl, and she plated her food quickly, taking a small amount.

"Take as much as you want, honey," Mom reassured her.

She looked down at her bowl, then back to the stove, gingerly adding more.

"Hayden, come on, buddy." Mom waved me over.

After scooping up a healthy serving, I joined Sierra at the dining table, Mom following shortly after.

"Thank you again for having me over for dinner." Sierra sat at the table, not having touched her food yet. I wasn't sure if she was waiting for us to start or what, so I took a bite of my food to let her know it was okay.

"Absolutely. Thank you so much for helping. Hayden loves to cook. He's been helping me with dinners since he was in elementary school," Mom gushed.

"Mom," I whined, the tips of my ears heating.

"Oh, shush, it's nothing to be embarrassed about. Right, Sierra?" She winked at Sierra, whose lips pressed together in a soft smile.

"Yeah. I think it's sweet," she murmured, bringing a spoonful of soup up to her mouth. "Whoa, this is really good!" She shoveled more soup and dumplings into her mouth, eliciting a laugh from both me and Mom.

"If you want the recipe, I can give it to you, but there's a secret ingredient." Mom smiled.

Sierra's eyes widened. "Secret ingredient? What is it?" She paused, her eyes bouncing around the room. "Are you allowed to tell me? If it's a secret."

"Love."

"Love?"

Mom nodded, amusement flickering in her gaze. "Yes, love. I firmly believe food always tastes better when it's made in a kitchen full of love and laughter."

After Sierra went home, Mom and I sat on the couch, watching TV. Dad wasn't home yet, and I was struggling to decide whether to bring up what I saw tonight.

"What's wrong, bud?" Mom must have noticed how restless I was, fidgeting and unable to sit still.

I furrowed my brow, trying to rack my brain for the right words to say. "Mom, if I thought someone was in trouble, but they won't accept help, what am I supposed to do? I know what to do in a life-or-death situation, but what if it's not? What if I can see someone struggling, but they won't listen?"

She looked at me with sadness in her eyes, but not the pitying kind. Mom placed her hand on my shoulder. "You show them kindness and empathy, bud. Keep showing up for them and letting them know you're there. I know it's hard, especially for someone with a heart as big as yours, but sometimes the best protectors aren't the loudest or the biggest or the strongest. Sometimes the best kind of support is the kind that sits with you in your most vulnerable moments." She patted me on the head. "You're a smart kid who knows right from wrong, Hayden. I know you'll do whatever is right. Just keep looking out for them."

I nodded. "I'm going to go to bed."

"Okay, honey." She pulled me into a hug, and I leaned into her a little more than normal.

That night, and every night after that, our conversation stuck with me. It didn't take much for me to decide; if and when Sierra decided she needed me, I'd be there.

One day, she'd find her voice. And when she did, I'd amplify it, even if it meant mine had to be a little quieter.

CHAPTER THIRTEEN

PRESENT DAY

With the amount of time we spent on the road between the months of June and September, having a week of rodeo close to home was a small blessing. As much as I didn't want to admit it, traveling all the time sometimes made me homesick—mostly for good, home-cooked meals and my own bed.

While the horse trailer I owned had a small kitchen, I was limited in what I could make. More often than not, I didn't have the time to cook anyway. The guys and I tried to stay away from fast food as much as possible, but that restricted the options we did have. I found myself bringing a lot of sandwiches and small snacks on the road.

Chicken and dumplings wasn't the only thing I knew how to make, although that was probably my favorite. My mom made sure I knew how to cook growing up and still shared recipes with me to this day.

Your future wife will appreciate it, she would say.

I never protested learning how to cook, though. It was fun, and I learned quickly to appreciate the work and creativity that it took. Anyone could follow a recipe; I was sure of that. But being able to make a meal your own was special.

Baking required following the rules, but cooking was forgiving enough that you could break them.

Sierra wasn't awake yet, but I still prepped ingredients for breakfast. My plan was to make cinnamon roll-stuffed French toast, eggs, and bacon.

I didn't have brioche or any kind of French bread, and I didn't want to run to the store at the risk of Sierra waking up before I could get back, so classic sandwich bread would have to do.

After cracking a few eggs into a bowl, I stirred in some spices and milk before dunking the bread slices in the mixture and setting them in the sizzling pan to cook.

In a separate frying pan, I started making strips of bacon, the savory aromas filling the kitchen. I hummed as the meal started to come together, everything around me fading into the background as I disappeared into my own little world.

A few minutes later, the creak of a door caught my attention, followed by the jingle of Pancho's collar soon after.

"Hey, boy." I laughed as he pranced up to me, immediately jumping up on my leg.

"Pancho!" Sierra scolded him from the hallway. "Sorry, we've been working on that."

She stepped into view, and my heart skipped a beat. Her hair, braided back into two plaits, hung over her shoulders, and she wore an oversized T-shirt that fell mid-thigh.

My mouth opened and closed, but no words came out, despite how hard I tried.

"Morning?" She raised an eyebrow in what seemed to be amusement at my tongue-tiedness.

"Morning good." Heat rose to my cheeks at the mistake. "Er, good morning." I internally groaned.

Why? Why was I like this?

"Pancho, come here." She called over her dog before asking what I was making.

"Cinnamon roll French toast, eggs, and bacon," I answered as I scrambled the eggs.

She hummed. "Sounds good." Without another word, she led Pancho out the front door.

"Get it together, Hayden," I muttered to myself. "You're friends, got it?"

Yeah, fucking right.

Pigs would fly, the ocean would dry up, and hell would freeze over before I'd ever be "just friends" with her. The cold, hard truth, though, was that Sierra *wanted* to be friends. I didn't know if she wanted to be more, given our history. I had to respect that, even if it cut me up from the inside.

I finished making the eggs, plating them up with a couple slices of French toast and a few strips of bacon. Reaching into the pantry, I pulled out a jar of peanut butter and a bottle of maple syrup, setting them next to Sierra's plate on the kitchen counter.

A few minutes later, the front door opened, and Pancho came barreling inside. He ran a few circles in the living room then collapsed into a heap on the kitchen floor with a loud sigh. Snores immediately rose into the air from the direction of the dog.

"A bit dramatic for someone who doesn't have a job," Sierra muttered, despite looking at the animal with all the love in the world. "Fucking freeloader."

I laughed, and her head whipped toward me, embarrassment creeping across her features like she didn't think I could hear her.

"The things we do for our pets, right?" I shook my head before gesturing to her plate. "Here, eat up. Do you want something to drink? Coffee? Tea? Milk? Orange juice? Water?" I listed off all the options.

She slid onto one of the stools at the counter. "Uh, coffee's good, thank you."

"Still milk, sugar, and a spoonful of peanut butter?"

"You remember that?"

"How could I forget? I always thought that combination was the weirdest thing about you," I teased, pouring her a mug, adding a splash of milk, a couple sugar cubes, and a spoon with a healthy amount of peanut butter on it.

"God forbid a girl have taste." She grinned, a glint of mischief in her eyes.

"Strange taste, but I like it. It's very you, Sierra."

Instead of responding, she took a bite of her French toast. Her eyes closed as she chewed, a low groan rising from her throat. As quickly as it happened, her eyes flew open with a rosy tint creeping into her cheeks.

She pulled on the end of her braids. "Um…breakfast is really good. Thank you."

My lips curled up, a million thoughts after the sound she made—only a few of them decent—rolling through my mind. "You're welcome."

"So, the fair is this week?" she mumbled between bites.

"Sure is. Have you kept up your skills in carnival games? I've improved my game, by the way," I added, a little glimmer of hope rising in my chest that she remembered.

Competitiveness flashed in her expression. "Is that so? I guess I'll have to be the judge of that."

Satisfaction bloomed inside me knowing there was still some of the fire I recognized inside her. Time may have changed us, but she still had a sliver of the girl I met all those years ago, and perhaps a small part of her still loved me as much as I loved her.

"You're on." I flashed her a wide smile as I dished up and joined her at the counter. "We'll have plenty of time to play games and eat fair food." We were all competing in the rodeo, but since we weren't traveling far, we didn't have to get back on the road right away to our next competition. We'd have plenty of time to have some fun.

She finished eating quickly, taking her plate over to the dishwasher to load it before whistling for Pancho.

"Thank you for making breakfast. You don't have to do that, you know?"

I nodded but shrugged. "I don't mind. You know I like cooking. What's making food for one more?"

"Right. Well, thank you. I'm going to take a shower and get ready for the day." She excused herself then headed down the hall toward her room with Pancho.

My phone started buzzing on the counter, so I tapped it to find that it was blowing up with notifications from our group chat.

The Silver Creek Cowboys (and Ellison) (plus Isa and June)

MIKEY

Juniper's going to be in town this weekend
so you all know what that means

COLTER

A chill night at home?

ELLISON

That sounds nice actually. Can we do that instead of whatever Mikey's about to suggest?

MIKEY

Don't steal my thunder!

And we all know a night at home would be the opposite of chill, am I right, Peach?

JUNE

Excited to see you all!

JAKE

Notice how she ignored what Mikey said?

ISA

ugh this isn't fair! i wish i could be in town too

ELLISON

Hop on a plane

Impromptu trip

ISA

i wish

MIKEY

Guys you're losing the plot here

Was there ever really a plot to begin with?

A bombardment of texts came through all at once.

JAKE

He lives!

REID

Nice of you to join us, buddy

COLTER

Guys, he's alive!

MIKEY

How's our boy and his...guest friend?

ME

I'm alive. I'm fine

Sierra's fine

JAKE

Just fine? Oop must have gotten into some hot water

MIKEY

Little lover's spat?

We're not lovers. We're friends.

REID

That's what they all say, right Honeybee?

ISA

You can deny it all you want, Haydie. The truth always comes out.

She said she wanted to be friends, so that's what we are.

Juniper, Colter, Reid, and Ellison all reacted with thumbs-down emojis.

MIKEY

Booooo

ISA

But aren't you guys like high school sweethearts? 🐻

JAKE

Damn, bro's got himself deep in the friend zone

What was the point of this text thread?

MIKEY

Yeah, guys, you stole my thunder!

June's going to be in town, so I say we all hit up Rudy's after the rodeo

ELLISON

Wasn't that the plan anyway?

MIKEY

Oh shh Firecracker. This way if we make it a special plan, none of you can bail out.

Haydie, bring your girl. We'll get you out of the friend zone, buddy

I rolled my eyes and turned my phone off. I'd deal with them all later.

On my way to my room, I noticed Sierra's door was still slightly open. The shower was running in the bathroom, and Pancho was chewing on a bone in her room. I had no idea how long she'd be, but I knew she normally kept her room closed to prevent Pancho from getting out.

As I grabbed the door handle, a flash of bright-blue fur caught my eye. I didn't mean to snoop or invade her privacy, but curiosity got the better of me. Instead of closing the door or moving away like I should have, I leaned back slightly, peeking my head in the gap between the door and frame. Sure enough, my suspicions were confirmed, and a blue stuffed tiger was neatly placed on the bed near her pillows.

She kept it. After all this time, she still has it.

sierra

SUMMER BEFORE SOPHOMORE YEAR

The Goldfinch fairgrounds were so lit up that you could practically see them from across town. Apparently that only happened during two weeks of the year: the Goldfinch County Fair and Gulch Days, the summer kickoff celebration.

I didn't plan to go to the fairgrounds, but my parents were fighting downstairs, so I fished out twenty bucks from under my bed and snuck out the window. If I had to listen to screaming, it may as well have been from people on rides or kids having fun. I'd have to figure out a way to get home that wasn't walking three miles in the dark, but I'd cross that bridge when I got there.

I'd never been to a real carnival or fair before. Ponderosa Valley had a small-scale fair, but my parents never took me, and I wasn't old enough to go wandering around town by myself. Not that anyone would have cared, but I had *some* self-preservation skills.

Lights from the rides and carnival games danced across the sky, and a symphony of music, laughter, and the happy screams of children surrounded me as I took everything in. The smell of fried food filled the air, combined with the distinctive musk of livestock and show animals.

Not really sure where to go, I wandered down the rows of carnival games, observing kids with their parents, teenagers hanging out with their friends, and couples on their first dates.

"Sierra!" A familiar voice called out my name.

I spun around to see Hayden, Keenan, and two of their friends, whose names I couldn't quite remember.

Hayden jogged over to me, despite the other boys telling him to wait up. "Hey!" he called out, waving his hand in a wild gesture. "Fancy seeing you here."

My cheeks flushed, warmth flooding into my body. "Hi."

"Are you here by yourself?" he asked as he looked around for my nonexistent companion.

I nodded. "Yeah, I, uh, needed to get out of the house." I didn't mention that I walked all the way here.

"Same. Well, that and I just got my driver's license, so Keenan practically begged me to drive him here." He laughed, and the sound was like honey. Warm and soothing.

By that point, the other three boys had caught up to Hayden, and he turned to look at them. "You can hang out with us if you want. We don't mind. Right, guys?"

His friends shook their heads.

"Oh…" I paused. "I don't know."

"Come on, it'll be fun!" Keenan tugged on my arm, not having much concept of personal space. I brushed him off, but he didn't seem to notice as he continued. "We can go into the funhouse with all the mirrors! Or go on the Zipper!"

"Only if you want to, but I…" Hayden's voice trailed off, fading into a whisper, even though the other boys had already moved on. "I just don't want you to be alone."

Oh.

"Well…I guess I could hang out with you guys," I conceded.

Hayden's face lit up. "Awesome! What do you want to do first?"

I shuffled my foot in the dirt. "I'm not sure. I've never been to one of these before."

"What?!" Keenan's mouth gaped. "We have to do *everything* now."

"I-I don't think I have enough money for that." I forced out an awkward laugh. "I didn't know what to expect, so I just brought this." I pulled out my singular twenty-dollar bill.

"That'll be enough to get you some ride tickets. And if you want to play games, I can pay," Hayden offered.

I shook my head. "No, I can't let you do that."

"You're my friend, Sierra. It's what friends do. We can make it even later," Hayden insisted, wrapping his arm around my shoulder, something that would normally make me shrink away. But with Hayden, it felt different. Safe somehow. Like I could trust him.

"Okay. But I'm going to pay you back."

"Deal." He stuck out his pinky finger.

I looked down at his hand then back up to him. "What's that?"

"Pinky swear. Lock it in."

After a moment's pause, I linked my pinky finger with his. Then Hayden brought his hand up to his mouth, kissing the knuckle on his thumb.

"Come on, you guys, we're going to leave you behind!"

Keenan yelled over his shoulder as he and the two other boys ran toward the mirror house.

"Um, what are your other friends' names?" I asked, slightly embarrassed by my terrible memory.

"Jack and Andrew," Hayden answered without hesitation or judgment.

I nodded then followed behind Hayden, trying to catch up to the three boys.

"Sierra, you've *got* to try these!" Keenan thrust a bucket of apple cider donuts under my nose, his mouth full of the sugary pastry. "They're so good."

I flicked my gaze toward Hayden, and our eyes met, both of us holding back laughter.

"Thanks." Chuckling, I took a donut out of the bucket and popped it in my mouth. Eyes widening, I took another one. "You're not wrong. These are delicious! It completely melted in my mouth."

"I *know*. They're my favorite," Keenan agreed. "Let's go play some games!"

We'd already gone on as many rides as possible, blowing through our tickets. My favorite was the Scrambler, even though I was squished between Hayden and Keenan because we didn't think about weight distribution.

"What do you want to play first?" Hayden asked me as we walked through the aisle of games.

I took in our surroundings, noting all of the different options. Balloon darts, a ring toss, one of those games where you raced horses with water guns, and a booth where you had to knock over milk bottles with bean bags were some of the options.

"Hmm…" I tapped my finger against my lips. "Balloon darts?"

"Sure! I'm really good at that one!" Hayden and I stepped up to the booth together.

"Hi, kids!" the carnival employee, an older man, greeted us. "You wanna play?"

"Yes, please." Hayden handed over a bundle of tickets. "You wanna go first?"

I pursed my lips, hesitating for a second. "I don't know if I'll be any good."

"Try it out!" The carnie handed me a couple darts.

Pulling my bottom lip between my teeth, I focused on the balloons, trying to decide which one to aim for. Settling on a balloon in the middle row, I pulled back my arm and then threw the dart. It flew through the air then hit the balloon with a *pop!*

"I did it!" I exclaimed, jumping up and down with excitement.

"Keep 'em coming! If you pop three balloons, you can win a prize!"

That was all the motivation I needed. I'd always been competitive, and now I was determined to take home a prize, even if it meant I'd have to hide it under the bed or in my closet.

Despite my best efforts, I only popped one more balloon. Shoulders slumping in defeat, I pouted my lips.

Hayden leaned in to whisper, "Which one do you want?"

I pointed to a stuffed tiger with bright-blue fur hanging on the wall. "That one's cute."

He puffed up his chest a little as he stepped up to the

counter. "I'm going to win it for you. Three more darts, please."

The carnie smirked then handed him the darts.

Pop.

Pop.

Pop.

Every single one of the balloons Hayden aimed for popped.

"Congratulations, son. Which prize would you like?"

He pointed to the tiger. "That one, please."

"Excellent choice." The carnie pulled the stuffed animal down from the hook, passing it over the counter to Hayden.

"Thank you very much!" Hayden smiled before turning to face me. "Here you go. What are you going to name it?"

My brows furrowed. "Name it?"

"Yeah! Don't you name your stuffed animals? Growing up, I had a stuffed dog named George. It looked exactly like our family's chocolate lab, so I named the stuffie after him."

The truth was, I'd never had stuffed animals growing up. My father thought stuffed animals were stupid, and they were also good bargaining chips for him if I did something he deemed as wrong or disrespectful. If I didn't want one of my belongings to be ripped up, I'd behave.

After a few moments of thinking, it came to me. "I'm going to name it Haze."

He laughed, his lips curling up like he knew exactly what the name meant. "Haze?"

"Yeah. Haze." I smiled back. "That way, I can think of this day every time I see him."

And you.
Hayden.
My first friend.
My *only* friend, really.

CHAPTER FIFTEEN

By the time Sierra and I arrived, Rudy's was already packed with people coming in from the rodeo and the fair. She won the barrel racing during today's performance round, so naturally I had to keep the competitive spirit going and challenge her to a round of carnival games before we met up with the rest of the crew at the bar. This led to us showing up a bit later than planned.

"Damn, it's busy," Sierra muttered as we pushed through the crowds trying to find our group.

The fair had a beer garden, but Rudy's had grown in popularity in our small town after Juniper, Liv, and Nico helped develop themed nights for the bar, including western swing and line dancing, barrel night—which was popular because you could get six shots and a mixer in a small plastic barrel for ten dollars—and bingo. Tonight was—to my dismay—karaoke.

"Hayden! Over here!" Jake's voice rose over the music and the person screaming into the microphone. I scanned the bar and saw his head poking above the sea of people.

"This way." On instinct, I took Sierra's hand to lead her through the masses. She didn't protest, probably because she didn't want to lose me. The minute we got to our group, though, she shook herself free from my grasp. It worked out in her favor—and mine—that Mikey handed me a beer at the same time, lessening the sting a bit.

"Hi!" Juniper came up to me, hugging me around the waist. Her eyes were a bit glassy, and it was obvious she'd been drinking a bit. "It's so good to see you!"

I hugged her back, chuckling a little at her drunken state. "Hi, Juniper."

Out of the corner of my eye, I saw Sierra talking to the other guys and Ellison.

"Good to see you again, Sierra. I hear Haydie over here has been a joy to live with," Jake teased.

She narrowed her eyes. "What makes you say that?"

"Oh, nothing. Just that our boy here says he's been—"

Lightning fast, I punched him in the ribs. Jake clutched his side, moaning and groaning about the pain. I rolled my eyes and then shot Jake a glare to send the message to quit messing around. "He's just being a dick. Don't listen to him."

"Okay…" Sierra's brows furrowed, but then Ellison and Juniper stole her away to the bar.

"What the fuck was that for?" I grumbled to Jake after they were out of earshot.

He shrugged. "Hey, I'm just trying to help you out. It's clear you're still in love with her, dude."

"And you think saying that she put me in the friend zone is going to help? How would you like it if I went up to Caitlin and did the same thing?"

Jake hesitated, allowing Mikey to pipe up and cut in. "It worked for Isa and Reid."

"Yeah, well, those two were idiots." Colter laughed, adding, "No offense, Reid."

Reid rolled his eyes. "None taken, I guess."

"Wait, weren't you the one telling me to tell Juniper how I felt about her before it was too late?" Mikey asked, putting his elbow on my shoulder even though I was three inches taller than him and it looked weird. When I didn't respond, he exclaimed, "You were! Dude, take your own damn advice!"

I made up some lame half-excuse, unable to look him in the eyes. "It's different."

"How? How the fuck is it any different?" Mikey's tone almost sounded annoyed, like meeting Juniper had turned him into a hopeless romantic all of a sudden.

An exasperated sigh escaped my lips. "It just is. There's a lot of history and baggage there that I'm not sure she—or I—is ready to unpack."

"Take your time, brother." Colter clapped a hand on my shoulder.

When I raised my brows at him, he shrugged. "People don't heal overnight, but if it's something you want—really want—to work out, it'll be important to talk. Untended wounds fester."

My mouth pinched into a thin line as I nodded. Colter understood my position probably the most out of all the guys. We all had our own demons and shit we'd gone through, but Colter had also supported Ellison through her grief and trauma from losing her dad in childhood. Everything he said was true. One day, Sierra and I would have to talk about what happened if we wanted to move forward and secure a future for ourselves.

No one said anything for a minute, all of us looking around at each other, just staring.

Jake finally clapped his hands together. "Alrighty, then. Let's get this party started, shall we? No more sad face. Turn those frowns upside down! Everyone, go put in a song right now, or else I'll choose one for you, and you probably won't like it." He pointed to the songbook right next to the DJ.

Sierra and the girls popped back to the group as he was saying this.

"No way in hell am I singing karaoke," Ellison protested, putting one hand on her hip as the other brought her drink up to her mouth.

"Come on, Ellie girl, have a little fun!" Jake scrubbed his hand through her hair, and she swatted his hand away. "You and Colter can sing *Grease!*"

"What are you going to sing?" Sierra nudged me with her elbow, a silly grin spread across her features.

I shook my head. "I'm going to sing nothing."

"You party poopers can go shit on someone else's night. The exit's right there. It's Juniper's first time back since she moved! The least you can do is have some fun!" Jake flung his arms around as he gestured toward the front door. I guessed he'd had at least two or three beers already. "I'm putting in songs for all of you if you don't get your asses up there right now."

"All right, all right. Let's go, Blaze." Colter wrapped his arm around Ellison's shoulders, leading her to the DJ booth.

"That's the spirit! Come on now!" Jake ushered the rest of us behind them, despite a couple grumbles from me and Reid.

After Jake handed in his song request, Colter and Ellison followed. Mikey put in a song, too, but I didn't know if it was a duet with Juniper or not. Reid wrote something down but stuck the card back in his pocket when Jake wasn't looking.

"Are you going to do one?" I asked Sierra as she flipped through the book of songs.

She raised her brows at me in this inquisitive way. "Am I going to get yelled at if I don't?"

"It's about fifty-fifty. Hopefully by the time everyone goes up, he'll be too drunk to notice."

That got a laugh out of her, and I grabbed her hand, leading her back to our table without ever putting in a song.

"Did you put in a song?" Jake came up behind me and grasped my shoulders after Sierra and I sat down at our table.

"Yup." I took a swig of my beer and nodded, lying through my teeth.

"Did you?" He turned to Sierra next.

She shrugged. "Couldn't find one."

Jake shook his head, wiggling his finger at her. "I'll give you a pass this time since you're new. But next time I'm going to sign you up!"

"Up next to sing, we've got Jake!" Evan, the new DJ, announced into the microphone.

"That's me. Prepare to have your minds blown, motherfuckers." Jake started to make his way to the DJ stand, smacking us all on the back as he passed.

After he grabbed one of the cordless microphones, giving Evan a nod, the opening notes of "Mr. Brightside" started to play.

Jake started scream-singing the first verse, and Colter shook his head. "Of fucking course he did."

It certainly had an effect on the bar, though, because when the chorus started, everyone in the building was singing at the top of their lungs. Jake hopped up on the bar and was leaning down over the sea of people jumping up and down. The floor shook, and the vibrations traveled up my legs.

"I had no idea he was this spirited." Ellison chuckled as we all watched him make a spectacle of himself.

"It's his alter ego coming out. He won't remember any of this in the morning." Reid laughed.

"And he expects us to follow this?" Juniper shook her head in disbelief, knocking back a shot. "I might need some more alcohol for this."

"You couldn't feed me enough liquor to do that." Sierra crossed her arms over her chest, her shoulder brushing mine.

"I'm with you there." I nodded, raising my bottle in agreement.

"What, you didn't put in a song?" Mikey asked.

"Nope," I said, popping the P.

Colter raised his brows. "You didn't put in a song, but how much do you wanna bet Killer up there put one in for you?"

"I don't know. Guess we'll find out."

Jake's song ended, and the crowd went absolutely wild as he hopped down. The guys sitting near the bar clapped him on the back, and he threw out a few cocky smiles at some of the girls nearby before stumbling back over to our group.

"How about that performance from Jake! Let's keep up the good mood, shall we?" DJ Evan laughed into the microphone. "Come on up, Mikey!"

"Ah, that's me!" Mikey chugged his beer, handing it off to Sierra before speed-walking over to the microphones.

He performed a very poor rendition of "SexyBack,"

and then Evan called up Colter and Ellison, who, to Ellison's obvious dismay, performed "You're the One That I Want."

Colter went all out, pulling out some ridiculous dance moves that made Ellison blush and roll her eyes as she stood next to him.

"Give it up for Colter and Ellison! Next up we've got… Hayden!"

My eyes widened and mouth gaped as Jake whipped his head toward me and winked.

"Go get 'em, Tiger!" He pushed me toward the DJ booth, despite my protests, even going so far as to threaten me, saying, "I'll drag you over there if I have to!"

I had no idea what song Jake wrote down for me, so this was truly the worst kind of roulette to play. I fiddled with the microphone in my hands as "Can't Take My Eyes Off of You" began playing.

"Are you kidding me?" I muttered, whipping my head toward Jake before lifting the microphone up to my lips. "Who do you think I am? Heath Ledger?"

The bar erupted into laughs, but I wasn't playing around.

Of course Jake would choose this song. If this wasn't an attempt at matchmaking between me and Sierra, then I didn't know what it was. I'd get back at him one day, though. I was sure of it.

Reluctantly, I started singing along with my eyes focused on the lyrics on the TV screen and my feet glued to the floor.

"Come on, Haydie! Give us a show!" Mikey yelled from our table, and I dared to look over at them.

Ellison was clapping along to the beat, encouraging the

rest of the group to get involved, and Jake was doing some kind of weird dance move.

By the time I locked eyes with her, Sierra had a big, radiant smile on her face. I didn't know if it was because she thought I looked ridiculous up here or what, but if making a fool of myself was how I could get her to smile, then so be it.

As the chorus started, I sang so hard I thought my lungs might burst. Walking over to the group, I took one of Sierra's hands in mine, lifting it to my lips during a break between lines before serenading her.

The way her face turned scarlet was enough to make up for the humiliation of Jake putting in a song for me.

"Wow, Hayes. I didn't know you were such a rockstar." Sierra giggled when I returned to the group. "If cowboying doesn't work out for you, I'd say we send you to Nashville. Or send in an application for you to be on one of those singing competition shows."

"Only if you come with me, Skip." I winked.

CHAPTER SIXTEEN

sierra

I woke up with a gnarly headache, a weird stain on my shirt, and Pancho standing directly over me.

The remainder of last night's karaoke outing was a bit fuzzy after Hayden's *10 Things I Hate About You*-esque serenade, but I could vaguely piece together taking a few shots of tequila and belting out "Man! I Feel Like A Woman!" with Ellison and Juniper.

"Do you need to go outside?" I rasped out the question to my dog, and he barked in response. I cringed at the high-pitched sound but pushed him off me and slowly rolled out of bed.

What *I* needed was a bottle of ibuprofen and a tall glass of water, but Pancho had the audacity to play games and wouldn't follow me out to the living room.

"Come on, then. Out," I commanded, and he woofed happily before leaping off the bed and prancing out the bedroom door.

The harsh sunlight filtering through the windows had me squinting, still groggy from sleep and very much hungover.

While the dog was outside doing his business, I poured myself a glass of water, swallowing down a couple of pain pills for the headache.

I had let Pancho back inside—he immediately ran back into the bedroom—and settled down on the couch when my phone started ringing.

I looked at the time. Seven thirty.

Who would be calling me at this hour?

My brows pinched together as I answered the call, croaking out a, "Hello?"

"Hello, is this Sierra Bayley?" a masculine voice asked from the other end.

"This is she." I suppressed a yawn.

"Hi, this is Deputy Grey with the Gulch County Sheriff's Department. I'm calling in regard to the fire investigation conducted a month ago. From our findings, we determined the fire as an accident, most likely due to the negligence of someone attending the rodeo. Unfortunately, with the damage done to the trailer and what evidence was left, we were unable to track down who it was. But the good news is that we don't need your vehicle anymore, so you're free to come pick it up at any time."

"Okay, thank you, Deputy Grey. I'll be over in Goldfinch later today or tomorrow to pick it up." I hung up the phone, taking a deep breath.

As much as I wanted to be relieved that I'd have my pickup back again, I wasn't. My trailer was still gone, and since they weren't able to track down whoever threw the cigarette, I'd have to cover most of the costs of buying a new one myself. Horse trailers weren't cheap, especially in this economy.

"Who was that?" Hayden stepped out of his bedroom,

walking into the living room where I was sitting on the couch.

"A deputy from GCSO."

He took a seat next to me. "Good news or bad news?"

I shrugged. "Both, I guess. The good news is they told me I can come get my vehicle, but the bad news is that they're sure the fire was accidental, and they're unable to track down whoever threw the cigarette. I'll have to buy a new trailer on my own."

"Damn." Hayden pouted. "I don't know, Skip. I find it hard to believe someone would be that careless around horses. Who just throws a cigarette butt into the window of a horse trailer?"

"I don't know, but it's fine. Don't worry about it."

It wasn't fine, but it was my problem to deal with.

Changing the subject, I asked, "Do you think you'd be able to drive me? To Goldfinch, that is."

"Of course. When are you wanting to go?"

"Today, if that's okay. Or we can go tomorrow. I don't want to throw off your schedule if you have something planned."

"My schedule's free. We can go now if you want."

I hesitated, lifting an eyebrow and cocking my head. "Are you sure?"

He stood, moving in front of me to place his hands on my shoulders, and leaned down so we were at eye level with each other. "Sierra, have I ever lied to you? We don't do that, remember?" He went as far as to take one hand off my shoulder and stick out his pinky finger, extending his hand toward me. "Want me to swear on it? I will."

My heart lurched in my chest as my vision darted down to his hand, memories of us as kids threatening to resurface. All the times we'd sworn on pinky fingers.

I pushed it down, though, and huffed out a breath, finally conceding. "Fine. Let me get dressed, and we can go. Is Pancho okay to come? I don't really want to leave him here by himself."

All he did was nod, grabbing his keys off the counter to toss and catch them in his hand. "Whatever you need."

"Right," I mumbled, heading back to my bedroom to change my clothes.

I shrugged on a crewneck sweatshirt over the T-shirt I slept in and swapped my athletic shorts for a pair of Wrangler jeans. After pulling my hair back into a high ponytail, I grabbed my wallet—double-checking that my ID was in there—and Pancho's leash.

"Come on, bud." I urged him to get off the bed.

He let out a sound somewhere between a huff and a grunt.

"We're going for a car ride," I continued.

That got his attention, and his ears perked up.

As I walked out the bedroom door, I said, "Go load up," and he sprang into action, leaping off the bed and sprinting out to the living room, his tongue lolling out of his mouth, eyes bright and full of energy.

"Hey, buddy." Hayden crouched down and was scratching between Pancho's ears. Pancho snuggled up to his leg and rolled onto his belly. "You're such a good boy, aren't you? What a lover."

What a traitor.

"Ready?"

Hayden's gaze snapped up to mine when he realized I was standing in front of them. He cleared his throat and stood, brushing dog fur off his jeans. "Yep. Let's get this show on the road."

He headed toward the front door, and Pancho walked

with him the whole way at his heels, tail wagging and butt wiggling like he was the happiest dog in the world.

Only Hayden could make my own dog like him more than he liked me.

"Do you actually believe that the trailer fire was an accident?" Hayden asked about thirty minutes into our drive.

I crossed my arms, not wanting to get into this. "Do you really believe that it wasn't? I get that your dad was a cop—"

"Is a cop," he corrected, and I rolled my eyes, unsure if the wording really mattered that much.

I still rephrased. "I get that your dad *is* a cop, but that doesn't mean everything has some nefarious motive behind it. It very well could have been an accident."

He looked as though he wanted to argue, but he took a deep breath instead. "I would rather it be an accident than someone doing it with the intention to hurt you. I just worry, Skip. Not even two weeks after the fire, someone messed with your saddle. Had you not checked the straps, you could have gotten seriously hurt. I'm not convinced it was all a coincidence."

I let out a dramatic sigh. "I appreciate the concern, but you don't have to worry about me. I'm a big girl. I can deal with things on my own. I've managed five years without you looking after me."

Hayden winced like my words cut him, and perhaps they did. But they were true. We hadn't been in each other's lives for five years, and had my trailer not burned down, we probably wouldn't be in this situation now.

His jaw hardened, and he swallowed. "Promise me that if something else happens, you'll tell me."

I hesitated.

"Please, Sierra. This is the only thing I'll ask of you." He extended his pinky finger.

Huffing out a breath of air, I took his pinky in mine. "Fine. But nothing else is going to happen." I wasn't sure if I was trying to convince him or myself more.

I wouldn't have been lying if I said the recent events put me on edge, but I thought if I ignored the issue and didn't show a reaction, whoever was trying to bother me or scare me would eventually get tired and leave me alone. It was probably a jealous competitor or a teenager pulling some sick prank. Or, like the GCSO deputy said, an accident, and the fire and saddle were completely unrelated.

For the next thirty miles or so, Hayden seemed to have his focus completely on the road, and I didn't want the topic of the trailer fire to come up again, so I played on my phone until Pancho started whining and we were forced to interact again.

"Sorry, can you pull over? He's going to keep whining if we don't let him out for a bit."

Hayden stopped at the next turnoff, and I clipped Pancho's leash on him, leading him to a grassy area. It was a bit gusty, so I hoped he would do his business quickly.

"How did you wind up with Pancho?" Hayden asked. "I know you played with Reggie when we were kids, but I wasn't under the impression you ever wanted a dog."

I crossed my arms to protect my body from the wind. "I definitely didn't when I was younger, but traveling and living by myself got lonely sometimes." I pursed my lips as his expression darkened. "Pancho was actually a rescue. I was in a rural area in South Dakota, and these people had puppies on the side of the road. They were just going to let them loose, so I gave them twenty bucks and took Pancho with me. He was six weeks old, I think.

"I don't regret him one bit. Not even when he's misbehaving. Sometimes, I think he saved me," I admitted.

A few years ago, before I got him, I was in a rough place. The anxiety caused by the fear that my father would somehow get out of prison combined with homesickness and grief of not speaking to my mom had accumulated and manifested into depression. Even though I had Lucky, Pancho gave me another routine to follow. And training him was unpredictable, so he always made things interesting.

"I'm really glad you two found each other," Hayden murmured.

I offered him a soft smile. "Me, too."

The rest of the drive to Goldfinch was quiet, but the tension had eased between us. Crazy what a little bit of fresh air could do for a person.

Once I'd gotten the keys to my pickup and loaded Pancho into the cab, Hayden stopped me before I could climb into the driver's side.

"You should stay," he blurted. "In Silver Creek. At least until the end of the season, that is. You still don't have a horse trailer, and I do. I don't want you to be stressed trying to buy a new one while competing and maintaining your spot in the standings."

"Oh, well, I—" I stumbled over my words. "I guess I could."

"It's really not a—wait, yes? You'll stay?" His features lit up, hope shining in his eyes.

"Yeah, Hayes. I'll stay." I offered a soft smile before clarifying. "Just until the end of the season, though. Then I need to figure out how to get a new trailer. Let me pay you rent, too."

"That's not necessary."

I stopped him, holding up a hand so he'd let me speak. "Yes, it is. You wouldn't let anyone else stay with you for free. Just because we… It's necessary. Please. Just let me do this."

"Okay, fine." He raised his hands in resignation, although I was convinced he would try to sneak the money back to me at some point.

"Thank you. I'll see you back in Silver Creek, okay?" I climbed into the driver's side. Pancho was already waiting for me to roll down the passenger-side window so he could stick his head out. When I reached over to close my door, Hayden grabbed it, holding on to it for a second.

"Drive safe. I'll see you at home." He closed the door gently, giving me a small wave before walking back over to his vehicle.

Home.

My brain latched onto the word and the weight it held.

Could Silver Creek ever be home for me? I wasn't sure.

I'd never really had a home before, and I questioned whether I deserved one, especially one where Hayden was concerned.

hayden

I'd convinced Sierra to stay with me for the rest of the rodeo season, and a weight felt like it had been lifted off my shoulders. She may not have believed that the fire and saddle tampering were related, but I had this nagging feeling deep down in my gut that told me otherwise. Maybe she was right, and I felt that way purely because of my dad being a police officer, but I also believed that one could never be too safe. Best case, nothing happened. Worst case, the events were related, and we had to put extra security measures in place to prevent further harm.

Next week, we'd head out on the road to Pendleton, Oregon. It gave me some comfort in knowing I'd be with Sierra at all times in case something went wrong. But also if something did happen while we were on the road, it would only solidify my theory that someone was targeting her—someone who was also competing in the rodeo circuit.

I pulled into my driveway after a long trip of thinking. My brain never shut off—couldn't shut off—when it came to Sierra. It was always either brainstorming ways to get her back, wondering how everything went wrong all those years ago, or dwelling on her safety.

Some may have called it obsessive or possessive, but it didn't come from a place of control. I just genuinely didn't know what I would do if I lost her again.

Sierra got home not too long after I did, parking her pickup next to mine. Dark spots formed half-moons under her eyes, and her shoulders were hiked up halfway to her ears. I could tell the last few weeks had taken a toll on her, and I wanted to do whatever I could to help relieve her stress.

She pushed through the front door without a word, and an idea hit me as I followed her inside. My plan wasn't anything too crazy, just something to take the edge off and, selfishly, spend more time with her.

While sleep was important, there was a difference between resting and wallowing in bed, and I feared the latter was what Sierra planned to do. Besides, other than going to Rudy's and running into town for errands, I didn't think she'd had much of an opportunity to explore Silver Creek.

"Grab a jacket, some of the sandwiches in the fridge, and Pancho's leash." I tapped her on the shoulder before she could get settled on the couch or disappear into her room. "Oh, and whatever other snacks you like."

"What? Why?" A puzzled look flashed across her face.

"It'll be nice to get out of the house for something other than rodeo for a change, don't you think? I know the perfect place." She cocked her head to the side, so I added, "Trust me, Skip."

"All right. Are you going to tell me where we're going, or is this another SGU football field situation?" she teased, standing and stretching her arms over her head.

"Well, it's definitely not illegal."

A laugh bubbled out of her. "Good to know."

While she grabbed Pancho's leash and a warmer layer, I went out to the garage. A couple fishing poles hung on the wall, and I moved them to the bed of my pickup along with my tackle box and some bait I had in the garage minifridge. At the last minute, I also decided to bring a blanket and some lawn chairs.

By the time I finished loading everything, Sierra was waiting in the living room.

"Got everything?" I asked.

She nodded and called Pancho to her side before following me out to the truck. Once we'd gotten settled with our seatbelts on, she threw me an expectant look. I knew Sierra well enough to know she didn't like surprises, but I had a feeling this one would be worth the wait.

"I know the last few weeks have been stressful, and I thought we could do something relaxing. Get some fresh air, too, and let Pancho run around." That was the only explanation I was willing to give her as we drove down the gravel road off my property and toward the Silver Creek.

It was already late afternoon, so it was unlikely there were many people still at the river, but we'd still have a couple hours before the sun set.

Open fields transformed into a wooded area, and I rolled the windows down as we got closer, the fresh, earthy scent of the running river filtering into the cab.

Only a couple of cars were parked at the pullout, and when Pancho realized where we were—even though he'd never been here—his ears perked up. Sierra's lips twitched like she was holding back a smile when I parked.

The crisp Montana air rushed into my lungs as I

hopped out of the pickup and retrieved the fishing gear and chairs from the back.

"Pick a spot, Skip." I gestured toward the creek.

Pancho was already in the water, paddling and splashing around.

"So, this was your surprise, huh? Fishing?" Amusement danced in her eyes, but she led the way, setting up camp on the far end of the creek away from the few other people here.

"It's calming." I shrugged.

She drew her bottom lip between her teeth, and I tried to look anywhere but her mouth. "I'm not gonna lie, I kinda think fishing is boring, but the fresh air is nice."

Laughing, I handed her a pole. "You probably just don't have enough patience for it." Knowing Sierra and how she was always moving onto the next thing, it made sense. Opening my tackle box, I pulled out a couple lures I knew worked well. "I don't know, something about the quiet is relaxing. I could sit out here all day, never even catch anything, and still go home feeling refreshed and happy."

After getting everything set up and bait on the hook, I cast my line and plopped down into my lawn chair. Sierra probably would like fly fishing because it was a bit more active than conventional fishing, where you had to sit and wait for a bite.

Despite her claims that she didn't like to fish, she sure knew how to cast a line. I didn't have to help her at all, and soon she was sitting next to me in her chair.

There was a good chance Pancho had already scared all the fish away, but any time spent with Sierra was time well spent, even if it was just two friends sitting at a fishing hole.

"If you get cold, let me know. I brought a blanket, too."

Her eyes cast downward as she shook her head, but there was a subtle smile on her face. "Always taking care of me, aren't you, Hayes?"

I wasn't sure how to respond, but luckily I didn't have to because by some stroke of luck she had a bite. The tip of her rod bent, and her eyes widened.

"Oh my God! I think I have one!" she squealed as she started to reel in her catch.

A few seconds later, we both burst into laughter because her big bite wasn't actually a fish but a huge chunk of moss.

I scrubbed my hand through my hair, fighting back laughter. "Damn, I really thought we had one."

"Just my luck, huh." Her shoulders shook as she bit her lip, plucking the moss off her hook and tossing it back into the water. "Took my bait, too."

"So far you're having better luck than I am," I pointed out, gesturing to my line that hadn't had so much as a single bite, from fish or otherwise.

She baited another hook before digging into the bag of sandwiches and snacks. "Do you want one of these?"

"Sure." I nodded, and she passed me one of the peanut butter and jelly sandwiches I had made a couple days ago.

Biting into her sandwich, she said, "I don't remember you ever being a big fisherman when we were younger."

"I wasn't. I didn't really get into it until after college when I moved here."

"It's a hobby that will stick with you until you're old. I can respect it." She paused. "I actually took up reading while I was traveling. I wouldn't call myself a huge bookworm, but I try to read at least ten pages of a book a day."

"Yeah?" I stopped what I was doing, wanting to be fully invested in her stories and let her know that I genuinely cared about what she did when we were apart.

"I made a habit of finding little free libraries all over the country." She huffed out a breath, which was half a laugh. "I'd take a book, then leave a different one that I'd found in another town or state. Maybe one day when I'm settled, I'll build one of my own."

"I think you and Isabelle—that's Reid's girlfriend—would get along really well. She reads like three hundred books a year."

Sierra blew a raspberry as she baited her hook. "I'm not quite at that level."

"What's been your favorite book you've read?"

By the look in her eyes, I never would have expected the answer.

"I have so many favorites. I read a fantasy once about a girl from a different realm who has been cursed to lose all her memories and start over on Earth every time she's killed by the man she loves. I also read a dark comedy about a female serial killer who gets into a fake marriage with the detective who's assigned to catch her. But the kicker is that they don't know each other's identities." She chuckled to herself. "You're not going to believe this one, but I actually also liked *To Kill a Mockingbird*."

A deep belly laugh escaped me. "Wait, is that the book Keenan had to read in high school? The one I grabbed from the library for him that one day?"

Pink streaked across her cheeks. "Yeah. Can you believe that?"

"That was the day you told me you got the

membership forms signed for high school rodeo." Conflicting feelings warred inside me at the memory. While I was happy she was able to compete in something we both loved, the memory of Sierra wincing in pain at a brush of my hand over her arm was burned into my memory.

There were so many things I would have done differently if I'd known what she was going through, had she let me in fully.

CHAPTER EIGHTEEN

sierra

OCTOBER, SOPHOMORE YEAR

I f you want to compete, you'll just need to get these forms filled out, then turn them in," Alyssa explained as she scrolled on the Montana High School Rodeo Association website. "You'll also have to pay your membership dues, but then you'll be able to enter into competition for the spring season!"

I pulled my bottom lip between my teeth as I read the requirements for the forms.

Both parent signatures are required.

There was no way in hell my father was going to let me participate in rodeos. He didn't even know that when I wasn't home, I was spending time at Hayden's place practicing. If he found out, there would surely be issues— if not for me, then for Mom, who usually was the one picking me up. Lately, though, I'd had Hayden just drop me off back at the school since he had his driver's license and have Mom pick me up there. At least then my lie of staying late after school wouldn't be a lie for her.

"You think you can manage that?" Alyssa pulled me back out of my thoughts.

I nodded, a little too quickly to be convincing, but I didn't think she noticed. "I'll get it done as soon as I can."

"Perfect. We—Hayden, Keenan, and I—are really excited to have you compete. I think you'll do really well, Sierra."

I dipped my chin, trying to hold back the smile but failing. "Thanks."

When I got back home that evening, having chosen to walk from the school, the air was already tense.

"Where have you been?" A gruff voice greeted me with accusation.

"I had to finish up some work at school." The lie rolled off my tongue with ease, like I'd been doing it for years—which I had. "Where's Mom?"

He ignored my question, lifting his nose to sniff the air. "Why do you smell like horse shit?"

I'm surprised you can smell anything other than alcohol.

I rolled my eyes, but it wasn't subtle enough, because he sprang up from his seat in his recliner and stomped over to me.

Digging his fingers into my forearm, he leaned in close to my face, his breath smelling of cheap booze. "Don't roll your eyes at me, you little brat. Show some respect."

Stand your ground. Don't show any emotion.

"Don't have anything to say for yourself?"

When I didn't answer, he gripped my arm tighter and flung me out of the way.

My shoulder banged against the wall, and fiery pain shot down my arm, but I didn't react. I couldn't. It would just fuel him even more.

"You and your mother are so ungrateful." He grabbed a beer bottle off the table next to his chair and paced back and forth, swinging it as he walked. "I do *everything* for you, and what do I get in return? Nothing but piss-poor fucking attitude."

The only thing we could do when he started to rant and ramble about how ungrateful and horrible we were was sit there and listen. Take the jabs like a goddamn punching bag.

"I'm *sick* of it!" His voice rose to a shout, and he threw the bottle on the ground, the glass shattering and bouncing off the floor.

My eyes widened, darting between the glistening shards just inches away from me.

"You tell anyone, and I mean *anyone*, about this?" He gestured to nothing in particular—or maybe everything. "You'll fucking regret it. I will make your life *hell*."

I believed him.

And that was what I was most afraid of.

Not even for me. Not even for Mom.

But for Hayden.

What would he do if he found out my best friend was the son of a cop?

Grumbling nonsensical words to himself, he plopped back down into his chair, turning on the television to some sports broadcast that was playing. Soon enough, heavy snores filled the room. I got up from my position on the floor and quietly swept up the broken glass before retreating up to my room.

Later that week, during my lunch hour, I went to the library and printed out all of the forms I needed to fill out for membership in the MHSRA. The forms were simple enough, asking for my basic information, what events I'd like to compete in—I only elected barrel racing—my school information, and signatures at the bottom.

Over the past few days, I studied different forms and paperwork my parents had lying around, practicing their signatures until I could perfectly forge them.

By the time I printed out the forms, the signatures were practically twins. The hardest part was getting a copy of my birth certificate, but I'd told my mom it was for a school project, and she didn't really question it. I was convinced she'd let me do pretty much anything I wanted if it meant I stayed out of her way and didn't cause her trouble with my dad.

I'd saved up enough money over the last six months to pay for the membership dues, too, doing odd jobs for neighbors and the Watkins family, so all I needed to do was get my transcripts and then submit the forms.

After folding up the papers neatly in my backpack, hiding them inside a book I knew my dad wouldn't bother to look inside if he snooped, I headed toward the doors of the library.

My mind was so occupied with the forms and everything going on that I didn't notice the person entering the library as I was exiting.

"Oof!"

"S-sorry," I muttered before realizing who I'd bumped into.

Hayden laughed. "On a mission?"

My lips flattened into a straight line as my cheeks flushed. "Something like that. What are you doing?"

He gestured toward the bookshelves. "I had to come grab a book for Keenan. He keeps forgetting."

"Ah." I nodded.

"I know you were just in there, but do you want to come with me? It shouldn't be long."

"Sure." It was becoming impossible to say no to him, even for something as simple as grabbing a book.

"Cool. Come on, then." He brushed past me, his hand barely grazing the spot on my arm covered in purple splotches, but it was enough for me to wince at the pain. The bruises were fresh, sensitive enough that even bumping into something hurt.

Hayden pulled back his hand like he'd been burned at the same time I tucked my arm close to my body. "Sierra?" he squeaked out my name.

I turned my head toward him, probably looking like a deer in the headlights, with bulging eyes and a gaping mouth. "Yeah?"

"You know I'm always here for you. But I just need to know. You'd tell someone if"—Hayden swallowed—"if someone was hurting you…right?"

My eyes narrowed, and I crossed my arms, tugging my sleeves further down past my wrists. "What are you trying to say?"

"I guess…" His voice trailed off, dejected. "I know people who can help. My dad can—"

"I'm fine, Hayden. I've told you this before," I bit back, unable to control my response—mostly out of the fear of what might happen if my father found out I'd told someone, especially a cop.

Best case scenario, we'd have to move again, and I'd lose the one friend I'd come to care about. I didn't want to think about the worst-case scenario. The best way to protect Hayden was to act like nothing was wrong.

"Pinky swear?" He stuck out his hand, his pinky finger raised.

"Yeah." It came out as a pathetic whisper because it was a lie. And I was sure both of us knew it was a lie. But I didn't take his pinky; I just changed the subject. "I got the forms for high school rodeo filled out."

Hayden's eyes widened. "Really?"

I smiled, even if it was a forced one, and nodded.

"Wait, and you already got the signatures and everything?" As if by magic, all the worry melted away from his features, replaced by pure excitement instead.

A small breath of relief left my lungs. "I did. I just need to ask the front desk for my transcript then submit the forms."

"This is incredible, Sierra!"

Before I could even process what was happening, Hayden's arms were wrapped around my middle in a bear hug and my feet were a few inches off the ground. His laugh filled the quiet library, and even when the grumpy librarian shushed us, his joy—the warmth of his happiness—enveloped me like a soft blanket on a cold winter day.

He put me down and continued talking as we walked through the aisles of books. I wasn't sure what he was saying, though. I was deep in my head about the logistics of all this.

I'd not only have to figure out how I was going to get to competitions but also how I was going to explain my absence to my parents. I wasn't sure spending every weekend at the school was a realistic—or believable—excuse.

Maybe I could get a job somewhere my parents wouldn't think to go. Working on the weekends wouldn't be a stretch, and getting a job would be nice to have some spending money anyway, or money to save for when I could finally get out of here.

"Earth to Sierra?" Hayden waved a hand in front of my face.

I snapped out of my daze, blinking a few times. "Hmm?"

"I'm good to go." He held up the book in his other hand. *To Kill a Mockingbird*.

"This is the book Keenan needed?" I didn't peg Keenan for a classics type of guy, or really a book guy in general.

Hayden snorted. "Yeah, apparently. I guess he needs to write a report about it for English class."

I puckered my lips like a duck. "Interesting."

Hayden chuckled. "Very."

hayden

Our impromptu fishing trip seemed to work, because by the time we had to get back on the road for the next rodeo, a little bit of Sierra's spark appeared to have come back.

She came out of the house as I was packing up the pickup and horse trailer. A baggy T-shirt hung loose off her shoulders, and she had on a pair of bootcut Wranglers.

"Morning," I greeted her.

She shielded her eyes from the sun. "Anything I can help you with?"

"If you want to grab Lucky's tack from the shed and load it into the horse trailer, that's about all I had left to do besides loading the horses. We'll be set to hit the road pretty shortly. Are you packed up?"

She threw out a thumbs-up since she already had her back turned to me, making her way over to the tack room.

Our trip to Oregon was one of our longer ones, lasting a full week before we immediately drove over to North Dakota.

This was also one of the few trips we'd be boarding our

horses at the rodeo site and staying in a hotel nearby. Since Sierra normally stayed in her trailer at an RV park, she hadn't been able to book a hotel, but I'd booked a double queen room. Jake was going to stay with me, but given the circumstances, he got booted to Mikey's room.

We'd also be leaving Pancho behind on this trip. Liv had offered to dog sit while we were gone, so on the way out of town, we'd have to drop him off at her house. He was already waiting in the backseat of the truck. The windows were slightly rolled down, so he was peeking his nose out.

"Ready to go?" I double-checked with Sierra after she dragged two duffel bags and a backpack out of the front door. "We're only going to be gone a week, you know."

She dropped the bags on the ground, huffing out a few labored breaths. "I'd rather be prepared and not need everything than need something and not be prepared."

I lifted one of the bags, thinking it'd be easy to toss it into the back of the pickup, but it was heavier than I expected. "What the hell do you have in here? Bricks?"

"No, just my entire rock collection," she deadpanned, rolling her eyes.

"Well, at least we'll have something to hold down the bed of the truck," I teased, tossing her second bag into the bed.

"Anything can happen on these types of trips." She shrugged. "If we somehow happen to get stranded on the side of the road, I have plenty of layers."

"If you say so. All right, Princess, let's get on the road." *That* nickname earned me a glare sharp enough to cut through bone.

She climbed up into the passenger seat, sparing me one more glance over her shoulder as she scolded me. "Never call me that again. I can handle Skip, but Princess is too far."

"Noted." I chuckled as I shut her door and made my way over to the driver's side.

The plan was to meet up with the rest of the group in Missoula, but a few hours into the drive, our text group was blowing up with notifications.

The Silver Creek Cowboys (and Ellison) (plus Isa and June)

JAKE

Not gonna make it in time to meet up guys

ELLISON

What happened?

JAKE

Flat tire. Had to stop in Livingston

COLTER

You guys alright if we just keep going then? We're almost to Butte.

That's fine. Sierra and I are right behind you, but we might still stop somewhere

It was about an hour past noon, and Sierra's stomach had rumbled a few times between Bozeman and where we currently were. I was starting to get a bit hungry myself, and I didn't want to wait much longer to eat.

MIKEY

We'll see you all in Pendleton, then I
suppose.

ELLISON

Drive safe. Send us updates plz!

"Guess we're not meeting up in Missoula anymore. Jake and Mikey got a flat outside of Livingston, so they had to stop. Colter, Reid, and Ellison are ahead of us, but they said they were just going to keep going," I explained, putting my phone back in the center console.

"What's our plan then?" she asked as her stomach growled. "Can we still stop?"

A chuckle rumbled low in my chest as I said, "Yeah, Skip, we can stop. I'm getting hungry, too."

About thirty minutes later, I pulled off the interstate into the parking lot of a small mom-and-pop diner. The building itself was small, with a red roof and a big, farmhouse-style sign that read *Ma's Roadside Diner*. A vintage flatbed truck sat out front, its dark teal body completely spotless and free from rust.

"What do you think?" I looked at Sierra for her approval.

She nodded, pressing her lips together in a pout like she was thinking. "Looks cute. Kind of reminds me of Ranger's. Let's do it."

I killed the ignition, and we made our way to the front entrance. Bells jingled as we stepped inside, signaling our arrival. A sign instructing us to seat ourselves was placed near the hostess stand, and a big dining room with a variety of tables greeted us.

We found a table for two near a window and sat down. Not too long after, a waitress with silver hair, round glasses, and a gingham apron strode up to our table with menus and two glasses of water.

"Welcome to Ma's! I'm Shellie, and I'll be helping you out today. Take your time to look at the menu, and I'll be right back to get some drink orders."

"Thank you very much, Shellie." I offered her a genuine smile before picking up my menu. "What have we got here?"

It was your classic American diner menu, with sandwiches, burgers, and an all-day breakfast.

"Look, they've got Elvis pancakes on the menu." I pointed out the breakfast item to Sierra. The pancakes had peanut butter, bananas, and bacon, just like Elvis Presley's favorite sandwich.

She tilted her head. "You know I can't pass up some good peanut butter pancakes, but the turkey bacon club looks really good, too. I'm guessing you're going to have the mushroom Swiss burger?"

She had me there. Like I'd told her a few weeks ago, old habits died hard. And I was nothing if not a man of habit. Why fix something that isn't broken?

"Are you two ready to get some drinks in?" Shellie popped back around to our table after helping the few other groups in the dining room. The place wasn't too busy for one thirty in the afternoon.

"I'll do a Coke," Sierra told her.

"Make that two." I gestured with my hands. "I think we're also ready to order, right?" I glanced at Sierra for approval, and she nodded.

"Sounds good! Are you wanting to put any appetizers in? Also, our special today is a steak sandwich with mashed potatoes and gravy." Shellie looked at me, but I pointed to Sierra to let her order first.

"I don't think we're going to do an appetizer, so I'll just have an order of the Elvis pancakes." Her eyes flicked up to mine, a blush creeping into her cheeks.

"And for you, darling?"

"I'll do the mushroom Swiss burger, please. With french fries." I handed Shellie both our menus as she scribbled down our orders on a notepad.

"I'll put those orders in and be right back with those sodas for you."

"Thank you so much." I dipped my chin in acknowledgment. Resting my forearms on the table, I leaned forward slightly. "So…"

Sierra's brows shot up. "So?"

"You always said you were going to get out of Goldfinch. Where'd you end up traveling to?" I'd resisted asking the question for this long.

I had to know where she'd been all those years, why she never reached out to me. I thought after the last time I'd seen her that maybe we were…something, anything. I didn't know. Maybe I was just a dumb kid with his heart on his sleeve and stars in his eyes, but the way she'd looked at me that night made me believe she felt the same way.

Sierra took a slow sip of her water before placing it back on the table, her eyes averting to the ice clinking around in the glass. "Everywhere. I wanted to see everything I could."

Everywhere but home.

"What was your favorite place you traveled to?"

She rolled her lips between her teeth. "It was this little town in Colorado called Cedar Bluffs. It reminded me a lot of Silver Creek, actually. It was small and close-knit, but the environment was rare. Everyone tended to mind their own business instead of getting involved in the gossip mill. It was nice."

I was sure she loved that. People in Goldfinch loved to talk. I couldn't exactly blame her for leaving after everything that had happened and the way the town reacted. Finding solace in a small town where who you were didn't matter was probably a nice reprieve.

"Would you ever want to go back?" My question came with a subtle tone of *Are you planning on leaving again?*, without actually saying it outright.

Her gaze flicked toward the ceiling this time. "Hmm… I'm not sure. Probably not. There's still so much out there I haven't seen, but I don't know, maybe…" Her voice trailed off. "I don't know if I'm ready to settle, but part of me wants to. Part of me wants to stop—"

"Here are those Cokes. Your food's on the way." Shellie interrupted Sierra's sentence, but I thought I had an idea of what she might have been trying to say, or at least what I hoped she was trying to say.

Part of me wants to stop running away.

"Well, I remember you always said you wanted to make it to Houston, Cheyenne, Pendleton, and Vegas. You've done Houston and Cheyenne."

She'd been at Cheyenne Frontier Days a couple years ago, and I thought I'd imagined her out in the arena. I wasn't able to work up the courage to approach her out of fear that I'd somehow scare her away. Honestly, if Pancho hadn't run up to me that day in Goldfinch, I didn't know if I would have had the guts to talk to her a month ago.

It wasn't that I was avoiding her. In truth, whenever we were in the same place over the years, all I wanted to do was reunite with her. But I think a small part of me knew that, for Sierra, coming back had to be on her terms. She had to be the one to choose to stay, and I wasn't going to take that power away from her. Even though the notion was painful, I was willing to be patient and meet her wherever she was. Be whoever she needed me to be.

"We're on our way to Pendleton now," I pointed out. "All that's left is Vegas."

She nodded, finally making eye contact with me, her emerald eyes shining with emotions. I hoped pride was one of them, because if nothing else, Sierra should have been very proud of herself and how far she'd come.

"Hey, Sierra?" I murmured, low and so soft I wasn't even sure she'd be able to hear.

"Hmm?"

"I'm really proud of you."

"Could we just get the check?" After we'd scarfed down our food—without too much conversation because we were both starving—I flashed a smile at our server, and she nodded, rushing away to grab the bill.

When she came back, she placed it on the table. Sierra reached for it, but I stopped her, placing my hand atop hers before handing my credit card to Shellie.

"Aw, how sweet. I just *adore* young love. You two look so good together," Shellie gushed as she took my card and whisked away before Sierra could correct her, "Oh, we aren't a couple," already falling off her lips.

Her cheeks flamed, and her eyes widened.

I shrugged, mischievous thoughts rolling through my mind. "Can't deny it, Skip. We *do* look good together."

Shellie brought back my card faster than I'd ever seen,

and she gave us her thanks for coming in. "You and your honey drive safe now." She winked.

Sierra ignored Shellie's statement, pushing back her chair to stand as I added a tip and signed the receipt. "Let's get back on the road or we'll end up getting to Oregon super late."

"I can drive the next few hours so you can get some sleep," she offered after I yawned on our way through the parking lot.

"Okay, yeah sure. That'd be great." A memory resurfaced, and I couldn't pass up the opportunity to give her a hard time. "Just don't crash, okay? I don't think I can take the fall this time."

"Hey!" She scoffed, tilting her chin upward like a petulant child. "You promised you wouldn't hold that against me!"

I chuckled, shoulders shaking in pure glee, replaying the first time Sierra tried to drive—after a bit of convincing—in my head.

CHAPTER TWENTY

hayden

MARCH, SOPHOMORE YEAR

"Are you sure this is safe?" Sierra drew circles in the dirt with her boot.

I patted the hood of my dad's old pickup. "Totally safe. I've been driving since I was like ten."

She grimaced, her nose wrinkling. "I'm not sure if that makes me feel better."

"Everyone around here drives young. Besides, we're just going around the ranch, not on the actual highways."

"What if we get in trouble? Or crash?"

I waved her off. "I'm not going to let that happen. And what my dad doesn't know won't kill him. Ask for forgiveness, not permission, right?" When she hesitated, I added, "Think of it as your first driving lesson on the road to getting your license."

"Okay…" She drew out the word, her bottom lip drawn between her teeth.

"We'll go slow. It's not like we're driving on a racetrack." I opened the driver's side door, gesturing for her to get in.

"I still don't know about this, Hayden." It looked like a

storm was raging in Sierra's mind, a raging tornado of things that could go wrong.

"Do you trust me?" I blurted.

She looked at me, eyes glazed with confusion. "Yes."

I did my best to reassure her, knowing there were risks but choosing to ignore them anyway. We were in a safe, controlled environment, and we wouldn't go more than half a mile away from the house. "Then we'll be fine. Nothing bad will happen, I swear."

"All right, then, if you say so." She climbed into the driver's seat, and I gently closed the door before racing around the front of the pickup to the passenger side.

"It's not a manual, so make sure you use only one foot for the pedals. That's super important, okay? You don't want to end up like my cousin, who ran into her house by accident because she was using two feet and accidentally hit the gas instead of the brake."

Sierra's head whipped toward me, panic settling in her eyes. "Why would you tell me that?" she screeched.

"So you don't make the same mistake she did, duh," I teased, flashing her a grin that probably looked goofy in hopes of easing her nerves. "Man, my family made fun of her for *years* after that. She never lived it down. My uncle put one of those *SLOW* traffic signs by their front door for a few months. Everyone called her Crash for like a year, too."

"Is that supposed to make me feel better?" Sierra scoffed.

I nodded. "Yeah, because you're not going to make the same mistake she did. I'll make sure of it. I'll keep you safe."

I could have been wrong, but I swore I heard her mumble, "Safe."

"Okay, first thing's first. Seatbelts," I said as I pulled my seatbelt across my body, clicking it into place.

Sierra put hers on, too, then reached for the key in the ignition.

"Ah-ah, not yet," I tutted. "Now, check your mirrors, and make sure they're adjusted so you can see. You don't want to do that while you're driving." Although, I had to admit, sometimes I forgot to adjust my mirrors and did exactly that.

"I may be wrong, but I've definitely seen you adjust your mirrors while driving," she quipped.

"Yeah, but I already have my license. I'm teaching you *good* habits."

To my surprise, she didn't argue further, fixing her mirrors then looking at me. "Okay, Teach, now what?"

"Now, you can start it. Then you want to put your foot on the brake and put the vehicle in drive. You're going to slowly ease up on the brake, then move your foot over to the gas and lightly press down on it."

"Okay." She took a deep breath as she took her foot off the brake.

We inched forward slowly, and she moved over to the gas pedal. But she gave it a little too much oomph, and we lurched forward. Just as quickly, we came to a screeching halt as she slammed down on the brakes.

My body slammed forward toward the dash, and I caught myself with my hand before my face smacked into it.

"Oh, God, I'm so sorry." Sierra let out a quiet cry, her hands immediately flying to cover her eyes.

I couldn't hold back the laughter that bubbled out of my chest. In response—and honestly, rightfully so—the back of Sierra's hand smacked into my chest.

"Don't make fun of me!"

Her response only made me wheeze, my words failing to come out. Once I'd somewhat composed myself, I tried to reassure her. "I'm not, I promise." I extended my pinky to her, but she just offered me a death glare, which triggered more laughing.

"It's like a rite of passage, okay? We all do it. Next time, just don't slam on the brakes because it makes it worse. Go again."

She huffed. "Fine."

That time was better, and we made it at least a few feet without Sierra panicking and jerking us back and forth with the brakes.

My eyes darted to her hands, currently white-knuckling the steering wheel. "You're doing great. You can relax. It's okay."

"Don't tell me to relax! That's like the worst thing you could say to a girl!" she snapped, eyes blazing with determination and a bit of stubbornness, but she still eased her grip on the steering wheel a little. "Okay." Pressing her foot back down on the gas, she inched forward slowly, much slower than she did before.

We crawled along the road at a snail's pace, but I could feel her nerves melting away, replaced by a new air of confidence.

"We can go a little faster," I whispered, careful not to seem like I was ordering her around, but we were going really slow. Maybe ten miles an hour, if that.

To my surprise, she didn't protest, and before I knew it, we were cruising around the ranch.

"This is so much easier than I thought!" Sierra proudly proclaimed.

I bit my tongue, resisting the urge to tease her about

slamming on the brakes and almost breaking my neck from whiplash.

"Take this turn, and we'll go down to the end of the property and back," I instructed as we approached a fork in the road.

"I didn't realize your family had this much land."

"Oh, yeah, this ranch is probably about two hundred acres. We have another patch of land, though, that's much larger. Most of our cattle are out there, but we'll move them back and forth every so often," I explained.

"Do you think you'll take over the ranch one day?"

I nodded confidently. "I think so. If I go to school at SGU, I probably won't ever leave. Well, besides competing in rodeos."

She nodded, but no words came out of her mouth.

Changing the subject to something lighter, I asked, "What's your favorite color?" I was sure I already knew it, but it wasn't something I'd asked her before.

"Purple," she answered immediately. "What's yours?"

I tapped my finger against my lips. "Well, it used to be yellow."

Sierra turned her head toward me. "What is it now?" One brow lifted in confusion, her eyes widening in anticipation.

My gaze met hers then flicked toward my feet as heat flared in my cheeks. "Uh…green. It's green."

We'd been so engrossed in conversation that neither of us noticed the tree up ahead—or the fact that Sierra was veering off the road straight toward it—until it was too late.

"Oh, shit!" On instinct, and against my better judgment, I reached for the steering wheel.

Sierra's head turned back toward the road, and she

screeched as we both grabbed the wheel, jerking it to the left.

Crunch!

We came to an abrupt stop…into the tree. If we'd adjusted a couple of seconds sooner, we would have missed it, but instead, the right side of the front bumper smashed into the tree.

Luckily, we weren't going fast enough for either of us to get injured, but an immense feeling of guilt—like a tsunami wave—crashed over me.

"Oh my god, oh my god, oh my god," Sierra mumbled over and over to herself, her head buried in her hands.

I reached for her, my hand hovering over her shoulder.

Her head shot up, eyes wild and cutting into me. "You said it was safe! You said we weren't going to crash!"

I did say both of those things.

"Are we going to get in trouble?" She gnawed on her bottom lip. "What if we get arrested? My parents will kill me!"

"Hey, hey, hey. It's okay, Sierra." I tried to think of what to do. Telling my dad the truth was the obvious answer, but it wouldn't go without consequences. Then it hit me. Unbuckling my seatbelt, I opened the passenger-side door.

"What are you doing?" Sierra raised a brow.

"Switch me spots."

"What? Why?"

"Because, if I tell my dad I crashed, it'll be a lot better than telling him you crashed. I at least have a driver's license," I explained before hopping out of the pickup to assess the damage.

Sierra unbuckled her seatbelt and got out, too, walking to the front of the pickup.

Running my hand over the hood, I reassured her. "It's not as bad as I thought. Hardly any damage. But we should probably still have him come out and check it."

"I'm so sorry." She hung her head, and I stepped closer to her, lifting her chin with my finger.

"Hey, don't worry, okay? I'll take the fall. It's on me for pressuring you to let me teach you how to drive in the first place."

Sierra rolled her eyes. "I'd hardly call it pressure. And you don't have to. I'm the one who wasn't paying attention. You don't have to take the blame."

I ruffled my hair with my fingers. "Yeah, well, I went to grab the wheel, and it freaked you out. It's all good. Maybe no more driving lessons for a while, though." I forced out a laugh.

We both looked at each other, then the pickup and back before we burst out laughing.

"What are the odds?" Sierra snorted. "My first time driving, and I freaking crashed."

"I won't hold it against you," I promised.

CHAPTER TWENTY-ONE

sierra

PRESENT DAY

After dropping off the horses, we pulled into the hotel just after dark. Thirteen-hour drives were not for the weak, even with the breaks we took. Honestly, I was a little bit in awe that I had been able to make those types of drives alone. I'd discovered recently that there was only so much of my own internal monologue I could take before I began to go crazy. It started to make a lot more sense why Hayden and his friends all traveled together. Being on the road could be lonely, so having a travel partner helped.

We parked the pickup and trailer in the lot next to the hotel and hauled all our bags—well, mostly my bags—into the lobby.

The front desk receptionist barely looked up from her phone as we approached the counter.

Hayden cleared his throat to get her attention. "Excuse me?"

She slowly lowered her phone, looking up at us through thick-rimmed glasses. "Yes? How can I help you?"

"We have a reservation. Under Watkins. For a double queen room."

The receptionist—Lydia, her tag read—tapped on her keyboard and clicked her mouse a few times before humming an acknowledgment. "Ah, yes. Right here. If you could sign and initial this for me. It's just our smoking and pet policies. Please write down the make and model of your vehicle as well in case we need you to move it. You'll be on the third floor. Wi-Fi is listed on the inside here, and breakfast is served from six to ten every morning."

Hayden set the pen back down on the counter, taking the room keys from Lydia. "Thank you so much." He tilted his head toward the hallway where Lydia pointed out the elevator, then hauled one of my duffels over his shoulder with ease, despite complaining about the weight when we were in Silver Creek.

My mouth gaped, and I had to stop myself from the worst thing that could possibly happen: *drooling*. What happened to the lanky kid I grew up with?

Not only did he grow up, but the man also grew *muscle*.

"Are you coming?" He glanced over his shoulder, amusement tinting his voice.

"Uh, yeah. Sorry." I stumbled over my words—and my feet—as I grabbed my remaining bags and followed him to the elevator.

The elevator door dinged, and we stepped inside, silence enveloping us. Neither of us spoke as Hayden tapped the third floor button and the doors closed. My eyes flicked over to him, but he stood facing forward as the motor whirred, lifting us two floors at a snail's pace.

This had to have been the most awkward elevator ride I'd ever been on, and for why? Hayden and I were two friends who happened to be sharing a hotel room—and twelve years of history. No big deal.

The doors couldn't open fast enough, and I exited the

elevator as quickly as humanly possible, taking a sharp right down the hall toward our room. Unfortunately, I didn't have a key, so I had to wait for Hayden to catch up.

Don't make this trip more awkward than it has to be, Sierra. Dammit!

It was all Hayden's fault. Hayden and his stupid adult muscles and his stupid memory of us as teenagers.

Argh! It turned out I was not the cool girl I thought I was. At least not when it came to Hayden Watkins. Never when it came to him.

The one thing that could make this whole sharing a room situation worse was if the hotel had a mishap and there was only one bed.

I closed my eyes, opening only one as the lock clicked and Hayden opened the door. Peering past the door, I let out a deep sigh of relief.

There are two beds. Thank fucking God.

"You okay over there?" Hayden raised his brows, the right corner of his lips turning up slightly.

Sweat made my palms sticky as I let out a nervous laugh, unable to stop the word vomit from spewing out. "Yeah, I'm great. Why wouldn't I be? This is perfectly fine. Everything is fine. I am *totally* cool."

Yeah, because that *was completely normal.*

It was the damn fishing trip and then being in the car —alone—together for thirteen hours. Factor in the diner, and my emotions were all over the place. My brain didn't know up from down or right from wrong at this point. However, I'd give it a good night's rest, and everything would be back to normal. I could go back to ignoring the fact that I was living with the first boy I'd ever loved—the *only* boy I'd ever loved—and had somehow convinced myself that I could be just friends with him.

Yeah, maybe that was a bit fucking delusional on my part.

"Which bed do you want?" I asked, waiting for him to claim one before setting my bags on a bed and then immediately throwing myself on it afterward. Once I was down, there would be no moving me for the night.

"You can have the one by the window." He gestured to the one furthest from the door.

I nodded, proceeding to do exactly as I planned and throwing my duffel on the foot of the bed. Before I could plop down, though, I caught a glimpse of myself in the mirror and groaned. My roots were already starting to show. I didn't *want* to do this tonight, but if I didn't do it now, I feared I wouldn't have time later.

Tearing open the zipper of my duffel, I pulled out the box of black hair dye and stomped to the bathroom.

"What're you doing?" Hayden poked his head in as I started to rip into the box.

Pulling out the supplies, I sectioned my hair into four parts. "Dying my roots. If I don't, then I'm going to look bald when the blonde grows back."

"Ah." He nodded, but I wasn't sure he actually understood. He was a guy, after all. I waited for the, *I liked you better as a blonde* comment to come, but it didn't. Instead, he said, "It's a good color on you, Skip. It brings out your eyes," before vanishing around the corner again. I heard the click of the television and the voices of whatever channel was on prior to Hayden turning on the TV.

The scent of chemicals wafted in the air as I mixed the dye, so I turned on the fan. I hated the smell of hair dye, but I hated my blonde hair even more. It reminded me too much of my childhood, and I thought black suited me better anyway.

Mom hummed as she ran the brush through my hair, long blonde strands falling delicately over my shoulders when she reached the ends.

I looked in the mirror in front of us, taking in both of our appearances. Twin pairs of eyes—although hers were more bluish than green—stared back at me. I had my father's nose, but that was the only part of me that looked similar to him. His hair was murky brown, and his eyes were an even darker, even more hollow brown. He had a tall, menacing stature, and while I wasn't even eight years old yet, I had a feeling I wasn't going to have his height either.

In every way that counted, I was my mother's daughter.

And he hated that.

Sometimes I thought he just hated me—not the way I looked— because his eyes would rake up and down me with disgust before he scoffed and moved on. Maybe if I'd looked more like him, he would be proud of me.

The truth was, I didn't want to be like him.

I didn't think Mom realized I heard their arguments some nights. How they weren't actually as quiet as they assumed they were. I heard the insults spewing from my father's mouth. The ones that only ceased with the slap of a hand across skin.

By the time I'd washed the dye from my hair and emerged from the bathroom, Hayden had turned off the lights. The TV was still running, a low drone in the background, but his soft snores told me he'd fallen asleep half under the covers.

Careful not to wake him, I pulled the comforter out from under his leg, dragging it up so it was covering his chest.

His lips curved into a soft smile, but he didn't wake up. He looked so peaceful, like an angel incarnate.

In a way, he was—an angel. He'd looked out for me for so long. Took care of me when all I wanted to do was push everyone away.

It was time I returned the favor.

sierra

The weather in Oregon was pleasant; the temperature was in the mid-seventies with a gentle breeze and little cloud cover.

I adjusted my cowboy hat, brushing the baby hairs out of my face as I peered out into the arena. The action had started not too long ago, and they were flying through the events, having already finished up bareback riding and half of steer wrestling.

There were three events between team roping and barrel racing—saddle bronc, breakaway roping, and tie-down roping—so even though I'd be riding around the rodeo grounds to keep Lucky warm before our race, I'd be lucky enough to get to watch Hayden and Keenan's run, especially since they were fairly early in the lineup.

The boys left me alone earlier, heading to warm up their horses, so I was enjoying the little bit of calm I had, though it didn't seem to last very long.

As soon as the team roping began, one of the rare barrel racers who was actually nice to me—Haley—walked up beside me, her hands in the pockets of her jeans.

"Hey, Sierra."

I was convinced a majority of the girls saw me as competition or a threat, so they kept their distance. Then again, I hardly ever made an effort to talk to them. I preferred to keep to myself, not letting anybody too close.

While there weren't any inherent threats to the people I befriended, I didn't want to let my guard down only to regret it later. I had to keep the people I cared about safe, and if there were fewer people for me to care about, that task would be much easier.

"Hi, Haley." My eyes swept over her. Her light-brown hair was pulled back into a neat braid, and she lifted her cowboy hat to brush some stray strands out of her eyes.

"Have you been here for very long? In Oregon, I mean?"

I shook my head. "No, we got here late last night. I had some loose ends to tie up in Montana, so we didn't make the trip early." Granted, those ends were tied a couple weeks ago, but taking a break from traveling for a short bit was nice.

"Ah, I see. My fiancé and I got here a couple days ago."

If I remembered correctly, Haley was from somewhere in Saskatchewan, so they had an even farther distance to travel. It made sense that they'd want a couple days to recover before all the action began.

"I'm glad you guys made it okay."

"Oh, yeah. We definitely didn't have to leave so early, but between you and me, I like dragging Bodhi around to do a little shopping. And he doesn't complain that I make his wallet so much lighter." She winked and shot me a grin before letting out a small giggle.

I returned her smile, shaking my head with amusement.

We stood in silence for a bit, watching the event.

"All right, folks. Our next roping team is a couple of cowboys from Montana. Hayden Watkins and Keenan Chase! Let's see what they've got!"

As the pair backed their horses into the roping boxes, Haley nudged me gently with her elbow. "Isn't that the team roper you're always hanging around?" When I nodded, she continued. "Is he your boyfriend?"

I puffed out a breath, trying to conceal a laugh. "No. Keenan is like an annoying brother."

She rolled her eyes. "No, I meant the *other one*. His partner. Hayden."

Sucking on the inside of my cheek, I averted my eyes. "Hayden's just a friend."

In the arena, Hayden had already roped the steer's horns, turning Peanut Butter around the corner for Keenan. He roped the hind legs with ease, and the announcer called out, "Five-point-six seconds for Hayden Watkins and Keenan Chase! Let them hear you!"

Haley shot me a look of understanding. "I see. Well, he seems like a good one, Sierra. Glad to catch up. I'll see you around?" Her eyes flicked to the arena, and we exchanged parting pleasantries before heading in opposite directions.

Fate must not have been on my side, because despite my pleasant conversation with Haley, shortly after she left, another one of the barrel racers shoved past me. Michaela Monroe.

Her blonde hair was curled into too-tight ringlets that fell mid-back. She looked like a beacon with her glittery, neon-pink button-up and stark white cowboy hat.

However, instead of leading me to safety like a lighthouse, she was a siren song, steering me to imminent doom.

Michaela was one of my biggest barrel racing competitors at the moment. We'd been flip-flopping positions in the standings all year. She also happened to be a Grade-A bitch, always picking apart my appearance and performances.

"Oh, sorry, Sierra." She stopped a few feet away before spinning around on her heel to face me, gaze fixed on me, no doubt scrutinizing something. "Your hair's gotten so long. I can't believe it doesn't get in the way while you ride."

I kept my gaze locked on the arena as I bit back a sarcastic comment, resisting the urge to ask how her tight curls don't give her a massive headache. I could be the bigger person…sometimes.

"Pure skill," I deadpanned, suddenly finding something on my nails to inspect.

She hummed, a subtle, patronizing mannerism that I'd gotten used to in our years of competing against each other. "Where have you competed this year? I haven't seen you around that much."

My eyes flicked toward her. "I've been in Montana the last few months."

"I was wondering where you were when I didn't see you in Reno or Cheyenne. Thought you might have disappeared off the face of the Earth again after Houston. Or maybe you just weren't good enough to make it to those ones." She let out a snicker that to any bystander would have sounded like we were old friends having a good time. However, I knew better.

"No, I just had different priorities this year. Clearly, it's been working out for me. Where are you sitting in the standings?"

The corners of her mouth fell into a frown. "Apparently. I'm sixteenth, but there's still a lot of season left. Anything can happen, you know."

"That's so true." Turning on a saccharine charm, I rotated my body toward her. "Well, Michaela, it's always *such a pleasure* catching up with you. I'd better go warm up my horse. Good luck out there today."

I heard her scoff as I walked away, my lips curling up in a satisfied grin.

Lucky chuffed and pawed at the ground when I approached him to warm up.

I took my time securing his tack, careful to double-check the straps for any damage, going as far as to triple-check the saddle was tight enough and wouldn't slip.

With the announcer and roar of the crowd in the background, I rode Lucky around a warmup pen a few times at a lope. We didn't do that for very long, but once we were going, we didn't stop moving, continuing to walk around the rodeo grounds because otherwise he got impatient and restless.

"Go get 'em, cowgirl." Hayden winked as he passed by me and Lucky as we stood in the queue for our race. The rider immediately before us had just finished, exiting the alleyway. Her time was decent, but I knew I could beat it easily.

I shot him a lopsided smirk before leading Lucky toward the alleyway.

"Sierra Bayley from the state of Montana! Here she comes!" The pounding of my heartbeat in my ears drowned out the crackle of the announcer's voice on the speakers and the roar of the crowd.

Lucky sped down the alleyway into the arena, and I guided him toward the first barrel, cutting around it with ease. Dust rose into the air, surrounding us in a hazy cloud. The second barrel came easy, too, and Lucky glided around it like it was nothing.

He ran toward the final barrel with my gentle kicks urging him on. Our position was solid, and we should have been able to make it around the last barrel without a hitch.

"Let her hear you, folks! Help her around the third and final barrel!" The announcer called out his encouragement as we approached the turn.

Everything was fine, until it wasn't. As we rounded the turn, my saddle started to slide ever so slightly. I gritted my teeth, willing all my strength into staying upright.

This can't be happening right now.

I engaged my core as we raced to the end of the arena past the time barrier without a hitch.

"Let's give her fifteen-oh-three!"

I huffed out a breath of relief as Lucky slowed to a walk, and we exited the arena. As I hopped off his back, Keenan and Hayden approached us.

"Damn, Skippy, thought we were about to have a repeat of Bridgers!" Keenan tugged on my braid.

I whipped it away out of his grasp, jabbing a finger into his chest, though my tone was anything but aggressive. "Watch your mouth, Chase. We don't speak of that day."

"Hey, I gotta hand it to you, though. You managed to finish the run without falling. That takes one strong cowgirl to do that."

Hayden nodded in agreement. "She's always been the toughest one out of all of us."

hayden

MAY, SOPHOMORE YEAR

Sierra started competing with us right from the beginning of the spring rodeo season in March. Over the past six weeks, we traveled around the state to compete in various rodeos, and I absolutely loved it. I could see this being a career I pursued in the future, despite my parents wanting me to go to school to get an education first, just in case.

It was a sunny day in the Gallatin Valley, just outside of Bozeman. This rodeo was duly named the Bridgers Rodeo and was one of my favorites. The area reminded me of Goldfinch, and the crisp mountain air always had a positive effect on my nerves.

"Have your parents come to any of these?" I asked while we sat around eating peanut butter and jelly sandwiches.

She shook her head as she lifted a hand to her mouth, still chewing a big bite.

"Oh, that's too bad." Alyssa gave her a sympathetic glance.

I didn't think Alyssa noticed, but I saw the flash of annoyance in Sierra's eyes as she swallowed.

"It's not that big a deal. I don't need them to be here."

"And you have my parents," I added, hoping to reassure her. I didn't exactly know why her parents didn't come to watch her, but it frustrated me a little. Sierra was really good, and it was unfortunate that her family wasn't here to witness it.

Her eyes flicked away before she stood, crumpling up the plastic bag her sandwich was in. "Yep." She walked over to the trash can to throw it away and didn't come back, disappearing around the corner instead.

"She's interesting, isn't she?" Alyssa stood up and placed her hands on her hips.

I shrugged. "I guess."

The way she said "interesting" made it feel like an insult. Was Sierra shy? Sure. Guarded? Absolutely. But she wasn't weird like Alyssa's tone insinuated, at least not to me.

"I wonder what her deal is." She was still staring, even though Sierra was long gone.

"What do you mean?"

She shrugged. "It's odd that her parents wouldn't be here, or at least come to *one* of the rodeos she competes in. Especially with how good she is. And they have to know about them. They signed the paperwork."

The urge to defend Sierra, even though the same thoughts had just rolled through my head, rose to the surface. "Maybe her parents work on the weekends. They could just be busy. I don't think it's that deep, Alyssa."

She raised her brows as she exhaled through her nose in amusement. "You're right, that's my bad. I shouldn't have made assumptions." Folding up her sandwich bag, she stood. "Well, I'd better go get ready to compete. You should, too. Go find Keenan."

I nodded, finishing the rest of my sandwich and handing her my garbage before standing and brushing the dust off my jeans.

Keenan and I had done pretty well, landing in the top five of the leaderboard. We weren't quite at the top, but it wasn't a bad spot to be in toward the end of the season.

"Our next young lady comes to us from Goldfinch, Montana. Sierra Bayley, let's do it!" The announcer's voice echoed, and my attention shot to the rodeo arena as Sierra and Buttercup exploded into a run. "I need you with me, folks! Let her hear you!"

The pair made it around the first barrel with ease, dust particles flying into the air as music played through the speakers and the crowd roared.

She looked like a natural out there. Her face was set in determination as they rounded the second barrel and charged toward the final one.

"Yup!" The announcer clucked his approval, but as she cut around the barrel, her saddle slipped, falling slightly to the side of Buttercup's flank.

"Oh, shit!" Keenan yelled, pointing toward the pair.

I jumped up from where I was sitting, but it wasn't like I could have done anything.

Sierra held her own, though, keeping her balance so she didn't fall out of the saddle.

"Whoa there! Looks like this cowgirl almost took a

tumble, but she's managed to hang on, folks. Help her home, everybody!"

Sierra managed to finish the run, albeit slower than normal.

"Eighteen-point-four-seven for Sierra Bayley. Next up is—"

I blocked out the announcer's voice as I ran over to the alleyway to check on Sierra, Keenan hot on my trail.

"What happened?" The thought slipped from my mouth as we reached her and Buttercup.

Keenan pointed to her cinch. "She didn't tighten her cinch enough. Actually, it's almost like you skipped over it entirely." He chuckled. "Hey, that's what we can call you. Skip."

"Oh, shut up," she snipped, her nostrils flaring. "It was an honest mistake. I got ahead of myself."

Keenan continued. "You're just lucky you didn't fall out there, Skippy."

"Hey! I still finished the run, didn't I?" Sierra drew back her elbow to hit him, but I intervened, stopping her before she caused rib damage.

"Come on, Skip." I winked, and even though she rolled her eyes at me, a soft smile pulled at her cheeks. "Let's get out of here."

"That nickname isn't going to stick, you know," she muttered as we walked toward the horse trailers.

I shrugged. "I kinda like it."

CHAPTER TWENTY-FOUR

hayden

PRESENT DAY

The second day of competition went well. Keenan and I placed fourth in the lineup with a decent roping time. Sierra, once again, swept the competition. The last time I checked, she was sitting thirteenth in the world for barrel racing.

The NFR was never a guarantee, but I held out hope that this would be her year. After Pendleton, we'd have two more multi-day rodeo events to compete in. Then it was the waiting game. It was unlikely that I would make it as a header—unlikely for Keenan, too, as a heeler—but I was content with seeing Sierra live out her childhood dream. In the stands or in the arena, I'd be cheering her on regardless.

After the rodeo concluded, we took the horses back to their "horse hotel" and then decided to meet up with the rest of our friends for dinner, finding ourselves at a steakhouse.

"So, when are you going to convince your girlfriend to finally move up to Montana?" Colter teased Reid.

He shrugged. "I told her the house is hers whenever

she wants to move. Even offered to build her a library in one of the guest rooms so she didn't have to get rid of her massive collection. Things are going really well with the bookstore, though, so it'll probably be another year. Who am I to tell her to shift her career goals when we're always on the road anyway?"

Mikey nodded in agreement. "June is the same way. Although, I'm sure if you asked Isa to move, she would in a heartbeat. Juniper would probably tell me to fuck off and then wait another six months after she'd already planned to move." He let out a boisterous laugh.

"She also just moved, though," Ellison pointed out.

"Yeah, but you know she's talked about going back to school. I don't know when it'll happen, but it's in the back of her mind. I can't imagine she'll leave her current job anytime soon, though. Working in this kind of research lab was her dream job."

Jake looked at me and Sierra. "So, Sierra."

My jaw ticked in anticipation for what he was about to ask.

She perked up, raising her brows at him. "Hmm?"

"You sick of living with Hayden yet?" he joked, nudging me with his elbow. "Or are you planning on getting the hell out as soon as you can? You know, if you ever need to get away from him, I'm building a guest house."

Her face paled, and my stomach churned.

"I-I," she stumbled over her words. "I'm very grateful that Hayden's letting me stay with him." It was both an answer and a non-answer.

The rest of the group nodded, although their stares were a bit blank as they seemingly tried to decipher the energy between me and Sierra.

Truthfully, they weren't wrong to be confused; this whole friends-but-not-really-friends thing Sierra and I had going was fucking confusing to me, too. As much as I wanted her to stay—for good this time—I'd already asked her to stay once. Convincing her to stay again would be like catching lightning in a bottle, but I was willing to try, even if it meant I got struck instead.

"How is the guest house going, by the way?" Colter asked.

"It's coming along. I'm hoping to have the framing and everything done before the first snow hits, but you never know what the weather will do."

Reid and Colter nodded like they were old farmers discussing the weather and crops.

Jake continued, a sparkle of pride in his eyes. "We're close to working on the roofing and siding, so I think by the time spring rolls around I'll have a second house, boys."

The guest house had been his secret project throughout the summer. I'd only found out about it recently, but it turned out he'd started work on it in late July and never told anyone about his plans. I thought Colter had been helping him with it some but was sworn to secrecy for whatever reason.

To be fair, though, none of us really went out to Jake's property. We all hung out at Colter's ranch or Reid's place since he had an arena. I used to go over to Jake's occasionally, mostly to carpool since his place was between mine and Reid's, but that was before Sierra moved in.

"Well"—Ellison clapped her hands, changing the subject when conversation about Jake's construction project lulled—"I know it's still early, but we're having everyone over for Thanksgiving this year. Our first official Silver Creek family Thanksgiving. You're more than welcome to come, Sierra. You, too, Keenan." She looked at my girl and my roping partner before she flicked her eyes to the rest of us. "I expect the rest of you to be there and to bring something. Beer, wine, a dish." She raised her brows at Reid at that. He was probably the best cook out of all of us. "We're making it a tradition now. No one's spending Thanksgiving alone anymore."

If you were a bystander, you would never have expected to see a bunch of cowboys biting back tears from welling in their eyes, but looking around the table, I noticed just that.

Mikey chuckled on a sniffle, breaking the momentary silence. "Look at you, Firecracker. Taking in all us strays. Never would have expected all this from you."

"How'd you think she ended up with me?" Colter's eyes gleamed with pride for his wife. "She's always had a soft heart underneath that tough exterior, haven't you, Blaze?"

When I first met Ellison, she was guarded and struggling through grief and her own mental health struggles. Not that she didn't have her struggles now, but she had a whole army behind her—we all did. But somewhere along the line, Ellison had taken on sort of a caretaker role for all of us cowboys.

It was what I loved most about our group of friends. Sure, we had each other's backs in the beginning, but watching my friends meet their better halves and heal along the way gave me hope for me and Sierra. Colter, Reid, and Mikey used to hold things in—I think we all have—but in the last few years, the women in their lives slowly chipped at the walls they'd built up, while simultaneously breaking down their own.

They showed them that vulnerability was their greatest strength, not an ailment.

"You've got us all mushy, Ellie. Only you." Reid shook his head with a smile.

Sierra turned her head toward me, and I offered her a soft grin. "I don't think I've ever seen this many men cry all at once," she whispered with a giggle.

"Not even when you made a bunch of those dudes from Great Falls cry at that rodeo?" Keenan teased, and her face flushed.

"They deserved it," she muttered.

"Hold up, what are you three whispering about over there?" Jake perked up.

"Sierra made a bunch of teenage boys cry when we were younger." Keenan shrugged, despite Sierra shaking her head in an attempt to get him to shut his mouth.

Mikey laughed, and Ellison's eyes widened.

"What?" she gasped.

"Looks like you've got some competition for being the scariest, Firecracker." Mikey was still laughing. "Man, does that mean we've got *three* Rottweiler girlfriends in the mix?"

"What the fuck does that mean?" Ellison scoffed.

"You know, you're protective and not afraid to punch dudes in the face, but then you're all lovey and cuddly with Colter," Mikey explained his thought process. "Colter's a golden retriever, and you're a Rottweiler."

She didn't look super convinced, but she still nodded. "Hmm, okay. As long as you don't call me a feral kitten, I'll take being a Rottweiler."

"I need to hear this story, though. How did you make them cry? Did you punch them? How old were you?" Jake leaned forward on his elbows.

"You want to tell the story, or do you want me to?" I raised my brows at Sierra, a laugh threatening to surface.

Sierra rolled her eyes. "Since Keenan has never been able to keep his mouth shut, I guess I'll tell it. Long story short, we were at a rodeo, and these bronc riders were talking shit about Hayden, so I told them off."

"Yeah, that's the SparksNotes version of it, Skippy. You gotta be more detailed. Tell them exactly what you said." Keenan laughed.

"I don't know what he said about Hayden, but it wasn't very nice, so I just told him he looked about as smart as he was good at riding broncs. He was the worst bronc rider in the association."

Both Keenan and I raised our brows, looking at her with expectancy to continue.

She sighed, her eyes rolling toward the ceiling. "Okay, and then I *may* have dislocated his kneecap because he didn't think I was strong enough to beat him up and tried to kick my feet out from under me, but assault is a crime, so, for legal reasons, that's a joke. If anyone asks, he took a really bad fall off a bucking bronc."

Jake coughed, almost choking on his drink. "Damn, that's brutal. Remind me not to get on your bad side."

She grimaced, her face contorting with discomfort at the attention. "It's really not that big of a deal."

"I'd take it as a compliment, Skippy," Keenan reassured her with a chuckle. "You're loyal. Maybe sometimes to a fault, but I'd rather have a friend who'd defend me to the grave than someone who lets people drag me through the mud."

"Well, I feel like you get enough shit as it is, Kee. You don't need strangers giving you a hard time, too." She smirked, mischief gleaming in her eyes where embarrassment once reflected.

"Nah, I think it's just 'cause you love me."

"I'll give you that one. I'd love you even more if you'd buy me some peanut butter cups, though," she teased.

The rest of the group had diverted into their own conversation, leaving the three of us in our own little world. Guess they had just wanted to hear Sierra's story.

"You and your peanut butter cups." I shook my head before turning my attention to Keenan. "Remember that time you couldn't make a decision on what to get at the gas station?"

He scratched his head. "Uh, you're going to have to be a bit more specific there, Hazey."

"The day we went to Ranger's," I elaborated.

"We went to Ranger's a lot," Sierra mumbled.

I groaned, rolling my eyes. "The time we went to Ranger's and you got something different than you get every single time. Then we went to the gas station, and you dragged me in even though Sierra said she forgot something and had to go back. Is that specific enough for you?" I huffed out a breath.

"Oh. That time. Yeah, I remember that." Keenan nodded before stuffing a fry in his mouth.

Sierra's face paled, and my brows pinched together.

"You good?"

Although her eyes glazed over a bit, like she wasn't fully here, she nodded. "Yeah. Yeah, I'm fine."

sierra

Chiming bells greeted us as we stepped inside Ranger's Grill.

"Take a seat wherever you'd like, kids!" Susannah, the owner of Ranger's, called to us as she passed by with a tray of food for a group sitting in one of the booths.

"Thanks, Susannah, good to see you!" Hayden replied as we headed toward one of the corner booths in the back. Keenan was going to meet us, but he usually ran late, so we beat him by a long shot.

I slid into the inside part of the booth facing the door, and Hayden slid in next to me. It was stupid, because we were friends, but butterflies took flight in my stomach anyway because this was the type of thing couples did. Or at least they did in the movies.

Shortly after we sat down, Susannah came to take our orders. "Afternoon, kids. What are we drinking today?"

"Can I get a cherry Coke?" I asked, adding at the last minute, "And a water."

She nodded, jotting it down on her notepad. "And for you, darling?"

"I'll do a regular Coke and a water, too, please."

"Got it. I'll be right back with those." She flitted around the corner, leaving us alone.

Coming to Ranger's Grill had become a sort of tradition between the three of us. Every Friday after school, we'd come here, and in the summer we were here even more frequently. Ranger's had the best burgers and fries, though, so who could blame us? It could get expensive, but with all the rodeo money I was making, it was worth it.

The clunk of boots against the tile floor announced his arrival before Keenan's voice called out, "Wassup!" He high fived a few of the people sitting at the tables near the front of the restaurant before sliding into our booth.

I had to laugh at his dramatic entrance. "Hey, Kee."

"Sues just took our drink orders, so figure out what you want to eat fast," Hayden teased.

Normally it took three to five business days for Keenan to make up his mind, even though he always landed on the same thing every time. But he'd get upset with us if we ordered for him, even though I was pretty sure we knew him better than he knew himself.

"Hold your horses, Hazey." Keenan held up a hand as he picked up his menu, perusing the options.

"You kids know what you're eating today?" Like clockwork, Susannah emerged with our drinks. She'd even put a maraschino cherry in mine, exactly how I liked it.

"He's going to need a minute." Hayden gestured to Keenan. "But we're ready, right, Sierra?"

I nodded, and Susannah focused her attention on me first.

I didn't even need to open my menu. "I'll do the aloha burger without tomato or onion."

The aloha was a quarter-pound beef patty with lettuce, Swiss cheese, pickles, pineapple, and sweet chili sauce.

"What do you want for your side, darling?"

"Regular fries, please."

"You got it. And for you?" Susannah asked Hayden after writing down my order.

"Let's do the mushroom Swiss burger today. With everything on it, and french fries on the side, please."

Keenan was still scouring his menu when Susannah looked at him.

"You ready, Keenan? Or do you need a little more time?"

"He probably needs more time," I teased, sticking out my tongue. "Or, you know, Sues, you can just put him down for chicken strips like normal."

Keenan rolled his eyes. "Ah, shut it, Skippy. I'll do a Mountain Dew and a bacon cheeseburger today, Sues, please. Tater tots for the side."

Both mine and Hayden's eyes widened with surprise. Even Susannah seemed to be taken off guard. Normally, Keenan ordered the chicken strips basket with french fries. Religiously, in fact. He hardly ever strayed away from what he liked.

"Switching it up today, Keenan, I see." Hayden pursed his lips while nodding. "Respect."

Keenan stretched out his arms behind his head. "Aw yeah, never let 'em know your next move, am I right?" He winked at me, and I fought the urge to gag and roll my eyes.

"You only did that because we were giving you shit. Are you sure you don't want to put in the chicken strips? I can flag Susannah over right now. I'm sure she'll come back, and Shane won't harass you too much about it."

"I'm *fine*. I'm a big boy."

Hayden and I exchanged an amused glance. He mouthed, *Bet he won't eat it*, and I had to hold back a giggle.

"How's the little filly?" Keenan didn't seem to notice our exchange as he leaned back in his side of the booth, stretching his arms behind his head. "What's her name again?"

"Peanut Butter," Hayden and I both said in unison.

"She's really good," Hayden added. "She's getting so big. Dad said it'll only be another year or so before we start training her to have a rider. She won't be in the arena for a while and still has a ways to go before then, but I have a good feeling about her. As much as I hate to say it, Bullseye is getting older. I'll most likely be able to ride him throughout college, but he'll be closer to retirement age once I finish school."

Keenan hummed in acknowledgment. "Can you imagine the rodeo announcer calling out, 'Hayden Watkins and Peanut Butter!'" He *giggled*. "Guess it's a good thing you're not a barrel racer, and they don't call out horse names for team roping."

"I like her name," Hayden replied defensively. "It fits her, and it's special." His eyes flicked to mine at the last part.

Keenan snorted, shaking his head. "If you say so, dude."

Susannah came back with Keenan's drink, and our food came out shortly after, so we didn't get too much conversation in between sipping on soda and munching on our burgers.

"Let's go to the gas station after this," Keenan mumbled, his words jumbled with the burger in his mouth.

"What was that? I couldn't hear you over all the food in your mouth," Hayden chided in a joking manner.

Keenan made a show of swallowing his bite and then overenunciated his speech. "Let's. Go. To. The. Gas. Station. After. This."

"What do you need at the gas station?" I asked.

He shrugged. "Dunno. Whatever I find."

"Do you even eat the snacks you buy from the gas station, or do you just hoard them like a squirrel before hibernation?" I teased, making a face.

"I eat them," he protested, but then he added, "just not always right away. I have to be in the mood."

"If you have to be in the mood, then why don't you just wait and buy the snacks you want later?"

He tapped his finger against his lips. "I like to stock up."

"But then you get sick of them and have like thirty of the same snack that you'll never eat," Hayden pointed out.

Keenan threw his hands in the air. "Let me live, okay!"

We all burst into laughter, clutching our stomachs and leaning on each other for support.

"You kids finished here?" Susannah chuckled as she approached the table.

"Yes, ma'am. Thank you. Tell Shane we said hello," Hayden said as we all threw bills on the table to pay for the meal.

"Will do. Come again soon." She gathered all the money, and we reassured her that we'd be back as we made for the door.

"To the gas station!" Keenan stretched out his arm like he was a voyager.

As we walked down the streets, fooling around like

teenagers did, the familiar, rusted-out truck parked at the gas station caught my eye.

Shit, shit, shit.

If my dad saw me with Keenan and Hayden, there'd be hell to pay later.

"Hey, guys, I think I forgot something back at the restaurant," I mumbled, fumbling through my pockets to make the lie more believable. "I'm gonna go back."

"Ah, I really wanted a candy bar," Keenan protested, gazing longingly at the gas station.

"Go ahead, I'll catch up with you guys." I waved him off. I just needed to get away before my dad came out, most likely with beer and a pack of cigarettes.

Keenan wasted no time to run across the street to the gas station, not even bothering to look both ways. Hayden didn't move, though.

"You sure? I can go with you?" His gaze bounced back and forth between me and Keenan.

"Yeah, I'm sure." I had already started walking backward, away from him. "Make sure Keenan doesn't blow all his money on stupid shit. I'll be right back."

"Okay…"

Out of the corner of my eye, I noticed the gas station door opening, a tall figure stepping out. Not thinking twice, I took off in a sprint without looking back to see if he'd noticed me.

Instead of running all the way back to Ranger's, I skirted around the corner into an alleyway. My chest heaved from exertion, and I leaned against the brick wall of the building next to me, hands on my knees and head down.

That was way too close. I didn't think my dad saw me and Hayden, but I'd find out later when I got home. The silly thing was that I didn't even run away for my sake. I wouldn't have cared if he saw me if I were alone. It was the fact that Keenan and Hayden were with me. Spencer Bayley wouldn't have taken kindly to the idea of me hanging around two boys, even if we were all just friends.

His favorite thing to do was isolate me and Mom. If we didn't have friends or anyone to help us out, we'd have to depend on him, even when he wasn't treating us properly.

The whole notion of it made me angry, and my hands balled into fists. One day I'd be free of all this. There'd be no one to control my life except for me.

I stood in the shadows of the alley for a few more minutes until I was sure the truck would be gone, and then I pushed myself off the wall and headed back in the direction of the gas station to meet up with Hayden and Keenan.

I didn't see them outside, so I looked both ways before crossing the street to go inside. The truck was nowhere in sight. My dad either went home or to a casino to blow whatever cash he had.

I heard the boys before I saw them and headed toward the sound of their voices.

"Dude, hurry up already. I want to make sure Sierra's okay!" Hayden whined as candy wrappers crinkled in the next aisle over.

"Don't rush perfection, Hazey!" Keenan retorted.

I was sure Hayden was rolling his eyes as he grumbled, "You already have like eight things. Who are you trying to feed? An army?"

"Yes, an army of one. Me."

I turned the corner, stepping into the candy aisle, and sure enough, Keenan had his arms full of gas station snacks. Pringles and Red Bulls, and bags of sour candy. He appeared to be deciding between Reese's peanut butter cups and KitKats.

"Reese's are superior," I announced, and they both jumped as they turned toward me.

"God, Skip, you scared me! I almost dropped my drinks!" Keenan clutched his goodies even closer to his chest.

"I'm just saying, if you loved me, you'd get the peanut butter cups and share them with me." I flashed them a grin, taking some of the drinks out of Keenan's arms. The last thing I wanted was for him to drop everything and make a mess.

"There, she made the decision easy for you. Come on, let's go." Hayden grabbed the bag of peanut butter cups with one hand and Keenan's arm with the other, leading him toward the cashier.

hayden

PRESENT DAY

Did you make sure to triple-check all of your straps?" I asked Sierra as she swapped out Lucky's halter and lead rope for his bridle and reins.

"Yes, I checked them." Irritation crackled in her voice. "You don't need to hover over me like I'm some kid, Hayden. I'm fully capable."

Fuck, she had a point.

"I'm sorry, you're right." I scrubbed my hand through my hair. "I didn't mean to micromanage you. I'm just worried, is all. I know there haven't been any issues since Billings, but…" My voice trailed off. I felt like I'd been waiting on edge for something to happen the last couple weeks. Instead of relief that nothing had happened, it was almost like dread was weighing down on me for the next time something *did* happen.

"What makes you so sure something's going to happen?"

I could tell she was trying to keep her tone neutral, but frustration peeked through in her question.

"I guess nothing. But if something does—"

Sierra cut me off. "Nothing's going to happen, Hayes. And if, God forbid, something does, I assure you that I can handle it myself. I'm a big girl." She let out a heavy sigh. "I appreciate your concern, but it's going to be fine. Weird coincidences happen all the time. It doesn't always have to be a bad thing. I'm going to warm up Lucky now, okay?"

"Okay, Skip." My shoulders drooped a little, because even though I knew she was right and she could handle herself, I couldn't get rid of the lingering fear of someone hurting her.

My eyes couldn't help but glue themselves to her as she rode away, her ponytail swaying behind her.

From behind me, I recognized Keenan's laugh and footfall as he approached me.

"Don't start," I dismissed him before he could open his mouth.

"Ah, come on, Hazey. Let me give you a little shit."

Shaking my head, I started to walk in the opposite direction. "I don't care what you have to say. How much did you hear?"

"Enough." He chuckled as he followed me. "You have to admit you sound a little bit like our dads. Sierra can handle herself. She doesn't need you hovering over her."

"I'm well aware of that, thank you very much. Sierra made sure to inform me of that like two minutes ago." I ran a hand through my hair. "Am I wrong for being a little concerned?"

He shrugged. "No, but there are different ways you can show your concern. Ways that won't push her away from you because you're being an overbearing worrywart."

Having Sierra call me out sucked because I was only trying to help, but having Keenan point out my behavior was worse.

I sighed, letting my shoulders drop. "I know, I know."

"Try to relax. She'll be fine, dude. I know you"—he paused—"care about her very deeply, but it's been almost ten years since we graduated high school. Times have changed, and that girl out there is strong as fuck. Not even that, she's even scarier than she was in high school." He laughed. "I'm just saying, I wouldn't want to cross her. She'll be fine. And if she's not, then she has you, and I have no doubt she'll come to you."

I sighed, knowing he was right but not wanting to admit it.

Keenan's shoulders shook as he visibly suppressed his amusement. "The best part about all of this is that you know I'm right. You just don't want to admit it." He patted me on the back and then turned back toward the arena. "Come on, she's going to run soon."

"She's number thirteen in the world right now, folks, and she's had some great runs the last few days. Sierra Bayley racing with her horse, Ace's Lucky Charm! Let's do it!" The announcer's voice should have prompted me to focus on the arena where Sierra was about to race, but a flash of movement in the direction of our horse trailer caught my attention instead.

"Where are you going? She's racing right now!" Keenan called after me, but I waved him off, my eyes stuck on the figure headed toward the trailer.

Keeping enough of a distance that the person—a blonde woman—wouldn't be able to see me, I tailed her. She didn't have a number on her back, so either she wasn't a contestant or she'd taken it off momentarily. I didn't recognize her from the back of her head either; she had no distinguishable features or clothing.

I thought I was far enough behind, but right before she reached the trailer and all of our equipment, she looked over her shoulder, a shocked expression flashing across her face. Instead of continuing toward the trailer, she ran off in the other direction.

"Hey!" I yelled, running after her. "Stop!"

She kept going, weaving through pickup trucks and horse trailers, until eventually she lost me.

"Fuck," I muttered just as the announcer called out, "Fourteen-point-seven-nine!"

By the time I trudged back to the rodeo arena, Sierra had already dismounted Lucky and was walking him back to the trailer to untack.

"Hayden?" Confusion laced in her voice. "What were you doing?"

I sucked my tongue behind my teeth before biting out a low, "Someone was trying to mess with the trailer."

"What?" I couldn't blame her for her disbelief.

"I followed her. She was headed straight for the trailer. I'd never seen her before, and when she looked over her shoulder, she saw me and ran away."

Sierra tilted her head a little. "Are you sure she didn't run away because a tall, muscular stranger was following her?"

I scoffed, rolling my eyes, trying not to focus too much on the subtle compliment she'd woven in. "No, Sierra, I don't think that."

She shrugged, a bit of petulance in her body language. "Of course you wouldn't. You're a man."

"Can you take this seriously, please?"

"Fine. You're positive she was headed for our trailer. Was she another contestant? What did she look like?"

"I'm not sure. She didn't have a number on her back, and I didn't get a good look at her face, but I didn't recognize her. She was wearing a long sleeve button-up and a white cowboy hat. Had blonde hair?" I tried my best to remember what she looked like, but to be honest, there wasn't anything that special about her besides the fact that she was trying to do something to our stuff.

Sierra pulled her lip between her teeth, although her posture did seem to stiffen a bit. "Don't take this the wrong way, but maybe you're being a bit paranoid, Hayes." We started walking toward the trailer, the clomp of Lucky's hooves against the gravel like a drumbeat rhythm. "You've been a bit on edge. Is it possible you were trying to find something to take issue with or someone to be suspicious of? I'm not trying to discredit what you saw, but nothing happened, right? The girl ran away?"

I nodded. "She ran, and I…" I looked away, running my hand across my face. "I ran after her, but couldn't catch up."

Sierra groaned, exasperation in her voice. "Hayden. You can't just run after random women. She probably thought you were going to attack her."

We're back to this again?

"I thought she was going to attack my trailer!" I defended my actions, although she had a point, even if I didn't want to admit it. I wasn't thinking about that, though. My mind was locked on Sierra's safety and that alone.

"Okay, well, nothing happened, so take a deep breath." She went through the motion with me, inhaling a long breath through her nose and then exhaling through her mouth. "Better?"

"Yeah." My heart rate had calmed a bit, the adrenaline starting to leave my body. "Sorry, Skip. I don't know what I was thinking. I just…"

She finished my thought for me. "You're looking out for me."

I nodded, and soon we were in front of the horse trailer. Everything looked fine, not a scratch or a dent in sight, and everything was locked up like it was supposed to be.

Maybe this was a good sign—the sign I was needing. Maybe Sierra had been right all along, and the fire and saddle incidents had just been weird coincidences.

Maybe we could go back home to Montana and both breathe a little easier knowing she was safe.

CHAPTER TWENTY-SEVEN

sierra

Loud chatter and the thump of bass drowned out everything else in the bar we found ourselves in after today's final competition.

The air felt hot and sticky from the warmth of bodies packed into the building, combined with the scent of spilled beer and liquor. The soles of my boots stuck to the floor with every step, but I gritted my teeth and bore it for the sake of Hayden and the rest of the guys. It wasn't like I had anywhere else to go.

I was sure if I asked Hayden, he'd pack it up and get us out of here right now, but he'd already done enough for me. The least I could do was spend a few hours in a bar, have a few drinks, and maybe, just maybe, be able to relax.

"Skippy! What are you drinking?" Keenan, who stood at the bar, attempted to yell at me over the sea of people.

Christ.

I pushed through the crowd to get to him. "You buying, Kee?" I nudged him in the ribs with my elbow, and he grabbed his side, pretending to be in pain.

"Ouch, first my ribs, then my wallet? You wound me.

What happened to being a strong, independent woman who can buy her own drinks?"

"Two things can be true at once, Chase. I can be a strong woman and still not spend a dime at the bar," I teased. "Besides, you guys cut a nice check tonight."

However, if we wanted to be technical, I also earned a nice check, placing in the top three.

"All right, fair enough. Just for you." Keenan flagged down the bartender. "What are you feeling then?"

"Could I get a vodka soda?" I asked the bartender.

He nodded and spun around, grabbing the bottles of liquor off the shelf to mix the drink.

Hayden appeared at my side. "Hey."

"Hi." I tilted my head to look at him. "Keenan's buying. Better take advantage of it while you can," I teased.

Keenan's head whipped toward me. "Hold on now, woman. I said I'd buy you *one* drink."

"It was worth a shot," I half whispered, half giggled at Hayden. "Maybe if you hurry, he won't notice."

"I heard that, Sierra!" Keenan protested, crossing his arms in mock disapproval.

"Just get me a Coors Banquet. I'll be over there," Hayden whispered in my ear, pointing toward a table near the back where the rest of the group was hanging out.

"Anything else for you?" The bartender slid my drink across the counter.

"Can I also get a Coors Banquet? That'll be it. It'll be on his tab." I tilted my head toward Keenan.

"You got it."

Once I grabbed the drinks, Keenan and I headed back to the table the group was at.

"Here's your beer, good sir," I joked as I handed it to Hayden.

"Why, thank you, milady." He winked before cracking it open and taking a long drink.

"Sierra's back, boys!" Mikey raised up his can of beer. "A toast."

I exchanged a curious glance with Hayden, and he shook his head as if to say, *Just go with it.*

Mikey cleared his throat, lowering his voice so it sounded more official. "Here's to kicking ass here in Pendleton and bringing home the hardware!"

"And here's to having Sierra and Keenan here with us," Ellison added, her gaze floating over the two of us.

"Cheers!" Everyone raised their drinks and clinked them together, a little bit of beer splashing on the table, but all seven pairs of eyes were sparkling and bright.

"How about a game of pool, fellas?" Colter stood, patting the table with one hand. "How are we splitting teams here?"

"Nose goes for whoever has to pair with Mikey," Jake blurted, tapping his finger to his nose.

"Hey! That's not fair!" Mikey protested as he crossed his arms over his chest.

Reid tapped his nose next, and Colter followed.

Jake let out a loud cackle. "Sorry, Hayden, looks like you're stuck with him."

"Think I'll actually sit this one out." He winked at me. "Guess it's all you, Colt."

Reid shrugged. "Suit yourself." The four boys and Ellison moved over to the pool table, leaving me, Hayden, and Keenan at the table.

"Not a big pool guy?" Keenan asked, nudging Hayden with his elbow.

Hayden took a swig of his drink, shaking his head with a smirk on his face. "Not a big fan of constantly losing because of Mikey."

Keenan nodded in understanding, shooting me a wink as he said, "I'm more of a Beerio Kart guy anyway."

Both Hayden and I groaned.

"Is that still a thing?" I grimaced just thinking about that cursed game.

"It can be if you want it to be. By the way, I know you guys cheated that one time we played."

I jutted out my lip. "I have no idea what you're talking about, Kee."

He dipped his chin, shaking his head. "I may have been drunk off my rocker that night, but your face turns beet red when you've drank too much, Skippy. There wasn't an ounce of color in your cheeks that night." A shit-eating grin spread across his features. "At least not from the alcohol."

"Get out of here." Hayden lightly shoved him, rolling his eyes playfully.

Raising his hands, he backed away from the table. "You're right, let me give you two some alone time." He wasn't paying attention, though, and bumped right into a girl, causing her to spill her drink all over him. Right before Hayden and I burst into laughter, I heard him turn on the charm and say, "Hey, how you doin'? Sorry about the drink. Let me get you a new one."

"He hasn't changed a bit." I huffed a laugh. "Think he'll ever settle down?"

After he broke up with his long-term girlfriend in college, it seemed like Keenan had entered his playboy era.

Hayden nodded toward Mikey. "If Mikey can settle down, anything is possible. Even for Keenan."

"I'll toast to that." Grinning, I clinked my glass against his beer.

An hour and a few vodka sodas later, Keenan was on the dance floor with the girl whose drink he spilled, Ellison and the others were still playing pool, and Hayden was at the bar, leaving me alone by our table.

I took a slow sip of my drink, eyes scanning the room like a hawk.

When my eyes flicked back to the bar, a girl was talking to Hayden.

But not just any girl.

Michaela.

Even from a distance, I could tell she was all over him, twirling her hair around her finger and laughing obnoxiously at everything he said.

Maybe it was the alcohol, or maybe it was just bold recklessness, but I marched up to Hayden just as Michaela said some bullshit about how she would have won the last race but her horse was being lazy.

"Hayes." I shot Michaela a side-eyed glance as I snatched the cowboy hat off Hayden's head to place it on mine, like a guard dog protecting her territory.

Apparently, I was the living proof of Mikey's earlier theory about the protective girlfriends in the bunch.

Hayden wasn't mine, but that didn't mean I wanted to watch him with another girl. Especially not one like Michaela.

She may have taken second place in the barrel racing

this week, but she wasn't about to take Hayden as a consolation prize.

She wrinkled her nose, looking me up and down, her eyes catching on my face. "Oh. Sorry, Sierra, I didn't know you were dating someone. I'm kind of surprised. He doesn't seem like your type."

I didn't say anything, just offered her a saccharine smile, the tension finally melting out of my shoulders once she was gone, swallowed up by the crowd of strangers.

Hayden chuckled beside me. "I've always loved the color green on you, Skip, but this is a new one."

I flicked my eyes toward him, fighting the urge to roll them. Whatever jealousy that had come over me was already disappearing. "Here." I took the hat—which was far too big for my head—off, holding it out to him. "You can have this back."

"Nah, keep it. It looks good on you." Hayden's lips quirked up into a grin as a slow country song started playing.

Couples gravitated to the dance floor like a mushy love fest.

Hayden grabbed my hand, pulling me toward the crowd. "Come dance with me."

"Hayes," I started to protest, but he cut me off.

"You don't get to stake your claim on me like that and not give me at least one dance, Sierra. You can claim 'friends don't dance'"—he put it in air quotes—"all you want, but friends also don't do what you did back there."

I drew my lip between my teeth, conceding with a nod. Hayden led me out to the middle of the hardwood, maneuvering between couples swaying back and forth to Lady A's "Dancin' Away With My Heart."

My hand found its place on his shoulder as the other grasped his, our fingers connecting like puzzle pieces. His palm was warm against my waist, but the heat between us wasn't stifling. The opposite, actually. Being in Hayden's arms was comforting. Safe.

My eyes darted around the room as I let him lead, my steps falling perfectly into place with his. My gaze bounced back to him, finding his deep-blue stare already trained on me.

"Funny, it feels like just yesterday we were dancing like this. Coldplay, though, right?" He smirked, and memories flooded my mind.

The high school gymnasium floor was covered in a black tarp, with string lights and a giant disco ball straight out of the seventies hanging from the rafters. Blue tulle and silver stars covered the gym as decorations for the "Starry Night" homecoming dance theme. Students crowded the dance floor and the snack and drinks table as conversational chatter floated around.

A DJ in the corner played school-appropriate pop music that was a little bit boring for my tastes, but what did I know?

I watched as the girls in my class flirted with their boyfriends or the ones they wanted to go out with. I wasn't really friends with them —even Clare and I had drifted apart once I stopped riding the bus. I just didn't have much in common with them. They liked shopping, getting their nails done, and talking about the various boys they had crushes on. They weren't interested in horses or rodeo, and there was only one boy who I liked.

Lilac satin hugged my body, and the applique flowers on the straps of my dress scratched my skin. I resisted the urge to pull the tiny petals off the dress, keeping my hands at my sides instead. The only comfortable part of my outfit was my brown cowboy boots.

I didn't plan on going to the dance at all, much less dressing up, but Mae was so excited. She didn't have a daughter, and with Hayden and I being seniors, this was her one opportunity to play dress-up with me. How could I deny her that?

Mae was more of a mother to me than my own. My mom wouldn't have cared if I wanted to go to a high school dance—be a normal teenager. She would have done whatever my dad wanted, which was to probably not let me go.

Truthfully, I hadn't seen my dad in a while. Maybe he'd skipped town or gotten arrested somewhere. Or better yet, maybe he'd gotten hit by a car.

Fingers tapped on my shoulder, pulling me out of my thoughts.

"Wanna dance?" Hayden asked as I spun around.

"Uh…I don't really know how to," I mumbled, fidgeting with my dress.

He took my hand, leading me out onto the makeshift dance floor. "I'll teach you."

The song hit its crescendo, and he spun me out—all of my daydreams of the past dissipating—then back into his arms.

"What's on your mind?" he murmured into my hair.

"Nothing, really. I'm just trying not to step on your feet or trip," I admitted with a laugh.

He hooked a finger under my chin with a delicate touch. "I've got you, Skip. I won't let you fall, remember?"

Too late for that.

My mind latched onto the lyrics, thinking about how perfectly they described my feelings toward Hayden. All these years, all this time apart, and we still wound up back in each other's lives.

Like planets set to always revolve around each other, forever in the same orbit. They may have been apart for some time, but eventually, even if it was only once in a lifetime, they'd find their way back to each other—find a way to align once again.

I wanted to believe this was mine and Hayden's once-in-a-lifetime chance.

Perhaps he believed it, too.

hayden

I couldn't get the image of Sierra stealing my hat last night at the bar out of my head. The memory flashed through my mind on a loop. I'd never seen her get jealous before—definitely not enough to fall into a Western stereotype—but I would be a lying man if I said I didn't like it.

We were getting back on the road early today, because the weather predicted a thunderstorm rolling in that afternoon.

It appeared that the weatherman was correct for once. Dark, imposing clouds swirled in the distance, and my best guess was that we'd end up driving through the storm regardless of the time we left.

Sierra grumbled as she dragged her duffle bags out of the room toward the elevator. "Remind me again why I brought so much shit?"

I laughed, not wanting to explicitly say, *I told you so*, but still thinking it in my head. "Here, hand me one of your bags."

She tilted her head as if assessing me, then gave a

resigned sigh, dropping one of the heavy-ass duffles. Somehow it felt like they were even heavier than they were when we left Silver Creek.

"Did you go on some secret midnight shopping trip? Or did you collect more rocks while you were here?" I teased.

Sierra kept walking ahead of me, but that didn't stop her from flipping me off and firing back, "I just couldn't help it. The rocks here are *so unique*."

I barked out a laugh and followed behind, throwing the bag over my shoulder.

"Do you think we're going to make it through the storm?" Sierra studied the sky when we got outside, her brows pinching together.

"Hopefully," I replied. "I don't have a lot of hope for missing it entirely, but if we're lucky, we'll be on the edge of this weather, and the rain won't be too heavy."

"Best get on the road then," she murmured, climbing into the passenger seat. "We still have to pick up the horses."

I nodded in agreement, throwing the rest of the stuff in the back of the pickup and rolling out the cover over the bed.

By the time we got the horses loaded and our wheels pointed eastward on the highway, rain was beating down on us, the windshield wipers doing their best to keep up. Puddles accumulated in the middle of the road, water spraying up every time we plowed through one.

Headlights of the cars that met us were blurred by the

torrential downpour, and horns blared as if that was their way of letting us know they were nearby. It didn't quell my anxiety. If anything, it made it worse.

"I think we're going to need to pull over!" My declaration was nearly drowned out by the sound of droplets smacking against the windshield.

"That's probably a good idea," Sierra agreed, worry lines creasing her forehead as I white-knuckled the steering wheel, trying to maintain control of the truck and trailer.

Turning on my hazard lights, I navigated us off the road at the nearest pullout so we weren't camping out on the shoulder in case, God forbid, the worst happened and someone ran off the path and hit us.

My phone screen lit up, and a slew of text messages came through from the group chat.

The Silver Creek Cowboys (And Ellison) (Plus Isa and June)

COLTER

Damn that rain is wild

ELLISON

Everyone okay? Jake and Mikey? Hayden?

MIKEY

thumbs-up emoji

We're alright. We pulled over.

ISA

OMG! not the kind of texts i wanted to get at 10am

JUNE

Hopefully the rain lets up soon. Keep us updated.

"Who was that?" Sierra's gaze fell onto my phone screen.

"Our Silver Creek group chat," I replied, the fact that Sierra wasn't in it dawning on me. "I just realized you're not in it. Let me add you."

"Oh no, that's okay, I don't—" She waved her hand dismissively, but it was too late.

The Silver Creek Cowboys (And Ellison)
(Plus Isa and June)

Hayden added Sierra to the chat.

Hayden changed the chat name to **The Silver Creek Cowboys (And The Girls)**

MIKEY

Whoa whoa whoa who just got added to the chat?

Sierra. I realized she wasn't included

ISA

AH FINALLY

GROUP CHAT OFFICIAL

JAKE

Does this mean what I think it means? 😏

SIERRA

What do you think it means?

Sierra's brows pinched together as she threw me a suspicious look.

JAKE

You know 😏

> No. No one knows what you mean

> But whatever you're thinking, no

MIKEY

Ah, so that's a yes

ELLISON

Do we even want to know?

JUNE

Probably not

"I have no idea what they're talking about," I muttered.

JAKE

I'm just saying, none of the girls were added to the group chat until...you know

He sent a few eggplant emojis.

ELLISON

JACOB

ISA

technically, i was added wayyyyy after that ever happened. like...a year after

REID

I thought we added Ellison because she lives in Silver Creek now

ELLISON

You did

JAKE

Okay well that's not important.

MIKEY

I mean, he's not wrong about the timing either

JAKE

Anyway I saw you take his cowboy hat last night, Sierra

ELLISON

How do you know they didn't get into a fist fight instead?

COLTER

She has a point. Sierra did tell us she dislocated some kid's kneecap in high school

SIERRA

Allegedly

No one got into a fist fight and no one was doing that.

JAKE

Knocking boots?

MIKEY

Doing the hanky panky?

Adding Sierra to the group chat was a mistake.

You know what, this was a mistake

MIKEY

We have her number now, so even if you two leave we're just going to add you back

JAKE

There's no getting rid of us now, Sierra

I smacked my palm against my forehead. "I am so sorry. I should have known, but I didn't think they were going to do *that*."

"They're not going to blow up my phone with notifications, right?" When I didn't confirm, she groaned, putting her head in her hands. "I'm sorry for ever asking who you were talking to." She muted the chat, but my phone continued to light up with notifications.

"It looks like we're going to be stuck here for a while." I sighed as I attempted to look out the window. "This rain doesn't look like it's going to let up anytime soon."

The silence in the cab—apart from the pounding of raindrops—was deafening, a chasm growing between us even though we were two feet apart.

I glanced over at Sierra, my eyes roving over her. "Tell me a truth."

"What?" Her brows knitted together.

"Tell me something true. Like, when I first saw you on the bus the first day of freshman year, I thought you were really pretty, but your eyes were so sad. All I wanted to do was get you to smile," I murmured before adding, "Truth."

"Okay." She looked down for a second like she was thinking. "I tried to avoid everyone when I first started school, but you were impossible to ignore. No matter how hard I tried, something kept pulling me to you."

I nodded, my lips twitching in a very subtle smile. "Taking the fall for you hitting that tree was the best decision I made in my life."

She rolled her eyes. "You didn't have to do that. Your dad was pissed."

"Yeah, but it was worth it because it meant you didn't get in trouble. Clearly, he wasn't that mad because I'm still here. Didn't get grounded for life."

Sierra tapped her nails on the center console. "I don't actually hate that stupid nickname you and Keenan gave me. If anything, I like it more because it's our thing. Truth."

"Keenan makes fun of me because I named my horse

Peanut Butter, but it's special to me because you were there to name her with me."

"I lied when I said I wasn't jealous when I saw you and Michaela talking."

My heart burst in my chest at the confirmation, but I still shot her a cocky smirk, flirting a little. "Oh, I know." I did my best to keep a blank expression as I said my next piece. "Truth, I've been really scared something's going to happen with all of the weird things going on. I worry someone's targeting you. I don't want to be overbearing, but I don't know what I'd do if I lost you again." The last part was hardly a breath off my lips.

She pulled her lip between her teeth. "I blame myself for a lot of things that happened back then. Truth."

"I waited and waited and hoped that you'd come back one day. That maybe it was all a bad dream and I'd have my best friend back… Truth," I whispered. The first time she left was devastating, but the second time… I was convinced the second time killed me, and for five years, I was a ghost—a shell of a person wandering around, searching for the one person that tied me to this world.

My eyes flicked down to her lips as her tongue darted out to wet them, then back up, emerald green staring into ocean blue.

"Skip." The name fell off my lips in a whisper. My hand cupped her cheek, my thumb brushing against the delicate scar tissue under her eye.

She leaned into my palm, gaze softening. Her eyes swept up and down my face, like she wanted this as much as I did.

The world around us seemed to pause, the raindrops and cars speeding by reduced to slow-motion frames.

My heart thrummed in my chest, a plea to close the

distance until the breaths between us were merely a whisper. My eyelids fluttered shut as I leaned in, our noses close enough to touch. The warmth of her breath tickled my skin, and my lips parted as I inched closer, my mouth nearly brushing hers.

My chance was gone in an instant, and reality came crashing back down.

Sierra drew in a sharp breath, and my eyes snapped back open as she sighed. "Hayes, I can't. We can't."

I pulled back, blinking. Thinking maybe I misheard her over the howl of the wind outside.

She turned away—the rift that separated us now miles wide—and her attention shifted to the passenger-side window. "The rain's stopped. W-we should get back on the road."

A pang hit me in the chest, but I swallowed my pride and nodded. I thought she wanted to kiss me as badly as I wanted to kiss her—close the five-year gap that had formed between us—but perhaps I was wrong…again.

We'd been in this situation once before. I knew back then why she hesitated. I just couldn't figure out why she still held back now.

sierra

SUMMER BEFORE JUNIOR YEAR

I smoothed my hands down the front of the flowy blouse Alyssa let me borrow for the concert we were going to tonight. The rose-colored top was so different from anything I had in my closet, with a frilly lace trim at the bottom and a deep V-neck that seemed to draw attention to my small chest in a negative way. I paired it with a pair of dark-blue bootcut jeans and my dark-brown cowboy boots.

Alyssa told me to leave my hair down and maybe put some curls in it. I wondered if Hayden would like it that way—not that I was trying to impress him or anything.

After giving myself a once-over in the mirror, I crept down the stairs. I'd heard my dad leave the house earlier, probably to buy cigarettes or beer at the gas station, but my mom was home, and I didn't want her to ask questions about why I was dressed up so nice to go to a fake shift at the hotel where I was a part-time front desk associate.

I made sure the coast was clear at the bottom of the stairs, but right before I headed out the door, I called out, "I'm leaving, Mom! I'll see you later!"

"Okay," she sighed from the kitchen, her voice gravelly and flat. "See you later."

I'd noticed she'd been acting a bit sluggish lately. Maybe she was just sick or wasn't getting much sleep.

I asked Hayden to pick me up at the hotel, so if either of my parents happened to drive by, my car would be there. He was already waiting when I pulled into the parking lot, a wide smile spreading across his face when I got out of my car.

Instead of letting me get in the passenger side, he rolled down the window. "Hold on, don't move."

I tilted my head to the side. "Why?"

He rolled the window back up, opened his door, and jogged around the front of his pickup to mine. "Okay, now you can get in." He gestured to the passenger seat after he opened the door, holding it for me. "Your carriage awaits."

My cheeks heated as I slid inside the cab. "Thanks."

"You look cute," he said, a bit breathlessly.

"Alyssa let me borrow this shirt." I fidgeted with the hem as I laughed nervously.

He nodded like he recognized the shirt. "Yeah, it looks like something Alyssa would have. It looks good on you, though."

I hoped my face wasn't as red as it felt. "It's a little out of my comfort zone, but she said I needed to dress up for the concert. Then she told me to do my hair like this." Normally it was pulled back into a braid or ponytail. If I kept it down, I kept it straight. Sometimes it had a slight wave because I had a bad habit of sleeping with wet hair, but it was rarely ever curled like it was today.

"I like it. I mean, I like how it looks on every other occasion, too, but yeah. It looks really nice." He stumbled over his words, a pink flush creeping across his cheeks.

"Thanks." Heat rose to my face in what I could only assume was a blush that mirrored his. "We should, uh, probably go?"

"Oh, yeah." Hayden gave me a small grin before putting his pickup in reverse. His right hand found the back of my seat as he turned over his shoulder to look out the rear window, and I swore my heart was beating a hundred times as fast as it normally did.

When we got to the fairgrounds, Alyssa, her boyfriend Dean, Keenan, and the girl he brought with him were already waiting for us.

"Dude, what took you guys so long?" Keenan teased, ruffling Hayden's hair when we got close.

Hayden pushed his hands away and smoothed out his hair. "Nothing, we're not *that* late."

"Uh-huh. Are you sure you two weren't—" Keenan started puckering his lips and mimicking exaggerated kissing noises.

I pretended to gag, gently pushing on his shoulder. "You jealous, Kee?"

"Nah, I've got my own girl." He winked at the redhead with him. "This is Ivy."

"Hi." She raised her hand in a small wave.

"Come on, guys. Let's go in, or else we won't be able to get a good spot!" Alyssa tugged on our arms as she passed by with her boyfriend.

We all followed behind the pair, handing our tickets to the fair employee at the arena entrance. We arrived a little too late to get right up front by the stage, but I didn't really want to be up there anyway. Big crowds made me uneasy because I didn't have a quick exit route. Part of me thought Hayden knew that, so he purposely made us a little late.

He squeezed my hand three times, giving me an understanding glance when we stopped on the edge of the crowd. I squeezed his hand back, a silent gesture of appreciation.

Big spotlights on the stage kicked on, and the strum of a guitar rippled out into the crowd from the speakers.

High-pitched screams and low whoops and hollers rose as the country performer ran on stage.

He urged the crowd on, pulling more cheers from them as he yelled, "Y'all ready for some real country music tonight?"

Hayden wrapped his arms around me, holding my back against his chest as we swayed with the music—a slow song between all the upbeat ones the band had been playing.

I didn't think we'd stopped dancing since the concert started. Keenan was teaching us all kinds of swing dancing moves. Sheens of sweat glistened on the boys' foreheads, and I was grateful for the slower pace, even if it was only temporary.

Keenan had his arm around Ivy, and he flashed a wide smile and a thumbs-up at us. I rolled my eyes but didn't see what Hayden's reaction was. If he had much of a reaction, he didn't show it, keeping his arms around my waist.

"Are you having fun?" he whispered in my ear.

I nodded against his chest, his warmth seeping through to my own body. "Do you think Keenan and that girl are going to start dating?"

Hayden shrugged one shoulder. "Dunno. He seems to

really like her, though. They met at a rodeo in the spring and have been talking since, I guess."

"That's good…" I hesitated for a moment. The question I wanted to ask lingered on my tongue, creating a sort of scratchy feeling. Finally, I spit it out. "Do you think you'll meet a girl at a rodeo? Or in college?"

He tensed behind me then shook his head. "No. I don't think so."

Relief washed over me, then guilt. What if I was holding him back?

"Do you?" he asked, repeating my question.

I shook my head. There was only one person who I could see myself ending up with, even if I knew I could never truly have him.

Through the remainder of the concert, my mind was stuck on Hayden. Imagining a future together.

The band finished their encore, and we said our goodbyes to Keenan, Ivy, Alyssa, and Dean.

Hayden drove us back to my car at the hotel, his hand tapping the steering wheel to Josh Turner the entire time.

When we parked, I turned toward him. "This was fun." My voice came out a bit unsteady, my heart racing in my chest. "I'm glad we went."

"I am too," he agreed.

I offered him a tight-lipped smile, neither of us saying anything as we sat in the dark parking lot of the hotel next to my car.

Hayden cleared his throat, his tongue darting out. "Hey, Skip?"

"Yeah?" My eyes couldn't help but be drawn to his lips, full and soft. I pulled my bottom lip between my teeth.

His hand reached out, grazing my cheek. I leaned my head into his hand, craving the contact. His palm slid to the back of my neck, and he leaned closer, his breath tickling my skin.

Hot breath tickled my skin, and the smell of cheap cigarettes burned my nose.

I pulled back, eyes widening in fear.

"W-what's wrong?" Hayden retreated, his hand falling to his side like I'd burned him.

I turned away, too embarrassed to look him in the face. "We can't. *I* can't."

"Sierra." My name fell off his lips in a soft plea.

"I'm sorry. I-I should go." I retreated from the pickup as fast as I could. "Um…thanks again for driving me, Hayes. I'll see you later."

"Sierra, wait," he started to say, but I'd already closed the door and opened my own, slipping into the driver's seat and turning the key in the ignition.

Stupid, stupid, stupid.

Kissing him would have been a mistake. Kissing him would have crossed a line that I wouldn't have been able to come back from—a line between friendship and something more. Even though it was a line I so desperately wanted to cross, staying friends was the best course of action.

Staying friends was the best way to make sure no one got hurt.

hayden

Nearly two weeks had passed since Sierra and I almost kissed on our drive back from Oregon. We didn't go home, having to simply pass through on our way to North Dakota for another multi-day rodeo.

The week in North Dakota was even less eventful than Pendleton, with zero suspicious activity around our equipment, trailers, and vehicles, giving me the hope I needed that we were in the clear. I didn't have to chase anyone down, and Sierra swept her events.

Luckily, we'd have two weeks before our final rodeo event in Billings, concluding the season until the NFR in December. Two weeks to breathe and hopefully get some well-earned relaxation.

"Morning," I greeted Sierra as she walked out of her room, her hair pulled up into a messy bun and a slouchy T-shirt hanging off her shoulder.

She narrowed her eyes at me. "Why are you so cheery this morning?"

"It looks nice outside. Thought I'd see if you wanted to take Peanut and Lucky out for a ride?"

"Caffeine first," she muttered as she beelined it for the kitchen. Little did she know, I'd already brewed a cup for her—adding all her fixings to it—when I heard her stir in her room, knowing she wasn't much of a morning person. "Did you make this?"

"Yeah." I shrugged. "It's no big deal. I was already making my own, so I made you a cup too."

"It's like boiling hot," she said with a deadpan expression. "What time did you get up?"

"About forty-five minutes ago." I couldn't lie to her, and she was already onto me as it was.

"You made me this cup, this piping cup of coffee, forty-five minutes ago?"

Rolling my eyes, I admitted the truth. "No, I made it when I heard you get up. You can be quite grumpy in the mornings, you know."

Expecting her to fire back with some witty comment, I suppressed a grin, but she just mumbled something that sounded a lot like, "Well, thanks," before grabbing the mug and joining me on the couch.

"Do you have any plans for the day?" I asked, flicking on the TV to a channel that was playing some old Western movie.

She shook her head, taking a small sip of coffee. "Not really, besides going riding now. I think it'd be good for Lucky."

"I thought so, too. And you haven't really had an opportunity to see much of the area, besides that one day we went fishing," I added.

"Is there really that much to see?" she teased, evidently beginning to warm up after getting some caffeine in her system.

"You'd be surprised. It's not Gulch County, but the landscape is pretty, even if it's mostly flatland."

She hummed in acknowledgment, downing the rest of her coffee before getting up to set the mug in the dishwasher.

Looking over her shoulder, she said, "Let me get changed, and then we can head out."

I exercised as much willpower as I could to not watch her hips sway as she disappeared down the hall into her room.

When Sierra reemerged, her hair was tied back into a braid. She still had her oversized T-shirt on, but instead of shorts, she was wearing a pair of Kimes.

"What are you staring at?" She looked down at her shirt then back up. "Do I have coffee on my shirt or something?"

I shook my head, unable to help the smile pulling at my cheeks. "No, you're perfect, Skip."

We got the horses tacked and pointed them toward the hilly area behind the house. Most of the property I lived on was flat, but there was a little bit of variety in the landscape to the east.

"Are you happy here?" Sierra asked as we rode toward the hills east of the house.

"I am," I admitted. "Like I said, it's different from Goldfinch, but it's different in a good way. It's quiet out here. Peaceful. I think…" I paused, turning my head toward her. "I think you'd really grow to love this place if you stayed here."

"Maybe." She gazed out toward the horizon, not making eye contact with me. I could have been wrong, but I thought I noticed her eyes glass over.

"Where do you think you'll go once the season ends?"

She tilted her head to the side. "I'm not sure."

I wasn't sure what I hoped she'd say. Part of me wanted her to stay here with me, but the other part knew that Sierra would go wherever the wind took her. She was independent, fiercely so. She always had been, and I would never hope to tame her or reel her in. I just hoped one day the wind would blow her back to me and she'd realize that she didn't have to carry all her burdens alone.

"Do you ever worry about what happens once you've achieved everything you've wanted?" Her question interrupted my swirling thoughts.

"What do you mean?"

"Is there a limit to what you can do? A limit to dreaming, to hoping?"

An odd sense of calm washed over me, and I shook my head. "I don't think so. I think dreams give us hope, and hope makes us stronger, able to endure difficult things. We'll always encounter challenges. That's just life. It's unpredictable. But having dreams and goals gives us the will to keep going, even when it's hard. Especially when it's hard." My eyes couldn't help but be drawn to her. All I wanted was for her to look back at me, too.

A silence fell over us, save for the hooves clomping against the ground.

"You're right," she finally spoke again, her voice a bit melancholic. "I guess I'm just not sure what's next. If I make it to the NFR, my dream since I was a kid, what's next? What else do I have to look forward to, to work toward?" A humorless laugh escaped her. "I don't know, I'm just rambling. It's stupid. Ignore me."

"What you're saying isn't stupid."

She snapped her head toward me, her emerald gaze holding mine.

"I think it's normal not to have everything figured out. You don't always have to be achieving things either. Maybe your next dream is to just *live*."

From what I knew about Sierra, most of her childhood had been spent just trying to *survive*.

Her teeth gnawed on her bottom lip. "Live." Eyes averting to the ground, she hung her head a little. "Yeah, that sounds like a pretty good dream."

A soft breeze tickled the back of my neck, a flock of birds soaring overhead. But what got my attention was a butterfly with orange wings fluttering on the wind across our field of vision.

"I think the universe agrees." I pointed out the butterfly. "That's a good sign right there, if I've ever seen one."

Sierra's eyes flicked up, and her lips curled into a lopsided smile. "Should we go back?"

I nodded, turning Peanut around. "Wanna race?"

A glint of mischief sparkled in her eyes. "You sure you're up for that challenge?"

"Always." Before she could respond, Peanut and I took off, speeding up into a trot, then a canter.

"Hey!" Sierra yelled behind us. "That's cheating!"

A deep laugh rose from my chest as I looked over my shoulder. "You're one of the best barrel racers in the world. I'm sure you'll catch up!"

When we got back to the house, I immediately hopped in the shower. We weren't outside for very long, but my body still felt like it was covered in grime and sweat.

The hot water rained down on my skin, providing much-needed relief in my aching muscles. Steam circled in the air around me, and I reached for the eucalyptus-scented body wash I'd found at the grocery store, not wanting to touch Sierra's fancy stuff.

I tried not to think about her as I lathered my skin in soap. It had been a long time since I'd been with anyone—five years to be exact—but that didn't mean I didn't torture myself over Sierra on the nights my resolve was weak and her lavender scent filled my nostrils like a phantom sense.

The guys had tried to set me up with girls before and had asked me why I didn't seem interested in women at the bars. The thought of being with someone else—of baring my soul to anyone but Sierra—just hadn't crossed my mind. Plus, during the very seldom times someone managed to get close, it was like my mind was wired to think about Sierra and Sierra alone. That kind of thing isn't fair to anyone, no matter which way you try to frame it.

I wasn't capable of shutting my brain off for the sake of getting laid, even if that meant it was going to be me and my hand for the rest of my life.

After letting the spray wash over me for a few more minutes, I turned off the tap and stepped out of the shower, reaching for my towel on the hook it usually hung on. Except my fingers only grasped the air.

"Shit." I opened the cabinet under the sink, hoping an extra towel was in there, but I came up short. Water dripped down my body, pooling onto the bathmat.

I didn't think Sierra was in the house because I was pretty sure I heard the front door shut before I hopped in the shower. I hadn't heard her bedroom door open or close in the last fifteen minutes at least.

I weighed my options. My phone was charging in my room, so I couldn't send Sierra a text to ask her to grab me a towel. I could yell for her, but it was unlikely she was back in the house, so that wasn't an option either. I could also just run into my room from the bathroom to dry off in there. It would only take a couple seconds since the bathroom was literally two steps away.

That was really my only option, unless I wanted to stand in the bathroom and air dry, which I did not want to do.

For good measure, I pressed my ear against the door. Silent as a mouse. The only noise I could pick up was the hum of the air conditioning and maybe the jingle of Pancho's collar in Sierra's room. She generally left him in there with the door closed when she ran errands, so I assumed he was just scratching his ears.

I took a deep breath, for some reason needing to hype myself up to walk around the corner naked.

This is fine. It's my house, and no one is here right now.

Twisting the door handle, I opened the door.

To my surprise—and hers—Sierra was not actually outside. She was in the house. In the hallway. Directly in front of the bathroom door.

"Oh my God!" she shrieked, covering her eyes with both hands, her cheeks already flaming. "I am *so* sorry!"

As embarrassing as the whole situation was, I didn't

miss the way her eyes flicked down and back up in the millisecond before she realized what was happening.

My hands flew to cover my crotch, water droplets still clinging to my chest and dripping off the ends of my hair. "No, I'm sorry. I thought you were outside. I, uh, didn't have any towels in the bathroom."

She was still covering her eyes as she turned away from me, toward her bedroom. "It's okay. It's your house. You're allowed to walk around naked if you want to." She opened her door, stepping inside while repeatedly muttering, "Oh my God," before slamming the door.

I chuckled a little at her reaction, despite it being a completely valid one. Wanting to tease her a little, I called out, "Nothing you haven't seen before, Skip!" then headed into my own room to grab a damn towel.

I immediately sent her a text once I was safely in my room.

Jokes aside, I really am sorry, Sierra.

Won't happen again.

She sent back a thumbs-up reaction, and I squeezed my eyes in a grimace.

Well, that could have gone ten times better.

CHAPTER THIRTY-ONE

sierra

I waited for five minutes before cracking the door to make sure Hayden was in his room. I didn't know if I could face him after our little run-in in the hallway.

"Nothing you haven't seen before, Skip!" His teasing echoed in my head as I paced the floor. My phone had buzzed with some texts from him apologizing, but how the fuck was one supposed to respond to seeing their childhood best friend turned lover turned stranger turned roommate naked in the hallway?

It wasn't like I could just say, *No big deal. You're right, I have seen it before.*

I mean, I could, but I didn't think that was the appropriate response. So, instead, I did what any normal person would do and reacted to the messages with a thumbs-up.

Okay, maybe that wasn't a great response either, but I panicked.

The coast was clear, so I snuck out of my room, tiptoeing down the hallway. I peeked around the corner to double-check he wasn't in the kitchen or sitting on the couch.

If that was the case, I guess I would be camping out in my room for the foreseeable future. I could always sneak out the window like I was fourteen, but I was all for practicality these days.

The rest of the house was empty, so I slipped on my boots and went outside, making sure to shut the door louder this time so Hayden would hear me leave. Not that he was going to be walking around naked again, but just in case.

I intended to drive into town to grab groceries for the house and run a few other errands, but about a mile down the road, an incessant *tap, tap, tap* against the pavement caught my attention. Turning down my radio, I strained my ears to figure out where the noise was coming from.

It almost sounded like a clicking, a consistent and steady rhythm as the vehicle moved forward. When I slowed down, the clicking also slowed.

I pulled over onto the side of the road to investigate, not wanting to keep going in case something was wrong and the noise wasn't all in my head. After turning on my hazard lights, I carefully hopped out of the pickup, walking around to inspect the body.

I rested my hands on my hips as I pulled my bottom lip between my teeth. Out of the corner of my eye, I noticed one of my tires had deflated. A flat tire shouldn't have caused that noise, but I couldn't drive long distances with a tire in that condition anyway. Luckily, I had a spare in the bed and a tire jack in the backseat. I came prepared for these types of things. As often as I was on the road, I didn't have the time to wait around for a tow truck or roadside assistance if I got stranded. I fended for myself, and I fixed things myself.

My eyes narrowed and brows pinched together when I opened the tailgate only to find that my spare tire was nowhere to be found. In its place was just a half-smoked cigarette, the butt still smoking, with a depiction of a blue camel on the label.

What the fuck?

Panic shot through my chest, my eyes darting around even though I was in the middle of an empty highway.

I squatted down to look at the tire, hoping my suspicions were incorrect.

Sure enough, there was a shiny, silver nail sticking out of my tire. If I hadn't caught it now, it was very possible that my tire could have blown out, leading to an accident.

I'd have to tell Hayden about this, but maybe I could swing it as an accident. I drove over a nail somewhere.

Unlikely.

As I thought more about it, a tingle ran down my spine. Nausea crept into my stomach, and my heart began to pound in my chest.

I only knew one person who smoked Camels.

CHAPTER THIRTY-TWO

OCTOBER, JUNIOR YEAR

The house was uncharacteristically quiet. I sat on the couch watching *Jeopardy!* with Mom while my father smoked a cigarette and read the newspaper.

Mom had asked him once to smoke outside because she knew the smell bothered me, but he told her that he'd do whatever the fuck he wanted in his house then nearly burned her with the end of his cigarette.

Alex Trebek read a question about a classic literature book featuring a character named Atticus. A question I actually knew the answer to because of the book Hayden and I grabbed for Keenan that one day in the library.

"*To Kill a Mockingbird*," I mumbled right before one of the contestants buzzed in and gave the correct answer.

"Good one." Mom smiled. "I wouldn't have gotten that one."

I shrugged. "One of my friends had to write a paper about it for a class."

The sound of glass shattering and a roar of anger from the kitchen startled both of us, prompting Mom to stand as though she was about to check on my father.

I got up slowly—reluctantly—after she did, not wanting to take any steps. Maybe if I didn't move, it would be like I was invisible, and he'd go away.

"What's wrong?" Mom asked, her voice soft. "Are you hurt? What happened?"

Something else—something heavier—crashed in the kitchen. It was loud enough that I was sure neighbors or people walking by the house would hear.

"Spencer?" Mom raised her voice in concern.

"When were you going to tell me that you let our daughter prance around at fucking *rodeos*?" My father came out of the kitchen, holding a newspaper in one hand and a half-smoked cigarette. "Says here: 'Sierra Bayley, Local Cowgirl, Wins High School Barrel Race.'"

"I didn't—" The look that flashed across my mother's face as her head whipped toward me was a mix of betrayal and confusion.

"Look at me when I'm talking to you!" He took a few steps closer to my mom, his hand shooting out like he was going to either grab her face or slap her.

"Hold on a second," Mom begged. "Please don't."

"Explain yourself then!" he screamed in her face. "I sure as hell didn't allow this to happen, so I'd better get some answers. Otherwise, you're not going to like what happens." He reached out again to grab her arm, but I interrupted.

"I signed up for it. I forged the signatures on the paperwork." The desperation in my voice seemed to get his attention as I added, "Mom didn't know."

After stepping away from Mom and crumpling the paper into a ball, he threw it in the trash then approached me. "I can't think of any reason why you'd want to hang around those people. Probably just busy *whoring around* like your sad excuse of a mother!" He was so close. The warmth of his breath tickled my face, and the scent of rancid tobacco hit my nostrils, but I stood my ground, still and unwavering as a statue.

"The only sad excuse of a parent is you," I spat, knowing my actions would have consequences.

"Sierra, don't…" Mom warned against talking back to my father, but her words trailed off into nothingness as he drew back his hand.

I braced myself for the hit, but nothing came. Instead, knuckles rapped against the front door.

"Gulch County Sheriff's Office. Open up!"

My father spun around, stalking over to my mom. "You bitch!" His voice came out in a growl that rivaled the sound of his palm making contact with my mother's face. "What the fuck did you do?"

Mom whimpered, "I didn't do anything," as she pressed her hand against her cheek, the skin already starting to welt.

The knock at the door grew louder and more forceful.

"Sierra," she gasped, eyes wide with terror. "Get the door, please." Rubbing her palm against her cheek, she put a hand on his arm. "Spencer, calm down. We have a visitor."

He made some sort of grunting noise, and my chest burned with disdain for the sorry excuse of a man I called my father.

The two of them disappeared around the corner toward the hallway, presumably so she could get him to calm down so we'd seem like a happy, law-abiding family. I approached the door, plastering on my best fake smile.

"Good evening, officers. How may I help you?" I

sweetly asked the Gulch County Sheriff's Office deputies waiting on the front steps.

"We received a call regarding a possible domestic disturbance at this address. We need to make sure everyone is safe."

"If someone comes to the door, no matter what, you tell them everything is all right, you hear me?"

All I could do was stand there, frozen in my spot.

"You hear me?" He raised his voice, his face mere inches from mine. "You don't say anything that could get me in trouble, or they'll take you away, too. You'll never see your mother again if that happens."

"Y-yes," I squeaked out, squeezing my eyes shut.

"E-everything is f-fine, officer."

His eyes softened, and he lowered his voice, not to intimidate but to soothe. "You're not in trouble. We're here to help. Are your parents home?"

I nodded, lowering my eyes to the floor.

"We need to speak to them, okay? It's important so we can make sure that you and everyone else are safe."

I took a deep breath and stepped aside so the officers could come into the house, then called out, "Mom, there are officers here that need to speak with you and..." I swallowed down the lump in my throat. "Dad." Bile rose in my throat even calling him that.

The officers ended up separating my mother and father from each other quickly. One officer took my mom into the bedroom to talk, while the other took my father outside, going across the street but still in view. The officer who went with my mom told me to stay put in the living room. I didn't know if they'd be talking to me or not, but the thought of being questioned made my chest tighten.

Although the voices in the bedroom were muffled, I could still pick out some of the things they were saying.

"*Can you describe what happened before we arrived?*"

"*Has your husband ever used a weapon against you or threatened you with a weapon?*"

"*Does he have a gun, or can he get one easily?*"

My dad didn't appear to actually be talking with the officer outside. His arms were crossed, and his mouth was set into a hard line instead.

My foot tapped against the floor, hands wringing together.

The officer said I wasn't in trouble, but what if I was?

What if they took me away instead of my dad?

What if I didn't see my friends again?

What if I *did* see my friends after this happened?

What would Hayden think?

A million questions swirled around in my mind, and my head started to spin, everything feeling light and floaty. I ran my tongue across the roof of my mouth, trying to get the tingling sensation to go away, but instead it just felt like I'd swallowed a mouthful of cotton.

Placing my head in my hands, I tried to think of something else, *anything* else. I squeezed my eyes shut, but I couldn't breathe, hiccups rising in my throat every time I tried.

Get it together!

I swallowed the lump in my throat, rubbing my hands against my legs, trying to dry off the sweat before the officer came back.

Breathe.

Blood roared in my ears. My hands trembled on my knees.

I'm dying. That's it.

No.

I focused on my breathing, inhaling for four beats, holding the breath, then exhaling. I repeated this over and over until my heart rate started to slow and the world around me came back into view.

I'm safe. I'm okay. We'll be okay.

After what felt like hours, the officer came out of the bedroom with my mom. He told us to wait while he went outside to talk to the other officer.

"Are you okay?" Mom asked, putting her hand on my knee.

I nodded, even though my hands were still shaking a bit. I was putting on a brave face for her, but deep down I was terrified about what would happen.

"What did you tell the officer?" I asked on a shaky breath.

She didn't make eye contact as she said, "The truth. I told him that we got into an argument."

I wasn't sure I believed her, but when I glanced out the window, the officers were putting my father in handcuffs.

"Mom." I sucked in a breath, pointing outside.

We watched through the windows as the police cruiser drove away with my father. Relief flooded through me at the thought of him spending time in jail, even if he inevitably would get out later.

The feeling didn't last long.

"Sierra, where's your wallet?" Mom whispered, still staring out the window.

"What?" My face contorted, disgust rising in my chest. "Why? Don't tell me you're going to try to bail him out!"

"Someone has to. W-we can't just let him—"

"Yes! Yes, we can!" I couldn't believe what I was hearing. "He deserves to be in jail for what he did!"

She shook her head, as though she was brainwashed by him in some twisted way.

"Mom! You need to leave him! Why won't you leave him?" My heart felt as though there were claws wrapped around it, trying to forcefully tear it out of my body.

"He's your father, Sierra!" My mother didn't sound like my mom anymore. "He's just frustrated."

I fought back the scream threatening to rise from my throat. "He *hurt* you, Mom! What if the next time, it's worse?"

She shook her head, as if in denial. "It won't be."

I blinked back tears, my jaw tense. "You don't know that."

"I'm not having this conversation with you, Sierra. I need to go to the police station to talk to them." As though she didn't quite know where to go or what to do, Mom looked around a few times. Then, like she suddenly snapped out of it, she grabbed her purse and walked out the door.

Nothing happened that night. A no-contact order was placed, so my mom couldn't do anything, but because he was charged with PFMA, he also had to wait until he appeared in front of a judge to have his bail and release conditions set.

But three days later, at his first appearance in court, the judge allowed for my father to be released on bond. The no-contact order was lifted after my mom insisted he be allowed to come home, and he gave an empty promise to attend counseling.

hayden

My hands fidgeted as I waited for Sierra in our usual booth at Ranger's. Ever since her dad got arrested again, it felt like a rift had formed between us.

Since the day I asked her if she was okay and confronted her about avoiding me, it seemed like she'd made even more of an effort to stay away. I tried not to let it bother me, but the truth was it felt like a thousand nails were being driven into my chest with a hammer.

> Here. In our usual booth

SIERRA

> I'm almost there

"Can I get you started with something to drink, Hayden?" Susannah stopped at the table.

"One regular Coke and one cherry Coke, please," I replied. "Sierra should be here soon. Can you add some extra Maraschino cherries for her?"

"Of course, dearie. I'll have those right out for you

kids!" She disappeared into the back, whistling a cheery tune as she went.

The bells on the front door jingled shortly after, and my head snapped up to see if it was Sierra. Unfortunately, it was just Clyde, one of the older gentlemen who always ate lunch here. I should have known. It was eleven forty-five on the dot, and Clyde was always punctual.

I tapped my fingers against the wood-grain table, impatiently waiting for Sierra to show up. She would show up.

"Here's those drinks." Susannah placed the glasses of soda and a couple of straws in front of me. "Should we wait for her to get here, or do you want to put in some food?"

"I'll wait. Thanks, Sues."

After putting my straw in my drink, I flattened the wrapper, folding it up before unfolding and folding it again.

Finally, after another ten agonizing minutes, Sierra walked through the front door.

She huffed out a breath as she sat down. "Sorry I'm late."

"It's okay."

Sierra leaned back on her side of the booth with her shoulders slumped, her eyes heavy with dark circles under them.

"How are you?" I asked a bit cautiously.

"I'm fine." She plunged her straw into her drink, taking a long sip. "Thanks for getting me a drink."

"Sues put extra cherries in there for you."

That put a smile on her face, even if it was small and appeared as though she was trying to suppress it.

"Hey, do you want to come over later? We've been training

Peanut Butter and trying to desensitize her to different things." My shoulders shook with a silent laugh as I thought about the things we'd been using in the training process.

"Oh, I don't know." She wouldn't make eye contact with me, choosing to stare at the ice in her glass instead. "Do your parents really want someone like me to come over?"

"What do you mean? My parents love you, Skip," I offered some words of reassurance, hoping it would ease her concerns.

She grumbled something under her breath, but I couldn't quite pick up what it was.

"Sorry?"

She rolled her eyes, and my heart cracked a little at the words that came from her mouth. "I don't want people to talk about you like they have been talking about me. Hanging out with me would just ruin your reputation. I'm sure your parents don't want you to be spending time with the kid of a criminal."

"What happened to you wasn't your fault," I whispered, reaching across the table to squeeze her hand.

She pulled it away, setting it in her lap. "You don't know that. You have no idea what happened. You weren't there."

I know enough.

"I know *you*, Sierra. You're a good person."

She let out a harsh exhale through her nose. "If I come over, will you stop talking about it?"

I nodded, even though she was the one who brought it up to begin with. I was just eager and willing to do anything it took to have my best friend back. "Of course. We can talk about whatever you want."

"Okay, I can come over for a little bit." Taking a sip of her drink, she made eye contact with me. "I missed you."

My heart lurched in my chest. "I missed you, too, Skip. Keenan and I haven't been the same without you around."

She clicked her tongue. "I'm sure Keenan has been just fine."

"Yeah, he's been hanging out with Ivy a lot more than he's been hanging out with me. I guess I've just not been the same without you."

"Sorry about that," she mumbled.

I shrugged. "It's all good now, right?"

"Yeah. Everything's good now."

"Mom, I'm back! Sierra's with me!" I called out when we walked into the entryway.

Mom rounded the corner to greet us. "Sierra! It's so good to see you, dear."

She reached out to pull Sierra into a hug. Sierra's brows pinched together, the corners of her lips falling, but she wrapped her arms around Mom, welcoming the embrace.

"Do you want some cookies? I just made a fresh batch of the peanut butter ones you love so much." Mom led us around the corner into the kitchen, the sugary-sweet smell of baking permeating through the air.

Sierra and I both slid onto stools at the counter, and Mom passed us the tray of cookies.

"Is Dad outside with the horses?" I asked through a mouthful of cookie.

"Don't talk with your mouth full," Mom chided before answering my question with a nod. "But yes, he's outside."

"We're going to go see what he's doing, right, Sierra?" I wiggled my brows. "I told Sierra that we've been desensitizing Peanut Butter to different things, and it's really funny."

"Okay, well, just make sure you're not in the way."

"We will!" I grabbed Sierra's hand with one of mine and a couple more cookies with the other, then pulled her toward the front door.

Dad was in one of the round pens when we got outside. He had a lead rope around Peanut Butter and was holding it in the hand that didn't have the umbrella.

"What's he doing with that?" Sierra asked, gesturing to the umbrella. "I've never seen anyone do anything like this with a horse. Not even at my grandparents' place."

"He's desensitizing her to 'scary' objects." I put quotes around *scary*. "Yesterday he was out here with a plastic bag."

"That's scary?" She laughed like she didn't quite believe me.

"Yeah, didn't you know? Horses are scared of everything that moves but are also scared of everything that doesn't move." I grinned, heading toward the fence.

"Buttercup's never been scared of anything," she commented.

"Yeah, that's because she's been desensitized to just about anything. She still gets scared, but her reactions are much more contained," I explained. "Watch when my dad opens the umbrella."

Dad stood a few feet away from Peanut, and he slowly opened the umbrella. She spooked a little, jerking her head away, but then calmed. He closed the umbrella and gave her a few encouraging pats. Eventually, as he repeated the motion, she reacted less and less, becoming bored with the object.

"See, he's introducing foreign objects to her and building her confidence. It'll prevent her from spooking or bolting later when she has a rider. The last thing we want is someone getting bucked off because she got scared by her own shadow."

Sierra snorted but leaned forward on the fence, resting her arms on the top panel.

"Hey, you two." Dad must have noticed us watching, and he approached the fence. "What are you doing out here?"

"I wanted to show Sierra what you were doing. The umbrella thing is kinda funny."

Dad chuckled. "Yeah, it's a little silly, but important. How was Ranger's?"

"It was good!" I replied.

Sierra had been quiet since my dad walked over.

If Dad noticed, he didn't say anything, but his eyes flicked down to her face, and his mouth flattened into a subtle frown. It was gone in an instant, though, as his gaze caught on our bare arms. Neither of us put on a coat when we came outside, even though it was starting to get chilly.

"You better get back inside before you catch a cold." He clicked his tongue.

I waved him off. "We're fine, Dad. I never wear a coat in the winter."

Giving me a more stern look, he pointed to the house. "Go."

"I should really be getting home anyway," Sierra mumbled, her boot scraping circles on the hard ground.

"All right," I grumbled, leading her back inside.

I didn't want Sierra to go back to that house. Not tonight, not ever. I wished she could live here with me, with a family who cared about her like mine did.

When we were back in the living room, she grabbed her coat, and I grabbed my keys to drive her back into town.

"Sierra, dear?" Mom stopped her on the way out.

"What's up, Mae?" She looked over her shoulder, a soft smile on her face.

"We're going to have a big Thanksgiving feast. You're more than welcome to join us if you'd like."

Shadows fell over Sierra's face, and sadness crept into her eyes, though it looked like she was trying to mask it. "I'll ask my mom. Thank you for the invite."

My phone buzzed as I was crawling into bed that night.

SIERRA

I talked to my mom about Thanksgiving

And?

SIERRA

She said it wouldn't be a good idea.

We're doing Thanksgiving at home with him

Oh

SIERRA

Yeah, so basically we're going to walk around on eggshells all day and hope he doesn't lash out at us

I can't even pretend like I'm working that night and come over anyway. My boss doesn't let me work holidays and they both know that

I'm so frustrated

I know and I'm sorry. I wish there was something I could do.

SIERRA

I just wish she'd think about me for once and not him

The moment I graduate and turn 18 I'm gone. I'm getting out of here with or without her.

I just hope that nothing happens before then

Do you think something will?

SIERRA

I don't know.

Three little dots appeared then disappeared then appeared again.

SIERRA

Hayden?

Yeah?

SIERRA

You can't tell anyone about this conversation

Please don't tell anyone

My heart felt like it was snapping in my chest. I didn't want to break Sierra's trust by telling my dad about what she said, but at the same time, I couldn't shake the thought of something happening to her if I didn't.

I was supposed to look out for the people I cared about. My dad always said I was a good kid; I was strong, knew right from wrong, and I could help lots of people. I had the power to keep them safe.

But how was I supposed to help Sierra when either option could end in her leaving?

sierra

S top it! Don't touch her!" a frantic voice warned the dark figure in front of me, but I couldn't pinpoint where the sound was coming from.

Was it me?

Was that my voice or someone else's?

Glass shattered around me, and I covered my head, shrinking my body to avoid the spray of broken shards raining down. A spark of pain jolted through me, and my hand shot to my face, warm liquid trickling down my cheeks.

Was I crying?

I closed my eyes, thinking if I sat here silently for long enough, this would all be a bad dream. I'd wake up any moment.

Footsteps disappeared around the corner, and I held my breath as I squeezed my eyes, my cheeks completely wet and stained now.

I didn't know how long I'd been sitting here. Ten or fifteen minutes?

Careful not to press my palms into the glass, I hauled myself to my feet.

A figure lay on the ground near the dining room table, but I stepped over it, determined to reach my intended target.

I reached for the phone, but before I could grab it, a heavy hand fell on my shoulder.

My head whipped around to look over my shoulder, but it was too late. In a swift movement, the dark figure standing behind me thrust a broken piece of glass into my back, and then I was falling...

Falling.

Falling.

Falling...until...

Sweat dripped down the side of my face as I jolted awake, my hand clutching my racing heart. Pancho whined as he paced in circles at the foot of the bed.

I took a deep breath, counting to four as I inhaled. Releasing the breath on another four beats, I repeated the box breathing exercise to calm myself.

"Just a dream, bud. Sorry to scare you." I patted the comforter, trying to calm Pancho down. Unfortunately, just like Lucky, he could pick up on my energy. When I was anxious, he mimicked my emotions, except he was ten times worse.

Instead of settling, Pancho barked, a high-pitched yip that echoed off the walls of my bedroom.

"Shh. I know. It's okay, I'm okay. See?"

Speaking in a soothing voice didn't seem to work, so I got out of bed, tiptoeing over to the door. It creaked as I opened it, and I winced at the sound, like I was fourteen again and sneaking out.

"Do you need to go outside?" I whispered. "Outside" was one of Pancho's buzzwords, so it got his attention right away, and he wagged his tail like he'd completely forgotten about my nightmare.

I walked out to the living room as quietly as I could, but the dog didn't seem to get the memo, practically sprinting down the hallway, his paws making loud thumps against the hardwood floor. I opened the front door, and he bounded out, disappearing around the corner to do his thing. He wouldn't go far, so I left the door slightly ajar and headed into the kitchen to get a glass of water.

Fumbling for a light switch in the kitchen, I accidentally hit the garbage disposal instead of the light above the sink, wincing at the awful grinding sound it made.

"Fuck," I groaned as I hit the correct switch and warm light slowly illuminated the kitchen.

I was in the middle of pouring myself a glass of water when footsteps approached from the hallway. I spun around, glass in hand, to find Hayden leaning against the island counter.

He lifted up a hand in greeting. "Hey. What time is it?" His voice, a bit groggy and raspy from sleep, caught in his throat.

"Two thirty or so. What are you doing?"

He came around the island to stand next to me. "Couldn't sleep. You?"

"Same. Bad dream. I accidentally woke Pancho up"—I gestured to the ajar front door—"and here we are."

As if saying his name summoned him, he poked his nose in the door, opening it so he could waddle back inside.

"Ah. Hey, buddy, did you protect Mom from her nightmare?" He scratched behind Pancho's ears, and the dog's tongue lolled out of his mouth happily.

I rolled my lips between my teeth, trying to ignore the flutter in my stomach at Hayden calling me Pancho's mom. I shouldn't have had that reaction. I didn't even know if I wanted kids. In my mind, there was too great a probability they'd end up like me—or I'd make them that way because the apple never falls far from the tree—but, then again, with Hayden as a dad, they had a sliver of a chance to turn out okay.

God, what the fuck was I thinking? Why couldn't I get the image of Hayden cradling a baby, cooing and whispering to it, out of my head? Why was the image there in the first place?

Shaking the thought from my head, I took a long gulp of water before placing the glass on the countertop.

"I should…" I mumbled with the intention of going back to my room, even if it meant I'd lie awake staring at the ceiling for hours.

"Wait." Hayden placed his hand on my arm in a featherlight hold that still somehow kept me rooted in place.

"Hm?"

"Do you want to go somewhere?" he asked, eyes darting to the floor.

My eyebrows pinched together. "Go somewhere?"

"Yeah. Go on a drive. I-I just know you, and maybe driving will help clear your head. I remember in high school you'd tell me that you were never able to get back to sleep after bad dreams and…" He didn't finish his sentence before backtracking. "Never mind, that was stupid. It's like the middle of the night."

Against my better judgment, I placed a hand over his. "A drive sounds nice."

His eyes—deep pools of blue—widened in disbelief.

If his eyes were the ocean, then Hayden was a siren song, drawing me in until I drowned in them, giving up every piece of my soul.

He walked to the front door. "You coming?" He looked over his shoulder, keys jingling in his hand.

"Yeah. Pancho, bed." Listening to the command, my dog padded back to my bedroom—albeit reluctantly and with his tail between his legs. He loved car rides, but he didn't need to come on this one.

Goosebumps immediately covered my arms when we stepped outside. There wasn't any wind, but the air was cold against my skin, and I wrapped my arms around myself.

"Do you want to go grab a jacket?" Hayden asked. He was smart and had a hoodie on already. The guy slept in them, though, and I didn't understand how he was never roasting.

I shook my head. "No, I'm good." Mostly stubborn, but if I went back inside the house, I probably wouldn't want to leave again.

"All right." He didn't sound like he believed me, and I didn't exactly blame him for that. It was only a matter of time before my teeth started to chatter and my body began to shake.

He cranked up the heat in the cab after starting it, but his pickup was old and took a while to warm up. It had been a few minutes since we left the driveway, and I could still see my breath in front of me.

I clenched my jaw so he wouldn't hear my teeth rattle, but he must have noticed my discomfort because he unbuckled his seatbelt and pulled off his hoodie. "Here."

"I don't want it," I bit out through a shiver. "You're going to get cold."

"Sierra, you're literally shivering. Take it." He thrust the army-green sweatshirt into my hands, the scent of his laundry detergent mixing with something woodsy.

"Fine," I grumbled, wiggling my arms into the sleeves. Before I pulled it completely over my head, I inhaled deeply, breathing in the aroma that was pure Hayden. Comfort fell over me like a warm embrace, and a calm sensation settled in my chest.

"Better?" His voice, so low it was almost a rasp, broke me out of the trance he'd put me in.

I ran my teeth over my bottom lip before nodding. "Yeah. Better." In an attempt to drown out my teeth still clanking together, I reached for the volume dial on the radio to turn it up.

"She Used to Be Mine" by Brooks & Dunn filtered through the speakers, and part of me regretted turning on music as my gaze flicked to Hayden's hands tensing on the steering wheel.

"What was your dream about?" Hayden's question came out soft—cautious. When I hesitated, he added, "You don't have to tell me if you don't want to. I don't want to pry."

"No, it's okay. Um. It was about that night." My gaze shifted to the floorboards. I hadn't told anyone about what happened nine years ago. Not Hayden, and not even the therapist the court recommended I see. That relationship didn't last very long, and it wasn't the therapist's fault, at least I didn't think it was.

sierra

EIGHT YEARS AGO

Stark white walls with watercolor paintings of mountains hanging on them greeted me as I stepped inside my new therapist's building. I'd never gone to therapy before, but the court had recommended it for both me and Mom.

A fragrance oil diffuser on a small coffee table dispersed a subtle aroma of chamomile, and an oscillating fan whirred in the corner. I awkwardly sat in a cream-colored chair in the corner, away from the other people who were waiting in the lobby.

I tapped my foot lightly against the wood-grain floor, picking at the skin underneath my nails as the lobby slowly started to dwindle in numbers. Some passed through to leave, while others walked down the hallways to their sessions.

"Sierra?" a kind voice called out my name.

I stood, glancing in the direction of the woman standing in the hallway.

"We'll be down this way." She waved me toward her, and I followed her down the hall and around a corner to a small office.

The space was cozy and welcoming. To the right of the door was a large bookshelf. Against the back wall, a leather, espresso-colored sofa with fluffy pillows was placed across from a blue armchair, each equipped with a small side table and a box of tissues. Natural light filtered in from the vermillion curtains covering a large picture window on the wall across from the door. A poster that read, *Things to Release*, with a bunch of balloons with writing in them hung on the wall, and the opposite corner of the couch housed a small desk.

"Have a seat." My therapist—a woman with dark auburn hair pulled back into a ponytail—gestured to the couch. "Make yourself comfortable. My name's Elena."

"Hi, Elena." I forced a small, pathetic smile as I sat on the couch, sinking into the leather cushion. At least it was comfortable.

The first couple sessions were easy, or at least they felt relatively easy. The way Elena had described it was that the first month or even two months were to get to know me as a person and earn my trust. At least, that was the way she put it. She wanted to earn my trust.

"I'll let you steer most of the conversations we have. I don't want to pretend that I know your life better than you do, because frankly, I don't. You're the expert when it comes to your life and your experiences. There may be times that I'll want to backtrack if we seem to be going off course, but for the most part, I want you to know you have the power in our sessions. I'm here to help guide the conversation and give you a safe space to talk."

It wasn't until a few sessions in that our conversations started to get deeper and more uncomfortable. Not in an inappropriate way, but in a way that I wasn't sure I was ready for.

"Tell me more about your relationship with Hayden." Elena didn't hesitate to get into the nitty-gritty after asking how I'd been.

"He…" My voice trailed off, because how was I supposed to describe Hayden and what he meant to me in the confines of just an hour? Less than, really, because of the time it took to talk about my week. "He was my best friend."

"I noticed you spoke about him in the past tense. Are you two not in contact anymore?"

"Not really. It's no fault of his own, I just…" I pursed my lips, my eyes darting to the floor as my brows pinched together. "I don't know."

"What are you feeling at this moment?"

"I'm not sure, guilty, maybe?"

"Why do you think that emotion is coming up for you? Walk me through what you're thinking and feeling right now."

"I guess I just feel bad because I could reach out to him. I still have his number saved. But I'm afraid?"

"You're afraid."

"I guess I'm scared that he'll be mad at me that I haven't reached out."

"So what if he's mad?" The question didn't come out accusatory; it was more like she was genuinely curious why that would matter.

"I don't want to disappoint him."

"Okay, and if he's disappointed?" She raised her brows.

I huffed out a breath, frustration starting to bubble up. "I don't know."

Elena tapped her lips a couple times before her face seemed to light up with an idea. "Have you ever heard of the wheel of emotions before?"

I shook my head.

She got up to grab something circular from the bookshelf. When she sat back down, she flipped over the circle. The wheel was broken up into six different sections, all of them in a different color. In each section, there were three tiers listing different emotions.

"Let's look at it this way." She handed me the wheel. "You said you feel afraid, right?"

I nodded.

"I want you to take a look at the wheel and the other emotions that can be attached to fear."

My eyes scanned the wheel of emotions. Fear was attached to many things—confusion, helplessness, anxiety —and they all stemmed deeper into other emotions like feeling weak and insignificant.

"I'll give you a moment to sit with that. But if you can identify it, what emotion do you think is attached to this fear? If you disappoint him or make him mad at you, what fear does that bring up inside you?"

"Um…" I cleared my throat, swallowing the lump that had lodged itself there. "I guess I'm scared he'll see me as weak or insignificant and then he'll leave. If he knows what happened, he won't want to be my friend or talk to me anymore." Tears burned behind my eyes, and I cleared my throat again. "I'll lose the one friend I have, even though it's stupid because I might lose him either way."

"Yeah," Elena said softly, reaching out to hand me a box of tissues.

"I'm okay." I wiped my eyes, trying to hold back the tears and be stronger than this.

"It's okay, Sierra. It's okay to cry. It's okay to feel. Close your eyes for me, yeah?"

I did as she asked, closing my eyes.

"I want you to take a deep breath. As you're inhaling, I want you to imagine the space where you're feeling these emotions expanding and then constricting as you exhale. Visualize it as a balloon expanding and deflating if you can, and take a few slow breaths with me."

Tears rolled down my cheeks as I breathed in and out until my chest stopped heaving and the tears eventually stopped falling.

"How does that feel?"

I opened my eyes. "Good."

"Good. I think we made some really good progress today, Sierra. We're almost out of time, so is there anything else you'd like to talk about before we wrap up?"

I shook my head, and we said our goodbyes.

I never went back to see Elena.

CHAPTER THIRTY-SIX

PRESENT DAY

Sierra disappeared into her head after I asked what her dream was about. I wasn't sure where she went, but I didn't think she realized tears were streaming down her cheeks until she sniffled a little.

"Oh, God, I'm sorry." She scrunched her face in a pained grimace, embarrassment radiating off her in waves. As if I hadn't cried in front of her plenty of times.

"Hey. It's okay, Sierra." I reached out to swipe away a stray tear, my finger lingering at the scar tissue on the apple of her cheek. "It's okay to cry."

"No. No it's not." She forced the words out through gritted teeth. "It's not, because it's all my fault."

I pulled over on the side of the road, because I wanted to give her the attention she deserved and I couldn't do that from behind the wheel.

I put the truck in park before opening my door and hopping out, ignoring Sierra's, "What are you doing?" to run over to her side.

Flinging open the door to a wide-eyed look, I murmured, "Come here," and opened my arms for her.

She unbuckled her seatbelt, wrapping her arms around me after turning so her legs were hanging out of the pickup. I stepped closer to her, nudging her legs apart so I was standing between her knees.

Sierra rested her head on my shoulder as I reached up to pet her hair. Hot tears dripped from her cheeks onto my shirt as I stroked my fingers through her dark strands, doing my best to soothe the ache I knew she was feeling in her heart.

"It's okay, I've got you."

"I'm sorry." Her chest heaved as she choked out another sob. "I didn't want you to decide to leave."

I wasn't sure what she meant, but I still did my best to reassure her. "I'm not going anywhere, Skip. I promise you. I'm right here."

She shook her head wildly, mumbling, "No. No. No," over and over again.

I cradled her head as I whispered into her hair. "I'm not going to leave you, Skip."

No one was around at this hour, so it was just us sitting on the side of an empty, dark highway with only the light of the cab and the moon and stars overhead. I didn't know how much time had passed, but by the time she let go of me and pulled away, my shirt was soaked with teardrops.

"W-we should go back," she whispered. "It's getting late."

"Are you sure?" I dropped my hands to the sides of her thighs, splaying my fingers out in a gentle hold. "We don't have to go back yet if you're not ready. We can stay here longer."

She turned away, forcing my hands to fall off her legs as she swung them into the cab. "Yeah, I'm sure. We should go."

A small hint of rejection settled in my bones, and I wondered if I did something wrong, said the wrong thing, but I pushed it away.

It's not because of you. It's just late.

We drove back to the house in silence. It wasn't until I pulled into the driveway, and the porch light on the house illuminated the inside of the pickup, that I realized she'd fallen asleep. Soft snores rose into the cab after I killed the ignition. After walking over to her side of the truck, I gently removed her seatbelt and lifted her into my arms, being as careful as I could not to wake her.

"Mmmm," she moaned as she snuggled her head into the gap between my neck and shoulder.

I managed to get inside the house without waking her up and padded down the hall to her bedroom. Pancho was asleep on the floor, and I stepped around him, laying Sierra under the white sheets and lilac comforter, pulling the covers up to her shoulders.

My body moved on its own accord, and before I could stop myself, my lips pressed against her cool forehead. She shifted a little but didn't wake up, her lips twitching up into a soft smile.

"Sweet dreams, Skip," I whispered as I backed away from the bed, out of the room, and closed her door with a quiet click before retiring to my own bed alone.

The next morning, I couldn't stop thinking about what Sierra said in the car. What did she mean by it was all her fault?

I didn't think anyone—least of all me—faulted her for what happened to her as a kid. She was just that, *a kid*.

She was still sleeping when I got up around nine o'clock, having not gotten much sleep after we returned to the house.

I made a quick breakfast of eggs, bacon, and a toasted bagel before scribbling out a note and leaving it on the counter for Sierra when she woke up.

> *Heading to Jake's for a bit. There's breakfast in the fridge if you want it.*
> *-Hayes*

It was a peaceful morning—a stark contrast to only a few hours ago. The sun beamed down on the earth through the clouds, creating dapples of light on the prairie. Birds sang, despite it being October, and the weather starting to cool down. Part of me wished I'd woken Sierra up so she could see this. So she could know that even after the darkest nights, the sun still rose.

I pulled into Jake's driveway, taking in the guest house he'd been working on. They'd made a lot of progress already. He had contractors come in and work on the house while we were on the road, so the roofing and siding were already finished. I assumed the next step was electrical and plumbing, then insulation and drywall. But Jake was right. I thought by the time spring rolled around, he'd have a nice little house here.

A tapping on my window got my attention.

"What's up, Hayden?" Jake's brows furrowed. "Everything all right?"

After killing the engine, I hopped out of the pickup.

"Yeah, everything's good. I just thought I'd swing by to see how the house is coming along. Feels like I haven't been out here in forever."

"You haven't," he pointed out as we started walking toward the house. "But that's okay. I'm really happy with the progress we've made."

"What do you plan to do with the house once it's finished?" I'd always kind of wondered what Jake needed a guest house for. He wasn't close with his family, and the rental market in Silver Creek wasn't exactly booming.

He shrugged. "I dunno. Rent it out as an Airbnb or something."

"To who?" I laughed.

"There's always people passing through looking for places to stay. Market it the right way, and it'll be fine. I can see the description now." He waved his hand in front of his face as though imagining something. "Quaint guest house on a Montana ranch. A quiet sanctuary to find solace. Eh? Eh?"

I snorted. "Let me know how that goes."

"What's the real reason you came over here?" He raised his brows at me.

My shoulders drooped as I released a sigh. "Sierra said something last night that I haven't been able to get past."

Jake tilted his head and flashed his palm in a request to continue. "Care to elaborate?"

"She had a nightmare, and I knew she wouldn't be able to fall back asleep without something to distract her, so I suggested we go on a drive. I was stupid and asked her what her dream was about, and she disappeared into her head for a bit. When she came back to me, she was crying. I told her it was okay to cry and she said it's not because it was all her fault," I explained as quickly as possible, leaving out the part about the sweatshirt and the song and everything else about last night.

"What was her fault?"

"That's what I'm confused about. I have no idea."

Jake looked like he was debating what to say, ultimately swallowing and biting the bullet. "What exactly happened with you two?"

I blew a raspberry. "Depends on how much time you have."

"As much time as you need, brother. If it makes it easier, you can help me do some work on the house."

"Ah, so you're hoping to get some free labor out of me, is that it?" I teased.

He rolled his eyes. "Forget I mentioned it. But you've never talked about Sierra before. Something had to have happened."

So, we were really doing this.

"Sierra and I were best friends. She moved to Goldfinch our freshman year of high school, and she was…shy."

"Really?" His eyes widened as he interrupted me.

"Guarded is maybe a better word for it. But she opened up as we grew older, and I…" My eyes shifted to the ground as I kicked around the dirt with my boot. "I loved her. I still love her, but things happened and it's not my place to say, but she's gone through a lot of pain in her life. I wouldn't wish what happened to her on my worst enemy. Anyway, I didn't see her for two years after I graduated high school. We reconnected while I was in college, but right when I thought maybe she was back, that maybe the girl I loved hadn't disappeared, she was gone without a word."

Jake blew out a puff of breath. "Damn, dude."

Scrubbing my hand across my chin, I nodded, lips drawn into a thin line. "Yeah."

"Have you told her how you feel?"

My hand moved up to my forehead, and I rubbed the skin above my eyebrows as I shook my head. "When she first moved in, she told me she wanted to start over. To be friends. I don't want to ruin whatever it is we have. Not when I have her back again. I-I don't want to lose her again. I can't lose her again."

"I'm not sure I'm the right person to be asking for advice." He forced out a laugh. "But I really think you're going to have to tell her how you feel. Imagine you don't and once she gets her trailer situation figured out she does leave. Are you comfortable with the idea of watching her fall in love with someone else? Are you willing to watch her move on, and are you going to be able to move on too?"

Fuck.

"That's probably one of the smartest things you've ever said to me. I kinda hate it." I laughed, but there was no humor in it. "I don't want to move on. I don't want *her* to move on. She's my one and only love, I'm sure of it. And I want to be hers, too. I just don't know how to say it."

He didn't offer me any more advice, having said what he needed to say, but he patted me on the back anyway. "I'm sure you'll figure it out. You always do."

On my drive home, after I put down the sun visor, the corner of a piece of paper or something of the like sticking out from under the mirror cover caught my eye.

I pulled on the corner and a polaroid photo—one I'd completely forgotten about—of me, Sierra, and Keenan before our senior year homecoming dance fell out. Keenan had his tongue out and was putting bunny ears behind my head. Sierra was holding up a peace sign with pouted lips, and I was looking at her like she was the only star in my sky.

hayden

I straightened my tie in the bathroom mirror upstairs as Keenan and I got ready for the Goldfinch homecoming dance.

I'd awkwardly asked Sierra if she wanted to go to the dance with me, but she gave me the same nonchalant answer as always.

"I'm not really a school dance person."

"Have you ever been to one before?"

She shrugged. "No, but you don't really want to go with me, do you? I'm sure there are plenty of other girls you could ask."

I could tell she was trying to play it off like she didn't care, but I noticed the way she stiffened as she waited for my response.

It took some persuasion from my mom, but she eventually convinced her to come.

Sometimes I worried that my feelings for Sierra were one-sided, but her body language told a different story. I didn't miss the way her cheeks would flush and her tongue would get all tied up when she was around me.

While Keenan was his usual self and went for the flashiest outfit possible, a hot-pink suit jacket and matching pants with black dress shoes, I went the more classic route with a black button-up, black dress pants, and a light-purple tie to match Sierra's dress.

"Come on, Keenan, your hair looks fine." I tugged on Keenan's arm as he raked his gel-covered fingers through his hair one more time.

When we walked down the staircase, I caught a glimpse of her in the living room, and my jaw practically hit the floor.

Her dress, a satiny-looking fabric, fell just above her knees, and her blonde hair cascaded down her back in loose curls.

"Wow." I blinked a few times before moving to stand next to her.

Keenan joined us before I could get another word out. "Damn, Skippy, you sure clean up nice."

Sierra rolled her eyes, crossing her arms over her chest. "Thanks."

"You look amazing," I breathed out. Words failed me in the moment, and I hoped she realized how breathtaking she truly looked.

"Thanks. Your mom did a good job." She let out a soft laugh as she spun in a slow circle.

"She had a perfect canvas to work with," I whispered, quiet enough that I wasn't sure she heard me, but the ghost of a smile flicking across her face said otherwise.

Mom entered the living room from the kitchen, holding a camera in her hands.

"Mom," I groaned, drawing out the word.

"Oh, shush, Hayden. Just a couple photos!"

It was never just *a couple photos* with my mom. Mae Watkins loved to capture every single moment, big or small.

"Come on, you three, get close. Act like you like each other!" She winked as she held up the camera, not waiting for us to squish together before snapping photos. She justified them as "candid."

Sierra was sandwiched in between me and Keenan, both of us having our arms around her shoulders. The camera shutter clicked as we looked at each other, making goofy faces before bursting into laughter.

"How cute! Hayden and Sierra, just you two now," Mom directed us.

"Does that mean I can get a picture with you, Mrs. Watkins?" Keenan teased, but I shot him a death glare.

If he started making MILF jokes, I'd beat his ass in the high school parking lot later. It wasn't my fault he didn't have a date to the dance because he and Ivy broke up. But, unfortunately, that didn't stop him from making the joke about taking my mom.

Sierra snickered at us, and my mom just shook her head with amusement.

Mom took a few more pictures of us, but right as we were about to head out the door, she handed Sierra a gift bag.

"What's this?" she asked, raising an eyebrow.

"Open it," Mom urged.

Sierra carefully took out the tissue paper, revealing a small, purple Polaroid camera. "Mae, you didn't have to get me something!"

"Now you can capture all these memories for yourself, dear. And you can take them with you everywhere you go, so you'll always have something to remind you of the people who love you."

To my surprise—and my mom's—Sierra wrapped her up in a big bear hug.

"Thank you so much, Mae. I love it."

Mom squeezed her back, and I swore I saw her eyes welling up with emotions. "Always, my dear."

"Come here, guys!" Sierra waved us over to take a selfie with her new camera.

Keenan threw his arm up behind my head, but I wasn't sure what he was doing. Sierra pouted her lips and threw up a peace sign after she told us to smile at the camera.

I didn't have time to react. The camera was flashing before I could even look at the lens; my eyes were locked on Sierra the whole time.

The first half of the dance had gone by fast, the DJ playing a bunch of upbeat songs and line dances to get kids out on the floor. Keenan was flirting with some girls, so I went to grab a couple glasses of punch and maybe a snack for me and Sierra.

However, when I turned around to walk back, she was standing out on the edge of the dance floor alone as people began to couple up. I wasn't sure what she was thinking, so I put the cups down and walked up behind her, tapping her on the shoulder.

She spun around to face me, blonde curls flying over her shoulder in the process. She looked as though she was trying to suppress her smile when she realized it was me.

"Wanna dance?" I asked as the opening chords of "Sparks" by Coldplay started to play over the speakers.

"Uh…I don't really know how to," she mumbled, fidgeting with her dress.

I took her hand, wrapping my fingers around hers,

leading Sierra out onto the makeshift dance floor. "I'll teach you."

Placing her hand on my shoulder, I rested mine on her back, our joined hands extended out.

"Follow my steps," I murmured. "You'll step backward with your left foot, backward with your right foot, then join them together. Then you'll do the same steps but forward. It's like moving in a box."

The song wasn't a traditional waltz, but my mom had taught me the steps as a little kid, dancing in the kitchen. She showed me how to two-step, swing dance, and waltz. Just like cooking, she'd informed me it'd come in handy one day, and as always, she was right.

Sierra's eyes flicked down to our feet as she watched our steps. It was like she was scared to mess up or step on my feet.

I took my hand off her back, using a finger to lift her chin. "Hey. Eyes up here."

Her pupils dilated, and her mouth gaped slightly, but no words came out.

"Trust me. I've got you, Skip. I won't let you fall."

Her cheeks flushed pink and her skin heated, but she did as I asked, keeping her eyes trained on me as we spun around the dance floor in time to the slow rhythm.

"See, you're getting the hang of it," I encouraged as I spun her out.

She giggled as I pulled her back in. "I have a really good teacher."

Sierra rested her head on my chest as the song ended, neither of us making any moves to pull away or step off the dance floor.

I was convinced Sierra had stolen a piece of my heart that night, and I didn't even want it back.

sierra

We were back in Billings for our final rodeo before the season ended. The final world standings, and the list of athletes who would make it to the NFR, would be announced in mid-October. I could practically feel the energy crackling in the arena, and my own body buzzed with emotions. Whether it was nervous energy or excitement, I wasn't sure. The last time I checked, I was sitting fourteenth in the world standings. This weekend could make or break my chances at making the NFR, so I didn't think anyone would blame me for being nervous.

However, under the surface, I also knew my nerves stemmed from something else. After finding the nail in my tire, I told Hayden it was just an accident, that I must have driven over something, but I could tell he didn't believe me.

Despite my denial, I told myself that I wouldn't let my guard down anymore. I wouldn't let fear stop me from performing my best, but I'd also be watching my back.

A hand pressed down on my shoulder, and I flinched, my heart jumping out of my chest.

"Whoa there, Skippy. You good?"

I released a sharp breath as Keenan squeezed my shoulder. "Yeah, sorry. Just a little on edge today."

"Nervous?"

I shrugged. "I guess. There's a lot at stake here."

He nodded. "Makes sense. I don't think you've got anything to worry about, though. You're one of the best barrel racers I know."

"Thanks." After gazing around the area behind the chutes, I asked, "Where's Hayden?"

Keenan tapped his lips as his head swiveled around. "Not sure. I thought he was behind me, but he must have gotten hung up talking to someone. I know his buddies, Colter and Reid, were close by."

"Ah."

"So, how are you two doing?"

My brows knitted together. "What do you mean?"

"I dunno. You two are living together, working together, and traveling together. Seems like ideal conditions for a lot of feelings to come up."

"We're just friends," I said flatly.

"Keep telling yourself that, Skippy." He patted me on the head like a puppy, and my lips drooped into a frown as I smacked his hand away. "You two were never meant to be *just friends*. That was evident from the start."

"What are you guys doing?" Hayden crossed his arms over his chest as he approached us, an amused expression plastered on his face.

"He's being annoying." I rolled my eyes as Keenan threw his arm around my shoulder. "Don't touch my hair again. My head is not for patting."

His hand hovered over the top of my head, but he lowered it at my warning.

"Come on, Skippy, you're no fun." Keenan leaned in, whispering, "Don't forget what I said. You guys? End game," before he stretched out his arms and yawned. "Let's get this show on the road, shall we? When's this rodeo gonna start?"

Hayden and I both rolled our eyes and shook our heads, but we still followed Keenan just as the rodeo announcer started speaking.

The jumbotron displayed a zoomed-in image of Hayden and Keenan as they set themselves up in the roping boxes. The steer was already in the chute, and eighties rock music played in the background.

"Let these cowboys hear you, folks. They hail from our great state of Montana, from two little towns called Goldfinch and Silver Creek if you've heard of them." The announcer rattled off some stats and then cried out, "And there they go, folks!"

Hayden and Peanut shot out of the roping box like a bolt of lightning. He swung his rope over his head, his gaze trained on the steer in front of him. In perfect timing, he threw the rope, the loop landing over the steer's horns.

Pulling the slack out of the rope, Hayden dallied as Peanut turned the corner. Keenan followed closely behind, his own rope flying through the air to catch the steer's hind legs.

"Give 'em five-point-four seconds! Things are starting to heat up here in Billings, and we're not done yet!"

I watched as Hayden led the steer out of the arena

then met up with Keenan on the fenceline to ride their way out as the next roping pair got ready to rope.

"Nice run, boys." I congratulated them as they passed by on horseback.

"Don't let us down, Skippy. Bring us home some hardware tonight." Keenan winked.

"Plan on it." I grinned, offering him a mock salute.

The next few events flew by in a blur, and before I knew it barrel racing was on deck.

"Sierra," a high-pitched voice muttered my name behind me.

Spinning around, I came face-to-face with Michaela.

"Michaela." I looked her up and down.

"Good luck tonight," she said, but I knew it wasn't sincere because of the jeering tone to her words coupled with the mocking grin on her face.

"I don't need it, but thanks," I retorted, pushing past her to get to Lucky. We were near the end of the lineup for barrel racing, so I had a little bit of time to catch my bearings. I wasn't going to let her intimidate me or throw me off. I had a race to win.

"For all of you rodeo fans watching tonight, we've got a real treat in this next cowgirl. She's been making waves all season long. Racing on her horse, Ace's Lucky Charm, we've got Sierra Bayley!" The announcer called out my name as I led Lucky into the alleyway, keeping him as calm as possible. I'd taken several deep breaths to slow my heart rate, and I was locked in.

Hooves pounded the dirt as Lucky raced down the alleyway toward the first barrel. I gritted my teeth as we cut around it, getting a little too close for comfort. I almost clipped it with my foot but was able to brush by without knocking it over. That was the last thing that I needed to happen in such a high-stakes race.

We adjusted well as we turned around the second barrel, dust flying in the air in a hazy cloud around us.

"Come on, come on, come on," I urged Lucky on. The last barrel was right in my sights, and then we'd be home free.

"Help her on home, folks!" The announcer's voice rang in my ears as we made it around the last barrel without a hitch, and Lucky took off into a gallop at top speed back toward the time barrier and alleyway.

My hair blew back behind me, the little tendrils that had fallen out of my brain whipping me in the face, but I wouldn't slow down, wouldn't waver.

Victory was so close, I could practically taste it.

"Fourteen-point-two-seven for Sierra Bayley and Ace's Lucky Charm! Now that's how it's done. Atta cowgirl!"

I glanced up at the jumbotron, relief rushing over me. The camera panned over my face, and I flashed a smile as we exited the arena and headed over to do an interview.

"So, Sierra. How are you feeling heading into the end of the season?" the reporter asked.

I took a deep breath, plastering my most convincing smile on my face. "Great. We're sitting in a good position in the world standings. Anything can happen, but I'm hopeful that we'll be headed to Vegas this year."

"Wonderful! What about the competition here tonight? Do you have anything to say about them?"

She was goading me; I could tell. But I would stay professional and not give her any ammunition to start drama.

"There are some incredible barrel racers out there

tonight. Whatever happens, any one of us deserves a spot in the top fifteen. Thank you."

With that, I took Lucky to one of the temporary stalls to get his equipment off and decompress from the day.

An unsettling tingle crept up my spine as I walked through the concourse of the arena after the rodeo had wrapped up. Somewhere in the last thirty minutes, I'd lost Hayden, Keenan, and the rest of the group. They weren't out by the trailers when I went out there to load up Lucky, so I came back inside to try to find them.

My eyes flicked to the right and then to the left as I passed by closed-up concession stands, but there was no one around.

I didn't want to turn around in fear that someone *was* following me, but curiosity won out, and I stopped, looking over my shoulder.

There was no one there, but the feeling that I was being watched lingered.

"Michaela?" I threw out her name, hoping it was just her lurking in the shadows. I could handle her, as annoying as she could be.

I inhaled a sharp breath through my nose, and the faint scent of cigarette smoke hit my nostrils.

I faced forward again and started walking a bit faster than I had been before, hands shaking from the adrenaline pumping through my veins.

The arena was eerily quiet, and behind me, lights started to flicker off from the lack of motion.

Not paying attention to where I was walking, I smacked

directly into a hard plane in front of me, letting out a squeak. Strong arms wrapped around me, steadying me.

"Oh, good, there you are. We were all looking for you. Are you ready to go home?"

Hayden. Thank God.

"Sorry. I got distracted, but I'm ready. Let's go." I swiveled my head one more time, making sure there wasn't anyone around.

The smell of smoke had dissipated, and I couldn't detect anyone other than me and Hayden. We were truly alone.

"Are you okay? Did something happen?"

I shook my head. "No, sorry. It's just kinda spooky in here when there are no people. Let's go."

I was probably just being paranoid, but I walked to the trailer a little bit faster than I normally would.

sierra

Deep breaths, Sierra." I gave myself a pep talk. I'd find out today if I made it in the top fifteen in the world standings. If I made it to the NFR and achieved my life-long dream. "If you don't make it, there's always next year." I splashed some cold water on my face and looked at my reflection. Water trickled down my skin and my eyes looked tired, dark splotches forming half-moons under them, but I was still alive.

"You ready?" Hayden asked when I finally came out of the bathroom.

I took a seat next to him on the couch, folding my legs underneath myself. "Ready as I'll ever be."

Externally, I looked cool, calm, and collected. The image of confidence. Internally, my heart was threatening to burst out of my chest. Not to mention, my palms grew sweatier by the minute.

"Do you want me to look first?" Hayden asked, squeezing my shoulder in an attempt to ground me. He already knew that he and Keenan weren't going to make it this year. They were too far down in the standings that making it in the top fifteen wasn't realistic.

I shook my head. "No, I just want to get it over with."

"I've got you, Skip." He kept his hand on my shoulder as I typed in the world standings list. "I'm right here no matter what happens."

Closing my eyes, I tapped the link. From beside me, Hayden drew in a breath, and my heart dropped.

Is that a good breath or a bad one?

I opened my eyes, expecting the worst.

14. Sierra Bayley, Goldfinch, MT, $159,234.89

I dropped my face into my hands, tears stinging the back of my eyes. "Oh my God. I did it."

Hayden alternated between rubbing circles on my back and squeezing my waist, pulling me close to his side. "You did it, Skip. You made it."

I picked up my head, jutting my bottom lip out slightly. Hayden's eyes were misty, and I could feel the tears trickling down my cheeks, but he pulled me into a bone-crushing hug. Although it wasn't stifling or constrictive. Instead it was full of pride.

"I'm going to Las Vegas!" I exclaimed once the reality of it all really set in. "I'm going to be competing at the NFR! Oh my God, I could *kiss* you right now!" My eyes widened at the realization of what I just said. "I-I didn't mean—"

Before I could finish my sentence, Hayden's hands were cupping my cheeks, heat radiating off them. But instead of pressing his lips to mine, like I so desperately wanted him to despite my backtracking, he placed a gentle kiss on my forehead.

His lips were soft and warm, and my stomach did backflips at the subtle gesture of affection.

Grinning, he pulled back. "You fucking did it, Sierra. You're going to the NFR."

Hayden's phone rang and he mumbled something—an apology, maybe—before answering. "Hello?"

A pause.

"Yep, we just looked." He shot me a wink. "No, that's okay. I didn't expect to. But yeah, she's…she's ecstatic. And I'm so proud of her."

A muffled voice on the other end of the line kept going on, but I couldn't pinpoint who it was.

"All right, we'll see you later. Bye, guys." He hung up the phone. "Sorry, that was Colter and Ellison. They wanted to tell you congratulations. And we're all going out to Rudy's to celebrate later."

I nodded, the shock of it all still buried deep in my bones. I stared at the standings on my phone for a while longer, both wanting the moment to really sink in and waiting for the numbers to change. Like it was all a fluke and there was a mistake.

But no, it was real. Everything I'd worked for, everything I'd dreamed about, had finally come true.

"I'm so proud of you." Hayden pulled me into his chest, resting his head on top of mine. We sat there like that for a while, our breathing matched and heartbeats synching.

"Are you upset that I made it to the NFR but you didn't?" I asked once the high had worn off. "You worked hard for it this year, too."

Hayden shook his head, wrapping me into his arms. "No, Sierra, never," he whispered in my ear before pulling back to look down into my eyes. "This is your dream. This has always been your dream. Watching it come true for you is more than enough for me."

"Are you sure?" I hated the way my voice sounded—small, meek.

"Yeah. Always."

I broke free from his embrace, standing a little too quickly. "I-I'm going to go take a shower." Unable to make eye contact with him, I rounded the couch and headed in the direction of the bathroom.

"Hey, Sierra?"

I glanced over my shoulder. Hayden had followed me and was standing at the end of the hallway. Turning around, I crossed my arms over my chest. "Yeah?"

"I love you." Hayden blurted it out like it was a secret he'd been keeping all these months. "I-I never stopped."

My mouth gaped, opening and closing, but no words came out. My arms came uncrossed and fell to my sides.

Hayden walked down the hallway to meet me, grasping my hands in his, both our palms aflame. "You don't have to say it back, Skip. It's okay. I just needed you to know that no matter what happens, I love you, and I see you, and I'm so fucking proud of you, okay?"

I love you, too, but that's what I'm afraid of.

Life wasn't kind to me—never had been—and fate always seemed to take away the things I loved.

sierra

JANUARY, SENIOR YEAR

I wrapped my arms around myself, hesitating to knock on the door of the address Keenan had texted me. This had to be the right place, the trees were practically shaking from the bass music blasting from inside the house.

> Are you here?

HAYDEN
> Yeah, are you?

> I'm outside

> I think?

HAYDEN
> Hang on. I'll be right there

Laughter erupted from inside, and I tapped my foot against the wooden deck.

This is dumb. I should just go.

I started to spin on my heel to turn around and go back to my car, but the door swung open before I could get to the steps.

"Hey, Skip."

I had to bite my lip to hold back the giant smile that threatened to spread across my face. "Hi, Hayes."

"Come on in." He leaned against the frame of the entrance, propping the door open with his foot. "Welcome to Keenan's humble abode. Er, well, his parents' humble abode."

If there weren't so many people and the house was free of the stench of cheap booze and sweat, I was sure the place was pretty nice. It appeared to have an open-concept living room and kitchen, with a hallway leading to what I assumed were bedrooms. But right now there were so many people packed inside that I had no idea how GCSO hadn't been called to respond to a noise complaint yet. Probably because it was far enough in the country that there weren't many neighbors.

"Looks…cozy?" I quirked a brow as I tried to figure out what to say.

"Yeah, maybe when the entire town of Goldfinch isn't packed in here like sardines in a can." Hayden snorted as he took my hand. "Come on, the basement isn't as bad."

He led us to a closed wooden door across the house.

"You're not going to murder me, right?" I teased. "Your dad's a cop, you'd be the perfect person to do it if you were. You probably know a hundred different ways to dispose of a body."

"I think if I was going to murder you, I would have done it by now, Skip," he retorted, shaking his head with amusement. "Besides, there's way too many witnesses right now for that."

"Fair." I laughed as he opened the door, revealing a set of carpeted stairs leading down to a basement. Colored lights illuminated the room below, and the chatter of more people drowned out the music filtering up the stairs.

"Over here." Hayden waved me along as he headed over to a brown leather couch that looked like it had seen better days. He patted the cushion next to him, and I sat, sinking into it.

I gasped, wiggling my butt. "This is actually a really comfortable couch." I wasn't sure I'd be able to get up; the whole thing practically swallowed me whole.

Hayden chuckled. "Don't judge a book by its cover. It's well loved. Do you want something to drink?"

I shook my head. "No, I'm good, thanks."

"All right." He rested his arm on the back of the couch behind my shoulder, tapping the fabric with his hand.

The TV in front of us had *Mario Kart* queued up on the game console, and a few remote controllers were placed on the coffee table.

"*Mario Kart?*" I asked.

"Beerio Kart!" Keenan answered from behind. I flinched, jumping in my seat, and he leaned over the couch so his face was right next to mine. "Sorry, Skippy, didn't mean to scare you. Hi, by the way. Glad you made it."

"What's Beerio Kart?" I asked.

Hayden rolled his eyes. "It's a stupid game Keenan learned from these guys at SGU."

"It's drunk *Mario Kart.*" Keenan nodded with a wild grin on his face. "It's so fun. You'll never play regular *Mario Kart* ever again after playing this. You in, Skip?"

I tucked a strand of hair behind my ear. "Sure?"

"That's the spirit! What do you want to drink? We've got beer, Twisted Tea, seltzer, and punch."

Hayden leaned in to whisper in my ear, "You don't want the punch."

"I guess I'll just take a Twisted Tea?" I wasn't much of a drinker. I didn't like the way my dad got when he drank, and my parents never had any good alcohol anyway. It was all too strong and bitter for my taste.

I'd had a Twisted Tea once after a rodeo when a bunch of us drove out on the backroads and got drunk. Hayden was the only one sober by the end of the night so he drove us all home. If underage drinking wasn't breaking the law, then the amount of people we had packed in the cab and bed of the truck was. That was a fun night, though.

"Coming right up. Hazey?" Keenan pointed at Hayden as he started to head up the stairs.

"I'll get something later. I wanna watch this." He winked at me.

A few minutes later, Keenan came back down with a Twisted Tea and a Solo cup with some mixture that smelled like literal death.

I coughed, holding back a gag, when he thrust it under my nose. "What the hell is in this?"

He shrugged. "Bunch of stuff. Tito's, some kind of tequila, Everclear"—he tilted his head like he was trying to recall what was in the concoction—"Malibu, pineapple juice, and a little bit of Sprite. It's punch! Want some?"

I pushed the cup away, wrinkling my nose. "I'm good. I value my life tonight."

"Your loss. It's fun." He sat down on the couch and handed me a controller, moving on from the topic like the conversation about the punch never happened. "Okay, here's how this works. It's the same rules as regular *Mario Kart* but with a few additions. Firstly, you have to finish your drink before you finish the race. The whole thing. But you also can't drink and drive. So, you can't be moving if you're drinking. First person to finish their drink *and* the race wins. You don't have to win the whole race and beat all the CPUs, by the way. That won't happen. You just have to beat me."

I blinked my eyes slowly, trying to comprehend this so-called *fun* game Keenan was trying to get me to play. "This sounds like a death trap."

Hayden snorted. "It is for Keenan. That punch is dangerous."

After choosing our characters—Yoshi for me, Bowser for Keenan—and our racecars, he handed me his remote. "You're a beginner, so I'll let you choose which racetrack we do."

I selected Coconut Mall, and Keenan nodded his approval.

"I'm so glad you didn't choose Rainbow Road. We'd never finish the race."

I handed his controller back after starting the game. The countdown reached zero, and Keenan immediately started chugging his drink.

I cracked my can and took a small sip, grimacing at the taste.

Keenan glanced over at me between swigs of punch. "Come on, Skippy, you're never gonna catch up to me like that."

Hayden whispered in my ear, "Give it a few minutes and he won't be paying attention to us. He won't even be able to stay on the road in the game. Drink half of it, and I'll drink the rest."

"Isn't that cheating?" I hissed, quiet enough that Keenan wouldn't hear.

"I mean, it's a stupid drinking game. Who cares if you cheat? It's not like he's going to ban you from his house. You're my girl, you know?"

I pulled my lip between my teeth, my cheeks heating, and not from the alcohol. Nodding, I did my best to drink half of the can then discreetly handed it to Hayden. He finished the drink, save for a little sip. He was right about Keenan. He wasn't paying attention to anything, much less the road. He'd been driving backward the last couple minutes.

Hayden handed me the can, and I drank the last bit of it before making a big show of crushing the can.

"I'm coming for you, Kee. Better get to driving!" I giggled, the small amount of alcohol already going to my head.

I passed by Keenan on the second lap after he ran into a wall. I leaned forward, sitting on the edge of the couch as I devoted all my focus to the race.

When I crossed the finish line, I let out a whoop of victory before jumping up off the couch. Hayden jumped up with me and wrapped his arms around me, lifting my feet off the ground.

"Damn, Skippy, you're really good at this," Keenan slurred, a drunken smile on his face. He wiggled his finger at me. "Giving me a run for my money."

Hayden and I exchanged a knowing look then burst into laughter. I had to clutch my stomach from laughing so hard.

"So, I got into SGU." A couple hours later after sobering up from Beerio Kart, Hayden—who was carrying a bright-red Solo cup with some kind of dark-brown liquid sloshing around in it—plopped down on the couch next to me, throwing his free arm over my shoulder and squeezing. "They want me on the rodeo team."

I leaned into his side, resting my head on his shoulder. "I knew you were going to make it. They'd be fools not to have you on the team."

He pressed his lips to my temple, murmuring into my hair, "I bet you'd make it, too, if you applied. You're the best barrel racer I know."

I sighed, slipping out from under his arm. This wasn't the first time Hayden tried to talk me into applying to SGU, and I was certain it wouldn't be the last, either. "I'm not going to SGU. I'm not going to any college, Hayes."

Out-of-state schools were too expensive. The only school that wouldn't put me in a massive pile of debt was SGU. A rodeo scholarship would have paid for my tuition, but staying in Goldfinch wasn't an option, not with my father so close.

"You still have time, though. It's still early and they're on a rolling application, so they don't have a deadline. You can get in. We don't even have to live in the dorms. We can get an apartment together, and we—"

I stood, raising a hand to stop him. "I can't, Hayden. You know I can't."

Getting an apartment with Hayden was even less of an option. The idea of my dad hurting him simply because I spent time with him was scary enough. Living together would increase the risk tenfold.

"I know. But I don't know why." He got up, too, forcing me to look up at him as he put his drink down and took my hands in his. He ran his thumbs over mine before lacing our fingers together. "I'd protect you, you know I would. You'd be safe with me."

But you *wouldn't be safe with* me. *You'd just end up getting hurt.*

I shook my head, squeezing my eyes shut to prevent the tears from spilling out. "Please don't. Don't do this. Not right now."

"I just…" Emotion welled in his eyes as he whispered, "I *love* you, Sierra."

I love you, too. That's the problem.

I loved him too much to put him in danger, loved him too much to subject him to the inevitable pain that came from loving me.

"I know. I'm sorry."

sierra

"Where's your costume?" Reid's girlfriend, Isabelle—who I'd officially met in person about twenty minutes ago—pouted with her hands on her hips.

We met at Colter and Ellison's house before going to Rudy's, and all of us were dressed up for Halloween. All of us except for Jake, that is.

"I'm not a dress up kinda guy." Jake shrugged.

"Why not?" I asked.

I'd always loved Halloween because it was the one day a year I could be anyone but myself. That, and because when I was younger, I never got to dress up. My mom was never allowed to take me trick or treating. Granted, when I got to high school and had a driver's license, or someone else to drive me around, I did what I wanted. The consequences still caught up with me, though, like they always did.

Jake stretched out his arms, yawning. "I just don't see the point."

"Yeah, that'll change." Colter smirked. He was dressed in khaki pants, a black cut-off T-shirt, red suspenders, and one of those plastic fireman hats from the dollar store. "Ellison was never a Halloween person and now look at her."

"Yeah, Jake, Ellison was never fun, and now look at her!" Isabelle teased. "She's even doing a *couples costume*! There's a first for everything!"

"Hey! I was fun!" Ellison protested, crossing her arms, covering the white tank top with black Sharpie spots that she was wearing. There was no questioning what she was meant to be with the dog ears and black eyeliner on her nose. "I just never saw the point in dressing up for Halloween after college. And I'm doing this for you, Isa." She pointed at the tiny blonde who was wearing a yellow corset with black lace accents, a black miniskirt, black and yellow striped socks, wings, and some kind of antenna.

Isa just shrugged. "I thought it was a fun idea. Besides, Rudy's is having a costume contest, and we have to go to support June."

Hayden raised a brow. "Juniper doesn't even work there anymore."

"Yeah, but I was part of the brainstorming for the themed nights, so it counts," she cut in.

"Man, I hope your costume isn't foreshadowing for tonight." Jake laughed at Mikey and Juniper, who were dressed as a prisoner and police officer, respectively.

Mikey just winked, saying, "She likes the handcuffs," as Juniper rolled her eyes. However, she didn't deny it.

"I think I know what you are, but who is she supposed to be?" Isa tilted her head as her eyes roved over mine and Hayden's costumes.

I raised my brows, mouth gaping even though she couldn't see my face under the mask.

"Isa, have you never seen the Marvel movies?" June gasped.

Isa grimaced, a flush spreading across her cheeks. "Guilty?"

"Well, that's an arrestable offense in itself." Mikey laughed. "Maybe you should be the one in handcuffs tonight."

"Okay, well, you still haven't answered the question." She rolled her eyes.

"She's a female version of Bucky Barnes's The Winter Soldier"—Hayden gestured to me—"and I'm Flynn Rider."

Isa pouted her lips. "Huh. All right, then."

"Wasn't it supposed to be a couple's costume contest?" Ellison raised her brows.

"Yeah," Juniper and Hayden said in unison.

Hayden added, "She told me she was going to be Rapunzel, but apparently she lied."

I shrugged. "Not a fan of blonde hair." When Isa and June looked at me suspiciously, I added, "On me. You guys look great as blondes."

"Now that we've got that all settled, should we get going?" Jake asked.

"No!" Isa protested. "You need a costume!"

"Just cut some eye holes into a white sheet and throw it over him. He can be a ghost," Ellison said dryly. "I'm sure we have one somewhere."

"That's so lame," Isa muttered.

"I'll be right back." Colter chuckled before disappearing into one of the bedrooms. He emerged with a *Scream* mask.

"Why do you have this?" Juniper took the mask from him, inspecting it. "And why was it in your bedroom?"

He shrugged. "You never know when you need a mask. According to Isa, all the girls on the Internet are obsessed with masked men. Thought Ellison might be into it, too."

Mikey burst out laughing. "Was she?"

Ellison rolled her eyes. "No. God, no. It doesn't help that he scared the shit out of me one day with it, and I almost broke his nose. I would have probably broken his dick, too, if he hadn't stopped me."

"Wait, wait, wait, I need more context. Was he naked and had the mask on?" Jake laughed.

"That's enough of this conversation," Colter interjected. "Just wear the fucking mask."

"Wait, we should get one of those," Isa whispered to Reid, just loud enough for me to hear. "It'll be like that book I read last month."

Suppressing a laugh, I shook my head at her, and she shot me a wink.

"All right, now that we've gotten that all figured out"—Juniper gestured to our whole group—"let's get going."

Rudy's bar was packed as usual, but instead of the normal rustic look, the place was decked out in Halloween decor. Fake cobwebs were draped across the bottle display behind the bar, a giant stuffed spider hung from the loft, and tonight's "barrels" were plastic jack-o'-lanterns.

The DJ was playing mostly Halloween remixes, but would occasionally throw in a country song or two.

"Are there no other bars in this town?" I nudged Hayden, leaning in to ask the question in a low voice. We were up at the bar waiting for drinks, and while it was so loud it was unlikely someone would overhear, I didn't want to offend anyone.

He shrugged. "There are, but they're not as special as Rudy's. If you'd come here three or four years ago, you would have assumed it was a completely different bar, but business has really boomed since they started the theme nights. It used to be mostly locals and regulars that came in, but now the college kids have started hanging out here. Normally, it would be annoying, but Rudy's a good man and he deserves the business."

"He's the owner, I'm guessing?" I asked.

Hayden nodded. "Not sure if he'll be here tonight, but I'll have to introduce you sometime. He's a hoot."

"I'm looking forward to meeting him."

"Here are those drinks, guys." Liv slid our drinks across the bar, taking Hayden's card and opening a tab.

We joined the rest of the group over at the pool table. Part of me wanted to ask if that's all they ever did—it seemed like all we ever did when we went out was gather around the pool table—but I thought better of it. It wasn't like there was much else to do besides drink, dance, and play pool or darts.

"Who wants to play?" Jake singsonged as he started passing out cue sticks before wiggling one in front of me. "Sierra?"

"You sure you want me to play?" I joked. "Last time I played, you all said I was worse than Mikey."

Colter countered, "We didn't say you were *worse* than Mikey. We just thought it was funny you both hit the eight ball in."

I rolled my eyes while grazing my teeth over my bottom lip. "It's all right. I'll sit this one out."

"Juniper? Isa? What do you think?" Reid asked.

Juniper shook her head. "Mikey and I are going to go talk to Liv and Nico."

"I'll watch with Sierra! Maybe we can go on the dance floor." Isa winked as she nudged me with her elbow.

I grimaced, my eyes darting toward Hayden in a silent plea for help.

He lifted a shoulder as if to say, *You're on your own*, a cheeky grin plastered on his face.

"Okay, then, let's do me and Ellison and against you three," Colter suggested. "We don't need a third person, right, Blaze?"

Ellison wiggled her eyebrows. "Yeah, we're good."

"Okay, well, this is already boring." Isa turned to me. "How do you like Silver Creek?"

I crossed my arms, leaning against the wall. "It's nice."

"Sorry, I'm sure you've been asked these questions like a thousand times already." She let out a nervous laugh. "You've known Hayden for a long time, right?"

"Yeah. Since freshman year of high school. Keenan, Hayden, and I were kind of our own little trio back then. We were a wild bunch."

Her eyes widened. "No way, really? Was Hayden a wild child back in high school? He's so quiet now, I can't even imagine him getting into trouble."

I laughed, shaking my head. "No. He wasn't wild. Keenan definitely took that title. Hayden wasn't quiet, though. He talked all the fucking time in the beginning, actually. As we got older, though, he started to get quieter, I guess."

Isa popped her lip. "Hm, interesting. I wonder why."

I had my theories, but it wasn't something I really wanted to share. I hated the idea that I was the reason he became quiet, so I pushed those thoughts down.

Pursing my lips, I shrugged. "I dunno. That was years ago."

"He seems like he's opened up a lot more just with you being here."

My eyes darted to the floor, my shoe scuffing the floor. "Maybe. I guess I wouldn't really know how he was the past five years."

Her mouth gaped into an O, opening and closing like she wanted to say something then changed her mind.

My phone buzzed in my pocket, and I pulled it out, mumbling a quick apology to Isa. A message from an unknown number flashed across the screen before another one followed quickly behind.

UNKNOWN NUMBER

> You'll drop out of the NFR if you know what's good for you.

> Clock's ticking.

My eyes widened.

What the fuck is going on?

Tapping Hayden on the shoulder, I muttered, "I'm, uh, gonna go get some fresh air." Without waiting for his response, I pushed through the crowds of costumed people to get to the front door. I sucked in a breath, the cool air immediately rushing into my lungs, providing some relief from the stuffy feeling I'd gotten when the texts came through.

I paced back and forth on the sidewalk for a few minutes, sweat pooling on my forehead and palms. I took a few shaky breaths before getting frustrated with myself.

I wasn't going to have a panic attack. Not here. Not now.

The front door of Rudy's opened and closed as people

filtered in and out, the music transitioning from muffled to loud, to muffled again.

Walking further down the sidewalk, I dipped into an alleyway, resting my back against the wall. I'd go back inside soon. I just needed to compose myself.

My phone buzzed again, and a shiver went down my spine. But then it buzzed another five times and I started to relax, pulling out my phone to see notifications from our girls' group chat that Isa made.

Cowboy Killers

ELLISON

Where'd you guys go?

JUNIPER

Bathroom. Gonna be busy for a minute.

Gotta see how well these cuffs work 😉 text when they announce the costume contest results

ELLISON

Gross

gif of someone gagging

Just kidding, kind of. Have fun

ISA

We're gonna need all the juicy details later

ELLISON

Sierra?

I stepped outside for a minute, I'll be back soon

The hair on the nape of my neck stood up, and the

feeling that I was being watched settled deep in my stomach. After glancing down the alleyway once, I walked back to the front of the building.

The night air was chilly and still, giving the atmosphere an eerie sensation. Maybe I was being dramatic or paranoid. It was Halloween, after all. But something about the string of events in the past few weeks didn't sit right with me.

I had a feeling I was being followed, but at the same time, I didn't want to alarm Hayden and his friends, or make them worry over nothing. Worse yet, I didn't want to put them at risk by getting them involved.

Closing my eyes for a brief moment, I breathed in on a count of four, then exhaled on four, repeating the action a few times to slow my racing heart before heading back to the bar.

Just when I thought I was calm, a hand pressed down on my shoulder, and I whirled around, ready to strike whoever it was with my fist.

Hayden held up both of his hands in surrender, surprise etched in his features. "Whoa, Skip. Easy there."

"Sorry." I exhaled a deep breath. "I thought…never mind. What are you doing out here?"

"They're about to announce the winners of the costume contest. Ellison said you stepped outside, so I thought I'd come get you." He regarded my face, looking a bit more closely. "Are you okay?"

My posture snapped straight, and I brushed past him, plastering on a fake smile. "Yeah, I'm great. Why wouldn't I be? Let's go inside."

I didn't let him respond before I pushed through the front doors of the bar, Hayden following on my heels.

"Welcome to the first annual Rudy's Halloween

Costume Contest!" Liv's bubbly voice echoed off the walls as she spoke into the microphone.

Cheers erupted throughout the bar, and she waited for everyone to quiet down.

"We've got some incredible prizes for our winners tonight, including a free branded trucker hat and a Rudy's T-shirt as part of our new merch launch"—she paused for whoops and hollers—"a fifty dollar voucher to The Copper here in town, and finally, for the first place winner, a two hundred dollar cash prize! We'll have three individual costume winners as well as a couples costume winner who will get the restaurant voucher. We had three amazing judges tonight, including our owner and namesake of the bar, Rudy!" She gestured to a kind-looking, older gentleman with white hair and patchy scruff on his jaw.

As Liv continued talking, I glanced around the crowd, trying to figure out if the person who sent me those texts was here. No one seemed particularly suspicious, and my stomach dropped.

"Without further ado, let's announce our winners!"

Nico handed Liv four envelopes like it was the Grammy's.

"In third place for our individual costume contest, the winner is…" Liv called out the name of a girl wearing butterfly wings, and she went up to the front to grab the hat. The next person who won was dressed as a pirate and got the T-shirt.

"Finally, our winner of the two hundred dollar cash prize is…" Liv paused for dramatic effect, and everyone started drumming their hands on their legs. "Sierra Bayley!"

My brows furrowed as my face contorted in panic. "What? N-no." I shook my head. "My costume wasn't even that good, why did I win?"

"Go on and get your money, Skip." Hayden laughed as he gave me a gentle push toward the front.

"Congrats!" Liv grinned as she handed me a plain white envelope. "I may have had a little bit of pull in you winning, but don't tell anyone. Your costume is great."

My cheeks flushed. "Thanks."

As I headed back toward Hayden, Liv announced the winners of the couples costume contest. Of course it was Colter and Ellison, Miles City and Silver Creek's very own "it couple."

Colter scooped Ellison up in his arms after taking the voucher, and she held it in the air like a trophy.

Mikey and Juniper were nowhere to be seen, and I laughed under my breath at the thought that they were still in the bathroom using the handcuffs.

"Can we get out of here?" I asked Hayden with what I was sure was a pleading look on my face.

"Yeah. Come on, Skip. Let's go home."

He led me back to his pickup truck, helping me into the passenger side.

After turning on the ignition, he didn't immediately start driving.

"Are you okay?" he asked, a tinge of concern in his voice. "Don't lie to me, Skip. We don't do that, remember?"

I bit my lip. "I was just a little overwhelmed tonight, but I'm good now. Promise."

It wasn't a complete lie. The texts *had* overwhelmed me, and now that we were leaving, I was starting to calm down again. My brain didn't feel like it was trying to attack me anymore, and my heart stopped pounding in my chest.

"Okay. You know I'm here for you, right? You've got me, Skip." He reached over and squeezed my hand.

CHAPTER FORTY-TWO

hayden

P ancho greeted us at the front door, his tail wagging like a whirlwind.

"Hey, boy. Did you miss us?" I got down to his level, patting his side before he rolled over onto his back.

Sierra stood next to us with her arms crossed and shoulders shaking as she laughed. "You are such a little traitor."

"Who can blame him? I'm a lovable guy," I teased.

"You're something, all right." She brushed past me, but Pancho didn't get up to follow her.

Sierra pulled off the mask covering her mouth and started unbuckling all the straps of her costume.

My eyes fixated on her as she shrugged off her vest and belt, leaving her in a form-fitting long sleeve and black yoga pants.

With a sigh of relief, she rotated her shoulder. "It feels so good to get that stuff off."

"I bet. That costume did look really good, though." I stood so I was closer to her level.

Her eyes averted away. "T-thanks. Well, I think I'm

going to go to bed. Long night." She seemed distracted, and I wasn't sure why. "Let's go, Pancho. Bedroom."

The dog huffed as he got to his feet, scampering away down the hall.

"Goodnight, Hayes." She raked her teeth over her bottom lip and turned around to follow Pancho.

"Sierra, wait." I reached out for her hand, placing her palm against mine. She paused in the middle of the living room, and I pulled her back to me.

Green eyes widened, and, through thick lashes, her gaze trailed up to mine.

"What are you doing?" she whispered. "Hayes—"

I didn't let her finish before my hand was cupping her cheek and my lips grazed hers, breaking weeks of tension between us. The kiss was gentle and slow. Soft.

I pulled back for a second, as if to silently ask if she was sure, but she didn't let the moment hang between us for long. Her lips were on mine again in an instant, hungrier this time. It was as though the feelings we'd withheld for each other had built up for so long that they couldn't be suppressed any longer. With a simple touch, the dam had broken, and it was time for the love we had for each other to finally be free. No longer caged, no longer confined.

Her lips parted, and I slipped my tongue inside to brush against hers. Her hands slid into my hair, and she pulled me closer.

When we finally came back up for air, I tried to catch my breath. "I've wanted to do that for so long."

"Can we just…take things slow?" she panted, her nose pressed against mine.

Our breaths mingled together in the air between us as she waited for me to respond.

I wished I knew what she was thinking. I wished I knew what I could do or say to ease her mind.

"Yeah. Always," I whispered against her lips. "Whatever you want."

Her breath hitched in her throat, and I swear she muttered, *Fuck it*, before her lips were pressed against mine again.

If emotions could be packed into a single moment, then this kiss was a well spilling over. My teeth grazed her bottom lip, pulling a quiet moan from her.

This was not slow. No, not at all.

"Is this too fast?" I asked, willing to stop if that was what she wanted.

She pulled back, lips skimming my jaw before she whispered, "No, don't stop. But I need to ask you something. Have there… Were there any others?"

"No." I shook my head, voice hoarse. "Only you. It's only ever been you."

She was my first everything. My first kiss, my first time, my first love, my first heartbreak.

It may have rendered me inexperienced, but once you've held the entire universe in your hands, there was no need to go looking for more. Even if it was only the one time, I could have died a happy man knowing I'd shared a part of myself with Sierra Bayley that no one else would ever have.

Sierra exhaled a breath, a sigh of relief perhaps, because when she said, "Me, too. I haven't been with anyone else," I think a feeling of relief settled in my chest, too.

After a moment's pause, she whispered, "Are we really doing this?"

I rolled my lips between my teeth. "Only if you want to. I'm all yours. Just say the word, Sierra."

Her tongue darted out to wet her lips, then she nodded, looking up at me through thick lashes. "Yeah, Hayes. I want to."

Thank fucking God.

Wasting no more time, I pulled my shirt over my head and tossed it to the side. Her eyes cut to my abs then trailed up my body to my face.

"Like what you see, Skip?" I teased. "What? Didn't get a good enough look when I got out of the shower that one day?"

She rolled her eyes. "In my defense, I didn't really have much of an opportunity to appreciate what was in front of me that day. You know, because I was a bit embarrassed to see the guy I was 'just friends' with naked. And without warning."

A laugh rose in my chest. "Come here. Lift your arms."

She did as I asked, raising her arms so I could pull her shirt over her head, revealing a black lace bra underneath. Reaching around her back, I unclasped it and let it fall to the floor, her breasts spilling out.

My heart skipped a beat as I took a good look at her. She was just as beautiful as she was five years ago, if not more. The girl I knew back then was still a bit timid, but the one in front of me now was so sure of herself. Like she'd finally found her voice.

I loved every single version of her that I'd gotten to know.

I ran my hands down the sides of her body before hooking my fingers in the waistband of her yoga pants and pulling them down her thighs. Lowering myself so I was on my knees in front of her, I kissed the flesh on the inside of her leg, moving up toward the lace-covered apex of her thighs.

Sierra sucked in a breath as I hooked my fingers in the band of her underwear and tugged them all the way off, baring her center to me—already wet and glistening with her arousal. With one hand, I palmed her ass, and with the other, I hooked her leg over my shoulder so I could lower my mouth to her clit.

"Hayden," she moaned as I licked a broad stroke up her center.

Sliding two fingers inside, I sucked on her clit. Her hips bucked toward my face in pleasure, and her arousal dripped down my hand.

"God, Sierra, you taste like heaven. I've waited five years for this."

Her hands slid through my hair, her fingers grasping and tugging on the strands while pushing my face closer, begging for more.

I buried my face between her thighs, savoring every minute, every taste.

My eyes darted up as she threw her head back, face contorting in blissful pleasure, her mouth agape as she let out a breathy moan.

I lifted her leg off my shoulder and put it back on the ground, ignoring Sierra's protests as I picked her up and walked down the hallway to my room, kicking the door closed behind me and laying her on the bed so her head was on the pillows. After taking off my jeans and boxers, I crawled up the bed, settling myself between her legs.

She reached for my cock, pumping it a couple times before swiping her thumb along the tip, sending a shockwave down my spine.

This was unreal. *She* was unreal, and I never wanted

this feeling of being with her—of finally having her again —to go away.

Moving her hand away from me, I moved back so I could lower my mouth to the space between her thighs. My fingers found her entrance, sliding inside with ease.

"Hayes, I"—she panted—"want you."

"Where do you need me, baby?" I murmured as my thumb circled her clit.

"Fuck, I—"

Her hips bucked up toward my hand, urging me to go deeper, faster. Curling my fingers, I hit that sweet spot inside her, and her resolve broke.

"Tell me what you need." I pressed a kiss to the soft flesh just below her slit. I may not have had a lot of experience when it came to Sierra, but I knew how to read her. It wasn't difficult to figure out what I could do with my hands, mouth, and body to make her feel good.

"Inside. I want you inside me." Her hands gripped the sheets. "Fuck me, Hayes."

I started to slide off the bed, but she stopped me, grabbing my wrist.

"Condom?" I asked, and she shook her head.

"No. Just you."

Our eyes locked on each other, hers brimming with lust and every emotion I never thought I'd see again. Trailing my gaze down her body, I watched as she slipped a finger inside her center, thrusting it in and out.

Lord have mercy.

Pushing her legs apart, I crawled so my body was above hers, hands pressing into the sheets beside her shoulders. "You sure about this, Skip?"

She nodded. "I've never been so sure of anything."

Bringing my hand to my mouth, I spit into it then took

my aching cock in my hand, stroking it before guiding it toward her slit.

I sank into her slowly, a small gasp falling from her lips from the initial push.

"You okay?"

"All good. Just go slow, i-it's been a while." She laughed, a breathy little exhale.

"Always." I took her hand in mine, interlacing our fingers as I inched myself in further, until I was fully seated inside her. "Breathe, love."

Her pussy clenched around me, squeezing my cock like a cobra.

"Fuck, Sierra," I moaned when I started moving, pulling out only to thrust back in.

Her fingers skimmed down her breasts to her stomach to her clit, rubbing circles on the sensitive flesh. Her hips rolled against mine, meeting me thrust for thrust. She pulsed around me, and if she kept this up, I was going to explode.

"Sierra, baby, I'm not going to last," I whimpered, the sound falling from my lips before I could stop it.

"Don't stop moving. I want you to come. I want you to fill me."

"Are you close?" I bit out through clenched teeth. It was taking everything in me not to come apart at the seams.

"Yes. Oh, God," she moaned, throwing her head back as her fingers moved faster. "Just like that, Hayes. Fuck me just like that."

My thrusts quickened, becoming frantic and messy. I drove my hips forward, slamming my cock inside her until she was a blubbering mess beneath me, crying out my name.

Her arousal dripped down my cock, the wet slap of skin against skin building with each thrust and combining with the desperate noises coming from her mouth.

The blood in my ears roared as I fell over the edge, my cock pulsing as my cum spilled inside her. My chest heaved as I drove myself deeper a few more times, her pussy squeezing every last drop out of me.

"You're so good, baby. Fuck, you're so good." The strangled breath fell from my lips as I gathered my bearings and pulled out of her slowly, my cock covered in us.

My cum dripping down the inside of her thigh did something to me, and an almost animalistic noise clawed its way out of my throat. I swiped a finger through the mess and brought it up to her lips. She sucked my finger clean, and I swear my dick got hard again.

After we cleaned up in the shower and Sierra went down on me, choking on my cock and making me come down her throat, we crawled under the covers, moonlight illuminating the dark.

"I love you. Always." I peppered kisses along her neck, and she squeezed my hand three times, like we were speaking in our own secret language.

Something inside me ached, though. I had her, but at the same time, it was like I didn't. There was still something holding her back. I could feel it. Somehow, Sierra was slipping through my fingers again, and I could do nothing to stop it. All I could do was hold her in my arms and pray she wouldn't disappear.

hayden

APRIL, FIVE YEARS AGO

Sierra was back in town to visit, a rare occasion since she really only came back to Goldfinch for court. Her mom moved away earlier in the year, so Sierra didn't have a place to stay. My parents offered to let her sleep at their house in my old childhood bedroom every time like clockwork, but she always declined. Part of me thought she felt awkward about the whole situation with her dad, since mine was a cop.

We ate dinner at Ranger's with Keenan and Ivy—who had gotten back together freshman year of college—just like old times, then came back to my apartment near campus. I had an early practice in the morning, but I would have stayed up all night with Sierra because that would have meant she was real and not just a figment of my imagination. She wasn't just a ghost of my past, coming back to haunt me.

I turned on one of Sierra's favorite movies, *10 Things I Hate About You*, and she snuggled next to me on my full-size bed. I was glad I wasn't in the dorms, because I wasn't sure how we'd comfortably fit on a twin-size bed together.

"I'm so happy you're here, Skip," I whispered into her hair as Heath Ledger serenaded Julia Stiles on the football field.

I wrapped my arm around her, tugging her closer to my side. She draped her leg over mine as she laid her head on my chest, putting her hand on my abdomen.

Ten or fifteen minutes could have passed, but I wouldn't have known. I hadn't been paying attention to the movie, wasn't even sure what had happened on the screen or who was in the scene at this point. I was fully engrossed in the girl next to me. My eyes tracked from Sierra's nose down to her full, pink lips and back up to her eyes.

"Hi," she whispered, her eyes locked on my mouth.

"Hey." Flicking my tongue over my lips, I cupped her face with my hands, drawing circles on her cheekbones with my thumbs. "Can I kiss you?"

"Please." She nodded, closing her eyes and parting her lips.

The kiss was soft, innocent. Nothing like how my classmates had described kisses with their girlfriends or their hookups. Her lips fit against mine like puzzle pieces, and it was like a chunk of my soul—a part I didn't know I was missing—found its way back to me.

I snaked one of my hands around her waist, the other entwining with her hair. Her hands found my jaw, and our mouths moved more hungrily. Like after finally getting a taste of each other, once was never enough. We were both starved for each other's touch, hands roaming up and down the other's body.

My tongue slipped inside her mouth when she took a breath, and hers tangled with mine, teeth clashing for a second. But it wasn't awkward or uncomfortable like most mishaps like that would be.

We made out for a while longer, then pulled back for air, our foreheads pressed against each other, chests rapidly rising and falling together.

"I've never done anything like this before," she admitted.

"Me neither."

Her eyes widened. "Never? You've never even kissed someone?"

I shook my head.

"But you're here, and I thought maybe…"

I pressed my forehead against hers again, our noses barely touching. "I'm yours, Sierra. I've always been yours. Only yours. But we don't have to—"

"I-I want this. Just…slow, yeah?"

"Slow," I repeated.

This time the kisses were deeper. I nipped her bottom lip then swiped my tongue over the spot to soothe the ache, and a soft moan fell from her lips.

Her hands slid under my shirt, roaming across my body, exploring every inch of my skin.

I lifted her hips, spinning us so she was on her back and I was on top. My hips ground against hers, the bulge in my sweatpants growing with each thrust.

She pressed a hand against my chest and for a moment, I thought she might have wanted to stop. But then she said, "Take off your shirt. I want to see you."

Sitting up on my knees, I pulled my shirt over my head. Gesturing for her to lift her upper body, I gently took off her T-shirt, leaving her in her bra. I cupped a hand over one of her breasts, and she sighed, the mere sound of it making my heart race.

Lowering my mouth to her collarbone, I peppered kisses across her chest. She unhooked the clasp on her bra, pushing the straps off her shoulders and letting the fabric fall to reveal herself.

I kissed the top of her breast before latching my mouth onto her nipple and sucking.

"H-Hayden," she moaned, her back arching off the bed, pushing her chest toward me.

Her fingers grasped my hair, tugging lightly on the strands.

One of my hands cupped her breast, while the other traveled down her torso to the waistband of her leggings. My fingers slipped under the fabric, playing over the soft skin below her abdomen.

Her gaze bounced up to my eyes.

"Is this okay?"

She nodded, and hooking my fingers into the fabric, I pulled down her leggings, tossing them to the side.

"What do you like?" I asked, my ears heating a bit because I was unsure of what to do—how to make her feel good.

"Maybe just"—she took my hand in hers, placing it on top of the already damp fabric covering her center and rubbing circles with my index and middle fingers—"like this."

I mimicked what she'd just done, and Sierra closed her eyes, a deep breath falling from her lips. "Good?"

"Mm-hmm."

My fingers dipped below the top of her underwear, finding the most sensitive part of her. Sliding a finger along her center, I glanced at her to see if she was okay with what I was doing. Sierra nodded, encouraging me to continue, and I slid a finger inside, moving it in a slow, steady rhythm. Her walls were tight around me, wetness coating my skin. With my thumb, I rubbed circles on her clit, how she showed me.

She grew wetter with every thrust, her center stretching around my fingers and her moans filling the low lit bedroom.

"Keep going, just like that," she sighed.

My dick twitched in my pants at the sounds she made, her pleasure urging me on, challenging me to make her come. If making Sierra feel good was an art, then I wanted to study it every chance I got, become a master at it.

Her head fell back, and her body arched off the bed. "I-I think I'm going to come."

Moments later, she unraveled around my fingers, gripping them like a vise.

"Holy shit," she panted, catching her breath.

"Yeah?" I let out an awkward chuckle, trying to keep my composure because *that* just happened.

She blew a raspberry. "Yeah." Sitting back up, she kissed me, running her hands down my chest toward my groin. "I want to"—*kiss*—"do something for you."

A soft whimper escaped my lips as Sierra pressed her hand over my hard length, squeezing gently before her eyes flicked to mine.

"Can I?"

I nodded, adjusting my position so I was on my back next to her. Straddling my thighs, Sierra took off my pants and boxers, slowly rolling them down my thighs to expose my length, hard and heavy against my stomach.

Her eyes widened as she stared at my naked body.

I hooked my fingers under her chin then lifted so she was looking back at me. "All good?"

"Um, you're just..." She pulled her lip between her bottom teeth. "Are you sure it'll fit?"

I couldn't help the laugh that bubbled from my throat, and I slapped a hand over my mouth. But Sierra started giggling, too.

"I'm sorry. That was so embarrassing." She covered her mouth with a hand. "But you're going to have to help. How do I?"

"Don't be embarrassed. I'm not laughing at you," I whispered, taking her hand and wrapping it around me. "Like this." With my hand placed over hers, I moved them up and down my length, showing her how it felt good.

My brows furrowed, pleasure wracking through my body, and Sierra stopped.

"Did I hurt—"

I shook my head before she could finish her sentence. "No. God, no. It feels good. You're so good."

"I'm not sure what I'm doing," she admitted shyly.

"You can use more pressure." She squeezed tighter, and I winced. "Maybe not that much."

"Sorry." She covered her face with her hands again.

"Hey, hey, hey. It's okay." I lifted her hands from her face, brushing away the strands of hair that fell into her eyes. Bringing one of my hands up to my mouth, I spit into it, then brought it back down to my cock, getting it wet. "Here. Try again."

She wrapped her hand around me, moving slowly from the base to the tip, back and forth. Her thumb brushed against the head, and a soft moan fell from my lips.

"Fuck."

Her lips curled up into a small smile, and she continued, moving faster. The pressure in my balls built until I was panting her name.

"Sierra. Oh, God."

I had to stop her. I had to stop her, or I was going to come.

I lifted her hand off me, and her face contorted into confusion.

"Hold on," I reassured her, pressing a soft kiss to her forehead. I rolled to the side of the bed, opening the drawer in my nightstand to pull out a condom. "Are you still sure about this?"

She nodded. "Yes. I want you. All of you."

"Come here." I patted the spot I was just lying in.

She moved, and I traded spots with her, tearing open the condom. Rolling it onto my length took a couple awkward moments, because putting it on yourself was different than how they taught you in sex ed. Settling myself between her thighs, my knees spreading her legs apart, I asked, "Ready?"

"Mm-hmm." Her eyes never left mine as I guided my tip to her center, pushing inside.

She let out a small squeak, and I stopped.

"Does it hurt?"

"A little," she admitted. "Just…go slow."

I nodded. "Always. Just relax."

Slowly, I inched myself further, her walls starting to adjust to my size. I moved until I was fully seated inside her then looked down to where our bodies joined.

"Move. Please, Hayden," Sierra whimpered.

I pressed my palms into the sheets next to her, slowly pulling out then pushing back inside her until we reached a steady rhythm, our heavy breaths completely in sync.

"Wrap your legs around me." I grabbed her thighs, lifting them so we were even closer. Her legs closed around my middle, and her hands grasped my arms, nails digging into my skin.

She was so warm and tight, her walls clenching around me, squeezing me. I wasn't going to last long in this position, but it felt so good.

I leaned close, our lips meeting in a messy, frantic kiss. Her tongue slid past my lips, and when I thrusted harder, she moaned, the soft cry bursting from her mouth.

"H-Hayes. Are you c-close?"

"Yes." My breath came out ragged in a half-moan. "Come with me, Sierra."

A few more thrusts and we were both there, her body shuddering under mine as I completely fell apart and the world around me faded into white noise.

"Hayden," she choked out, back bowing off the sheets.

I was still coming, spilling inside the condom as her body convulsed around mine.

My chest heaved as I lowered it to hers, pressing my forehead against hers, our breaths mixing together in the air. Sweat dripped down my brow, and I wanted to pull back, but Sierra placed her hands on my cheeks.

"I'm so glad it was you." She didn't give me time to respond before her lips were on mine. Gentle and loving.

What she didn't realize was that to me, she was all-consuming. Even though it was both our first time, I didn't think I ever needed to experience sex with anyone else. I was confident that nothing would ever compare to the feeling of her wrapped around me, our bodies the closest that they could ever humanly be.

A couple hours later, after cleaning up in the shower, we lay under the covers wrapped up in each other, the sheets messy and our breathing starting to slow into a steady pattern.

"You're perfect. You're everything to me," I murmured into her hair.

Sierra stirred, sitting up like she was going to leave, so I sat up, too, prompting her to look at me, her green eyes seeming to glow, even in the absence of light.

"Sierra." Her name came out as a whisper.

"I—"

"Please don't go." I blinked back the tears welling in my eyes as I brushed a strand of hair behind her ear, thumb stroking the pink scar under her eye. "Stay. Even if it's just for tonight."

She opened her mouth like she was about to protest but then decided against it, instead cuddling into my side, resting her head against my chest.

We just lay there together in the silence, eventually moving into a more comfortable position. My hands never left her hair, fingers brushing through the strands, as I started to fall into a gentle slumber.

I was convinced she was the greatest love of my life.

My one and only.

Our souls were intertwined. There was no me without her.

When I woke up the next morning, Sierra's side of the bed was cold, the sheets and comforter neatly made.

She was gone.

And I didn't even get to say goodbye.

sierra

PRESENT DAY

A loud crash and the sound of glass breaking in the living room jolted me out of sleep.

"What was that?" I hissed.

"I don't know, but stay here." Hayden crawled out from under the covers and threw on a shirt, his back muscles rippling as he pulled it down his torso.

God, Sierra, stop that.

Snapping out of my trance, I jumped out of bed, too. "I'm not just going to sit here. What if there's someone out there? They can't take on both of us."

Hayden let out an exacerbated sigh. "Fine, but stay behind me."

His bedroom door creaked as he slowly opened it, letting the light from the hallway and the main parts of the house filter in.

"Is someone there?" he called out.

"What are you doing?" I hissed. "This is how literally everyone in movies ends up getting murdered!"

He looked back at me, rolling his eyes. "No, the worst

thing is investigating the scary noises, which is what we're already doing. Besides, this isn't *The Conjuring*, Skip."

When we stepped into the living room, the evidence was plain as day. The window above the couch had been broken, shattered into a bunch of tiny pieces now covering the floor and the furniture.

"Don't move." Hayden ordered as he looked around the room, sweeping it for threats. Gingerly heading toward the couch, he stopped, stooping down to pick something up off the ground.

"What is it?" I took a step forward, careful not to step on anything sharp.

He held up a brick, covered in soot and something red.

TIME'S UP, it read, in what I hoped was paint.

The brick landed with a thud as Hayden shot up to his feet, spinning around and stalking down the hall back to the bedroom. "We're leaving."

I followed, a little bit in shock. "What?"

"I said, we're leaving, Sierra. It's not safe here."

"It was probably just a prank. Just some college kids being dumb after Halloween," I blubbered, not being convincing in the slightest.

"Sierra, someone burned down your trailer, cut your saddle, and put a nail in your tires. I know you said you thought it was an accident, but I've never been convinced given everything that's happened. And now this? That's not a prank, that's a pattern. Has anything else happened?"

I bit my lip, wringing my hands together.

"Goddammit, Skip. You have to tell me about these things! Everything. I want to know everything that has happened in the last three months since the fire."

"I've been getting text messages. But I didn't think they were a big deal. I just thought"—I hesitated, knowing how utterly stupid I must have looked—"I just thought someone was trying to scare me or pull a prank, or I don't know, had the wrong number."

Hayden ran his fingers through his hair before bringing his hands back down to flex them, popping his knuckles in the process. "What did they say?"

"What?"

"What did the texts say?"

I could tell his patience was wearing thin, but not necessarily with me. Hayden had always tried to protect me, and while I was grateful, on the other hand, it was only putting him at risk.

"The first ones I got were after the fire, saying how lucky Pancho was and to quit while I was ahead. I-I didn't know what it meant, and I guess I was in shock from everything that had already happened, so I just brushed it off. Then I got another one. Last night."

Hayden sucked in a breath. I could feel the anger radiating off him, something I'd never experienced before with him. He was the most level-headed person I knew, but at that moment, it felt like he wanted to burn the world down. Not only that, but like he would burn the world down *for me*.

"That one told me to drop out of the NFR."

Hayden's mouth gaped, opening and closing like he was trying to figure out the best way to approach this. "Why would you keep these from me? You promised you'd tell me if anything happened. We swore not to keep secrets anymore."

"I didn't want to be any more of a burden than I already am."

He winced, his face contorting into disappointment or sadness, or something of the like. "How many times do I have to tell you before you'll finally believe it, Sierra? You're not a burden to me. You *never* have been."

"I'm just…" *Trying to keep you safe.* My brain filled in the gap where my mouth could not.

He stepped closer to me, cupping my face in his hands. "I know what you're trying to do, but it's not going to work, Skip. I lost you once, and I'd be damned if I let that happen again. Don't push me away. Please."

"Where are we even going to go?" I bit my bottom lip.

"Goldfinch. We're going to stay with my parents until we can figure this out. My dad's still a deputy, and there's a whole department who will protect you."

Familiar beige walls decorated with family photos greeted me as we stepped into the Watkins family home. The scent of peanut butter cookies wafted through the air, and an immediate sense of comfort enveloped me. Nothing about Hayden's childhood home had changed, and if I didn't know any better, I would have thought I was fourteen again, walking into the house for the first time.

"Mom?" Hayden called out.

Pancho had already barged into the house, because he lacked manners, and was trying to get old Reggie to play with him. His attempts were unsuccessful, and the Corgi continued to lie on the floor despite Pancho's happy barks.

"In here!" Mae's voice drifted out from the kitchen.

"Hey." Hayden wrapped his arms around Mae, pulling

her small frame close to him. "I brought someone to see you."

I walked around the corner, and Mae gasped, her face lighting up with happiness.

"Sierra, dear. It's so good to see you again." Mae's eyes glassed over, the beginning of tears welling up. She pulled me into a tight embrace once Hayden let her go.

"Hi, Mae."

"You look so good, honey!" She pulled back to regard me. "That hair color looks wonderful on you. Really brings out your eyes."

"That's what I said, too." Hayden nodded, shooting me a wink.

Mae freed me from her hug and took a couple steps back. "What are you two doing here?"

Hayden and I exchanged glances as if asking each other, *Do you want to tell her?* He raised his brows at me, and I sighed.

"There's been some…things happening."

Wow, Sierra, could you be more vague?

Hayden cleared his throat. "She's been getting threats. For a few months. It's escalated to the point I don't feel safe having her alone at the house. Someone threw a brick through my living room window."

"Oh my goodness." Mae gasped. "Are you two okay?"

We both nodded as Hayden replied, "Yeah, Mom, we're okay. A little shaken up, but that's why we're here."

"Well, you know you're welcome to stay as long as you need, son. And you're always welcome here, Sierra." Mae reached forward to squeeze my shoulder. "I'll make chicken and dumplings for dinner. Your favorite." She winked.

"Sounds good. I think we're going to just go around

town, yeah?" Hayden looked at me for the last part, like he wanted to ask if that was okay, and I nodded.

"Your dad's on day shift, so he should be home for dinner. He'll be happy to see you both," Mae added as we headed toward the front door.

Neither of us said a word as we drove back into town, the only sound coming from the tires of Hayden's pickup kicking up dust and gravel on the backroads. That was, until we passed by the tree I'd crashed into all those years ago.

My eyes cut to Hayden, who appeared to be holding back his laughter.

"Don't even think about it," I muttered, although the grumpiness was more of a front to hide my own amusement.

"I didn't say a single thing." Hayden grinned like a little kid as he put one hand on the top of the steering wheel and the other on the seat back of the passenger side.

I rolled my eyes. "You were thinking about it, though."

He squinted, eyes lit with a twinkle of mischief. "Actually, no, I was thinking more about the stadium break-in, but now that you bring up the tree, I—"

"Nope. I'd much rather talk about breaking into the football stadium," I cut him off.

"Should we go see if we can break into the stadium again?"

"I never thought I'd ever hear you say those words," I teased. "Keenan must be rubbing off on you."

He shook his head with a smile. "Better not. We could walk around the campus, though, for old time's sake?"

I nodded. "Yeah, that sounds nice."

Hayden parked in one of the lower guest parking lots, and we began the trek up a hill to the campus quad.

Most of the leaves had fallen from the trees with it being early November, but there wasn't snow on the ground quite yet. I much preferred SGU in the spring, when flowers were starting to bloom and the grass was damp with morning dew because the temperature wasn't as scorching as it was in the summer.

"This is a nice little hike," I huffed out a breath.

"Try doing it in the winter when the sidewalks are covered in ice." Hayden laughed. "It was a miracle if you never slipped and fell at least once. Cowboy boots probably weren't the best footwear because they have no traction whatsoever, but that was all I wore."

"I probably would have fallen all the time and embarrassed myself," I admitted.

"Couldn't have been worse than when I saw someone slip and fall while riding their bike across campus in the winter. Don't know what they were thinking, but it made for a good laugh. Maybe all the times I slipped were karma for laughing." He closed his eyes and stuffed his hands in his pockets as he reminisced.

I tried to imagine myself as a student, what my life could have been like if I'd gone to college with Hayden. Maybe we would have held hands while he walked me to class, even if it made him late to his own. We'd meet up for lunch in the dining hall and train together in the student athletic center.

But then I remembered why I couldn't have gone to SGU.

That was the thing about what-ifs, nonsensical daydreams, romantic delusions. They always disappointed you in the end.

"I never actually gave you a tour of the campus when you were here. This building over here"—he pointed to a tall brick building surrounded by cottonwood trees—"was where I had my Introductory Algebra class."

As he talked about the building, my eyes scanned our surroundings. I froze, a black metal bench beneath a tree that forked in two directions catching my eye. It had only been five years, of course the campus hadn't changed that much. Of course that damned bench would still be there.

"Sierra?" Hayden turned around, concern painting his features. "Are you okay?"

It was as though I had tunnel vision, everything around me blurring so my eyes could only focus on that bench and tree.

Hayden always said we never kept secrets from each other, never lied, but what were you supposed to do when you finally had the person you wanted most in the world after being ripped apart time after time—after you let them slip through your fingers like sand? What were you supposed to say when you were the one who let them fall after promising you'd always catch them?

I wouldn't have forgiven me if I were him.

I didn't know if he would if he really knew the truth of why I left again and again.

SGU's campus was beautiful this time of year, autumn colors covering the landscape like a Renaissance painting.

The last of the court dates had been earlier in the summer, and the court found my father guilty of his charges. He was going to prison this time. There was always the chance he could get out, but for now, temporary relief washed over me.

I didn't need to be here, probably shouldn't have come back, but I wanted to see Hayden. Surprise him. Make up for the last time I snuck out of his room without a word.

This time things could be normal. We could be happy.

That night in April, I lay on Hayden's chest, feeling his breaths slow until he fell asleep. Then my phone lit up with a text. A reality check that Hayden wouldn't be safe as long as my dad was around.

And I knew I had to go.

No matter how much I wanted him, how much I needed him, I knew I could never have him. Even though he owned a piece of my soul, there'd always be a part of me that wanted better for him. Knew he deserved better.

I hadn't talked to him since, and maybe it was selfish of me to show up here now, but it was like Hayden and I were connected by an invisible thread. I could never stray too far without his heart tugging mine back.

I caught a glimpse of him ahead, and I started jogging toward him, resisting the urge to call out his name like we were in high school again.

But then I realized he was with someone. Hugging someone, embracing someone in his arms.

A girl.

She was pretty, with long brunette hair and a smile that sparkled even from three hundred feet away. The way she was looking at him…I recognized it.

It was how I always wished I could look at him. How I wished I could be the person he deserved, someone who could love him without fear.

Even though my father was gone, I couldn't promise nothing would happen ever again.

Or worse, that I wouldn't be the one to hurt him.

What if I turned out to be a monster? What if, by not choosing to do whatever it took to protect Hayden, I was no better than the man who was supposed to shield me from the horrors of the world?

It's better this way.
He's better without you.
He's…safe.
Before he could turn around to see me, I spun on my heels.
And I left.
For good that time.

hayden

Sierra wasn't moving, completely frozen in place in the middle of the sidewalk.

"Sierra?" I called her name again before returning back to her, placing a hand on her shoulder.

She jumped, her panic-filled gaze darting to mine.

My stomach twisted in knots, nausea churning in my gut over all the scenarios of why she wasn't responding to me playing in my head. "Is everything okay?"

Her mouth gaped and her brows raised, her eyes going blank. "I-I came back," she stumbled over her words.

I furrowed my brow. "What? You came back?"

She nodded, tears welling in her eyes. "That fall. The next semester after we—" She shook her head like she was clearing a memory. "After the last court date when my dad got sentenced."

Maybe I was imagining things. "You came back."

"Yes." Her voice shrunk.

"Y-you. You didn't reach out. I had no idea." My chest constricted with this new information, a burning sensation rising in my throat.

"I know. I wanted to come back to surprise you." She hung her head, avoiding my gaze. "I saw you."

I flinched, tripping over my feet as I took a few steps backward, needing to create some space between us. I had so many questions.

Why didn't you come talk to me?

Did I not mean enough to you?

Was it something I did?

"You were with a girl. I-I thought you had moved on, that you were better without me. You looked happy. Safe." Sierra pulled her lip between her teeth, sadness creeping into her gaze.

She always had been the girl with the sad eyes.

"You deserved someone better than me, Hayes. Leaving was the only way I could keep you safe."

My fists clenched at my sides, and I was sure if I pressed my nails into my palms any harder, they would bleed. But that was the irony of it all, wasn't it?

A wave of emotions—disbelief, betrayal, grief for what could have been—washed over me.

"That wasn't your decision to make!" I yelled, louder than I had intended. Her body recoiled, and guilt sank into my chest. Yelling at her made me no better than the person I was trying to protect her from. I lowered my voice, but hurt still interlaced in my tone. "You should have told me."

Her response came out small, nothing like the Sierra I'd seen the past few months. Dejected almost. "I know. I'm sorry."

I took a few steps toward her, wanting to pull her into my arms and soothe all the hurt she was feeling, but she backed away from me.

My heart dropped. "Skip."

"I can't. I-I need to go somewhere."

Panic settled in my stomach. Where? Where was she going to go?

I reached for her arm. "What about the threats? It's not safe."

The whole reason we were here was so I could protect her. Was I already failing at that?

She pulled back, shaking her head. "I just need a minute alone to clear my head. I'll come right back."

I hesitated, unsure of how to respond.

Maybe it was because of some unhealthy attachment I had to her. Maybe it was because I was being selfish, but I didn't want her to go. I wanted to work this out, fix things. At least come to an understanding and move past the secrets, past these little miscommunications that had been plaguing us over the last decade.

Please don't go.

Don't leave me here again.

I'd bleed myself dry for you if you would just stay.

But I didn't say any of those things. Instead, the words, "Please don't run away again," fell from my lips, soft as a whisper.

She sighed. "I'm not going to run away. I promise."

"Pinky swear?" I extended my hand, pinky sticking out.

She linked her pinky finger with mine, bringing her hand up to her mouth to lock it in before murmuring, "Pinky swear."

I placed my hand over hers, squeezing three times. "I'm not leaving. I'll be right here when you're ready to come back, okay? I promise. I'll be right here for you, always."

She nodded, squeezing my hand in response.

"I love you."

She didn't say it back.

sierra

Throwing my hands in my pockets, I walked down the hill toward the parking lot Hayden's pickup was in. All I needed was a couple minutes to clear my head, to get the image of that day out of my system, and then I could go back. We could talk about it. I'd be ready this time.

I'd face it head-on instead of running away again.

I had to. For our future.

I'd fight for him this time because Hayden was it. In every imagination of my future, every single version of me, whether I was living in Montana or competing in rodeo or not, Hayden had a place in it.

Yes, I'd decided. I would hold my head up high, and I'd go back to him. I'd swallow my pride and do whatever it took to make it right. I'd get down on my knees and beg if that's what it took.

I loved him.

I *loved* him.

I nodded to myself over and over again, like I was giving myself an internal pep talk, which I sort of was.

"You can do this, Sierra," I murmured as I turned around with the intention of walking back up the hill.

A twig snapped behind me, and I spun around. "Hayden, I told you—"

"You." His voice—one I'd heard piercing through my nightmares the past five years—dripped with vitriol. He looked different, as though his time in prison had aged him. I wouldn't have recognized him if I hadn't heard his voice.

I couldn't move. It was like my feet were frozen to the ground, my muscles completely devoid of any feeling. Pins and needles pricked my fingers and toes as he stepped toward me.

"This is new." He reached out to grab a strand of my hair, letting it slide through his fingers before it fell back over my shoulder. "But still, there's no mistaking it. You look just like your mother, Sierra."

"What do you want?" I backed up slowly, as if the man in front of me was a wild animal and not my father. "Why are you here?"

Maybe if I stalled long enough, Hayden would catch up to us. He had to have been coming after me, right? He was too stubborn to actually let me go.

"I'm here because you ruined my life! I spent five years in prison because of you and your sad excuse for a mother. Five years in that hellhole because you were too *weak*." He spat out the words like they were poison on his tongue. "I didn't want it to come to this, but you didn't listen to my warnings. You *never* listen, do you?" Reaching into his pocket, he pulled out a revolver, the metal glinting under the street lamps as he flipped it in his hand. "You should have quit in August when I set your trailer on fire."

My eyes widened, images of the incidents that had occurred over the last few months flashing before my eyes.

The trailer fire. Pancho. The fear that I'd lost him to the smoke gripping my heart like claws.

The cut strap on my saddle. Thinking it was Michaela trying to sabotage me.

The nail in the tire of my pickup.

The lingering smell of cigarette smoke and the sensation that I was being watched.

The *brick* that he threw into Hayden's window.

Broken glass shattered on the floor, blood dripping down my hand. White, searing pain jolting through my face.

"How did you…"

"You're all over social media. I figured it would be harder and you'd be more careful, but it was so easy to track you down. You ruined my life. I had dreams! Goals! And now…" He laughed, the sound sinister and grating in my ears. "Now, it's only fair that I make sure yours never become a reality. We can make this easy, or we can do it the hard way."

He cocked the gun, a wicked grin spreading across his features.

"Go to hell," I hissed, against my better judgment. I should have stayed calm. Letting my emotions get the best of me would put me in a compromising position. I knew that. Getting mad at him would only provoke him.

He sighed as though he was disappointed in my response. This was the first time he almost seemed fatherly. But the sentiment vanished as quickly as it appeared. "I see." Taking a few steps closer to me, he raised the hand holding the gun. "The hard way it is."

Before I could react or run, a hard metal object came

crashing down onto my temple and the entire world went black.

sierra

MAY, SENIOR YEAR

Graduation was only a couple days away.

All I had to do was survive the next couple days, walk across the stage to get my diploma, and then I was done. Free. I was one step closer to finally getting out of this shithole and leaving the past, and all the pain it caused, behind me.

I had a little bit more pep in my step as I came home from school, tossing my backpack on the couch without thinking too much of it. I had nothing to hide.

I ran upstairs and threw on some more comfortable clothes—leggings and a tank top. I planned to go over to Hayden's house anyway for dinner under the guise that I was going to work. It had worked for me the past few years; I didn't see why I would ever stop.

As I pulled my hair back into a braid, the front door slammed shut. I could hear my father's heavy steps across the hardwood from upstairs, but I took a deep breath. I wasn't going to let him ruin my last week of high school. I was so fucking close to freedom, I could practically taste it.

A nervous ball of energy settled in my stomach, but I

pushed it aside. I would go downstairs and grab my backpack to take up to my room, do my homework, and then I'd leave.

I crept down the stairs as quietly as I could, careful not to make my presence known. It was no use, though. When I reached the base of the staircase, he was standing with his arms crossed and something in his hand. My backpack and its contents were scattered across the floor like he'd been rummaging through it for something.

You're a fucking, idiot, Sierra. You knew he was going to do something like this. Shame on you for thinking it was safe because you had nothing to hide, I thought as I kicked myself for leaving my bag on the couch.

"Hi?" I tried as hard as I could to keep a flat tone.

"What the fuck is this?" He waved the thing in his hand, and I realized it was a polaroid picture—one of me, Hayden, and Keenan during homecoming.

"Give it back!" I lunged for the photo, but he lifted it above his head.

"Answer the question. What the fuck is this?"

Frustration clawed at me, but I leveled out my voice. "It's a photo."

"No fucking shit, Sierra! Who are those boys? Is that who you're whoring around with these days?" He brought the photo down so he could take a look at it.

"That's none of your business," I muttered.

He squinted, staring at the picture more intently. "That kid. He looks fucking familiar." He flipped the photo around and pointed at Hayden. "Now that I think about it, they both do."

Hold your tongue, Sierra. Don't do anything stupid.

"Wait, no. I know what it fucking is," he growled. "They're the kids of those deputies who work for GCSO!

What the hell are you doing hanging around them? I warned you, you little bitch. If you got me in trouble, there'd be hell to pay. Now answer the fucking question."

My heart pounded in my chest.

"What. The. Hell. Are. You. Doing. Hanging. Around. Those. Boys." He bared his teeth like a feral animal with every word, enunciating each syllable.

"Please give me the photo back." My teeth ground as I extended my hand palm up.

"Yeah, I don't think so," he huffed, and then he ripped the photo right down the middle.

A cry tore itself from my throat, and I lunged at him against my better judgment, clawing at his arm to get the torn-up pieces.

He smacked me away, and I backed up a few feet, putting space between us.

"You've been hanging out with those sons of *pigs*, and you just expect me to be okay with it? Who the fuck do you think you are? Other than a good for nothing *slut* just like your mother." He spat out the words as he stalked toward me with a murderous expression on his face.

My mom raced into the living room before he could get to me.

"Stop it! Don't you dare fucking touch her!" Mom screamed at him, putting herself between us. "If you lay one hand on her, I'll leave. I swear it this time, Spencer. I will fucking leave, and I will take her with me."

"What the hell did you just say to me?" He spat in her face then reared back his fist. A sickening crunch pierced through the air as his knuckles made contact with Mom's face. The momentum sent her flying backward into the wall, and her hands flew up to her nose, the blood already flowing through her fingers.

"Mom!" I cried out, reaching for her.

"Sierra, don't!" she pleaded as my father stepped toward her.

"Stop!" My throat was already raw from screaming, from begging him to stop. "Please don't! Don't hurt her."

"I'm so sorry," Mom whispered.

All I could do was watch as he grabbed her throat, pinning her to the wall. His muscles rippled as he squeezed her neck, cutting off her air supply.

My feet were a thousand pounds, heavy chains wrapped around them to keep me in place.

Do something!

You can't let him do this!

Lunging forward, I wrapped my arms around his middle in an attempt to pull him off of her. When that didn't work, I kicked the back of his legs. I'd dislocated that boy's knees, I could do the same to him if I had to.

"Please! Get off of her!"

"You little brat! She deserves this! You both do!" Flinging me off his back, he released Mom from his grip for just a second. It was enough for her to slump to the ground, motionless.

Instead of going back to her, he walked into the kitchen. I didn't know what he was doing, so I took the opportunity to help Mom.

"Mom." I got down on my knees in front of her limp body. "Wake up. Come on, Mom. Please wake up. Mom!"

Before I could even react, his heavy footsteps returned. The moment I spun around to face him, it was too late. The bottle was already flying through the air before it shattered against the wall, glass shards raining down on us.

I tried to cover my head and protect Mom, but a sting of pain shot across my face.

Another bottle smashed against the wall, and then another, until the living room was a war zone, a battlefield covered in tiny little shards.

Rhythmic thuds against the floorboards filled my ears. Footsteps. Were they coming closer or were they retreating?

I braced myself to be hit, but the impact never came. The house was suspiciously quiet, but I didn't dare move a muscle.

I lay on the floor for minutes…hours?

I wasn't sure how long it'd been, but eventually, I hauled myself to my feet even though I felt weak, so weak. Taking in my surroundings, I surveyed the damage. Mom was still unconscious, and blood dripped down her face. Glass, some pieces speckled with red splotches, covered the hardwood, and sticky liquid pooled on the ground. Beer or blood, I couldn't tell.

The tang of copper filled my nostrils, and I pressed my fingers to the skin under my eye, wincing with the sting of pain that came with it before my hand retreated back down under my gaze.

Blood clung to my fingertips, and I squeezed my eyes shut, a lightheadedness threatening to overtake me. I'd deal with my injury later. I needed to help her.

Keeping my footsteps as light as possible, I stepped into the kitchen. My father had fallen to a drunken heap on the floor, but he was still breathing. I could tell by the rising and falling of his chest.

On my way over, I had debated grabbing one of the jagged pieces that covered the floor. It would be so easy, too easy, to plunge one of those pieces into his back, stab him like he'd stabbed us. Even if it wasn't literally, but psychologically. My scars may not have been visible, but I'd bore them for years, had taken blow after blow, cut after cut.

Yes. He deserves this. I won't be his punching bag any longer.

Leaning down, I picked up a piece of glass.

I can end everything right now. All the suffering. All the pain.

No one—not me, nor my mother—would ever have to live in fear again.

The sharp tip cut into my fingertip, but I let it fall back down to the floor. I didn't do it—couldn't do it—because if I went to prison because I got rid of him, it would affect the people I loved. So, instead, I reached for the phone on the counter and dialed three numbers.

"911, what's the address of your emergency?" The dispatcher's voice on the other end of the phone line crackled in my ear. "Hello? Are you there?"

Despite the shake in my voice, I spoke as clearly as I could. "Hi, yes, I'm here."

"What's the address of your emergency, hon?"

"2210 Sparrow Lane in Goldfinch." The address rattled off my tongue as I looked around, making sure my father wasn't getting up and couldn't hurt us more than he already had.

"Can you tell me what happened?"

"My…my father. He hurt us—me and my mom. Um…" My voice cracked as I walked back over to my mom. She was still unconscious, though she appeared to be breathing, just much slower than normal. "She's not moving. My father choked her then threw glass bottles at us. T-there's so much blood."

"Is he still there?"

"Yes. But he's not awake, either. He was drunk."

I heard typing in the background as the dispatcher listened.

"Okay, hon. Can you stay on the line? We've got officers on the way. They're five minutes out, okay?"

"Okay." I let out a deep breath, whether it was from relief or sadness, I wasn't entirely sure.

As promised, red and blue lights flashed outside the window a few minutes later.

My gaze caught on my mother, still lying motionless on the floor.

She stepped in to defend me. To protect me. She's not moving because of *me*.

I need to leave. I need to leave before anyone else gets hurt trying to defend me. The only way I can protect the people I love…is if I disappear.

CHAPTER FORTY-EIGHT

Sierra hadn't come back yet, and it was starting to get dark. We'd need to get back home soon if we were going to make it for dinner.

It was a long way, but maybe she started walking back to the house. If that was what it took for her to get her emotions in check, I wasn't going to interfere. We all had different ways to regulate our emotions, maybe walking was hers.

I dialed the home line anyway.

"Hayden?" Mom answered on the second ring.

"Hey, Mom. Did Sierra go back to the house?"

She hesitated on the other end of the line before replying, "No? Was she supposed to?"

Fuck.

Where could she have gone?

"No worries, Mom. I just wanted to double-check. We'll be home for dinner shortly." I did my best to mask the panic in my voice, tried to keep it steady.

"Hayden? Are you sure everything's okay?"

A lump in my throat constricted my air, and I swallowed it down.

Fuck.

I took a deep breath, forcing out the words. "She's gone, Mom. I don't know where she went. She said she would be right back and…"

"Oh, honey." Mom's voice broke a little. "Try calling her, okay?"

I nodded, even though I knew she couldn't see me. "I'll call you back, okay? I love you, Mom."

"I love you, too, honey."

The line beeped as she hung up, and I immediately dialed Sierra's number.

Come on, Sierra, come on. Pick up.

"Your call has been forwarded to an automated voice messaging system. The person you're trying to reach is unavailable. At the tone, please record—"

I hung up and dialed again. I'd call as many times as it would take for her to answer. We could figure this out. I'd talk it out with her all night if I had to.

"Your call has been forwarded—"

"Damn it! Come on, Skip." A plea ripped itself from my throat, the words floating up into the sky, reaching no one.

I jogged down the hill where the pickup was parked to see if she was waiting for me there. Maybe her phone just died, and she'd be leaning against the pickup, scowling at me even though it was obvious she was just trying to hide a smile.

When I got to the parking lot, she wasn't in the cab. She wasn't waiting by the pickup either, and a smattering of dark red staining the sidewalk greeted me instead.

My heart instantly hammered in my chest, worst-case

scenarios playing through my head. Something happened, and I wasn't there.

A feeling of helplessness washed over me as I placed my hands on the top of my head, my face tilting toward the sky.

Dammit! Where are you, Skip?

"Sierra!" I called her name but received no response. I ran around campus, back to the spot we originally separated, thinking maybe she had turned around and I'd just missed her.

When fifteen minutes had passed and I still hadn't found her, I dialed the next person I thought of.

"Hello?" my dad answered with a confused tone.

"Dad, Sierra's missing." I barely spat out the words through heaving breaths. "We got separated on SGU's campus, and now I can't find her and she won't answer her phone. Mom said she wasn't at the house, so I—"

"Slow down, son." Dad cut me off. "Take a deep breath. What happened?"

"We came to stay with you guys for a bit because Sierra's been getting threats for months. Back in August her trailer was set on fire and then her saddle got cut at a rodeo in Billings. She thought they were all a coincidence, but then someone threw a brick through my window so we came here because I didn't think it was safe back home. But then we came to campus and got into an argument. We got separated and now she's gone, Dad. A-and I'm worried that it might be…"

My dad sucked in a harsh breath as though the same idea dawned on him, too. I heard him typing furiously in the background, and then a noise of frustration ripped from his throat.

"Hayden, I need you to stay calm," he started to say,

and my heart felt like it was beating a mile a minute. "Sierra's father was released from prison four months ago."

"Why wasn't she notified?" I growled, my jaw clenching.

"The courts did try to notify her, but they were unable to reach her."

"Fuck!" I didn't mean to lose my cool, but Spencer Bayley was dangerous. "She changed her phone number, and she moves around so much that she wouldn't have a permanent address. This is not good, Dad."

"I know. If it truly is her father, then we need to approach this very carefully. We'll have SAR units deployed and dispatch will send out a BOLO. We'll find her, Hayden. Don't worry. Just stay put, okay?" It wasn't a request, rather an order. "Please, Hayden. I know you want to find her, but I need you to stay where you are."

It was like he knew exactly what I was thinking. And normally, I wouldn't disobey my father, but this was different. This was Sierra. The love of my life.

I thought I'd lost her to her father once before when she didn't show up to our high school graduation, and the same fear I felt back then creeped into my bones. I couldn't lose her to him again.

I *wouldn't*.

"Okay," I lied, knowing the moment I hung up the phone I was going to run all over town looking for her. I'd run myself into the ground if that's what it took.

"Thank you. We'll find her, son. I promise."

The minute we hung up, I hopped in my pickup and peeled out of the parking lot. If I had to drive around town all night I would. I wouldn't sleep, I wouldn't eat, I wouldn't stop until Sierra was safe.

I navigated to my police scanner app and turned the

volume all the way up. The second I heard something regarding Sierra, I would be on my way. I knew it wasn't smart to intervene, and I should leave the police work to my dad and his coworkers, but I couldn't just sit around and wait.

My mind filed through all of the places she could potentially be, places her father might drag her to, but I came up short. My mind couldn't operate the same way as a criminal's.

If I were a piece of shit who kidnapped my own daughter, where would I go?

Somewhere secluded for sure, but where?

Parking my truck at Ranger's, I ran down the street toward the gas station her father liked to frequent. A bell chimed as I flung open the door, heading straight for the counter where an employee had headphones on.

"Excuse me?" I slammed my hand down on the counter, scaring the young man.

He jumped, ripping his headphones off his head. "Huh?" He shook his head, blinking a few times. "S-sorry. How can I help you?"

"Did a woman about twenty-six years old, five-foot-five, jet-black hair, and green eyes come in with an older man by chance?" I rattled off the question.

"No, sorry, we've been really slow." He gestured to his phone where some animated cartoon with a pirate wearing a straw hat was playing.

"Okay, thanks." I pursed my lips and nodded, then rushed out the door back into the cold. The sun had gone down now, and time was of the essence. I ran around the block, keeping my eyes peeled for any signs of a struggle while listening to the police scanner.

Voices crackled on the radio. "We've got tracks leading

into the Jasper Wilderness near Bluebell Basin. SAR units dispatched to the area."

The part of Jasper Wilderness where SAR units were dispatched was a scarcely trafficked area with no trails for hikers. Only experienced backpackers and hunters frequented it, and rarely in November.

It was isolated and quiet. An ideal location to dispose of a body.

My lungs burned as I sprinted to my vehicle, speeding all the way out of town toward the base of a popular trail. I'd park there then figure out how the hell I was going to get to Bluebell Basin.

The trailhead was dark, the pine trees looming overhead and reaching into the night like skyscrapers. There were no police vehicles to be found, and I couldn't hear the crackle of their radios, so I started walking into the brush with a flashlight.

I was taking a huge risk, creeping into the forest like this when police were looking for a suspect, but it was one I was willing to take, even if it was fucking stupid.

I knew the general vicinity of where they said the tracks were, I was just going to be taking a roundabout way. Probably the best, considering my dad and his coworkers would have questions if I ran into them.

I hiked through the woods, careful not to make too much noise as to not alert Sierra's father of my presence.

Red and blue lights up ahead told me that I was close to the area, and I continued on, pausing every few seconds to listen for footsteps or a sign of struggle.

Voices up a few hundred feet or so caught my attention, and I moved as quickly as I could without drawing attention to myself. A small clearing was up ahead, and I hid behind a tree when a few silhouettes came into view.

"Put the gun down, Spencer," a deputy tried to reason with the man I knew was Sierra's father. Prison had hardened him even more. His eyes were hollow, and his appearance gave the impression that he hadn't shaved or showered in days. I feared what he would do to Sierra if they couldn't reach a resolution.

On the bright side, she was on the opposite side of the clearing from Spencer. He didn't have a gun to her head, so she must have been able to get away from him at some point.

"Don't take another step or I'll shoot." His voice was calm, steady; he was a fucking sociopath.

"Drop the weapon!" one of the other officers ordered Spencer as officers raised their guns. "Put the gun down, Spencer, and no one will get hurt."

"You boys almost convinced me, but I don't think so." Spencer raised his gun and pointed it toward Sierra. "I have nothing to lose anymore, so shoot me if you have to, but I'm taking her with me." His finger flirted with the trigger as he slowly squeezed it.

"Look out for your friends, Hayden. If they're in trouble, help them, okay?"

My dad's voice echoed in my ears.

Maybe I wasn't able to help Sierra before. I couldn't save her from the pain she endured as a kid, but I could save her now.

"Stop!" The scream ripped itself from my throat as I threw myself forward out of the bushes, in front of his line of fire.

Bang!

Bang!
Bang!

CHAPTER FORTY-NINE

sierra

I braced myself for the white-hot pain of bullets, squeezing my eyes as though accepting my fate.

The sound of three gunshots echoed through the forest, but the pain never came.

My eyes flew open just as my father's body crumpled to the ground, the tang of blood and smoky smell of gunpowder mixing in the air.

Relief flooded over me as I ran my hands over my body, checking for any signs of blood or wounds.

Nothing. Nothing hurt. I was safe.

It's over. It's okay. Everything is—

"Two-six-three to control." An officer spoke into his radio. "Shots fired. Suspect is deceased. Person down. A civilian. We need immediate assistance."

A civilian?

My vision focused on the additional body in front of me.

Hayden.

Lying still on the ground a few feet in front of me was Hayden.

No, no, no.

He'd put himself between me and the gun. *Why* would he do that?

My knees buckled, and I fell to the ground, crawling over to him. The world around me blurred, hot tears staining my cheeks.

Blood marred the fabric of his shirt near his shoulder, but I had no idea where the exit wound was or if there even was one. My hands searched his body, trying to find the place where I could stop the bleeding.

There was so much blood.

"Hayden!" I cried out.

He didn't say anything, eyelids fluttering as his mouth opened and closed like he was trying to say something. He rasped out a barely audible, "Skip," then his eyes closed.

"No! Hayes, come on. Wake up. Stay with me! Please," I begged, hunched over Hayden's motionless body, tears both staining my cheeks and dripping onto his face. "You can't leave. Please. You told me you wouldn't leave. You said you'd be right there waiting for me to come back! You promised!"

A sob ripped itself from my chest. "I'm sorry! Please, don't leave me."

This was all my fault. If we hadn't gotten into that argument, if I hadn't left, this wouldn't have happened.

Strong arms lifted me away from the body, even though I kicked and screamed and fought against them.

Eventually, my limbs stopped moving from fatigue.

Lights flashed and sirens blared around us. Someone's radio crackled near me, Roy's, or maybe the other officer's. But I was numb. All I could think about was Hayden.

I'm sorry.

I couldn't protect you.

I'm sorry.

I love you.

My heart poured out all the things I didn't get to say to him.

I'm sorry.

I failed you.

sierra

An incessant beeping echoed through the hallway, bouncing off the sterile, too-perfect walls of the hospital in Goldfinch.

I sat in one of the hard, uncomfortable chairs in the waiting room, wringing my hands together and tapping my foot so hard I was sure the receptionist would get annoyed with me and tell me to stop. But I was also sure they were trained not to do that, given they worked in a hospital and these types of places were the source of a lot of stress for most people. They probably had more empathy than I gave them credit for.

The paramedics arrived on the scene in record time, racing Hayden to the hospital after Roy carried him back down the mountain. When he looked at me after they drove away with his son, his face was ashen, as though he'd seen a ghost.

"I'm so sorry," I stammered, tears welling in my eyes. "I didn't know he was going to do that. It's all my fault. If I hadn't…"

Roy patted me on the shoulder, stopping me from finishing my sentence. "It's not your fault, Sierra. Please don't blame yourself. This is Hayden we're talking about." Wiping his eyes, he let out a shattered breath. "He's nothing if not my son, and I should have known he wouldn't stand by and wait. He loves you."

"I know." I bit my lip hard enough to draw blood.

"Come on, I'll drive you to the hospital." He placed a hand on my back and led me to his pickup, his lights still flashing.

"Sierra?" Mae jogged over to me. When I stood, she yanked me into her arms, squeezing me like I'd vanish if she let go. "I was so worried when Hayden called and said you weren't with him. Are you okay? Are you hurt?"

"No, no, I'm fine," I reassured her. "I have a minor concussion, but I'm okay."

She pulled back, emotion glistening in her eyes. "Oh, thank goodness. I don't know what I would have done if something happened to both of you."

Tears burned behind my eyes, my vision blurring until my cheeks were damp. "Mae, I'm so sorry. I didn't mean to put him in danger."

She took a step back, but her hands still clasped my arms in a protective way. "Honey, no. This is not your fault. Please, tell me you understand that." She raised her brows, giving me a stern look. "You were just a child, you hear me? You were an innocent person dragged into a horrible scheme by a monster. Do not blame yourself."

More tears leaked from my eyes, because that look was what a parent should have been like. A parent who cared enough about me to be stern, but also empathetic and kindhearted.

Nodding, I wiped my eyes. "Yes, I understand."

"Good." She brushed a loose strand of hair out of my eyes. "You deserved so much better, Sierra. I'm so sorry we weren't there to protect you."

She pulled me back in, holding me there for what felt

like minutes. But I reveled in it, sank into her touch. A mother's embrace.

Mae had always been more like a mother to me than my own.

"Mrs. Watkins?" A nurse appeared from the hallway.

Mae perked up and released me from the hug. "That's me."

"Your son is out of surgery. Everything went smoothly, and he's awake if you'd like to come see him."

"You'll be okay?" Mae asked me, her brows furrowing in concern.

I nodded. "Yeah, I'll be okay. Go."

She squeezed my hand three times. "Okay. Love you, Sierra."

"I love you, too," I murmured, but she was already disappearing down the hall with the nurse.

I sat in the lobby, tapping my foot as I waited. The TV was playing a kid's cartoon and my eyes caught on the screen for a little while, but mostly it was like I was in a dream state, disassociated with the world around me.

Heavy footsteps approached my chair. When I looked up, Roy was standing over me.

"He can have more visitors now if you'd like to see him," he said. His mouth was flattened into a thin line, so unlike the Roy I'd grown up knowing. His eyes had a blankness to them.

"I would. If that's okay."

"Of course it's okay, Sierra." His expression softened as he helped me up, and we walked down the hall to the room Hayden was in.

My heart lurched in my chest at the sight of him. Despite the tubes and wires hooked up to him, a bright smile that spread to his eyes appeared on his face when I stepped in the door. Bandages covered his shoulder under his blue hospital gown, but he appeared to be in good spirits.

My vision blurred, and I blinked tears away.

"We'll give you two a minute." Mae kissed Hayden on the forehead before squeezing my shoulder as she exited the room with Roy.

I practically ran over to his bedside, not wanting to have any more distance between us. Never again. "I thought I'd lost you."

Tears rolled down my cheeks, and Hayden reached out to wipe one away.

"I told you I wasn't going to leave, Skip. I pinky promised, remember? And I never break a promise."

My chest tightened as I whispered, "I'm sorry, Hayes. I'm so sorry. I should have stayed with you."

"Hey, hey, hey." He squeezed my hand with the little strength he had. Funny, even when he was the one lying in a hospital bed, he was still the one to comfort me. "You know who we were dealing with. Who's to say it wouldn't have happened another time, and I wouldn't have been able to get to you? Don't blame yourself for a single second, Sierra." His tone turned stern. "This is not your fault. Do you understand that?"

I nodded. "I-I was just scared. Scared that you were gone and I'd never get the chance to tell you I love you, too."

"You love me, Skip?" Emotion glistened in his eyes even as his lips curled up into a boyish smile.

"Yeah, Hayes." My lip trembled as I blinked back tears. I pulled my bottom lip between my teeth, biting back a laugh. "I love you. I never stopped, either."

"Hey, nurse! Did you hear that?" Hayden yelled, his words echoing off the walls. "She *loves* me!"

"Shhh." I giggled, pressing a gentle kiss to his lips.

"I love you, too, Skip. In every single universe. Every single lifetime." He raised my hand up to his lips before locking eyes with mine. "I loved you ten years ago, I love you today, and I'll love you a hundred years from now."

"Even if we aren't alive anymore?" I laughed.

He nodded. "Even if all that's left of us is the dust of our bones."

I leaned down, pressing my lips to his, tasting the salt of my tears. My forehead pressed against his and our breathing synced, but neither of us made any moves to pull away.

When we finally separated, it was my turn to scold him. "No more playing Superman, okay? I know you were trying to help, but I don't need saving. Not when it comes at the risk of your life."

"Skip," he protested.

"No, Hayes. Listen to me, please," I pleaded, hoping the emotion reached my eyes as well so he knew how serious I was. "You've helped me so much, baby. I don't need you to save me because all I need is to have you by my side, supporting me. And I can't have that if you risk your life."

"Okay." He nodded, understanding reflecting in his gaze.

"Thank you."

"I love you, Skip."

"I love you, too, Hayes. Always."

hayden

TWO WEEKS LATER

"Do we have everything?" Sierra asked as she balanced a casserole dish in her arms along with a big container of peanut butter cookies that my mom had sent home with us.

We were heading out the door to go to Colter and Ellison's place for Thanksgiving. It was both a Thanksgiving dinner and a "Welcome Back, Hayden" party, apparently, even though I'd been out of the hospital for a few days now.

I was lucky enough that the bullet only hit me in the shoulder on my left side, damaging the soft tissue surrounding the joint. The exit wound was fairly clean and fortunately none of my bones were fractured. The doctors implied that someone was looking out for me that night because there wouldn't be any long-term effects that would impact my rodeo career. The blood loss and shock caused me to pass out, but I was cleared from the hospital relatively quickly, after undergoing surgery to remove any bullet fragments, with orders to take it easy for a while.

"We should have everything," I replied, holding the

front door open for her and pressing a kiss to her head as she passed by after shooing Pancho back to her bedroom. "Don't worry, love. They won't be mad if we forget something."

Her cheeks flushed, but she quickly mumbled, "I know. I just want to make sure I'm contributing."

Even though Spencer was gone, Sierra had been a bit jumpy the last few weeks, and understandably so. Instead of buying a new trailer and getting back on the road, she'd insisted on staying with me longer, though I wasn't opposed to that idea. I wasn't opposed to the idea of her staying with me forever.

She'd also opened up about everything that had happened the last few months, and even before then. The true story about what happened that night back in May our senior year and what caused her to leave the first time. The guilt she felt surrounding not being able to protect the people she cared about and the fear that someone else would get hurt trying to help her. The anxiety attacks and the therapist she saw for a while. Her fears of being abandoned again by the people she cared about.

I'd suggested reaching out to Elena about coming in for a session, because even though it'd been years, it might be beneficial. A quick Google search told me she still worked in Goldfinch. We could both see her, because God knew it would benefit me, too.

After Sierra called me out in the hospital for risking my life, I came to the realization that growing up, I'd developed a bit of a savior complex. All I'd wanted to do was help people, even if they didn't need or want it.

I knew now that sometimes the people I cared about just needed support. But even though Sierra was right—I couldn't support the people I loved if I risked my life and wasn't around—never once did I regret taking that bullet for her. Not even for a moment.

Admittedly, the first few nights in the hospital, I woke in a puddle of sweat, nightmares of losing Sierra to her dad's twisted plans haunting my sleep. In every scenario, I didn't make it to her in time—I wasn't there to save her, and I had to watch the life drain out of her eyes as I held her in my arms.

I wondered if that was how she felt when she thought she was going to lose me.

She sat watch at the hospital every minute she could, despite my insistence that she needed to rest, too, and could go home. That I would be fine. Part of me thought she believed that if she let me out of her sight, I'd disappear on her, but that couldn't have been further from the truth. Sierra Bayley was stuck with me. There was no world in which I would ever leave her. Not now, not ever, really.

If I was the sun, then Sierra was my moon, creating light in times of darkness.

I rang the doorbell when we got to Colter and Ellison's place, and I could already hear the shuffle and chatter of people inside.

"Come in!" Ellison called out to us, and I opened the door, revealing all of our friends standing underneath a store bought banner that read *Happy Birthday* but *Birthday* was crossed out and replaced with *Thanksgiving*. Someone had also written in smaller letters *Homecoming, Hayden* underneath the *Thanksgiving* as well.

"Welcome home, Hayden!" everyone cheered, except Mikey, who said, "Happy Thanksgiving!"

I huffed out a laugh because the sign and all their antics were oddly fitting.

"How are you feeling, buddy?" Colter gently wrapped his arm around me as he led both me and Sierra into the kitchen where a whole spread of food was waiting.

"I'm feeling fine. This one"—I squeezed Sierra's shoulder—"has insisted on babying me for the last couple weeks. At first it was cute, but now I'm ready to get back to normal life."

Sierra sputtered out some words in protest as she set down her trays, but I pulled her into my arms and kissed her on the forehead.

"I like when you take care of me, Skip."

"Is everyone here now?" Isa asked from her spot on the couch next to Reid.

Ellison counted everyone in attendance—her, Colter, Reid, Isa, Mikey, Juniper, Jake, Keenan, Sierra, and myself —then nodded. "I think so?"

A knock at the door got everyone's attention.

"Uh, honey, were you expecting anyone else?" Colter raised his brows.

"Not that I'm aware of?" She furrowed her brows as she headed toward the door, opening it to a shivering Caitlin and Whitley, her three-year-old daughter.

"Caitlin! What are you doing here?" Ellison pulled her into a hug before squatting to her niece's eye level. "Miss Whitley, it's so good to see you."

"Hey, sis," Colter greeted her.

"Sorry to barge in, guys. I hope you don't mind that we're here." Caitlin sounded like she was out of breath.

"No, not at all," Ellison reassured her while the rest of us awkwardly observed the exchange. "I thought you guys were spending the holiday in Washington?"

Caitlin pulled her bottom lip between her teeth and shook her head. "Had a change of plans. Adam had an emergency business trip. I thought Mom might be home, but it looks like she went to Bozeman instead."

Out of the corner of my eye, I noticed Jake roll his eyes, his fists clenching at his sides.

"Well, we're so happy you're here!" Isa jumped up from the couch, prompting the rest of us to welcome the pair into the house. "Whitley, what do you like to eat?" She took the little girl's hand in hers, leading her over to the living room as Caitlin offered her a grateful smile.

"I like patotoes!" Whitley squealed, her blonde pigtails bobbing as she jumped up and down excitedly. "And turkey!"

"Wow!" Isa giggled at her mispronunciation of potatoes. "Good thing we have both of those things! Are you going to eat so much and grow up to be a big girl?"

"Yeah! I'm gonna be big like him!" She pointed at Jake.

Jake grinned as he scrubbed his chin.

"Well, now that everyone's here, should we eat?" Ellison asked, gesturing to the kitchen. "Go ahead, guys. Help yourself."

"We turning on the football game?" Jake called from the kitchen.

Isa and Ellison both rolled their eyes at him.

"If you insist." Ellison let out an exaggerated sigh. "Men and their football."

"Don't lie, Ellie girl, you love it, too," Jake fired back. "Colter's told me all about how competitive you get during playoff season."

She shrugged. "Guilty." Immediately shifting back into boss mode, she gestured for the guys to get moving. "All right, come on. Let's get this line moving, boys. We've got a little girl who needs to eat!"

"I want turkey and mashed patotoes!" Whitley cheered, sending us all into a fit of laughter.

I cleared my throat once everyone was seated with food. "Before you all ask me the same questions over and over again, yes, I'm feeling better. No, I'm not in too much pain. I'm ready for everything to be back to normal, so please don't treat me like I'm breakable. That's all, thank you."

A few mouths gaped, but then several people shrugged and went back to eating.

"If that's what you want, Haydie, we've got you." Mikey nodded.

"Guess that means you're going to be opening the chute the next time we practice roping," Reid teased.

Sierra shot me a stern look, but I grinned.

"You've got yourself a deal."

It was late when we stumbled through the front door of my house. Sierra changed into pajamas then let Pancho out as I put away the leftovers Ellison sent home with us.

Pancho ran back toward Sierra's bedroom when she let him back inside, and she started to follow him, but I stopped her before she disappeared down the hallway.

"Sierra, wait."

She turned her head to look over her shoulder. "Hm?"

"Do you want to…" I cleared my throat, swallowing the nervous lump. "Do you want to sleep in my room tonight?"

Her head swung to her open bedroom door, but then she turned around to face me. "Yeah. I do, Hayes."

"Come on, then, love." I took her hand in mine as I joined her in the hallway and led her back to my room.

Sierra whistled for Pancho as I changed into sweatpants and a loose T-shirt, but the naughty little devil ignored her.

She snorted, rolling her eyes. "Whatever, I guess. He can have a room all to himself." She closed the door then flopped down on the bed, rolling onto her side.

I rolled so we were lying face-to-face and reached out to brush a strand of hair behind her ear.

"Has that room always been vacant?" she asked, propping herself up on her elbow.

I nodded, wondering if I should tell her the real reason why.

"But there's furniture in there and everything. Why didn't you get a roommate?"

Fuck it, I thought. I wasn't going to keep secrets from Sierra anymore. Not after almost losing her again.

"It was always meant to be yours." I scraped a hand through my hair as I waited for a reaction. Her eyes widened a bit, but she didn't respond, so I continued. "The room was always meant to be for you in case you came back. Maybe it was delusional, but I wanted to hold on to the hope that one day you'd reach out to me and we'd reconnect. I nearly did rent it out, but at the last minute panicked and backed out. It's always belonged to you, just like I always have. I know that's probably weird and creepy but—"

She didn't give me time to finish my sentence because her hands cupped my jaw and her lips smashed against mine.

"I can't believe you did that," she murmured against

my lips. "But I always kind of wondered why you had a purple room in your house."

"You don't think I'm crazy?" I asked, pressing my forehead to hers.

She laughed, a soft, breathy one. "No, I do, but you're *my* kind of crazy. I wouldn't change you for the world, Hayes." She planted a kiss on my cheek as she said, "I love that you can be a little crazy," then one on my jaw with, "I love that you're fiercely loyal to the people you care about," a kiss below my earlobe as she whispered, "I love that you'd take a bullet for the people you love, even though that was a stupid fucking thing to do," and finally, with a kiss and nip to my neck, "and I love that even though you can be a little overbearing and overprotective, you never tried to fix me. Instead, you showed me I was never broken to begin with. That I'm strong, capable. Worthy."

"I love you, Sierra. So much." A whine slipped from my lips as her hand trailed down my stomach, her mouth biting and sucking the sensitive flesh on my neck before her tongue darted out to soothe the sting.

sierra

My hand slipped beneath the waistband of Hayden's sweatpants, cupping his hardening length. A groan slipped from his lips, and he gripped my waist as I nipped his earlobe between my teeth.

"How's your arm?" I asked, not wanting to go any further if he was in any sort of pain. The doctors had told him to take it easy, and I was sure sex was on the list of activities to hold off on.

"It's fine," he bit out through a moan, his hand sliding down to squeeze my ass. "Don't stop."

Hooking my fingers in the waistband of his sweats and boxers, I pulled them down to his knees. His cock lay hard against his stomach, and I wrapped my hand around it, pumping the length a few times. His hips bucked as I swiped my thumb across the crown, pre-cum gathering in a bead at the tip.

I scooted further down the bed, toward Hayden's knees, as he rolled onto his back. I took his length into my mouth, swirling my tongue around the tip and using a hand to stroke it while I sucked.

"S-Sierra," Hayden moaned, his fingers grasping the top of my head.

I bobbed up and down, taking him deeper and deeper while my eyes bounced up to his face. He'd thrown his head back in pleasure, mouth gaped. My eyes watered as his tip hit the back of my throat, but I kept a steady pace.

"F-fuck, Sierra. I'm going to come if you keep this up."

I sat up, his cock coming out of my mouth with a pop. "That's kind of the point, babe."

His length was wet with my spit, and I grasped it in my hand, pumping it a few more times before taking off my clothes and throwing them to the side.

Hayden, after seeing what I was doing, pulled his shirt over his head and kicked his pants off so we were both naked.

My hands dragged down my body to my clit and, using two fingers, I rubbed circles on the sensitive spot. Hayden pumped his cock as he watched me touch myself, lust shining in his gaze.

"Come here, love." He patted my leg, and I moved my body so I was straddling him.

Hayden guided his cock inside me as I sank down on him, a sigh falling from my lips at the sudden fullness.

I rocked my hips, adjusting to his size. His fingers dug into my waist, holding me down.

Leaning forward, I moved up and down on his cock, my breasts bouncing in front of me. My hands gripped the sheets next to Hayden's body, and he leaned forward to kiss me, pinching my nipple with one hand and cupping my jaw with the other.

"You're so good, Sierra. Keep doing that," he gasped, falling back onto the sheets.

"Hayes," I moaned while I rode him, long locks of my

hair falling into my face as my back arched. "You're so b-big."

Every time I had sex with Hayden felt like the first time, his size stretching and filling me. Emotionally, it felt that way, too, like he was breaking down all the walls I'd built up around my heart the past five years.

My pussy clenched around his cock, and he bucked his hips, meeting me stroke for stroke.

Sitting back up, I pressed a hand on the center of his chest as I rocked my hips back and forth. Hayden's length brushed against my clit with every movement, sending shockwaves through my body.

His nose scrunched and eyes squeezed as I ground my hips against his, so I paused for a moment.

My face twisted in concern. "Are you okay? Am I hurting you?"

Ocean-blue eyes stared into mine as he shook his head. "No, Sierra, you're not hurting me. The opposite, actually. I want to fuck you so badly." He lifted me off him, moving as though he intended to switch our positions.

"But your shoulder," I started to protest.

"We'll take it easy. I'll be careful, I promise." He planted a kiss on my forehead. "Will you get on your hands and knees for me?"

My core clenched as I crawled up to the headboard on my hands and knees, switching spots with Hayden. Over my shoulder, I watched Hayden pump his cock in his hand then guide it toward my entrance, slipping inside with ease.

A heavy sigh turned into a moan as he started to move, sliding deeper and deeper with each thrust. My back arched as he pressed his weight into me, my body tightening like a coil around him.

This position, this angle, was too much all at once.

Every nerve in my body was on edge, pleasure racking through my veins.

"Oh, Sierra, fuck," he cursed, gripping my hips so he could pound into me harder and faster. "You're… squeezing me so tight."

"Hayes." My eyelids fluttered as an orgasm crashed over me. My heart pounded in my chest, my entire body begging for more of him. "I'm coming, Hayden." His name fell off my lips like a prayer, and my back bowed off the bed, breasts pressing deeper into the soft sheets.

"I'm almost there, love," Hayden breathed out in a half moan, half stutter.

I didn't think I could come again so fast, but when his pace quickened, stars scattered around my vision as he brought me over the edge for a second time. His cock twitched, and my name accompanied with a string of expletives fell from his mouth as his cum spilled inside me.

After gathering his composure, he slowly inched out of me with a sigh. His release dripped down my thighs, and he quickly grabbed a towel to clean up, wiping the cloth across my inner thighs before pressing it against my center.

He flopped down on the bed next to me. "Come here." He patted his chest, and I rolled so I could rest my head on him.

His fingers raked through my hair, scratching my scalp. I sighed, snuggling closer to him to absorb his warmth.

"I could get used to this," he whispered with a smile.

"Me, too," I admitted, and for once, it wasn't a lie. With my father gone, the fear that had found a home inside me had started to dissipate. I could really picture myself staying here with Hayden and the horses and his rowdy group of friends.

"I love you, Skip. With everything that I am. You're not

just my moon and stars, you're my entire universe," Hayden murmured into my hair, his hand sliding down to my back where he started rubbing slow circles.

"I love you, too, Hayes. Always have, always will."

sierra

The bright city lights of Las Vegas greeted us in a flashy, larger-than-life welcome for a girl from a small town in Montana.

I resisted the urge to press my nose up against the glass of the passenger-side window like a child outside a candy store. I'd traveled all over the world in the five years since I'd graduated high school, but I hadn't yet had the chance to make it out here.

"How's it feel?" Hayden chuckled when he noticed me staring.

I twisted to face him, a wide grin on my face as I replied, "You know how people always talk about singers having their 'I made it' moments? Kind of like that. But also a bit like a dream. Don't pinch me, but I worry if I blink, it'll all vanish."

He reached over and took my hand in his, squeezing it gently. "*You* did this, Skip. It's not going to disappear, because it's real. You're real, and you're here."

Tears of happiness welled in my eyes, and Hayden's eyes softened.

"Hey, what's wrong?" He released my hand to wipe a stray tear that had started to fall.

"Nothing's wrong. Really. I'm just…proud. I'm not sure eighteen-year-old me was convinced I'd make it to today, much less the NFR," I admitted.

Hayden, with one hand on the wheel and the other cupping my cheek, smiled. "You should be proud of yourself. You should be so damn proud, Sierra. Soak it all in because you made it."

In reality, I'd only have about fifteen minutes to soak it all in because the minute we arrived at the hotel, it would be boots on the ground. I'd get Lucky settled first and foremost, but practice for the grand entry as well as the NFR welcome reception and back number ceremony would be that night.

Then, in addition to early morning practice runs before competing every night for ten days straight, I'd have meetings with sponsors, interviews, and autograph sessions during the day. I knew I'd hardly have time to breathe, but, for whatever reason, it didn't make me nervous. Instead, a wave of calm washed over me.

If that scared, fourteen-year-old version of myself who didn't know if there'd ever be an end to the pain and suffering could only see me now. I liked to think she'd be proud, too.

Purple silk so dark it almost looked black clung to my body as I waited for the back number ceremony to begin. We'd already had a red carpet-esque event where Hayden stood by me the whole time as we took hundreds of pictures.

We separated as he went into the audience, and I joined the rest of the competitors. I had no idea what to expect, but I noticed a lot of familiar faces other than the obvious ones in Colter, Reid, Jake, and Mikey.

A hand clasped down on my shoulder, and my body tensed before a low chuckle followed.

"Sorry, Sierra, didn't mean to scare you," Colter apologized, lifting his hand off my shoulder to scrub it across his facial hair. "Pretty incredible, isn't it?"

This definitely wasn't Colter Carson and Reid Lawson's first rodeo. In fact, this was their fifth appearance at the NFR, and they'd brought home plenty of hardware in the last five years.

"I keep waiting for the moment I wake up and this was all a dream." I laughed. "I'm sure it'll feel more real tomorrow when I'm in the arena, but right now it just feels…surreal."

Reid joined us next. "I remember the first time we made it and felt the same way. You worked hard to be here. Especially considering everything that happened the last few months, you deserve this."

"Thanks, guys." Heat creeped into my cheeks at the compliments. I wasn't used to people acknowledging my achievements, much less being happy for me.

"Knock 'em dead out there." Colter winked before he and Reid walked off to talk to some of the other cowboys.

From the stage, the man who was hosting the back number ceremony greeted the crowd. "Welcome to Las Vegas, everybody! It's time to kick off this year's Wrangler NFR!"

A video played, and then they were calling up the top fifteen bareback bronc riders in the world. Each event would be called one by one, with barrel racing being second to last, right before bull riding.

"It's time to announce your top fifteen barrel racers in the world!"

In a single file line, all of the barrel racers walked down the runway toward the stage. Cameras flashed from the audience, and people held out their hands to high five some of the girls. We lined up on the side of the stage, and the number fifteen barrel racer was announced.

Then it was my turn.

"She's a cowgirl from Montana, and she's come all the way to Las Vegas for her first ever NFR! Back number one-oh-seven, Sierra Bayley!"

A smile so wide I was sure my cheeks would ache later spread across my face as I received my back number and walked to the center of the stage. Spotlights shone on me and cameras flashed as I waved to the crowd then walked down the runway.

"Looking good, Skip." Keenan and Hayden met me after I grabbed all the gifts competitors would receive from sponsors, including my official NFR jacket.

"Thanks, Kee. This will be you guys next year." I ruffled the hair on Keenan's head, but threw him a death glare when he reached to touch mine. "Ah-ah," I tutted. "Don't mess up my hair, Chase."

"That's not fair! Why do you get to mess up mine?" He pouted.

Hayden laughed. "Because you're not the one who's about to have a hundred more pictures taken of her."

"So, what do you want to do to celebrate tonight?" Keenan nudged me with his elbow as we walked.

"Sleep?" I laughed, which turned into a yawn. I'd been going since six this morning.

"Skippy," he whined. "You're *killing me*. Come out for one drink at least. Please?" He pouted his lips and gave me puppy dog eyes.

I rolled my eyes. "Fine. One drink. Then I'm getting a jumbo slice of pizza and going to bed."

"That's the spirit! Look at us. Hazey, Skippy, and Kee back together again in Sin City. I could be a poet. Or a rapper." He nodded as he chuckled to himself.

Hayden and I raised our brows at each other before letting collective snorts at his antics.

"Just like old times." Hayden threw his arm around my shoulder and tugged me close to him as we headed out to take more pictures.

hayden

Keenan, the girls—Ellison, Isa, and Juniper—and I sat together in the front row as night seven of the NFR commenced. Colter and Reid were on track to win their first world championship buckle, and Mikey looked like a solid contender for the NFR average title in bull riding.

Sierra had competed well, too, and my heart burst with pride seeing her compete at the most important event in professional rodeo.

"Has Sierra decided what she's going to do after the NFR is over?" Ellison asked. She knew how badly I wanted Sierra to stay in Silver Creek, and I was pretty sure she'd been dropping hints to Sierra about it the whole week.

I shook my head. "Not sure yet. I'm not going to pressure her, but ever since the…" I cleared my throat. "Since the incident, she's been a lot more relaxed. It took some time, but part of me thinks I could convince her to stay."

"That's so cute!" Isa squealed, her eyes sparkling with excitement and pure joy for me.

"You two are so good for each other," Juniper agreed. "From what I've seen, at least."

Keenan smirked. "They've always been great together. I think they just needed to get out of their own way. For the longest time, you both tortured yourselves into thinking you couldn't be happy."

I threw him a glare, and he shrugged.

"It's true. You may not think you were self-sabotaging, Hazey, but in a weird way, you were. Sure, Sierra was more obvious about it, but I don't know. You focused so much on protecting her. And she did what she thought would protect you, too."

I had to agree, even though I didn't want to. Sierra had left without saying goodbye, but I now understand that, in her own way, it was an act of love. What she thought was her final gesture of love toward me was leaving to guarantee my safety. While I was angry about it for a while, and didn't get how she could make that decision for me, I learned to understand the way her mind worked. After so many years of trauma and abuse, she did what she thought was best for both of us.

"Yeah, I know," I grumbled.

Keenan patted me on the back. "All that to say, I'm so glad you two are finally together. It's been a long time coming, and I know you make each other so happy. I'm proud of you guys."

A small smile tugged at my lips. "Thanks, Keenan."

Music blared over the speakers, and the microphone crackled as the announcer started talking. "It's night seven of the NFR, and we've got more barrel racing coming your way. She came into the NFR number fourteen in the world, and she's been sitting pretty in the middle of the leaderboard this week. A cowgirl from the state of

Montana, she's riding on Ace's Lucky Charm! Sierra Bayley!" He dragged out Sierra's name as she and Lucky raced down the alleyway.

"Let's go, Sierra!" the girls cheered as the pair rounded the first barrel, keeping their turns sharp and precise.

I sat on the edge of my seat, my hands grasping the plastic.

"Whoa there, Hazey. Loosen up or you'll snap that seat in half." Keenan chuckled at my white knuckles.

"What?" My eyes flicked down toward my hands, and I lifted them from the chair, though it didn't stop them from shaking.

"She's doing great, dude. Look." He pointed toward the arena where they were heading toward the third and final barrel.

Once they made it around, cutting through the cloud of dust that rose from the ground, they sprinted toward the alleyway. Sierra's hair flew behind her, her legs kicking Lucky's flank as he pushed with all his might. She patted his neck encouragingly as they crossed the time barrier and slowed to a stop.

"Thirteen-point-four-eight seconds for Sierra Bayley and Ace's Lucky Charm!"

A zoomed-in angle of her face projected on the jumbotron. She looked over at the section we were sitting in, a beaming smile on her face before she threw me a wink and waved at the crowd.

"That's my girl." I slumped back in my seat, finally able to relax knowing she kicked ass out there.

The minute our hotel room door slammed shut behind us, Sierra's lips were on mine. One of my hands tangled in her hair as the other gripped her waist, walking her back toward the bed.

"My little barrel racing star," I murmured as I nuzzled my face in her neck. "You were incredible out there tonight."

"You think so?" She pulled her bottom lip between her teeth as the backs of her thighs hit the bed.

"I know so. Watching you under those arena lights?" I blew a raspberry with my lips. "You looked like a queen."

She raised up on her toes, planting a kiss on my lips. "I had my lucky charm in the stands today."

I made a *tsk* sound. "Skip, you don't need luck. But I'm glad I can be here for you. Now, will you let me treat you like the queen you are tonight?"

She nodded, raising her arms so I could pull her blouse over her head. Reaching around her back, I unclasped her bra, letting her breasts spill out. Her nipples were already hardening, and I rolled one between my fingers, pulling a sigh from her lips.

Wrapping my arms under her thighs, I lifted her onto the bed then dropped to my knees before her. After taking off her jeans, slowly rolling the fabric down her legs, I kissed a trail up from her knee to the inside of her thigh, my eyes darting up to hers.

She sucked in a breath as I dipped my index finger under the band of her underwear and swiped it up her center before swirling her arousal over her clit. Slipping the same finger inside her, I looked up as she pulled her bottom lip between her teeth. Adding my middle finger, I curled them a couple times as she tightened around me.

"I love seeing you like this," I murmured, knowing it

was just going to get better and better the longer we were together. Although I felt like I knew a lot about her—what made her tick and what made her feel good—I wanted to become an expert on how to make her body react to me the way it was right then.

"I need more," she bit out through gritted teeth, wiggling her hips to push my fingers deeper.

I pulled my fingers back, despite her protests, to hook them in the band of her panties and take them down her legs. I helped her get one leg out, then she kicked the tiny piece of cloth somewhere behind me.

Pushing her legs further apart, I settled myself between them. My mouth lowered to her clit and sucked on the sensitive flesh. Her thighs tightened around my head as I lapped at her entrance, licking a broad stroke up her slit.

"That feels so good, Hayes. Please," she gasped, "keep going."

Her praise made my stomach flutter. With one hand, I pushed her thigh away, and with the other, I slid two fingers inside her to work in tandem with my tongue. My thumb worked circles over her clit and my mouth savored every taste of her.

"F-fuck," she moaned, hips bucking toward me as her head fell back. "Oh, God."

She was close, I could feel it in the way her thighs trembled around me.

I buried my face between her thighs, my tongue flicking every sensitive part of her until she fell apart at my hands. Shattered breath fell from her lips as her first orgasm crashed over her, wetness coating her thighs and my tongue and fingers.

When I came back up for air, her chest was heaving and her face flushed.

"This is hardly fair, you know." She gestured to my fully clothed body.

I laughed, immediately pulling my shirt over my head. "I can fix that."

She reached for my belt buckle, and I let her undo it as well as the button and zipper on my jeans. Soon, the only thing between us was my boxers, my cock straining against them.

"Take them off, Hayes," she whispered, her tongue darting out to lick her lips.

Sierra scooted back on the bed so she was closer to the headboard, and I crawled toward her after taking my boxers off.

Pressing a gentle kiss to her lips, I murmured, "Hey, Skip."

"Hi, Hayes."

"How do you want me, love?" I asked, spitting in my hand and fisting my cock.

"I want to look at you," she answered.

"Come here, then." Scooping my hands underneath her thighs, I pulled her close.

Kissing down her neck, I reached her breasts, taking a nipple into my mouth to swirl my tongue around it. When I lightly nipped the bud, Sierra's breath hitched, and I licked away the sting.

After swiping a finger through her slit, I wrapped one of her legs around my waist, guiding my tip toward her entrance.

The head of my cock slowly sank into her, inching deeper and deeper as our bodies joined together. I started moving slowly, grinding my hips against hers at a torturous pace.

She wrapped her other leg around me, hooking her

ankles at my back to force my thrusts to go deeper. Her fingers grasped my arms, nails piercing my skin as I started pounding into her.

Her eyes fluttered shut, and I leaned down to kiss her forehead.

"Eyes open, love. You said you wanted to look at me."

Sierra's back arched as her eyes widened, her green irises practically glowing. A pink flush spread throughout her cheeks, and her pouty lips parted in a moan.

I hooked her legs over my shoulders, creating an even deeper angle. Her breasts bounced each time our bodies met, skin slapping against skin.

My hands glided up her body to her nipples. Rolling one between my fingers, I used my free hand to palm the other.

"Will you come inside me again?" She gasped as my cock hit her G-spot.

Fuck.

My head fell back as my balls twitched. "Are you sure?"

"Yes. Please. I want to feel it again."

Hugging her legs against my chest, I rammed my hips toward hers, pounding into her in messy, desperate thrusts.

A choked sob rose from Sierra's throat, and she clamped a hand to her mouth to muffle her cries. A whimper fell from my mouth as her pussy clenched around my cock, pulsing and squeezing me.

"Baby, I'm almost there," I breathed out.

Her needy moans kept me going, and soon we were moaning each other's names and holding on to each other for support. Her legs fell off my shoulders, and I gripped her thighs as they wrapped around my waist again.

My name fell off her lips in a desperate plea, a prayer,

and it sent me over the edge. My vision blackened at the edges and my cock pulsed as I spilled my cum inside her.

Her walls tightened around me, and I knew she'd reached her high, too. I continued to move, staying with her as she came down from her orgasm, a fresh glow painting her cheeks.

"I love you," she whispered. "So much."

I inched myself out of her slowly, her pussy releasing my cock with a wet pop. A mixture of my cum and her arousal dripped out of her, and I swiped a finger through the mess.

"I love you more, Skip." Bringing my finger up to my mouth, I sucked it clean.

Her eyes rolled back at the sight, and it only urged me on. Without thinking, I dipped down between her thighs to lick and suck my own cum clean. It was something I never thought I'd ever do, but when it came to Sierra, I was a starving man. After the first taste of her, I was convinced I'd never get enough.

"Who are you?" She huffed a nervous laugh.

Wiping my mouth, I laid my chin on her stomach. "Yours, baby. I've always been yours."

"Come here." She beckoned me with a crook of her finger, and I slid up next to her pulling her into my arms.

Sierra rested her head on my chest, and I raked my hand up and down her back, stopping every so often to twirl a strand of her hair on my finger.

"I'm so proud of you, baby. Let's get cleaned up." With one last kiss to her forehead, I carried her to the bathroom to run a hot shower.

sierra

Ladies and gentlemen, you've traveled from all around the world to Las Vegas, Nevada. You've watched as the top fifteen cowboys and cowgirls in the world competed in events from barrel racing to bull riding, and we've reached the pinnacle event. Tonight, we will crown nine new world champions. Are you ready? Let me hear you!"

An uproar from the crowd drowned out the rest of the announcer's welcome.

With my head dipped down, I leaned against a wall, taking deep breaths in and out.

One more race.

One more night.

It was unlikely I'd be taking home a buckle tonight, but the experience of making it to the NFR outweighed any disappointment I may have had. Besides, any feelings that rose up in me were just a product of my competitiveness. Now that I'd made it to the top—to the most important rodeo event of the year—I never wanted to lose the view.

Making it to the NFR had sparked something in me, a drive I knew I always had but was scared to tap into.

I knew my friends were all proud of me, but most importantly, *I* was proud of me.

From behind the chutes, I watched as Colter and Reid secured their first world championship win. My cheeks ached from smiling as they waved and tipped their hats at Ellison and Isa.

Jake competed well, too, but he was in the same boat as I was. Neither of us would take home a world championship or average championship this year, but we still had the jacket and back number to prove our presence here.

The energy in the arena built in anticipation for the bull riding, but barrel racing came first.

Lucky stomped the ground with his hoof as we waited for our turn to run the cloverleaf pattern. I patted his neck as I tried my best to keep my energy calm and collected.

"We did it, buddy. We made it. Let's enjoy this last ride, yeah?" I cooed at him, and he huffed in response. I liked to think he agreed. Nothing was on the line here, so we could just relax and do the thing we loved most: race.

The cowgirl who was up before us finished her race and walked her horse out of the alleyway as I mounted Lucky.

"For one final ride in the Thomas & Mack, let's hear it for Sierra Bayley and Ace's Lucky Charm!"

"Let's do this, bud," I murmured as I took a deep breath and put my trust into my horse.

Lucky burst down the alleyway like a flash of lightning, and I was convinced he ran faster than he had all week. He turned toward the barrel, all of it muscle memory and passion, and I guided him around the barrel, careful not to tip it over.

The smell of dust and livestock surrounded us as we

continued on the pattern. Lights flashed all around us, and even though I was locked into the race, I also let myself soak it all in.

Our second barrel was successful, and we raced toward the third and final one. Country music sent us home along with the roar of the crowd as Lucky galloped toward the time barrier.

"Thirteen-point-three-six seconds for Sierra and Lucky! What a way to end her first NFR!"

Happy tears streamed down my face as I untacked Lucky, giving him extra treats and pats for a race well done.

"We did it, Lucky. You've been beside me this whole time as I've chased this crazy little dream, and we made it. Let's do it all again next year, yeah?" I pressed my forehead to his nose, laughing as he chuffed happily.

The drive back from Vegas was long, but we made it in a couple days after a long night of celebrating Colter and Reid's first world championship and Mikey's average championship win.

We picked up Pancho from Liv's house when we got back to town, knowing the little devil would be overjoyed to see us.

Hayden and I hadn't really discussed what was going to happen now with our living arrangement. The most logical answer would be that I'd move out, buy a new trailer with my earnings and continue to travel around.

For once, though, I didn't want to lean into logic.

"Now that the season's over, I guess I have to decide

what I'm going to do. If I'm going to…" My voice trailed off because saying, *Go home*, didn't sound right. "I guess I'll have to figure out where I'm going next."

As if he read my mind, Hayden immediately said, "Stay. This is your home, isn't it?"

My gaze bounced down to the ground. "I don't know. I've never really had a home before."

"You do, though. And you have." He hooked his finger under my chin, forcing my watery eyes to look at his. "No matter what, you'll always have one with me. No matter where we are, no matter how far you go, you can always come home. Let me be your home."

A loose tear rolled down my cheek, but I nodded because he was right.

I knew it now.

Home wasn't always four walls. Sometimes home had a heartbeat and blue eyes deep enough to drown in. Sometimes home remembered your favorite childhood meal and favorite color so they could incorporate those tiny things into their life with you in mind. Sometimes home would follow you to the ends of the Earth, in every lifetime, even when you tried to push it away, thinking you didn't deserve it.

I'd spent twenty-six years trying to find a place where I truly belonged, a place I could call home. Little did I know I'd stumbled upon it at fourteen years old on a school bus.

I was confident Hayden Watkins was my soulmate. Regardless of where this life would take us, I knew even when we were dust floating along in the wind one day, my soul would still belong to him. Our lives would always be intertwined, like stars destined to revolve around each other for eternity.

Love was what bound us together after all these years,

even when it seemed like the world and all its forces were trying to tear us apart.

Pancho barked happily as he ran around us in circles, his butt wiggling the entire time as though he understood exactly what Hayden was asking.

I laughed, looking down at the dog. "What do you think, Pancho? Should we stay?"

He yipped a high-pitched bark in response.

"Well, I think that settles it." I grinned at Hayden. "We'll stay."

"Let's go home, Skip." Hayden scooped me up into his arms, carrying me toward the house, toward our future.

Resting my head in the crook of his neck, I whispered to no one in particular, "I'm already there."

TWO MONTHS LATER

sierra

"Do Colter and Ellison always celebrate every holiday like this?" I asked as I added pink and white heart sprinkles to the top of the peanut butter cookies I made earlier.

Hayden shook his head. "No, they don't. And now that I'm thinking about it, it's kind of weird that they'd have *everyone* come over for Valentine's Day, right?"

"I feel like they've been acting weird." Biting back a smile, I asked, "What do you think they're going to announce? Oh my God, what if she's pregnant? The last time we saw them she was sick, wasn't she?"

"I mean, it's also Caitlin's birthday?" Hayden suggested, but from his tone I didn't think he believed that reason.

"Is Cait even going to be there?"

"Probably not. Her husband is kind of…" He pursed

his lips and widened his eyes, even though his gaze was trained on the floor. "We don't like him very much."

I grimaced. "Yeah, I gathered that from Thanksgiving."

"Well, Nosy, are you ready to head out so we can find out what the special occasion is?" Hayden teased, throwing his arm around me as I put the cookies into a plastic container.

"Yeah, let's do this thing." I grinned, following him out to the pickup.

Lilac-colored cosmos bloomed in the planter boxes we'd put in at the front of the house, and a welcome mat covered in muddy paw prints decorated the front porch.

Shortly after I'd officially moved in, we moved all of my belongings from the guest room into Hayden's. As much as he wanted to keep the room purple, we decided to paint it a pretty light blue-gray color and turn it into an office. Although Pancho still took a liking to the room and often slept in there on a fluffy purple dog bed.

Lucky and Peanut grazed in the pasture, and our brand new, upgraded horse trailer was parked in front of the barn. Since I wasn't buying a new trailer for myself, Hayden and I agreed to put our funds together to upgrade his.

Our house had little bits of our personality woven throughout it, but our love was truly what made it a home.

"Should we get another dog?" I blurted as we pulled out of the driveway. "Or maybe some goats? A cat?"

"Whatever you want, love. We can have all the animals."

I smirked, ruffling his hair. "You've always been good at taking care of things in need."

He shook his head. "You've never *needed* me to take

care of you, Skip. You've always been so strong, you just needed a little push to find your voice."

"Are you regretting helping me find it?" I teased.

"Never." He took my hand in his, bringing it up to his mouth to kiss my palm.

The whole gang pulled us into hugs when we walked into Colter and Ellison's house. Isa flew in from Houston, and Juniper was back from Minnesota to visit for this special occasion.

Hayden took the container of cookies from me and set them on the kitchen counter as Isa and Juniper pulled me into their conversation, all of us making small talk.

Reid passed out mimosas to the girls, but I noticed he only poured orange juice into Ellison's glass.

My eyes widened, and I tilted my head at Hayden, lips pursed into a smile. He winked at me before going back to his conversation with Mikey and Jake.

A few minutes later, Colter cleared his throat, getting everyone's attention.

"So, I'm guessing you're all wondering why we wanted to host a party today." Ellison pulled her bottom lip between her teeth. "And no, it's not because we just like Valentine's Day."

I coughed and said, "I knew it," earning a chuckle from Hayden.

"We're having a baby!" Colter blurted.

Hayden and I pretended to be surprised as the whole group of us cheered.

"Wait, oh my God!" Isa squealed, launching herself at

Ellison to hug her "I'm going to be an auntie!" Tears welled in Isa's eyes. "When are you due?"

"End of August," Ellison replied.

"Wait, does that mean…" Jake counted on his fingers before laughing. "NFR baby?"

Colter nodded, a stupid grin on his face. "NFR baby."

"Atta boy." Mikey slapped him on the back, and Ellison rolled her eyes.

"We're so happy for you guys. I can't believe you made me keep it a secret, though," Reid teased.

Isa put her hands on her hips. "You kept this a secret from me!"

He pressed a kiss to her forehead. "My love, you have a big mouth when you get excited."

She pouted, grumbling, "I know."

"Aw, I always knew Colter was going to be the best daddy," Juniper teased.

"He's already got *big* Daddy energy." Mikey wiggled his brows, earning groans from a few of us. "What? It's true!"

"All right, settle down, y'all." Colter laughed, gesturing for the volume to lower.

It was a fair point. The guys were acting like it was NFL draft day or they just won the lottery.

"Should we all toast to a happy, healthy preg—" Colter reached for a cupcake to hold in the air but was cut off by the sound of his phone ringing. His face contorted into concern as he saw who was calling. "Sorry, baby, I need to take this."

"Who is it?" Ellison asked, and Colter whispered in her ear. Her face blanched, and she followed him into the bedroom as he answered the phone, leaving the rest of us stunned in their living room.

"What's going on?" Juniper furrowed her brows.

"I have no idea." Isa pulled her lip between her teeth.

None of us knew what to do while we waited, all of us just awkwardly standing in the living room, a stark contrast to the happy atmosphere a few minutes ago.

"Hey, you just finished your guest house, right, Jake?" Hayden asked, breaking the silence.

"Sure did!" His expression brightened. "It looks super nice. We could have a house warming party next. Gotta get some furniture in there and make it all homey, but it should be usable in the next couple of months."

Congratulations floated around the circle, but the air was still tense as we waited for Colter and Ellison to come back.

If I strained my ears, I could make out some muffled voices from the bedroom. Someone sounded like they were crying, and I hoped everyone was okay.

A few minutes later, Colter and Ellison emerged from the bedroom.

"Sorry, guys." Colter's voice had an edge to it, and he looked absolutely pissed. Ellison looked like she was fighting back tears, a few wet streaks already painting her cheeks.

"Is everything okay, man?" Reid asked, his brows furrowing with concern.

"It was Caitlin." Colter's jaw ticked. "Adam just served her divorce papers."

closed-door modifications

For those who want a reading experience without explicit sexual content (or for those who want to easily find the spice), here are the chapters that include open-door scenes. Please note that each of these chapters include explicit sexual content that is fully consensual.

If you would like to skip the spice, please note the starting points in parentheses that will provide you with the best reading experience. Fully skipping the chapters with spice starting points will cause you to miss out on important scenes and plot points.

- Chapter 42 (page 304 to page 308 ending before "I love you, always.")
- Chapter 43 (page 311 after "'Slow,' I repeated" to page 316 ending before "I'm so glad it was you."
- Chapter 52
- Chapter 54 (page 379 to end)

acknowledgments

The Dreams We Chase is easily the most difficult book I've written, and not only because of the sensitive and heavy topics. Grief is weird and some days, this story felt impossible to write, despite yearning to start it for months. Other days, the words flowed easily onto the page, like its own form of therapy. I hope this story impacted you the way it impacted me, that you felt seen, and were able to feel a glimmer of hope that even on the darkest of days there is a light at the end of the tunnel, and you are stronger than you could ever know. If you've ever felt hopeless, just know I'm so happy you're here and so proud of you for hanging on.

I would be nowhere without my support system—the people who you may not know, but still find a way to shine through in all of my stories.

To my fiancé, for supporting me through this little dream of mine and introducing me to the most soul crushing, heart wrenching, angsty anime that fueled and inspired the emotional devastation of this book. It's probably a good thing you didn't influence me to watch them sooner. You know, for the sake of the readers.

To all my author and Bookstagram friends that I've made along the way for pushing me on the days when I feel like there's no motivation left and when my creative well seems like it's gone dry. Without this community of talented and kind people, I surely would not be where I am today. There are far too many people to name, so just know if you've ever received a long-winded voice note, been bombarded by serial text messages or DMs, or opened your inbox to several reels, memes, and/or TikToks (or all of the above), you hold a special place in my heart. Thank you for putting up with my chaos.

Thank you to the officers at the GCSO for your guidance in ensuring the events and legal aspects of this book were as accurate and handled with as much care as possible. Sorry to Jackie, especially, for keeping my writing a secret for months and depriving us of book chats. Thank you as well to the readers with law enforcement backgrounds who were just as willing to jump in and answer my questions.

Thank you to the team of people behind the scenes of every release. Authoring may seem like a one-woman show, but I truly couldn't do any of this without you.

Copy Edit and Proofread: Andrea Halland, Editing by Andrea
Beta Readers: Caprielle, Casey, Elle, Kait, Karlee, Leila, Samantha, Shaylene, SJ, Sydney, and Tiffani

To my content and ARC teams, thank you for loving on my characters, screaming about my books every chance you get, and creating beautiful content. It brings me so much joy to see your creativity and passion for books shine through your reviews and posts.

If you've made it this far, thank you. I would be remiss not to recognize the people who have helped me along the way in my writing journey, but nothing would be possible —my dreams wouldn't be achievable—without you, the reader.

thanks for reading

If you enjoyed *The Dreams We Chase*, I would greatly appreciate if you left a review on Amazon, Goodreads, or any other platform!

For more updates on the H.K. Green Universe, subscribe to my newsletter.

about the author

H.K. Green is a contemporary romance author based out of Montana, writing raw, emotional stories that will break your heart then put it back together.

Inspired by real-life, relatable challenges, her books feature found families, a healthy dose of sarcastic banter and emotional angst, strong female leads, and the men who'll do anything to give them the world.

When she's not writing, she can be found curling up with all kinds of books, hanging out with her rescue animals, going to rodeos or her family's farm and ranch, and spending time with her real-life book boyfriend.

You can connect with H.K. Green on Instagram and TikTok @authorhkgreen and learn more on her website at www.authorhkgreen.com.

www.ingramcontent.com/pod-product-compliance
Lightning Source LLC
Chambersburg PA
CBHW051255130726
47987CB00004B/1535